THE TRAVELING TYRANT
AUDACITY OF POPE

by
Richard Marsden

TYRANT INDUSTRIES

THE TRAVELING TYRANT: AUDACITY OF POPE
By Richard Marsden
Copyright 2018, All Rights Reserved

ISBN 13 - 978-0-9992903-0-9
ISBN 10 - 0-9847716-7-0

Edited by – Cara Patterson
Cover Art by – Ksenia Kozhevnikova
Formatted by – Henry Snider

THE TRAVELING TYRANT SERIES

Paradisa Lost
Casual Fridays
Audacity of Pope
High Stakes
End Road
The Truly Most Greatest Battle Ever

For John, the Wise

1

THE UPPER ARM -THE MERCILESS IN SPACE-

Mordid wished he hadn't quit smoking. He had nothing to do while waiting around, nor could he blow clouds of pale, acrid smoke into people's faces when there actually was something to do. He couldn't start back up either. One, there was not a single cigarette left in the fleet. Well, not one he could get his hands on. His employees were only loyal to a point, and every soldier that reeked of nicotine claimed they had "just" smoked their last one. Two, the love of his life, or rather, the love of the moment, and he had quit the indulgent habit on the same day— and incidentally, she had shot him not long after that. The urge to take a deep drag on the cancerous stick brought a pain to his chest. The healed bullet wound and the craving acted in concert as a healthy reminder for him to take more care when choosing a woman. However, were there a cigarette in easy grasp, or a pretty face, he doubted he'd resist either for long.

He drummed his fingers atop a long gray desk. He sat, slouched in a high-backed seat, staring out a broad window at the endless sea of stars. Pale, cold light shone from above, illuminating his meeting hall where he and his treacherous, but useful, command staff would bicker about the fleet's day to day operations.

Currently, the room was empty.

Eryn was busying herself glorifying all things Mordid. Thrask was probably training his soldiers while rubbing unconsciously at his chest where Mordid had placed a pulmonary collar that linked his life to Mordid's. Rodriguez had the fleet to handle, and Mauss was uncharacteristically late. The man was old. Perhaps he had finally died of natural causes, the most unnatural of deaths in a mercenary company.

Mordid was just about to reach into his pocket for his communication device when the door slid open.

"Finally," Mordid said.

The tall, gaunt man entered. Mauss was clad, as was his custom, in a uniform that was a little outdated for the 20th century military theme Mordid chose for their mercenary band. Mauss, like his uniform, dated from another time and another Tyrant. The old spider had survived the reigns of prior masters and had engineered the deposing of one Tyrant for another. Mordid knew this firsthand.

Mauss not only was old-fashioned in his style of dress, he was old-fashioned in his style of work. In his hand, he held a manila folder. No datadisk was in his hand, no holopresentation was at the ready. Mauss was a pen and paper guy.

He approached Mordid and placed the single folder atop the table. His thin, skeletal finger tapped it.

"Just the one? One offer?" Mordid frowned. Normally, there would have been dozens, sometimes even a hundred inquiries for his services. The last job on Pristine had gone swimmingly well, his lady troubles aside. The client was happy, the sinister investors who kept him in business were pleased, and besides getting shot and having to put Helen to the torch, all was well. Mauss should have had two armloads of papers from clients begging for hired guns. The Upper Arm and Corporate Worlds were always shy of fleet and manpower, and Mordid was happy to oblige. For a price.

Mauss flicked his wrist and the folder spiraled across the table.

Mordid slapped his hand atop it, stopping the folder's

2

mad flight. He picked it up and opened it. His eyes scanned through the offer and Mauss's handwritten notes to the side.

His gaze fell upon the suitor for his affections and military power.

"No."

Mauss tilted his head. The lights embedded in the ceiling cast a reflection on his shiny, bald scalp. "Why ever not?"

Mordid shook his head. "This smacks of religion and all the turmoil it has to offer, and I don't want to get involved in that. And you did see mentioned here that they want a relic transferred to the Khan system? How many mercenary companies have sped off to that deathtrap, hmmm?" Mordid smirked. "I'm the reckless one, and you're the voice of reason, remember?"

"Look at the last page."

Flipping through the papers, Mordid flung them aside one by one, causing them to land haphazardly upon the desk.

Mauss sighed.

Mordid made his way to the bottom of the stack and read out loud, "Blah, blah, for your esteemed services we promise to pay—" He clamped his mouth shut. His gaze darted up toward Mauss.

"This is for real?"

Mauss nodded. "I was late because I was checking and rechecking all of my sources. The origins of the contract I've not figured out, yet. How they found us, why they chose us, and all that. But that offer and that number with all those zeroes is very much real."

Licking his lips, Mordid reached out across the table and, with delicate movements, put the papers he had so willfully tossed aside back in order. His hand caressed the archaic manila folder, and he shut it. Mordid stroked his pointed beard and stared at the most valuable stack of papers in the galaxy.

"Well?" Mauss prompted.

Mordid sucked in a breath and exhaled in a dramatic fashion. "I'm tempted. I'm *more* than tempted. That is a ridiculous sum of money." He pursed his lips. "And yet something in the back of my mind is still telling me to say no." He rose and circled the table, staring down at the folder. "You said you can't confirm how the offer came to us? They didn't deliver it?"

"No," Mauss said, "it arrived in the hands of one of my agents in the Upper Arm, who in turn directed it to me by shuttle. My agent said he was using the, ahh… facilities, when the contract was slid under the stall door. Usually, I know a little bit more about the employer and their motives. Not this time, I'm afraid. I only know that the offer is from them and that they were specifically looking for us." He cleared his throat, "Or rather, you, Tyrant."

"Massive amount of money, shady delivery, a specific target in mind." Mordid arched a brow. "A trap?"

Mauss nodded. "A possibility. However, have you ever angered them? Done something to make them wish you harm?"

Mordid mentally recounted his long list of enemies. The list was almost as enormous as the sum of money being offered, but *they* were not on it. He had quite purposefully steered his ship, both literal and proverbial, away from them.

"No."

"It's up to you," Mauss said, "I have other offers for you to look at should you turn this one down. However, I felt this one needed your undivided attention before I pulled out the less," he cleared his throat, "appealing prospects."

Avarice and caution fought a brief war within Mordid. He stared intently at the folder, as if doing so would somehow divine something about its true purpose. Staring didn't work, and greed boldly trounced hesitation. He focused his stare upon Mauss.

"They have the money?"

Mauss nodded. "You know they do."

"Accepted." Mordid straightened and thrust his jaw out in a very Tyrant-like manner. "I'll have Admiral Rodriguez take the fleet to Reconquista. The Mexican will be delighted to be going to his home away from home."

Diplomat Mauss nodded. He scooped up the folder and tucked it under his arm. Striding toward the exit, he paused. He turned to face the Traveling Tyrant.

"Mordid."

"Hmm?"

"When we get to Reconquista, try not to piss off the pope. The Holy Father and his minions are bound to be sensitive and I'd loathe to lose out on the largest contract you, or any Tyrant for that matter, has landed due to some social miscalculation." Mauss cocked his head and opened one eye wide, fixing his stare upon his employer.

Smiling, Mordid said, "I'll keep my hands off the nuns. I'll charm the zealots. They'll love me." He gave a thumbs up.

"Hmmph." Mauss spun on his heel and left through the automatic sliding door.

#

The makeshift chapel Rodriguez sat in was bathed in darkness. Only a solitary light added its illumination to the chamber and was directed, like a spotlight, upon a massive, wooden crucifix on the wall. The wooden pews were clean, polished so by the loving hands of his bridge crew. Mexicans at heart, if not by birth, and Catholic to a man.

A few of his men sat in silent contemplation, huddled in the pews with their hands clasped and their eyes shut. There was an altar, where the shipboard priest would deliver his sermon and prepare the Eucharist for the devoted followers to the one true faith. Today, it was unattended. Rodriguez had the priest, Father Oroyo, sent on an errand to the other end of the *Merciless*. It was for the best if the good father remained ignorant of what was transpiring. Today, Rodriguez had more than prayer planned to take place in the chapel.

Valdez, Rodriguez's First Officer, sat next to his admiral, hands gripped in tight prayer, but his dark eyes were focused firmly on Rodriguez.

"Why are you staring?" Rodriguez asked.

Valdez gazed at the great cross instead. "Admiral, you look pale as an Upper Arm space-born. He does not know. He *cannot* know."

"Mordid is crafty, Valdez," Rodriguez whispered. "He will let plots simmer, rise, and then, just before they boil, he will act." He licked his lips and found them to be dry. "Too many secrets. If just one of them gets discovered…" he trailed off.

"They won't," Valdez assured him. "God is on our side. The Earth ship will not be found. Mordid will never know we arranged the contract. He will never know who his guest is. The Holy Father will return from exile. You should be happy. Our people, driven away like criminals, will return triumphant. All thanks to you."

He wished he could be so certain of victory and of maintaining a level of secrecy. The chapel was clean of listening devices, thus making it a perfect place for clandestine meetings. However, Mordid's command staff, and the Tyrant himself, actively spied on each other, which meant on him as well. If anyone in his crew talked, that would be the end of it. The pope would never return to the Eternal City of Rome and the true faith would be denied the right to flourish on the world that created it. Perhaps worst of all, the next Traveling Tyrant would not have the colorful name of Rodriguez.

"I have faith that you will be right, Valdez." He reached over and patted him on the shoulder. "But I cannot help but worry. So much is at stake."

The man nodded. "*Si*. I will confess, admiral, that there is one thing about all this that bothers me." He smiled and his teeth flashed in the inky shadows of the chapel. "I relish the idea of dodging the bull. Should you or I die, such is God's will. I don't fear that."

"Let's be clear, Valdez, that I prefer to be a living saint, not a martyr," Rodriguez said.

"Oh, naturally!" Valdez beamed. "However, should it come to that, it is the will of God." He leaned close and lowered his voice. "But the Holy Father is risking himself. Earth Space is bad enough. The bastards on Earth could be lying—"

Anger boiled up inside Rodriguez at the thought of it. "If they harm him, they'll have blood on their hands, and not just his."

"True." Valdez pursed his lips. "Beyond us having to trust Earth Government, why does the Holy Father want to go to the Khan system? There is nothing there but endless war for no gain. Why not head directly to his goal? Why fly into war?"

Rodriguez shrugged. "Someone has to win, eventually, but

I agree. It has bothered me as well. Of all the places to go, there are much safer ones and much more secure routes. Perhaps he wishes to enter Earth Space through all the chaos and confusion of that Corporate Worlds warzone? He did not say, and my correspondence with Reconquista is clear. The Holy Father needs to be taken to the Khan System." He sighed. "I doubt I will be able to ask him why in person, even if he's a guest on this very ship!"

"Maybe he wants to preach to the aliens on the other side?" Valdez laughed in soft tones that were appropriate for a church. "New converts."

Rodriguez shook his head. "No, Valdez. All the aliens on the other side of the Khan system are dead. There are no souls for our Holy Father to save there, only loot for the corporations to pick over."

"Eventually," Valdez whispered.

Rodriguez's lips twitched. "*Si*, eventually." He cleared his throat. "Valdez, speaking of the dead."

His first officer needed no further prompting. Valdez rolled his shoulders and said, "Say the names and I'll make it happen. You'll make sure Oroyo forgives me for my sins?"

"Naturally."

"Who?"

Rodriguez lowered his voice, so that the whisper barely carried. "When we deliver the Holy Father to Earth Space, we will deliver Mordid as well. For this to be successful, that means Mauss, Eryn, and Thrask will need to be handled. Preferably, all at once. Look for such an opportunity in the weeks ahead."

Valdez nodded, but his expression tightened.

"A problem?"

"No, sir." Valdez shifted in his pew. "Well, yes. I do not like the idea of killing a woman." He shrugged and looked up at the cross.

Rodriguez chuckled. "No problem, *mi amigo*. Eryn isn't really a woman. She is a monster. You don't mind arranging the demise of a monster do you?"

"No."

Rodriguez smiled and absently reached up and stroked his long moustache. "*Bien*."

#

The door to the Tyrant's meeting chamber opened, and Jenkins straightened and squared his shoulders, doing his utmost to look like the elite officer persona he had adopted. Karlson, looking old and worn as ever, did the same, putting on a respectable show for the boss. Bulks, the third man on Tyrant guard duty, continued to pick at his nails and didn't even bother to look up as Mordid strode out of the room. Jenkins doubted Bulks even saw Diplomat Mauss enter and leave the meeting chamber.

Fortunately, Mordid paid Bulks, the sloppy End Roader, no mind. The stocky Tyrant with his intense blue eyes and pointed black goatee walked down the long and poorly lit halls of the *Merciless* with his hands clasped behind his back and his head bowed low. His iron-gray coat swished about his boots, which clicked on the deck with each hurried step.

Jenkins recognized when his master was in a foul mood. Whatever Mauss had told the Tyrant must have been upsetting. He followed after him.

"We done yet?" Bulks asked.

Mordid continued walking.

"Shut up," Karlson murmured.

Bulks snorted and thankfully remained quiet, taking up the rear.

The halls were empty, and the few crewmen and soldiers that wandered about were quick to see their angry employer and find other pathways to take. The ship was massive and had never been fully crewed. It was cheaper to keep just a bit beyond a skeleton crew for operational purposes and hordes of soldiers and marines at the ready for the real work. This meant vast sections of the *Merciless* were deserted.

They reached an elevator and entered it. Soft mind-numbing music, at odds with the stark militaristic tone of the ship, greeted them.

Mordid was not chatty. He leaned against the back wall of the elevator and stared at his glossy black boots.

Jenkins frowned. Shifted from one foot to the next. He opened his mouth.

"Not now, Jenkins," Mordid snapped without glancing up.

"Yes, sir," he replied.

"Testy, today, ain't he," Bulks whispered, but not quiet enough for the Tyrant not to hear him.

Mordid arched a thin, black brow and stared at the inbred soldier. He then turned his blue, piercing gaze onto Jenkins.

The Tyrant was Jenkins's patron, and it was by his grace alone that he had the honor, and highly paid task, of guarding his person. Jenkins took a step closer to Bulks and kicked him in the shin.

"Ow."

Karlson offered his own kick.

"Ow!"

The elevator halted, and Mordid's lips formed a brief smile.

The doors opened revealing the busy bridge of the *Merciless*. Music played here as well. Not the slit-my-throat-please music of the elevator, but instead, distinctive, fast-paced music, laden with lyrics in Spanish. A Mexican flag hung on the wall and the crew, to a man, had swarthy skin, black hair, and short, compact forms. Most were adorned with prominently displayed crucifixes. Some were crafted in gold, others silver, but more than a few were made from wood and looked as if they had been carved by amateur, but no doubt devoted, hands.

"Gentlemen," Mordid said to Jenkins and his team. "I shall be on the bridge for a bit. Why don't you call it a day and send the next shift to gaze at and protect my most glorious form."

"Yes, sir," Jenkins said.

Mordid nodded and walked onto the bridge and was greeted by a chorus of cheers and comments in a swift, foreign dialect that Jenkins could make no sense of. However, his employer understood their speech and responded in kind.

I need to learn Spanish, Jenkins thought.

Karlson pressed a button on the wall, and the elevator doors slid shut, blocking out the garish sights and sounds of the *Merciless's* command center.

Whirling on Bulks, Jenkins said, "You're an

embarrassment. Easy-going is one thing, but when the man is in a bad mood, you have to learn to keep your mouth shut and at least pretend to be a soldier."

Bulks's large eyes and jutting jaw marked him as an End Roader. They all had a similar look, courtesy of being born on a planet with a distinct lack of genetic diversity. The man shrugged. "Who cares? We need to make sure Mordid don't get hurt none. Guess what? He didn't get hurt none."

"That's not the point," Jenkins said. He wagged his finger at Bulks. "We need to impress him. He's our ticket to pay raises and promotion."

"You mean *your* ticket," Bulks said. He smiled, displaying a few prominent gaps between his yellowed teeth.

Jenkins rolled his eyes. "Fine. My outfit is a volunteer one. Transfer out of the squad if you don't like it."

Bulks's large eyes blinked like a frog's. "Leave?" He laughed. "Aw, no. No, sir! I like it with you. With Herrin."

The elevator halted and the doors opened.

Bulks pushed past the pair and said over his shoulder. "See ya later." He added, "sir," about halfway down the hall.

Jenkins stared at his back while Karlson pressed the button again. The doors shut, and he pressed another button to ensure it would be a long wait.

"They're undisciplined. All of them," Karlson said.

He was right. Herrin's chosen men, three in all, were uncouth and brilliant examples of a stereotype. Since they had been hand-picked by Tolfus Herrin, the knife-wielding medic, they had spent more time in the brig than in training. They didn't socialize with the rest of the squad, and they didn't take orders very well. Herrin had been useful back on Pristine. Reliable and ruthless. His chosen men, though? Not so much.

"I promised Herrin he could have his pick." Jenkins sighed and leaned against the wall, taking up the same position Mordid had before. "Maybe I'll just be sure to assign them to duties where Herrin is involved." He looked at Karlson. "He picked them. Let him handle the lot."

Karlson grunted. "Bad idea, sir. They're undercutting your authority. You're an officer now, remember?"

"You mean I can't sweep the problem under the rug?" Jenkins asked.

"Well, of course you can. A good officer just knows *how* to do it." Karlson ran a hand through his salt and pepper hair. "It's only a matter of time before we see action again. You saw how Mordid looked. Something is up."

"True," Jenkins said. He pushed himself off the wall and paced back and forth through the elevator. "I take it you're suggesting that bad things should happen to them?" While he had no love for Bulks, Rendstrot and Umbradax, Herrin had saved the pair of them more than once. He shook his head. "I can't do that to Tolfus. He is creepy, violent, and murderous, yes. However, we owe him."

Smiling, Karlson said, "I'm not thinking something quite so sinister, sir. Just that they are a reckless lot, and if we were in combat, that recklessness might not be an advantage." He added, "To them."

"Ah," Jenkins said. He grinned. "Let nature take its course."

"Right!" Karlson said, "And the next time Mordid says, 'Hey, do something dangerous,' you send them into danger and not me. Remember on Paradisa when I had to play bait for that bug that ate half the squad?"

He recalled. Karlson threw the grenade at the alien beast, and Jenkins made the shot to detonate the weapon, along with the creature. It was the event that first brought the Tyrant's beneficial attention upon him. He owed Herrin, but he owed Karlson more. If Karlson wanted the End Roaders removed, then so be it. So long as Herrin was spared.

"How self serving, Karlson," Jenkins mock-chided.

"Thank you, sir," he replied.

They had a plan. When the bullets flew, it would be the End Roaders leading the charge.

#

Sweat poured down Thrask's body. He was stripped to the waist and pounding his fist into a leather bag suspended from the ceiling. The exercise room smelled of musty clothing, stale sweat, and oil.

He powered his right fist into the bag, sending it reeling on its chain, and followed up with a series of jabs with his left. Were it a man, his sternum would have been broken and his kidneys bruised so badly he would urinate blood. Alas, the bag wasn't a person. It was just toughened leather filled with sand.

Thrask had only one workout partner today. Not that the man had any interest in exercising. Tolfus Herrin was content to sit on a weight lifting bench and sharpen his knife. His blonde hair bobbed with every pass of the whetstone, and his large, pale eyes only glanced up from the blade's keen edge when Thrask delivered a sufficiently loud and rattling punch.

"Herrin, I just got word today that we're going into action." Thrask breathed hard, clenched his fist and slammed it low into the bag. The thing spun on the chain, only to be sent reeling the other way by a cross stroke.

"Dangerous and profitable, I'm thinking. Am I right?" the End Roader asked.

"Yes." Thrask continued pummeling the bag, keeping an eye on the knife-wielding medic between blows. "And that means some opportunity for me." He ceased his rigorous workout and felt his heart thunder in his chest. However, with every beat of his heart, he felt the machine fused to it tick. The accursed thing jutted up from his slab-like pectoral, like someone had rammed a tin can into him. The flesh around the pulmonary collar was reddish and bruised, never quite healing. Damn Mordid! Damn Eryn! The thought that Mordid put it there sickened him. The thought that Eryn had hijacked it so that her life and his were twined in a one-sided manner was downright infuriating. Damn them both!

"I take it you want my help?" Herrin sheathed the knife at his side. He offered a thin smile. "The last time didn't go so well."

Thrask touched the machine linked to his heart. "No, it didn't. But we'll get this out yet. Sooner or later. Eryn might have a leash on me, but that means Mordid doesn't anymore." Thrask leveled his gaze upon Herrin. "I think I want to settle the score between him and me."

Herrin shrugged. "That's your business."

"Our business." Thrask glared at him. "I pulled you out of the brig. I made you what you are. Your record is clean; you're a recognized doctor. Meanest one I ever met, and murderous, but doctor none the less. That comes with extra pay." Thrask jerked his thumb at himself. "All that is because of me. I'm the ticket to success."

Smiling, the End Roader said, "I'm grateful, but I'm not stupid. If you go after Mordid, then you run afoul of Eryn. The two are a couple. Sorta."

"Kinda," Thrask agreed.

The pair had affection for one another, even if they tried to hide it. However, Eryn was deadly and ambitious, and Mordid was the Traveling Tyrant. Tyrants didn't have friends or family and certainly not love. Lovers maybe, but not love. Not if they wanted to stay a Tyrant.

Thrask said, "So, I want something maybe a bit more subtle. An open coup won't cut it."

"You're looking for an accident?" Herrin's teeth flashed as brightly as his blade. "For Lady Fate to play her cruel hand?"

Thrask nodded. "Right. Besides, Mordid thinks he owns my life. He's not afraid of me. Not so long as I got this." He lowered his chin to glance at the device. It looked like a can had been rammed into his chest. "Eryn does own my life, so she'll not expect much from me either."

"Leaving Diplomat Mauss and the Mexican admiral to worry about," Herrin said.

"Mauss has spies everywhere, but if we keep this between the pair of us and look for the right time rather than try to force the issue, he'll be none the wiser. As for Rodriguez?" He shrugged. "He's too new to plot against his master so soon." Thrask smiled. "Soon as Mordid is dead, they'll be at one another's throats anyway. It will be a great time for you, me, and some assistant to go down to the infirmary and get this thing out of me. Finally."

Herrin bobbed his head from side to side, considering. "Hmmm…"

"Hmmm what? You owe me. You were a step away from being marooned or jettisoned into space." Thrask approached him until his broad shadow fell across the much smaller and wiry man.

Unperturbed, Herrin stared up at him with his overly large eyes. He waved his knife about. "You're asking for a lot, and I want something in return. I want a fair trade."

He was expecting that. Crossing his muscular and sweaty arms, Thrask asked, "What do you have in mind?"

"Jenkins's job. He didn't serve you too well, but I will." Herrin rose.

That was easy! He was going to offer him the job when he became the Tyrant anyway. "Done. I'll need a good bodyguard after the Tyrant's taken care of." Thrask extended his large hand toward the End Roader.

Herrin took it, and for being slight of frame, his grip was surprisingly strong. "A deal then, General."

"A deal," Thrask replied. He released his grip. "For now, do your job and look for a chance to act. We need Mordid isolated and then your Lady Fate needs to act."

"It ain't your fault what happens to the stupidly careless," Herrin said. He eyed his blade before sheathing it.

"Exactly!" Thrask returned his attention to the bag. He'd be rid of Mordid, the collar, and then Eryn. After that, things would be different. He pounded away at the bag, imagining it was Mordid and then Eyrn with alternating, powerful punches.

2
THE UPPER ARM -RECONQUISTA-

How the Mexicans fled Earth, launched themselves into the most remote parts of space and still managed to find a desert to live in amazed Mordid, and it annoyed him. He shifted, uncomfortable under the blazing sun of Reconquista, while sweat soaked his black uniform and his gray coat begged to be slipped off his shoulders and abandoned. However, each time he tried, Eryn put a hand on his shoulder. Appearances must be maintained.

He glanced at her. She was clad in black, taller than he was, smiling and sweat-free. She caught his gaze and whispered, "Don't whine."

"I'm not."

"You look good."

"I'm hot."

She nodded. "Yes, you are."

Mordid's personal landing craft, behind him, provided scant shade against the glaring sun. Before him stretched a sea of people. They were dressed in frocks, suits, sheets, and all manner of religious attire. Most of them had dark skin and dark hair, but the crowd had its fair number of people who were not clearly of Mexican descent. Mordid spotted a few pale-skinned types, so

15

common in the Upper Arm and the unique nationality leftovers that were prevalent in the Corporate Worlds. The Catholics of Reconquista were organized and viable enough to woo non-Mexicans to a place that seemed godforsaken to him. They must have been doing something right.

Then there were the nuns. Eryn, sadly, did a fantastic job of keeping his fleet nearly female-free, and those that did work for him, worked for Eryn, which meant they were atrocious to look at. The maid who cleaned his room, with her missing teeth, oversized eye, and robotic vacuum-foot, he didn't consider much of a woman. And clearly, Eryn didn't consider her one either. For Eryn, there was but one woman in the fleet.

Reconquista was blessed in some small measure. It did not have an Eryn who insisted upon her matriarchal status and demanded she remain the fairest in the land. The nuns, though clad head to toe in black, had pretty faces, and despite the voluminous clothing, they still managed to show off their womanly figures. Mordid squinted his eyes and tried to imagine just what they might look like beneath all those robes.

As if sensing the objects of his attention, Eryn whispered, "Don't even think about it. They're all taken by a higher power."

He frowned.

Beyond the crowd, Mordid made out pale buildings, some of them quite enormous, with red, terra-cotta roofs.

Clad in black and looking miserable, Jenkins and his full team of men stood near Mordid. The crowd was kept several paces back by their stern gazes and leveled guns, but they had steadily surrounded the ship in a curious sea of humanity.

Several of Eyrn's busybodies, consisting of mostly men and a handful of unattractive women, filmed, recorded, and buzzed about Mordid like bees.

Eryn leaned close to his ear. "Have you ever seen so many people?"

"No," Mordid said. He tugged at his coat. "I don't like it. They could go all feverish on us. Next thing you know, we're being sacrificed or turned into cult members." He shook his head. "I don't like how glassy-eyed they look." He frowned. "I don't like religion."

16

She laughed. "That's the burning light of faith you see in their eyes. God loves them. I hear it's a good feeling."

Mordid rolled his eyes. "They're blind and stupid."

She continued to tease him. "What? You don't believe in God? Religion, sure, it can be terrible. But, you do believe in an Almighty, mmm?" Sarcasm dripped from every word like poison from one of the countless knives she was likely hiding on her person.

"Of course I do."

She blinked, clearly taken aback. "Yo-you do? I always imagined you to be an atheist. Or, or do you really worship 'the other guy.' I thought that was just a nasty rumor. If it's true, we can always change our theme to something more sata—"

"No," Mordid interrupted. "I believe in God. He's a mercenary, just like me. He has to be. He hedges all his bets. What are disasters? God's punishment. What are good times? Miracles." He peered at Eyrn. "Only a mercenary would choose someone to be a saint *after* their death. No surprises that way. You never hear about a living saint who then loses his status, right? God is always making sure. He is always making solid bets. Oh, I believe in God all right. He always wins, and he always bets on winners." He puffed his chest out. "And me, being a winner, I naturally think he loves me." He glared at her. "Do my eyes look glossy and faith-filled?"

"No," Eryn admitted. She blinked and fixed a smile upon her face. "Let's keep your religious attitudes to yourself, though. We don't want to make our employers angry."

"Not until they pay us, at least," Mordid quipped.

"True. Ah! I think the relic is coming."

There was a disturbance in the crowd, like a rippling. Heads turned, arms reached out, and people wailed, cried, and shouted. A few even fainted. A ring of soldiers, clad in white, armed with medieval halberds, marched through the throng, pushing them back. Mordid made out several figures within the protective ring. Some were clad in brilliant red robes, others in more simple attire. Leading the group was a stooped Mexican with a balding head, wisps of frosty hair and a black suitcase handcuffed to his wrist.

"Do your thing," Eryn said and stepped back.

Mordid extended his arms wide and waited for the company of men to reach him. When they were within shouting distance, he bellowed, "Welcome! I, Mordid the Traveling Tyrant, am here to guarantee the safety and delivery of your most sacred relic!" His voice thundered across the desert landscape, amplified by Eryn's team of propaganda agents and their speakers. It was perhaps a bit too loud, given that everyone winced, even Mordid.

Stunned by his voice, the crowd went silent.

The ring of soldiers forced their way to Mordid's ship. He maintained a smile as his men in black squared off against those in white like pieces on a chessboard.

"I take it that is the relic?" Mordid asked, quieter now that his PR team had lowered his voice so as not to deafen the crowd further. He extended his hand toward the suitcase. He was curious what it contained. Finger bone of a saint? A piece of the True Cross? "I shall guard it with my life, and for a healthy paycheck."

The man chained to it offered a smile. "You must be Mordid." He looked at the suitcase. "This stays with me. Unless you'd like to cut off my wrist?"

"Maybe I sh—"

Eryn stepped behind him and offered a kick to his heel.

"Should show you to your quarters," Mordid said. He looked at the group, then back at their spokesman.

The leader with the suitcase nodded. "I am Cardinal Pedro Chavez, and this is…"

He introduced an assortment of cardinals, bishops, archbishops, and so on. Mordid began to understand why the crowd had vacant stares most of the time. He shook his head, clearing his mind, and gestured toward the ramp leading into his landing craft.

"After you, Pedro."

The old Mexican offered an even wider smile than Mordid's, but the men around him scowled and narrowed their eyes.

The crowd started to murmur once more and press

forward. Apparently they were just as curious about what was in the suitcase. The soldiers in white formed a defensive barrier, using the hafts of their halberds to keep the curious at bay.

"Time to go, sir," Jenkins said.

Pedro and his entourage boarded the ship. Mordid followed after him. He could hear Eryn shout orders to her crew and Jenkins do the same.

Inside the ship, it was blessedly cool and dark. Mordid would be glad to leave Reconquista behind. Too bright. Mordid was an Upper Arm man, one born under manmade light, not the sun. At least, that was one of his origin stories.

Mordid said to the gathered guests, "Take the path to your left, and you'll find a few spacious rooms and seats. Buckle in; we'll be heading to the *Merciless* shortly."

The communication device in Mordid's pocket buzzed. He reached in and fiddled with a few of the dials.

"*Hermano, are you ready to leave yet?*" It was Rodriguez.

"Yes," Mordid said, "I have the relic, and we're just packing up now. You should come down and visit before we leave. You must miss home."

"*Is it still bright, dry, hot, and too crowded?*"

Mordid smirked. "Not homesick, I see."

"*No. Besides, we have problems. I just detected a fleet of ships entering the system. They are not pilgrims.*"

Cursing, Mordid pressed the device closer to his ear. "How many?"

Static crackled in his ear. "*Not many, but they seem intent. Get back here. Fast.*"

"I'm on my way." Mordid thrust the device into his pocket. The ramps closed, and his various employees made their way to their seats.

Eryn came up alongside him. She looked down and opened her mouth, but her cheery expression changed to something terse and intense. She could read Mordid all too easily. "What's wrong?"

"We're on the clock." He moved to his seat and sat down.

Eryn blinked. "That was fast. Someone must want what is in that suitcase very badly."

Mordid nodded. Worse, whoever it was had almost timed the attack perfectly. Either someone on his end, or someone on Reconquista, had spoken too freely. He frowned. Who would want to stop a relic from reaching the Khan system? He shut his eyes as the ship shuddered while its engines powered up.

"Something isn't right about this deal," he murmured to himself. Then again, he sensed that from the start.

#

THE UPPER ARM -THE MERCILESS ORBITING RECONQUISTA-

The view before Rodriguez was of the prow of his ship. It was a mighty, if old, warship. Her hull looked like a knife, and her paint was a dull gray, blazed here and there with the red fist emblem of the Traveling Tyrant.

Mordid was on his way, and by the time the enemy was close enough to do him harm, it would be too late for them. The Tyrant, and more importantly, the Holy Father, would be safe aboard the *Merciless* and encased in layers upon layers of battle-worthy metal.

The flicker of light among the sea of stars indicated the position of the enemy fleet as it closed in. It was a small group and no match for the Tyrant's fleet. No match for Rodriguez.

Valdez hunched over a console, his hand planted on the shoulder of the helmsman. His dark eyes widened. "They've launched smaller ships." He growled, "Lots of them."

"Fighters?" Rodriguez tilted his head and narrowed his eyes. Such ships were swift and could be a danger. Not to the *Merciless* of course, but to the Holy Father and the shuttle he was aboard.

"*Si.* A cloud of them, coming in fast." Valdez looked at his admiral with a worried expression on his face. "Very fast."

Stroking his moustache, Rodriguez nodded. "They wish to assassinate him." He pressed a button on his captain's chair and was greeted by a static-laden, but serviceable, channel. Both fleets were trying to use electronic means to shut down one another's communication. For now, he could get through.

"To all ships, this is Admiral Rodriguez. Launch fighters

and engage the enemy. A bounty to each man who makes a kill. A paid vacation to whoever kills me three!" He grinned. Nothing like incentive motivated his murderous pilots. He saw the battle screen soon enough flash with over a hundred friendly green dots, all of them eager to challenge the foe. The *Merciless* had her own complement of interceptors, which were leading the counter charge.

Valdez shook his head. "Admiral, a few of them might make it through and threaten him."

There was no need to say which "him" Valdez meant. Rodriguez pondered sending the Holy Father back to Reconquista to wait the battle out, but he didn't know what was happening on the planet. Perhaps that was the enemy's true purpose? Their fleet certainly wasn't large enough to win an outright battle. Perhaps they were hoping to force the Holy Father back, back to some trap? No! The Holy Father would be safest on board his ship, under his care.

"God will not allow him to perish." Rodriguez watched as one of the fast approaching red dots on the battle screen vanished. Then another and another. "Neither will our pilots," he said with a smile.

Brief flashes of orange decorated the black void of space. He could make out agile shapes, twirling like fireflies in the night and the blazing dots that indicated tracer rounds firing in great volume and the streaking light of missiles and the glimmer of beamers.

"Should we open up on them?" Valdez asked.

Shaking his head, Rodriguez said, "No need to kill our own today. Look. The enemy dies." He gestured to the screen where every second one of the angry red dots disappeared. The main enemy fleet halted its progress as elements of the Tyrant's host moved into position to block them from reaching the flagship.

"Their capital ships are breaking off," Valdez said. He clapped his hands. "They are fleeing!"

Normally, victory brought a rush of exhilaration to Rodriguez. He would praise the Virgin Mary, whoop and holler and drive his men into a frenzy of celebration that culminated with him breaking out a bottle of authentic Mexican tequila from the days when there was a Mexico back on Earth. However, this time, something wasn't right. A swarm of the red dots remained on the screen, threatening and close. They were tiny, insignificant fighters that were so near he could make them out with the naked eye.

The enemy fighters were sleek and silvery ships, of a make and model that spoke of money and sophistication. They were not the bulky, durable ships he'd expect from an Upper Arm mercenary outfit. They weren't economical and plain, like so many of the ships manufactured in Corporate Space either. No, the ships were elegant.

"Earth," he spat.

"What?" Valdez strode across the command deck and peered out the window. "What is happening?" He shot a look over his shoulder at Rodriguez. "What are they up to?"

They all knew the secret, and there was no need to be coy. An Earth Government ship was shadowing their fleet. The captain of said vessel had promised the pope's return to Earth, with freedom, in exchange for Mordid, dead or in chains. Likely dead. A hero for a villain.

"Valdez, take command. I will see how our deal is progressing. Mordid's ship is almost here. Make sure it arrives." He stared at his second in command.

The younger man turned to face Rodriguez and saluted. "I swear on my soul that it will!"

"*Bien.*" Rodriguez stormed off the deck and into the halls of his ship. Crewmen scurried about to their battle stations, unaware that the fight was nearly over. It could hardly be called a battle. That worried Rodriguez. Too easy.

Ignoring the salutes of the men, Rodriguez made his way toward a secure communication hub, one that he had repeatedly checked for listening devices and tampering. Within the chamber was a series of monitors, chairs, and machinery.

He shut the door and sat down. With heavy punches into the console, he sought out the same channel he used when speaking with the Earth Government captain who silently trailed their fleet.

The screen fizzled a moment before into view came the smiling, dark face of the agent of Earth. Behind the blue-clad officer was a brightly lit room, holographic controls, and crewmen busy at work. The captain of the vessel was in a chair that was, of course, far nicer than the seat Rodriguez had to take when ruling over his vessel.

"A social call, Admiral?" the captain asked.

"You know why I am contacting you," Rodriguez snarled. "Those are ships from Earth Force attacking us. Do you go back on your word so quickly?"

The captain shrugged. "I'm sorry you think that. However, those ships are not from Earth Government. They are not members of Earth Force. Earth, yes. Government, no. Our armed forces, no."

"What?" Rodriguez crossed his arms. "Explain."

The captain nodded. "Of course. The fleet that is harassing you consists of older ships. We no longer use them."

That in of itself was unsettling. From what he had seen of their behavior, Rodriguez was thankful he heavily outnumbered his attackers. If Earth Government ships were even more superior to them… well, that couldn't bode well for the future.

"Who does?"

The captain sucked in a breath. "I can't say for certain. I can guess, though, if you like." He clasped his hands together. "Please, don't take my word for it. It's just a theory I have."

"Out with it, snake." Rodriguez glanced over his shoulder, ensuring the door was sealed and shut. He returned his gaze to his Earth counterpart. "Who do you *think* is causing me trouble?"

"Well," the captain said, "when I told you Earth Government was ready to have the pope return, I didn't mention that the current Earth-approved pope might be upset about losing his job."

Rodriguez blinked. "You gave the anti-pope a fleet?" He stood up. "Are you stupid? Of course that sinner would want to kill the Holy Father!"

"Calm down, Admiral." The captain waved his hands, and his tone remained level and cool, while his smile remained plastered in place. "Earth Government does not outfit anyone, other than itself, with the tools to do harm. I am simply theorizing that the soon-to-be former pope may have used his resources to illegally get a hold of some of our outdated war material. For years, we have allowed *our* pope to exist. If he caught wind that he was to be, uhhh, demoted as it were…" he trailed off.

"Damn him." Rodriguez puffed his chest out. "Well, it doesn't matter. I have defeated the false pope, or whoever it is that has 'borrowed' your outdated equipment."

The captain nodded. "I'll admit you have done so marvelously. I don't know why they bothered with the odds so stacked against them. Religion brings about desperation, I suppose." He blinked, and for a moment the man's plastic smile wavered. "I'm sorry, I didn't mean that as an offense. I'm not terribly religious."

"Hmmph. Few on Earth are. They just pretend to be, so everyone feels good. No longer. The *true* pope will be among you sinners, and he will not smile and say all is well. He will call sin out." Rodriguez cut communications and stood up from the chair. He stroked his moustache and thought a moment about the attack and what the Earth agent had said.

The attack was too easy to defeat. Too easy meant he might be missing something. His blood chilled as he pondered what the true purpose of the enemy was. There were too many unknowns. What the Earth captain theorized made sense, but that did not make it true.

He reached into his decorated tunic and produced a communication device. He turned the clunky dials to reach his most trusted man.

"Valdez."

"*They are all dead or running for their lives, Admiral!*"

"*Bien.* I want the ship searched." He continued to twirl the end of his moustache, binding the hair in a tight knot, then releasing it. "Every deck. Every bay."

There was a pause followed by, "*Por ciudad?*"

"*Si.*" He didn't elaborate why they needed to be discreet. Better to explain that in person. Later. He returned the device to his pocket and exited the room. Glowering, he stomped his way back to the bridge, just in time to see Valdez, and a few others leaving. They were armed.

Rodriguez gave a curt nod and watched as Valdez and his fellow Mexicans spilled out into the cavernous ship with steely glints in their eyes. He prayed that they found nothing, and that the assault on their fleet was as the man from Earth said it was—born from desperation. However, he had not become an admiral of one of the largest mercenary outfits in the galaxy by being reckless. No, he had become an admiral by being cautious. If the attack was a ruse for something more sinister, he'd find out about it. And then he would destroy it.

#

The craft rocked once more, and the lights flickered. The guests screamed, except the man with the suitcase, who sat serene and quiet throughout the ordeal. Jenkins envied him.

Mordid, red with fury, pounded on the door leading to the ship's cockpit.

"Fly better, Nums or I'll do it myself," he shouted.

Over the intercom the pilot replied, *"Be my guest, sir. In the meantime, might I advise you stay buckled in."*

The ship jerked once more as another shot glanced off its hide. Jenkins felt his stomach do flips, and he gripped the arms of the restraint seat. Looking at his boss, he said, "Sir, I think Nums has the right of it."

Mordid swayed on his feet and made his way to the nearest seat. He flung himself into the chair and strapped in. "If I die, remind me to fire the lot of you!"

"Sir," Jenkins said, "if there was a bullet I could throw myself, or Karlson, in front of, I would. I think we're all in Nums's hands now."

Eryn, her expression tight, smiled as she squirmed in her seat. "Dear, tell Jenkins why you picked Nums to be your personal pilot."

Mordid sneered. "Shut up. Now is not the time for chiding me on any of my decisions."

She grinned and looked at Jenkins. "He thinks he's funny and quirky. He didn't bother to see if he was a good pilot. For all he knows, Nums is a washout from a half-dozen other outfits.

One bit of wit and the Tyrant thinks you're gold. It's a vanity thing by the way. He thinks he's very witty, and so when he sees it in others, he actually sees a bit of him in them."

Karlson groaned. "Is he a washout pilot?"

She laughed.

"What do they want, can I ask that?" Jenkins peered at Mordid.

"The suitcase. It contains a relic of great importance going to a place of great danger. I think they want to destroy it." Mordid frowned. "Or they could be after me specifically. Always an option."

Jenkins waited for the ship to fall apart around them. Of all the deaths he could imagine, one at the hands of the frigid, eye-popping vacuum of space was the least appealing. He internally laughed, without humor, at the thought that right now he'd prefer to be shot, burned, or even drowned.

"*That's not good. We sort of need that piece.*" Nums said through the intercom.

"What's not good?" Mordid barked.

"*Hmm? This thing still on? Oh! Good news, sir! Our fighters have driven them off. But we've taken some damage. The landing may be a bit rough.*"

"We should pray," the man with the suitcase said.

Mordid nodded. "I agree. Everyone, bow your heads and pray to Nums. With enough happy thoughts we might be able to make up, through faith, what he lacks in piloting."

The guest smiled once. He bowed his head and murmured a prayer that the others in his party repeated.

Jenkins was not a religious man. Being in the line of work he was in, it was hard to feel religious. However, he wasn't against asking the Big Guy for help when he couldn't help himself. He bowed his head and whispered a few half-remembered phrases involving a valley, a rod, and shadows, though he wasn't sure what order they went in or how a rod would defeat impending darkness and death, let alone compensate for Nums's skills or lack thereof.

The ship lurched and with it, Jenkins. His eyes flew open, and he sucked in a breath. The lights flickered out, and shouts and cries replaced the prayers.

Just as fast, the ship stopped moving, and the lights returned. The astonished and panicky yells faded. The men murmured to one another, and Mordid and Eryn exchanged a long glance.

The door to the cockpit opened, and the short, wide-eyed and smiling Nums appeared. "Huh! Dumb luck, sir. We ended up nailing that landing! Amazing, given we're missing a good part of our landing gear."

"A miracle," the man with the suitcase said.

Mordid unhooked himself from his seat and stood up. He clapped his hands together. "It is. All praise Nums, our new God."

Nums blushed. "Aw, thanks, sir. I don't need to be turned into a deity, though."

Eryn cleared her throat and the tall, sinuous woman stood. She looked over to the guests, then stepped to Mordid's side and placed a hand on his shoulder. "We'll leave it as divine. How's that?"

"That reminds me of Pastor Kestor and his lot back on Paradisa," Mordid said. He snapped his fingers. "Jenkins, take our guests to their room."

Jenkins waved Karlson over. The harried old soldier rounded up the bodyguards and chose a few to tag along with Mordid and the rest to stay with him.

The ramp of the ship opened, squealing and clanking. As cool air greeted them, a landing bay filled with soldiers, marines, and crewmen in dark militaristic attire. When Mordid strode off the craft, Jenkins saw their expressions lift. He could sympathize. Without Mordid, there was no pay.

Jenkins walked over to the leader of the guests. "Come with me, sir."

"Of course. Your prayer was interesting. Oh, and call me Pedro." His brown, wrinkled face filled with yet more creases as he smiled. "But the intent was heartfelt. I think it helped."

"You heard that?" Jenkins turned his eyes away. "Good ears for an old man."

"One in my line of work does a lot of listening."

Jenkins led the party off the craft and looked back at the shuttle. The bottom was blackened and twisted, while along the hull there were a few scorch marks.

He heard Mordid talking to Admiral Rodriguez through a command communication device. The admiral was giving Mordid a report on the situation.

"Well, good work, *amigo*. I'll add another made-up medal to your chest shortly. Any idea who tried to kill me this time?"

"*No.*"

"Awesome."

Mordid thrust the device back into his pocket. He took Eryn by the arm and, though he lowered his voice, Jenkins could still hear him.

"They had no chance to begin with." He moved closer to her. "Rodriguez said it was essentially a suicide run."

Eryn peered at the damaged craft. "Really? No chance at success?"

Jenkins detached himself from Pedro and his men and stepped a little closer to the pair.

"Almost none." Mordid's blue eyes narrowed. "If I wanted to destroy the relic, or me, I would have sent a lot more ships and done it right. So, we're facing incompetents, or there's something I'm missing."

Jenkins cleared his throat. "Sir, maybe the attack was meant as a distraction? If it killed us, great, but what if they had something else in—"

"Mind your own business," Eryn hissed. She opened her mouth to say more, but Mordid pulled her aside. His arm hooked with hers. Though she was taller, Mordid was bulkier and acted as an anchor.

"Good thinking, Jenkins." He smiled, contrasting Eyrn's slit-eyed glare and deep scowl. Mordid's blue eyes flickered with amusement. "However, our guests are tired." He raised his voice. "Take Pedro and his boys to their room. I'll do some more thinking on this matter. Gentlemen, you are in good hands!"

Jenkins heard some of the withered cardinals and bishops gasp and complain.

"Boys?!"

"He's insolent."

"No respect."

Mordid ignored them and led Eyrn aside where they huddled close in a conspiratorial manner. Whatever was said between them was too hushed for Jenkins to make sense of.

Patting him on the shoulder, Karlson said, "Come on. We can angle for Tyrant-points later."

Lingering a moment, Jenkins nodded and approached Pedro and his entourage. He waved to the men Karlson had picked to go with them. "Let's go."

The other bodyguards remained near Mordid, warily watching the bay for any signs of threats to their master. Even aboard the *Merciless,* he wasn't safe.

Jenkins and his party marched out of the bay and down a long, gray hall. Crewmen scurried out of the way like mice as the collection made its way into the bowels of the ship. Their voices echoed, their boots slapped on the deck, their robes swished. Jenkins stared at the metal deck intently with each striding step.

Jenkins halted. "Karlson, Umbradax."

The group halted. The salt-and-pepper haired Karlson tilted his head, and the inbred Umbradax made his way to the front. He idly scratched his crotch, unashamed that religious folk were about.

"Take Pedro to his room. Work out a guard rotation. I want two men on the door at all times," Jenkins said.

"Okay," Umbradax said.

Karlson's brows knitted. "You're not coming with, sir?"

Jenkins flashed a smile. "I'll be along later. I have a suspicion."

Karlson growled, "Sir, we have a job to do. An important one."

"No, you do. I'm delegating." He winked and departed, leaving the group so he could go wander the many halls and decks of the *Merciless* on his own. He had a hunch that the true attack on the relic had yet to occur, and if he could prevent it, then he'd be a hero to the company, and of course to Mordid. A happy boss was a well-paid and favored Jenkins.

#

Thrask marched down the hall, saluting to soldiers as he passed them by. This portion of the ship was where his men were stationed, where they trained and readied themselves for the next mission. Thus far, Thrask had little for them to do. Mordid had revealed almost nothing about the current job other than they had to deliver an item to the dreaded Khan system. It was some sort of holy relic. That part was nonsense.

At first, Thrask was excited by the mission. The Khan system was where careers were vaulted into the heavens and burned to the ground in equal number. If Mordid was going into that war zone, Thrask was sure he'd be able to bust up heads, obliterate rival mercenaries, and make a serious name for himself. Alas, the Tyrant had told him no such thing would happen.

It was a navy job. Transportation and nothing else.

He cursed and continued on his way to the gym where he could work out some of his frustrations on a punching bag or drown his annoyance in the welcome pain of lifting weights.

"Slow up, boss," a voice said from behind him.

Thrask restrained a shout. He whirled to find himself staring down at the bug-eyed End Roader Herrin.

The man smiled. Thrask crossed his arms and glowered.

"Don't sneak up on me."

"Habit."

"What is it?"

Herrin cleared his throat and glanced up and down the hallway. There were only a few people moving about. He moved closer and whispered as he spoke. "Mordid's guests are here safe and sound, but something is wrong."

"Hmm?" Thrask tilted his head. "How so?"

"One fellow, Pedro by name, has a suitcase handcuffed to his wrist. I take it that's the trinket that needs delivering," Herrin said.

Thrask shrugged. "Mordid let that slip, eh? Yeah, it's some relic or other. So what?"

"We were attacked on route to the *Merciless*. Jenkins and Mordid both came to the conclusion the attack was cover for something else." Herrin shrugged. "Beats me as to what. The attack seemed plenty real to me. We barely landed in one piece."

Thrask punched his hand into his open palm, and the clap of flesh on flesh sounded like a gunshot. "Attacked? I didn't know. No one did. No alarms were sounded, and no messages were sent to us. Namely, none were sent to me. The damn navy is awful secretive." He pondered a moment. Rodriguez had handled the attack on his own. That was his right, but to be left out made Thrask suspicious.

"You said Mordid thought the whole thing was a ruse?"

"Something like that," Herrin said. "I couldn't eavesdrop every little thing, but yeah. He's suspicious. So is Jenkins. Neither is entirely stupid."

"If they're concerned, then so am I. It could be an opportunity for us, Herrin." Thrask smiled. "However, we need to get a bit more information. Who do you think knows the most about this attack?"

Herrin pursed his lips. He then met Thrask's gaze. "The admiral. He'll know the most."

"Damn right he will, and so will his little band of Mexicans. They're a tight lot." Thrask smiled, baring his teeth. "So, I think you and I should go ask one of his cousins, or whatever they are, a few questions." Thrask checked himself from laughing out loud. "I have just the plan."

Herrin returned the wolfish smile. "I'm all ears, boss."

Thrask jerked his head. "Follow me. I need to stink up the bathroom closest to the bridge." He turned and navigated his way through the ship to the deck closest to Rodriguez's nest.

As they neared the bridge, more and more of the marines, crewmen, and others around them were those who were firmly in the pocket of the admiral. Thrask was mildly uncomfortable. He much preferred to be surrounded by his own cohorts, and in truth, every moment off the ship and on a planet, no matter how hellish it was, was better than wandering around the *Merciless*. He glanced at the various cameras placed sporadically above doorways. The ship was riddled with spies. The entire command staff, and Mordid, spied and counter-spied. He'd be seen wandering where he shouldn't, but so long as he sufficiently terrorized one of Rodriguez's men, all would be well. He'd have the information he needed. His presence would be debated over, but that wouldn't change a thing.

The bathroom nearest the bridge was dim, like the rest of the craft, and like so much of the *Merciless*, it was empty. The stalls were gray, as were the walls, and the urinals were a shocking and contrasting polished white. The smell of chemical cleaning supplies nearly made his eyes water.

"Pick a stall and when one of Rodriguez's exiles comes in, do your thing." He pointed at Herrin. "Scare him. Don't kill him. We need information, and we need him to wet himself so that he won't cry to Rodriguez."

Herrin nodded and slithered into a stall. He shut the door and whistled a tune.

Thrask stuffed himself into a different stall. He groaned as he shut the door. He was a massive man and simply not meant for the tight confines of inter-galactic waste facilities. He glanced at the toilet and wrinkled his nose. The navy apparently didn't teach its men to flush. He reached out to press the button to dispose of the filth.

The toilet burbled.

Apparently the navy didn't teach its maintenance men to do their job either. Someone had thought the best solution was to just pour chemicals atop the waste.

Sighing, Thrask stared at the ceiling, trying not to ponder the contents of the toilet and trying to avoid thoughts like, "How could one man produce so much?" or "Was this a group project?"

"Ugh."

Herrin said from his stall, "You okay, boss?"

"Yeah," Thrask replied. "I'm just fascinated by someone's efforts."

At least the smell of chemicals overpowered whatever stench was emanating from the toilet.

The door opened, and Thrask waited a moment. He heard footsteps, followed by the sound of a zipper lowering. Thrask opened the stall door and peered through the crack.

Perfect!

The man attending the urinal was short and wiry, with a deep black moustache that framed his mouth and a haircut as short and flat as Thrask's. Most importantly, he was a Mexican, and around his neck hung a golden crucifix that Rodriguez's men were so fond of wearing.

"Herrin," Thrask said, "mind the door."

The End Roader slithered out of his stall and barred the exit.

"You," Thrask said to the Mexican. "I have some questions."

The man ignored him and continued to go about his business.

"Hey," Thrask drew closer. "I'm talking to you, sailor."

The man zipped up, flushed, and turned to face Thrask. He scowled and looked up at him. His eyes narrowed, and he reached into his tunic.

Sensing a weapon, Thrask balled his fists up, and his muscles coiled like a spring. If the idiot drew a gun, he'd smash him in two. He had no compulsions about interrogating a paraplegic.

The man pulled out a pair of oversized, reflective sunglasses. Despite the dimness of the bathroom, he placed them on his face, and Thrask saw his own square-jawed, battle-scarred reflection in each lens. He frowned.

"Listen up. You're going to—"

The jab came faster than Thrask could react. Pain blossomed through his nose, and he staggered back. He snarled at the Mexican, who had both his fists up, and one of them had a bit of slick, red substance on it.

The Mexican hovered on his feet, circling left then right.

"Are you kidding me?" Thrask shook his head. "Fine, we'll do this the hard way." He lunged and swept his hand out to grapple the much smaller fellow.

With ease, the Mexican bobbed under the swipe and delivered two jabs. Both landed squarely on Thrask's face.

"Ah!" Thrask stumbled back again and rubbed his nose. Blood stained his hands. Insolent Mexican! Narrowing his eyes, Thrask charged and delivered his own powerful punch, and a kick for good measure.

The Mexican side-stepped the punch and responded with another pair of jabs. The kick was dealt with by backing up, so that Thrask's foot ended up making little contact. Just as Thrask's heavy boot landed on the ground, the Mexican stepped in.

The tiny, but immensely strong, Mexican slammed his right fist just under his jaw. Thrask felt his head snap back, and his vision began to darken.

"Boss?" Herrin said, alarmed.

"I'm fine." He groaned and leaned against one of the urinals. His opponent danced in place while Thrask caught his breath.

He spit, and a glob of blood stained the white porcelain with vibrant red. He shook his head clear and sized up the Mexican. "Hmmmph. Someone taught you to fight, eh?"

His opponent flashed a momentary smile.

"Oh crap," Herrin said.

Thrask didn't take his eyes off the Mexican as he said, "What is it?"

"I know this guy," Herrin said from behind him. "Boxing champion of the fleet. I won a couple hundred off his title fight." Herrin groaned. "I, I don't even know if he speaks English."

The boxer shuffled closer, and his fists flew.

Thrask brought his arms up to fend off the attacks, and he tried to circle, but there was little room to maneuver. When he covered his face, the boxing champion punched him in the gut. When he lowered his hands, his nose was targeted. Pain filled Thrask's body as blow after blow landed, and for all his efforts he was able to land only parting shots in return. Every punch, kick, and attempt to grapple was met with an elusive slip and a series of vicious counterstrikes.

"Hurry up, boss," Herrin said.

"Trying!"

Roaring, Thrask barreled toward the boxing champion. He'd force him in a corner and take away any chance he had to move.

The man threw himself wide at the last moment and his hand pushed hard on Thrask's elbow, forcing him to turn toward the stall he had been hiding in. A punch to his kidney had him gasping, and another push sent him headfirst toward the toilet.

34

He screeched as he fell to his knees and his nose was greeted with a smell so foul that he choked back vomit. Thrask tried to rise, but something small, strong, and ferocious jumped on his back. Small, muscle-corded arms wrapped around him as the Mexican proved he was not only a first rate boxer, but an adept wrestler as well.

Thrask tried to rise, but the man on his back pushed him closer and closer to the contents of the toilet.

"Herrin!" Thrask bellowed. His words echoed in the stink-stained bowl. Filth and chemicals worked in combination to choke him as much as his attacker.

Closer and closer his head was pushed to the floating mix of human waste. Just as his nose was about to touch something a horrid shade of brown, the pressure on his back relented. Flinging himself away, Thrask collapsed outside the stall and breathed in cleaner air with great gulps. His eyes watered, and blood trickled freely from his nose. Through blurry vision, he saw Herrin's knife sliding in and out of the Mexican's body. To the little fellow's credit, he belted Herrin several times before falling to his knees.

Herrin's blade darted in a final time and the boxing champ collapsed in a pool of his own blood. The inbred, murderous medic jogged over to Thrask.

"You don't look good, boss."

Thrask groaned and, wobbling, made his way to his feet. Herrin had a gash over his eye and a bruise on his cheek.

"You don't look much better." Thrask stared at the corpse. "I didn't want him dead. There are enough cameras around that they'll find out it was us." Thrask sighed, "Unless…" he trailed off.

"Unless what?"

He didn't like the only option available. "We'll need to talk to the old man. Mauss will be able to clear this mess up or at least erase any recordings of us traipsing near the scene. He'll also be interested in what Rodriguez is up to." Thrask rubbed his sore neck.

Herrin nodded. "I take it, Mauss's help won't be for free?"

"Nope. He'll want something. If not right away, eventually. The buzzard has been here the longest, and it isn't because he's lucky." Thrask shrugged. "If I'm ever made the Tyrant, it'll probably be with his blessing." He gazed a moment at the body.

"Come on," Thrask said, "let's go see Mauss."

Herrin stopped by the blood-stained body and reached into his own pocket. He put something in the corpse's hand before standing.

"What's that?" Thrask asked.

"An opportunity I've been waiting for. Before we go, let's stop by an infirmary. I can treat you." He winked and cleaned his knife with a few towels taken from the wall-mounted dispenser.

Thrask shrugged and he left the restroom, wincing with every step. He muttered under his breath. "That bad, eh?"

From behind him, Herrin said, "Medically speaking, you're quite the mess. I'm sure a little pain will be worth your trouble in the end, boss."

Thrask focused on the pain coursing through his body. His nose throbbed with every beat of his enslaved heart. To mitigate the pain, he imagined Mordid going through an equal, if not greater amount of suffering. Everything was the Tyrant's fault, but soon enough he'd have his revenge.

With every pained step, Thrask mouthed the Tyrant's name followed by a crude curse.

3

THE UPPER ARM -THE MERCILESS ORBITING RECONQUISTA-

Mordid watched Pedro Chavez and his collection of religious fans depart. He stepped close to Eryn so that his body guards didn't listen in. They were a good lot—Jenkins had impressed him on more than one occasion—but some things were best left unknown to them. Besides, men like Jenkins were a bit too ambitious.

"Well?" He said.

Eryn's brow arched. "Well what?"

"We are being paid a ridiculous sum to get a suitcase to the Khan system. Right out of the gate, we get jumped, and the attack is ill planned?" He took her by the arm and walked through the landing bay, sidestepping crates and navigating around brightly painted cranes and stacks of ammunition.

She said nothing, but her eyes fixed on his.

"They want the relic. Do you remember that job we did on the Hioshi Company?" Mordid nudged her.

Her eyes flickered. "Yes. We staged an attack so you and I could slip in and plant a listening device. They're here!" She looked at the guards and opened her mouth.

Mordid yanked her closer. "Not yet. We'll tell the boys

that we may have unexpected guests later. First thing is first. I want that relic."

"Why?"

He grinned. "Because the enemy, whoever they are, want it. They either want their hands on it or they want to destroy it. But I think they want their hands on it. That means it'll be much safer in my hands anyways. Chavez just doesn't trust me yet. He should have handed it over to begin with."

Eryn gave short laugh. "And you think stealing the relic from him will win him over?"

"Well…" he trailed off and tried to think of another way to phrase it.

"You are just curious. Someone tells you 'no' and you can't let that sit." She poked him. "Is that the real reason?"

"Partly," he confessed. He sighed and looked at the tops of her polished boots. "Eryn, there is something *wrong* with this job. It's too good to turn down. I'm worried that the relic is something a bit more than a splinter from the Holy Grail or a page from a saint's favorite magazine." He turned his gaze upon hers. "I need to know what it is. I can't be a proper Tyrant unless I know all the angles."

"I see." Eryn licked her full lips, and with her pale hand she flicked aside few errant strands of raven-black hair from her face. "And I agree. However, let's be subtle about this, just in case the relic *is* something mundane and you're wrong."

He couldn't help but smile. His mind worked through various plots and schemes to get at the item, but Eryn was right. He needed to be sly about it. He needed to take a look at the item and then either steal it, for safekeeping of course, or slip away, undetected. Chavez had to stay happy. A happy Chavez meant a fulfilled contract and thus happy shadowy investors and thus a well-paid and happy Mordid.

He didn't have to think long.

"I have a plan," Mordid declared.

"Oh?" Eryn lowered herself to gaze at him at eye level. "Is it a good one?"

Meeting her maddening stare, Mordid said, "We need to act fast because I think someone else is on this ship with the same plan as us. So, we waltz on down to Chavez's room. Distract the guards, slip in, and then hide. I can't imagine our guest always has that thing chained to his wrist."

"You better hope not." She stepped back.

"Hey!" Mordid flashed his most winning of smiles. "It'll work. Just a peek at what's in the suitcase and then I can be on my way. He'll never know because we aren't going to delegate this one. The personal touch!" He tugged his coat about his broad shoulders.

She looked him over. "Let's do this right. Come with me to my room. We'll get dressed up there." She approached the guards and cleared her throat. "Mordid believes there may be some stowaways onboard. The hostile variety." She looked them over. "I don't want an alarm to be raised—we have a guest to impress—so you lot are to search the ship. Discreetly."

Mordid, following her lead, added, "My eternal love for whoever brings me back the unwanted guests alive. I want to know what they are up to."

They stared at him.

"Shoo. Go. I'll be fine." Mordid waved them off with both hands.

The men, reluctantly but obediently, wandered away, leaving Eyrn and Mordid relatively alone in the landing bay.

She offered her hand to him. "To my room?"

He looked at her extended hand and slapped it. "Great idea! I love your room. Knives. Cameras. More knives." He shook his head. "My favorite part is the picture of your genocidal grandfather over your bed. Who wants to sleep with the dreaded Sanovich watching over them?"

Her skin flushed a brilliant shade of red. "I've never shown you my bed."

Mordid passed her by and gave Eyrn a long look. "My dear, I know everything. All your secrets. All." Which wasn't true, but it helped keep his employees on their toes. He suppressed a laugh as he saw Eyrn go from a plum-red hue to a deathly pale shade.

"Everything," he said, casually, as if it were no great task in prying into Eyrn's affairs.

Which was still a lie. He knew precious little about her plots. He knew less about their mission. What was the relic? Who wanted it? Who might be aboard? Why was the pay so high? Why were they going to the Khan system? That system was for vainglorious fools after loot that best not be touched. Frowning, he placed his hands behind his back and stalked his way to Eryn's chambers.

Her room was as he remembered it from prior visits. Orderly. Neat. Threatening. She liked to collect and display things, many of which were instruments of pain and suffering. Eryn's primary task was head of PR. She made his face the one that all the clients in the galaxy wanted to see. Hence, she had on display several recording devices. She also doubled as an interrogator. It was more of a hobby really, but one that she was skilled at and that explained the variety of sharp things she had on shelves and hanging on the walls. He wondered if she named them.

She had gone into her bedroom to change, and no doubt to look for a surveillance device as well. She wouldn't find one. He had wandered her rooms on more than one occasion while she was off doing tasks. No door was locked to the Tyrant and no security camera was safe from his altering hands, or rather Mauss, and he was all too happy to help Mordid scheme and spy on Eryn.

When she emerged, she was wearing a skintight suit of ebony. She was coated neck to toe, and it almost looked as if she were wearing nothing at all but a black coat of paint and a belt wrapped around her waist with a variety of tools hanging from it. If he didn't know how utterly dangerous and murderous she was, he'd be exhilarated by the sight. Not that she wasn't fetching, despite her history. He genuinely liked her. However, he was the Traveling Tyrant and she was as much a rival as an asset. Still, he could feel his heart pound a bit louder.

"Do I get a suit like that?" Mordid asked.

She arched a brow. "No. I figured you could wear this." She flung a piece of black fabric at him.

Catching it, Mordid unraveled the cloth to reveal a hood with slits cut out for the eyes. Right where the forehead would be was a phrase embroidered in contrasting white in a garish font.

"Bad Girl," Mordid said and narrowed his eyes at Eryn.

"It's the only one I had for you. Sorry." She beamed.

"Hmmph," Mordid said and tucked the hood into his belt. "Let's go."

She nodded. "I'll lead the way."

Graceful and sleek in her movements, Eryn passed by Mordid and exited the room. She escorted him through the warrens of the *Merciless,* choosing corridors that were empty. When there was a passerby, she pulled Mordid with her into the nearest available closet or unused room, of which the ship had many.

The *Merciless* was originally built to single-handedly descend upon hostile planets with overwhelming force and awe. At full capacity she could be teeming with thousands upon thousands of soldiers, marines, technicians, fighter craft, bombers, tanks, and more. She had been built long ago, though, and military theory had changed since the time she had been launched. These days no one was fool enough to pile all of their resources into one ship. A single ship might malfunction. A lucky shot might cause her to detonate from stem to stern. A wise mercenary, like Mordid considered himself, spread his men and material out through numerous craft. Thus, nowhere near full capacity, the ship was in many ways ghostly.

Its emptiness aided him and Eryn in their journey to Chavez's guest quarters located deep within the ship.

His communication device buzzed. Frowning, Mordid produced the item and toyed with the dials.

"*Amigo, where are you?*" Rodriguez said.

"Bathroom. I do some of my best thinking here. Go ahead and get underway to the Khan system without me."

"*No rush, no rush. When you complete your thoughts, come to the bridge. The men like it when you belt out a command. It inspires!*"

The channel went dead. Mordid put the device into his gray coat.

Eryn smirked. "He already knows what system to go to. I don't find him the type that needs his hand held." She smiled wider, and her eyes became small, suspicious slits. "He wants to know where you are. I'd be careful, Mordid."

He plucked the fabric from his belt and pulled on his hood. "I am careful. And a bad girl." He tapped his forehead.

She pulled on her own hood. It lacked any embarrassing writing. Mordid was about to complain when she darted past him down the gloomy, gray hall. At the far end, she peered around the corner and then flattened herself against the wall.

Grumbling, Mordid followed after her with much less grace and stealth. He whispered, "Whose on guard?"

"Karlson and one of the new End Roaders. I can't remember his name." Eryn nudged him. "What's the plan to distract them?"

Mordid said in quiet, discreet tones, "Lead them on a long and merry chase and don't get killed. And do NOT kill them. Then slip away."

"We don't have time for that," Eryn objected.

"I don't, you do." He pushed her out into the hall.

Before Eryn could say a word, Mordid heard the shout of "Hey!" in unison from the pair of guards.

"Bastard!" Eryn screeched. She ran away, thankfully down a different corridor acting as the perfect bait.

Mordid sighed a breath of relief that she was good enough to play along. He sighed again when Karlson and the End Roader tromped past, guns leveled. Karlson was shouting into a communication device. The pair never even thought to glance down the hall Eryn had emerged from. The boys would need some reminders on how to guard a door. But for now, their incompetence was Mordid's gain.

Despite his initial good fortune, Mordid had little time to act. He darted toward the door and pressed the button. The door would not open for just anyone, but Mordid's finger was a universal key on the ship.

The door slid open, and he passed inside.

The rooms were lavish. Nothing but the best for his guests. The main room had plush chairs and a holographic entertainment system, and on the walls hung numerous pictures of Mordid engaged in monumental events, some of which had actually happened.

He could hear talking from one of the many side chambers, and he ducked low as he made his way over. Taking a quick glance, Mordid took stock of his situation.

In the next room, he saw several of Chavez's men clustered around a table. Chavez was at the head of the table, and the suitcase was there. That was not good. Slightly better, though, was the fact that it was not chained to the wrist of Pedro Chavez.

Mordid scratched his pointed beard under his "bad girl" hood. The relic was within his grasp, but at the moment he could see no discreet way of taking a peek or possession of it.

He heard voices behind him. Looking in the direction of the new sounds, he saw the shadow of men approaching from yet another room.

There were numerous places to hide, but the best was a long couch against the far wall. Above it was a picture of himself giving the thumbs up gesture and an overly-excited smile. He ran to the couch, shifted it aside, and placed himself behind it just as he heard the voices from the adjoining room grow much louder.

"Hello?" a raspy voice asked as men entered.

Mordid kept silent.

"We're in here," Chavez said.

"Oh! Coming."

The voices diminished soon after.

He'd done it! For what good it was worth. Mordid frowned. The plan was a hasty one, and fluid like so many of his actions. It was one of his key traits. He had a level of unpredictability that made guessing his plans of action difficult. However, he was also unsure what to do next. On more than one occasion he was just as confused as his foe. This was one of those moments.

Sighing to himself, he waited for an opportunity to present itself.

#

"Shall we plot a course to the Khan system, Admiral?" one of Rodriguez's helmsmen asked.

"Not yet," he said. He paced the deck and felt the eyes of his men track his every move. The bridge was lacking half of its men, and all of its charm. He gazed at the brown, hot, and dusty world in the view port. There they were, hovering above their birthplace and instead of good cheer and stories of their youth on Reconquista and its neighboring systems, they were silent.

It wasn't a surprise. The mood of the crew matched that of its master. Naturally. He brooded and so they brooded.

Walking across the bridge, he listened to the rhythmic sound of his boots atop the deck. A prayer flew from his lips, then a curse, then a prayer again.

His communication device buzzed. Blinking, Rodriguez pulled it out and pressed a button.

"*Valdez?*"

"*Si!*" his first officer answered. "*We found a ship. It is very fancy. It's a transport craft and in one of the empty bays. The exterior doors were shut. So, either someone let them in, or they have the technology to open the doors themselves. We did not find a soul on board. Admiral, I've never seen technology like this.*"

"Assassins." Rodriguez let out a long breath and reached a hand up to stroke his moustache. They must have slipped in during the attack on Mordid's craft and, given the fact the ships were from Earth, it was highly likely they had the means to "pick the lock," so to speak. He had hoped Valdez would have found nothing, and that the attack was simply ill-conceived and a failure. Now the evidence was overwhelming. The false pope's minions were here and they had state of the art technology at their fingertips. If the true pope were killed…

He banished the thought.

"Get to the Holy Father's chambers. We don't know where the enemy is, but we do know where they are going. I'll meet you down there," Rodriguez said.

"*You?*"

He could hear the surprise in Valdez's voice.

"Yes. Me. I want to handle this personally. Keep things as quiet as you can, Valdez. If you do encounter the assassins, then you must kill them all. No prisoners. The ship, I want it under guard. I'm suspicious why Earth ships, apparently older ones, are getting so advanced!" It was best if Mordid was kept in the dark, but scavenging the Earth invader was too good to pass up. As for Mordid, if he found out about the Holy Father, he'd only ask more questions, and that is something that could not happen. Ignorance would be the end of Mordid and the rise of Rodriguez.

"*This ship is amazing. It will be done!*"

Grunting, Rodriguez put his device away and turned to face his crew. They had anxious expressions and wide eyes.

"I shall be back. If anyone asks where I am, say I'm in…" he thought a moment, "the bathroom." He forced a smile. "Tell them I do my best thinking there."

Lupe, one of his men, bolted up from his seat. He pulled a pair of bulky headphones off. "Admiral, I was listening in on some of the channels." Which was his job. "Mordid's guards are reporting an intruder." He swallowed. "Near the quarters of the Holy Father."

"So it begins." He nodded his thanks and strode off of the bridge. Rodriguez placed a hand firmly on the butt of his pistol. "With me!"

He and his men broke into a run.

#

The ship was gargantuan. With its long corridors, uniform gray paint scheme, and dim lighting, Jenkins had been lost on more than one occasion and discovered empty bays, rooms, and closets. He was surprised he didn't bump into a white-bearded janitor asking if his thirty year shift was over yet.

He had a sense invaders were aboard. However, they could be hiding anywhere within the maze-like confines of the *Merciless*. Yet, if they were after the mysterious suitcase, he knew they would have to head toward Pedro Chavez's quarters eventually.

He wandered the halls and paths near the guest's quarters, looking intently at every face he saw. There were few on that level, and he recognized most. There was a squad of marines assigned to patrol that portion of the ship, to whom he nodded. Deckhands who were unarmed and unassuming enough paid him no mind. He also saw one of Mauss's agents pass by. He looked viperous. However, he was one of *their* vipers, so he was allowed to pass. There was also Karlson and Umbradax, stationed at the door. He avoided them, not wanting to explain himself just yet.

He was getting bored and wondering if his hunch was

wrong. Passing down an empty hall, he paused as he heard a sound. Noises aboard a mighty ship were not unusual. Even on an empty portion of the vessel there were creaks, groans, and even the echoes of conversations, not to mention the continual and monotonous hum of machinery.

The cocking of guns was not altogether unusual either. Except that he was nowhere near where the army was stationed, and the marines were generally armed with beamers.

Pressing himself flat against the nearest wall, Jenkins edged toward a branch in the hallway. He peered around the corner and smiled. By an open door, a pair of men stood, and they were not dressed in any attire befitting an employee of the Traveling Tyrant.

They were wiry sorts, and he at first thought they were twins. They had mocha skin tones and shaved heads. They were foreign, or at least not like the people he normally associated with—the dregs of the Upper Arm and the Corporate Worlds. Yet there was something altogether familiar about them.

They had no scars, no facial imperfections, no pock marks, or anything remotely ugly about them. They were, in a word, beautiful. It clicked. They were men of Earth whose genetics had become one giant melting pot of uniformity and whose wealth had done away with pesky things like wrinkles. He had seen their holographic images on countless advertisements in the Corporate Worlds. Seen their placid and smiling faces in endless propaganda pieces Earth Government sent to the Upper Arm speaking of "unity, prosperity, and equality." He had seen them plenty of times, but never in person.

They looked perfect. Jenkins glanced at his own hand. It was sickly pale. Upper Arm folk were like cave fish. These men? Mocha models.

What were they doing aboard the *Merciless*? They were about as far from Earth Space as one could get. As far as Jenkins knew, the Earth Government was so bureaucratic and inefficient that they'd never extend their claim beyond the systems that were already theirs. That was what he'd been told, at least. What everyone believed. Earth Government was stuck. It did not grow. That's what the Corporate Worlds did, with Earth's permission and a share of tax. The Upper Arm was beyond that. It was the no man's land of the galaxy. Earth was bureaucratic, but beautiful. The Upper Arm was anarchic, ugly, and free.

He drew his pistol and approached the two.

They were dressed in black bodysuits that hugged their forms perfectly with bits of glossy armor worked into the fabric. Their weapons were sleek, and the two were busy checking them over.

"Alright, how about you put those down," Jenkins said and flashed a smile.

The pair looked up, surprised.

One inched his gun up.

"I wouldn't do that." Jenkins waved his pistol to ensure he had their rapt attention. "I only need one of you alive."

The two exchanged glances and set their weapons down. They held their hands up.

"Good thinking." Jenkins drew closer and gestured with his free hand to the wall. "So, what are you boys doing so far from home?"

They obeyed his nonverbal command and put their hands against the wall. The two remained silent. Jenkins saw that on the back of their hands were blue, faded tattoos. They were hard to make out against their skin, but he was certain they were crucifixes.

Jenkins kicked their weapons farther down the hall and took a glance into the room they had emerged from. He was greeted with the sight of two more men who looked as uniform as the ones he had up against the wall, except they were armed and leveling their guns.

"Ah hell," Jenkins said and leapt aside.

No sooner had he done so, one of the men against the wall spun. His foot snapped out and slapped into Jenkin's hand, sending his pistol spiraling into the air.

It landed in the man's hand. He grinned, baring perfect, white teeth.

Jenkins backed away, frowning as the four similar-looking men approached. One of his assailants took aim. The others followed suit.

He shut his eyes and readied himself for the hail of bullets that would cut him down. So much for single-handedly saving the mission and becoming a hero for the company.

"Wait," one of the men said.

Jenkins popped an eye open. "Isn't that my line?"

Three of them lowered their weapons, and their eyes betrayed confusion as they eyed the speaker.

The fourth said calmly, "We don't want to alert anyone. No gun play. We kill him." He sniffed. "By hand."

"Ah," everyone, Jenkins included, said in unison.

The four sped toward Jenkins, who in turn ran. He didn't get far.

Pain burst through his back as he felt a foot land at the base of his spine. He rolled, but they were on him a moment later. Their hands and feet flew in rapid succession, striking, slapping, and crashing into him. Jenkins grit his teeth as he felt hammering shots to his face, to his stomach and atop his feebly upraised arms.

He rose, but one of the intruders grabbed him by the arm, while another slammed his knee into Jenkins's throat before he could let out a cry for help. He wheezed and tried to pull away, coughing up blood.

The grip on Jenkins's arm relented, but more hits landed. The pain from each new strike blended with the rest. It was a chaotic mess. They were everywhere. Punching, kicking, elbowing, and pushing him about. He attempted a wild swing of his own, but his opponents were evasive and knew a lot more about hand-to-hand combat than he did. With his vision reeling, Jenkins lurched toward the wall. He propped himself against it and saw the men looming toward him.

Spitting and cursing, he hurled himself at them, flailing his arms about. They backed off, but in doing so left an escape route open. The room they'd been hiding in was still open.

He had no idea what lay in store that way, but he couldn't go any other direction. They had him hemmed in. Jenkins charged ahead past them and their snapping fists and darting feet, into the room beyond.

Like so many rooms within this part of the *Merciless* it

was gray and bland, but not entirely empty. There was a waste chute against one wall and a pile of equipment in the center of the room.

He ran toward the stacked up guns, boxes, and machinery, leaping over it on his way to the only viable escape route—the garbage chute.

"Don't let him escape!" one of the men shouted.

Jenkins didn't halt for an instant; he threw himself toward the silvery, metal flap of the chute and shut his eyes. He had no idea where it went. For all he knew it dropped a hundred feet into an incinerator, but it would be a little longer left to live than had he stayed.

The flap collapsed as he dove in. Metal encased him, and he screamed as he bounced, head first, into the unknown. His cries echoed, and he crashed into a pile of refuse. He hurt, but he was alive.

Looking up, Jenkins saw the light from the room he had escaped. The silhouette of a head appeared.

"Can we do something loud now?" the shadowy figure said to his cohorts.

Jenkins looked around with bleary-eyed vision. He had landed in a large refuse bin. The bin had a ramp leading to a large, rectangular room filled with other such bins and a mass of knee-deep waste. The walls had been painted a bright green, but the paint had faded and was scored and pitted to reveal raw metal beneath. There was a faded sign posted on one wall that said something about the cold, cruel, and hard vacuum of space along with a picture of a man exploding. The chamber smelled of sweaty socks, rotted food, and oil.

"Nice try," Jenkins said up to his attackers, spitting up a bit of blood as he did so. He rolled out of the bin and reached for the communication device at his side. The bulky, black item was cracked, and wires jutted out from it at odd angles. He frowned and dropped the useless thing. Scanning the room, he noted a door against the far wall. He'd just have to go get help in person.

Just then, Jenkins heard a banging from the chute above.

Were they seriously throwing themselves down after him? He blinked and backed away from the bin, half expecting the men from Earth to land one by one in the garbage room.

A solitary grenade landed instead.

"For you," he heard from the chute.

The grenade exploded.

#

Herrin might be an inbred murderous soldier, but he was handy with a knife and did a decent job of dressing and treating his wounds. Thrask was thankful he had him hauled out of the brig.

As Thrask sat on a bench in an infirmary, Herrin used a rag to clean away the last bit of blood from the general's face.

The doctor was absent, having been told to "go away" by Thrask in the most unfriendly of tones.

"Feeling better, boss?" Herrin asked. He discarded the red-stained rag on the floor without a second glance.

Craning his neck side to side, Thrask mumbled, "I feel like I went toe to toe with a boxer."

"Champion boxer," Herrin corrected.

Thrask grunted. He looked over the room. It was like a hundred other infirmaries he had been in. There were tables, white curtains and the smell of medical equipment in the air. Getting out of here was top on his priority list. Lately, nothing good had come from his ventures into medical rooms. Then again, only through surgery could he truly be repaired. He turned his eyes onto Herrin.

"You're pretty good at this, Herrin. You're a doctor, right?" He reached up and grabbed his chest, feeling the metal underneath his shirt.

Guessing his thoughts, Herrin shook his head. "Sorry. I might be able to help in a surgery like that, but there's no way I could do it on my own. Not yet, at least. Besides, I'd hate to experiment on you, boss."

"Just a thought," Thrask replied. He jumped to his feet and reached into his pocket. He pulled out a tiny, clear container filled with white pills. He popped one in his mouth to let the medicine dull the swelling and pain.

"Doesn't matter anyway. I'm not quite ready to be rid of it. Not till he's gone." There was no need to say who.

Thrask moved for the exit and looked at Herrin. "Time to go see the old buzzard." He snapped his fingers. "Oh, I have a question for you."

They left the room. Outside, the pale-faced doctor waited in the hall. He eyed Thrask with open suspicion.

Thrask reached out with his broad hand and grabbed the doctor's frail wrist. Thrask placed the doctor's trembling hand against the cold steel buried in his flesh. Only the fabric of his shirt separated the doctor's flesh from the pulmonary collar's rhythmic ticking.

"You can tell Mordid it's still here." Not that Mordid had any power over him anymore, but there was no reason to let him know that. Not yet, at least. It would be a delightful surprise when Mordid's smug grin was replaced by a look of terror when he realized his collar was broken.

The doctor's head bobbed, and when Thrask released him he scurried into the infirmary and out of sight.

"What's the question, boss?" Herrin asked.

Thrask stared daggers at the back of the doctor before making his way down a shadowy corridor in the direction of Mauss's abode. Herrin fell in behind him, silent as ever.

"Where did you learn your trade?" Thrask asked.

"You mean knifing people?"

He threw a quick look over his shoulder at Herrin. "No, patching them back up."

Herrin smiled and his pale eyes flashed. "On End Road I learned both. We don't have proper doctors there, and I was handy with a knife so…" he trailed off.

Thrask belted out a laugh. "Are you telling me that because you had a knack for putting a knife in someone that automatically made you a qualified doctor? Nice planet."

From behind him, Herrin said, "Not too much a difference I figure. Though killing is easier than saving. When I go back, I'm sure I'll be able to teach them proper."

"Go back?" Thrask turned down a hall, and his eyes focused on the various cameras hanging from the ceiling. Shady, nervous sorts from all branches of the company were milling about, going in and out of rooms. Everyone in an army uniform, upon seeing

Thrask, turned their backs and promptly sought escape.

They were in Mauss's territory now—a den of informants looking for the old man's favor in the hopes of promotion, or perhaps guided by good old-fashioned blackmail.

He paid the nervous soldiers no mind. Thrask wasn't after traitors. Not today.

"Yep, back." Herrin said. "I owe it to my family. It's expected that no matter what, you don't forget who your kin are. On End Road, it's easy. There are only four families. We're close."

"Eh?" Thrask faced him. "Only four? I heard rumors of inbreeding, but—"

Herrin's eyes hardened.

Thrask stared him down. "What, you haven't heard that one before?"

"Doesn't mean I like it." Herrin cleared his throat. "Boss," he added. Shifting from one foot to the other, Herrin said, "In the early days, all those rumors were true. The four families were small and isolated. Things are different now. You don't get too many fishy-ones."

"Fishy-ones?" Thrask regretted asking the moment he did.

"Yeah. Flippers. Strange eyes. One arm, or maybe one too many arms." Herrin laughed. "All the stuff of nightmares. But you don't see too many of them anymore. The genetic pool isn't quite so stagnant. Still, my third cousin Earl is fishy. He's blind, but he's also the strongest man I've ever seen. He's bigger than you, boss. The family uses him like an ox to plow the fields. Earl likes it, too. I saw him just laugh and laugh for three days on end as he plowed away. He's ugly as sin, but he's Earl Herrin and I'm Tolfus Herrin. We're kin. I'd do damn near anything for him. If he asked. Not that he can speak, but you get the idea."

"Huh," Thrask said, unsure what else to say, or if he wanted to know any more about Herrin's homeland.

"You should visit one day. Plenty of recruits are there just looking for the opportunity to leave for a spell."

"Yeah, I'll think about it when I'm in charge." A thought occurred to him. "Those other End Roaders you put in with, Jenkins's lot?"

"What of em?"

Thrask sniffed. "They are all Herrins?"

"Of course!" Herrin put a hand to his chest, and his eyes widened. "I'd never consort with the others. Boss, I'd murder a man if I found out he was from one of the other three families. You don't know what *they* are like. Calling them cannibals is both true and a compliment given what else they're up to. Anyway, Bulks is from a branch founded by Margus Herrin, Rendstrot's family ties into great Shamus Herrin and Umbradax's line traces back to Kyleene Herrin, who was my great, great grandfather's second wife. We're all Herrins though. I'm direct line, so I get the fancy name. Tolfus. I'm named after a mean son of a bitch that carved out a good part of End Road for us Herrins."

"Hmmph!" Thrask turned and continued his way through Mauss's lair. The halls became more crowded, and the quiet ship soon bristled with activity. Mauss's agents worked here, spying for, and probably on, the Tyrant. Besides being a place for traitors to wag their tongues, it was also where information was gathered and sorted through, and where contracts were found, discarded, and negotiated. It was the boring part of the job Thrask was grateful he knew little about. Mauss found the work; Thrask pulled the trigger. He liked that relationship.

He approached Mauss's door and rapped on it. The camera above the doorway focused upon him with a *whizz* and *click*. The lens glittered.

"I don't care if you're busy," Thrask said up to the camera.

The door opened. From within, Mauss's voice ghosted out. "The End Roader stays."

Thrask nodded to Herrin. "Wait here."

Herrin flushed with anger but shut his mouth and nodded.

Thrask entered, and the door shut behind him. Mauss's room was darkened, like so much of the *Merciless,* and consisted of a door leading to the man's personal chambers and a desk. Upon it sat a variety of absolutely archaic, but apparently functional, computers.

Adding to the room's antiquity were the scraps of paper and collection of pens on the polished surface of the desk.

Mauss sat in a chair; his fingers were linked together and his eyes were set in a permanent glare. The skeletal man offered barely a hint of a smile and gestured to a seat across from him.

"General Thrask, it is so rare for you to visit."

Thrask snorted and strode toward the desk. He pushed the chair aside, and choosing to stand, he planted his hands on the top of Mauss's desk.

"I want information," Thrask demanded.

Mauss leaned back. "Eryn's more subtle. I'll admit though, I do like how you get right to the point." He tilted his head. "Information about what?"

He had no time for lengthy word games or negotiation with Mauss. "You are aware that Mordid was attacked not but an hour ago?"

The diplomat of the fleet shrugged. "So? We are in a dangerous line of work. These things happen."

"Yeah, yeah." Thrask leaned over the table and tried to use his physical mass to overwhelm the ancient figure seated before him. "But something isn't right. The attack was too easy. So my sources say."

"Source," Mauss said.

Thrask eased back from the man. "Eh?"

"Source," Mauss repeated. "You have one. Tolfus Herrin. He was aboard Mordid's ship under Jenkins's command when it came under attack. He told you what you are now telling me; otherwise, he wouldn't be outside standing guard." Mauss peered intently at Thrask. "I am the one in the business of learning things, Thrask. I know everyone's plots, schemes, and dreams." His lips twitched.

Undaunted, Thrask said, "That's why I'm here. Admiral Rodriguez kept the attack quiet."

"Mordid's decision, I'm sure," Mauss said.

Pressing, Thrask said, "The Mexican knows who attacked us. He probably even knows what their real purpose was! He was on the bridge when it all happened. I tried to get one of his weasels to talk, but that didn't work. Our ship is minus one Mexican."

Apparently unconcerned by the admission of murder,

Mauss said, "So where do I fit in, General?"

Thrask clenched his fists into meaty balls until his knuckles stung. "If you're good at unraveling all of our plans, then tell me what Rodriguez is up to. This mission pays a lot, and I for one won't let the contract be wasted by high command." Not entirely true. His primary goal of the day was to find some leverage over Rodriguez, but if it helped preserve the contract, all the better.

Mauss said with a thin smile, "I like the way you think, and so I'll tell you this. The attack was a ruse, and there is danger aboard the ship. I will also tell you that there are multiple parties trying to thwart it. They think they are being clever, but I do have eyes everywhere." Mauss sighed. "You have nothing to worry about, General. No need to kill anyone." He sighed. "Anyone else, that is."

Thrask snorted. It looked as if whatever opportunity he imagined might be presenting itself was in fact not. So much for thwarting one of Rodriguez's schemes.

"Fine. I'll leave it to others to deal with this threat. I want you to clear up the matter of the dead Mexican. I'll owe you one." He turned his back on the diplomat.

"There is another threat that needs looking into, General," Mauss said. "You can repay me for cleaning up your bathroom mess right now."

Turning, Thrask eyed him. "Oh yeah?"

"Rodriguez is up to some very wicked games. I might have the information I need to break him. I might even share it with you. You could be the one to topple him and move one step closer to the top." Mauss made a gesture with his hand. "If I so choose."

Thrask asked, "And what would make you choose to do that?"

Mauss tapped the top of his polished and cluttered desk with a thin finger. "I'm quite predictable, General. I do what is in the best interest of the investors. If I felt the company were at risk due to Rodriguez's games, then I'd shed light onto them. I'd expose him and crush him." He sniffed. "Currently, the company is not at risk. I have no reason to embarrass or destroy him. Or anyone, for that matter." He stared intently at Thrask.

"Then we're done here?" Thrask rubbed his head. He hated verbal games. He much preferred a straight conversation, or better yet, a situation where he could just give orders and be promptly obeyed.

"Maybe. If you find out some information for me, I'll share some with you, and you can choose how best to use it." Mauss licked his lips. "We'll also consider us even on the affair of your murderous escapades."

Thrask rubbed his jaw and pondered. Mauss was a sinister fellow, but he wasn't a liar. He was the master of making bargains, not breaking them.

"Fine," Thrask said, "tell me what you want, and in return you give me information on the admiral."

Nodding, Mauss said, "We have guests aboard, and one of them has chained to his wrist a suitcase. It contains a relic that we are transferring to the Khan system."

Thrask might not consider himself the best at keeping pace with the various machinations of the command staff, but this one was easy.

"You want the relic?"

"Yes."

Thrask frowned. "Subtle-like I assume?"

Mauss nodded. "I didn't say it would be easy. However, if you know the attack was a diversion, then Rodriguez knows as well. Mordid knows. Eryn knows. Others as well, I'm sure, but those three for sure."

"Throw Jenkins in there, the rat. Hmmph. They're going to be clustering about our guests, I gather?"

"Yes. They all have an interest in protecting the relic. I have no idea if it's a concentrated effort. Knowing us," he sighed, "probably not." Mauss pointed at Thrask. "Which means there will be a lot of confusion very shortly. I'd call that an opportunity to act."

That didn't give him much time. The time to act was now.

"I'll get the bauble and you'll give me a noose to hang Rodriguez with?" Thrask glared at him. "And I can choose to threaten him with it or use it?" Rodriguez in his pocket was perhaps better than dead. A dead admiral meant a new admiral.

Mauss shrugged. "I'll give you rope, General. You'll have to tie the knot on your own." He looked Thrask up and down. "General, if you do this for me, we'll be more than even. I have my eye on you. I sense great potential."

He didn't like how even compliments sounded mildly dangerous coming from Mauss's lips.

"Good," Thrask said. It was not the most witty of answers, but it got his point across. Wit was Mordid's department.

Thrask exited the room, and as soon as the door shut he drew Herrin close.

"I have something very dangerous for us to do."

Herrin blinked. He had in his hand a communication device. He glanced at it, then at Thrask. "Sure. Oh no, did you kill the old man? We can cut his body apart and—"

"No," Thrask interjected. He leaned close to Herrin's ear and whispered. "In a few minutes, half the command staff and who knows who else will be mixing it up near the honored guests. While on the ship, did you notice a guy with a suitcase chained to his wrist?"

Herrin nodded. "Sure, I saw him. The relic guy."

"I want that suitcase. You need to not be seen or caught, and it has to be done fast. Oh, and the guests can't find out. We need to be," Thrask spat the next word out, "subtle."

"Tricky, but I'll try." He held up the communication device. "I had this turned off, so I'm a little late, boss. I just got word from Karlson that an intruder was sighted near the guest quarters." He offered a meek smile. "He wonders where the hell I am."

Thrask cursed. "Bah! It's happening already. Come on. I'll provide a distraction while you get that damned suitcase and bring it to the gym."

The End Roader grinned. "Sure thing." He glanced at the door and then back at Thrask. "Will he handle the trouble in the bathroom?"

"Yes. No one will see footage of us on the deck, and he'll make sure no one remembers seeing us either." Thrask shrugged. "Someone else will get blamed."

"Perfect," Herrin replied.

4
THE UPPER ARM -THE MERCILESS ORBITING RECONQUISTA-

Hiding behind a couch with barely a plan, yet an unquenchable desire to know what was in the suitcase, was hardly relaxing for Mordid.

He squatted and his muscles strained and his back tightened up, sending little jolts of pain through him whenever he placed his weight on one foot or the other. The pain in his chest from Helen's gunshot ached. He listened to the conversation from the other room, but it was too distant, muffled, and muted for him to make much of.

Eryn would lead Karlson and his crony on a chase, but it wouldn't take long before the rest of his bodyguards showed up to keep the relic safe. He suppressed a smile at the irony. However, outwitting the likes of them wouldn't be too difficult. Other than Jenkins, they were only good at pulling triggers and standing in the way of impending danger. Karlson's only talent was not being dead after all these years.

Someone rapped loudly on the door.

Mordid risked a little peek over the back of the couch and watched as one of Chavez's men shuffled in. He approached the door without concern and pressed a button. It slid open silently, and Admiral Rodriguez burst in, followed by several members of his bridge crew. He drew his pistol, and his dark eyes flashed.

"Is he safe?" Rodriguez demanded.

The baffled religious figure before him staggered back a few steps. "What? Oh, yes." He straightened his robes and then wrung his hands together. "Is there a problem?"

Mordid remained behind the couch, ducking every moment he thought Rodriguez's eyes panned his way.

Rodriguez looked over his shoulder and said to his crew, "Wait outside."

The men saluted and left. The door shut.

Rodriguez returned his attention to Chavez's minion. "No. Not yet, at least."

Mordid watched as from the other room Chavez and his party emerged. They pushed toward Rodriguez and spoke in a flurry of Spanish.

Damn it all! Mordid knew some Spanish, but when so many were speaking the language at once and in unison, it transformed their words into utter gibberish to his ears.

Though he was desperate to know what Rodriguez was saying and Chavez in return, he was more concerned about the suitcase. Chavez didn't have it, which meant it was still on the table unattended.

Grinning, Mordid crawled out from behind the couch. He tiptoed across the room, keeping a firm gaze on Rodriguez and company as he slid his body close to the wall. They were wildly gesturing, talking in a rapid staccato, their voices increasing in volume.

Almost there. Mordid eased closer toward the next room. He could see the edge of the table and atop it the glossy black exterior of the suitcase. His eyes fixed upon the prize.

He took another step.

So long as they remained distracted with one another, he could make it.

The conversation halted.

Mordid slowly, almost sheepishly, turned toward the group and sucked in a breath. They were all staring at him, and Rodriguez had his pistol leveled.

"*Hola*, bad girl," Rodriguez said. He gestured with his pistol. "Put your hands up."

Sucking in a breath, Mordid raised his hands in a hesitant manner. He glanced over his shoulder and sighed. The suitcase was within sight and almost within his grasp, but there was no way to get it now. His plan, bold as it was, had failed.

He reached toward his hood, ready to reveal himself and present the truth, or at least a version of it. He doubted his client would be pleased, but not all gambles paid off.

The door rattled as someone on the other end pounded on it.

"Open up!" came the thunderous voice of Thrask. "And get these Mexicans out of my way!"

His booming knock and raucous words were like a grenade in the room. Rodriguez ducked, and the religious flock jumped and turned to face the source of the noise. It was the perfect distraction.

Mordid knew he'd been caught. However, he'd peek inside the suitcase before calling an end to the game. The little journey wouldn't be for nothing, and if his client was angry, at least Mordid's curiosity would be sated. Mordid sprinted into the adjoining room where the suitcase was left.

"Stop!" Rodriguez shouted after him.

The door rattled once more, and Mordid heard Thrask cursing and roaring away. The cries of the guests mingled with the repeated commands of Rodriguez and the bellows of Thrask, all of which Mordid ignored.

The suitcase sat where Chavez had left it, on a table in a small sitting room. There were numerous chairs clustered around the table, and, besides the suitcase, there were a variety of electronic devices and a few steaming cups of Wake Me Up!

He grabbed the suitcase and fumbled with the hinge. Just as it clicked, Mordid's breath caught in his chest with the anticipation.

Rodriguez's fist, rings and all, struck him a moment later.

The suitcase flew from his hands, and Mordid landed atop the table. The wood buckled under his weight. The suitcase and caffeinated drinks mingled momentarily in the air, before landing atop Mordid.

He let out a cry as steaming liquid spattered over him. A boot to his side followed up the dousing of piping hot Wake Me Up!

Groaning, Mordid rolled up to his knees. He saw Rodriguez looming above him, his face twisted into a snarl and his moustache bristled with agitation. In his hand, he clutched a pistol, and he brought the butt of it toward Mordid's skull.

Giving his own war cry, Mordid lurched to his feet, wrapped his arms around his admiral's waist and propelled Rodriguez to the far wall. As Rodriguez struck it, a portrait of Mordid fell and clattered on the floor. The admiral gasped, and a cough burst from his lips.

Mordid rammed his knee into the man's crotch and ripped the pistol out of his hands. The weapon spiraled through the air and landed among the debris strewn across the floor.

"You fool, it's—"

Mordid was unable to finish his sentence.

Rodriguez's normally brown skin was red with pain and fury. He slapped Mordid so hard it sounded like a gunshot. No sooner had Mordid registered the sting of the blow, he felt Rodriguez's hands grasp his coat. Violently, he was shaken and lifted off of his feet.

"Where did you get this?" Rodriguez said as he realized it was Mordid's coat, but not that it was actually him! He then slammed his forehead into Mordid's nose.

"Gack!" Mordid slumped, and pain rocketed throughout his skull. He was prevented from collapsing by Rodriguez's iron-fisted hold on his gray coat. Like a puppet with sliced strings, Mordid dangled.

Mordid had a knife hidden in the back of his belt. He'd cut out Rodriguez's heart and get a new admiral. These things happened. He reached for the concealed weapon and drew it. As Rodriguez hauled him close, Mordid placed the tip of the blade against the man's stomach.

"Stop!" Pedro Chavez shouted. He stood in the doorway, his frail hand extended and his eyes wide and flashing. Behind him, the religious entourage peered, clutching at Pedro's plain robes and thin arms. Mordid could not tell if they were hiding behind him or trying to keep him from getting involved.

The pair froze. Mordid reached up and pulled his hood off.

"Mordid?" Rodriguez released him. He stepped back several paces and rubbed his hands along his uniform. His expression was suitably one of complete shock.

Landing on his feet, Mordid slid the knife back into the little hidden holster on his belt. Rodriguez would never know how close he came to bleeding to death.

"Yes, me." He reached up to touch his nose and winced for his efforts.

Pedro's face darkened. He approached the two and stared at Mordid. "Why are you in my room?"

"I own the fleet. It's as much my room as yours," Mordid said. He wanted to sound confident, but his crunched nose made every word come forth with a nasal twang.

From the other room, Thrask emerged, pushing aside the cohorts of Cardinal Chavez. He looked as if he'd gone through a beating of his own.

"Everyone out of here! Now!" Thrask pushed past Chavez and reached a bear-like paw toward Mordid. He grasped him by the shoulder and guided him out of the demolished room and back into the front entrance. The others gathered there.

"Back away from the Tyrant or I'll rip your arms off," Thrask threatened as he pushed Mordid ahead of him.

In the room, Mordid saw some of his bodyguards, Pedro's men, a confused looking Rodriguez and an undisguised Eryn. Behind him, Thrask loomed. As well he should! A dead Mordid was a dead Thrask. Everyone was talking at once, and fingers pointed accusingly in every direction. The entry room was crowded and chaotic, with the volume of conversation rising by the second.

Shrugging off his pain, Mordid whistled, piercing the cacophony with the sound.

Everyone stared, and the conversations ceased.

"Time to quiet down. You," Mordid pointed at his guards. "Man the door and wait for me." The men nodded and obeyed.

He pointed at Eryn next. "You, out."

She visibly stiffened but likewise obeyed. He'd tell her later how things went.

Looking over his shoulder, he said to Thrask, "Thank you, General. You have impeccable timing. I'll take it from here."

"Hmm?" Thrask shrugged. "If you say so." He glanced into the ruined room. "Hey, get back to your post, soldier."

Herrin slipped from the room with the suitcase and bobbed his head with a murmured, "Yes, sir."

Mordid hadn't even seen Herrin until he was leaving- a quiet man. No matter. As soon as the entry was much less occupied, he faced Chavez. "Pardon me for the difficulty."

"Pardon you?" Chavez shook his head. "Not so easily. I am a guest here on this ship. Your job is to see the relic safely transported and you try to steal it?" He glared. "I am having doubts about our contract."

Raising his hands, Mordid said, "Again, pardon me. I was merely going to move the relic somewhere safe. I suggested we do that earlier, and you balked."

"Where is safer than here?!" Chavez drew closer. "You are outrageous. You break into my room—"

"My room," Mordid reminded him.

Pressing on, Chavez said, "You tried to steal the relic. Do you deny that? Or is it yours, too?"

"No, no. The relic is yours. However, it's in danger, and I was trying to discreetly shift it in such a way that no one, not even you, knew where it was. Hence my poor disguise." Not entirely true, but the truth was the last thing he wanted to confess.

"Danger?" Chavez poked Mordid square in the chest. "From who? You?"

"No," Rodriguez said. "Mordid is right; it is in danger. During the attack, intruders snuck aboard the ship. My men just found their transport craft, and I came here straight away. Their ship is a stealthy thing that no doubt has placed equally stealthy, and very bad, men aboard the *Merciless*." He eyed Mordid. "It was only one ship, so the assassins are few."

Mordid nodded. Assassins? Why not thieves? Mordid kept the admiral's choice of words in his mental pocket for later. Either was possible, but Rodriguez sounded confident as to their motive. "I surmised something like that myself. Hence, with your permission, Cardinal Chavez, I'd like to move the relic. Separating it from your party will increase the likelihood it won't be found."

Chavez shook his head. "No. Absolutely not. You must guarantee its safety and that of myself and my followers. Fail in any aspect of that and the Holy Father will not pay you. That is final." Chavez stepped closer still, nearly nose to nose with Mordid.

"I suggest," Chavez said, "that you focus on keeping enemies off your own ship rather than trying to pilfer the treasures of your clients."

Chavez's men echoed him with angry murmurs and frowns.

Mordid flashed a smile. It only hurt his split lip a little. "Of course." He looked past Chavez at Rodriguez. "Well, subtlety is still not out of the question. How many know there are unwanted guests aboard?"

The admiral stroked his black moustache. "My bridge crew and I. Assume everyone who was in this room. Mauss was not here, but knowing him, he probably knows too. He is much like the devil—around even if you don't see him."

"Let's keep it quiet then. Do not alert the *Merciless's* crew." Mordid stepped around Chavez and placed a hand on Rodriguez's arm. "Move the guests elsewhere, but do it quietly. I want everyone to think they are still here. I even want guards."

Rodriguez planted his hands on his hips. "Ah, bait?"

"Exactly. If we raise the alarm, then they'll be just that much harder to catch. Whoever is aboard are professionals. Think you can set the trap?"

Rodriguez nodded. "I will see that our guests are moved. As for catching the invaders?" Rodriguez paused a moment as he thought. "I'll station a squad of marines in the room. They'll be confused about why, but they'll shoot at any assassins that wander in."

"Good!" Mordid patted him on the back. "You hit like a bull." He noticed that Rodriguez again used the word "assassins."

Rodriguez laughed. "I hope you do not take it personally that I thought you were a *bandito*."

"*No problem*." Mordid returned his gaze to Chavez. "*Si?*"

Chavez tugged at his robes. He regarded a few of his compatriots and then stared at Mordid. "No problem. However, Mordid, I ask in the future you keep me apprised of your…" he cleared his throat, "plans. I would have been willing to assist in any way."

"Really? Can I see the relic?" Mordid glanced at the doorway.

"No. Unless you wish to convert to the Catholic faith here and now?" Chavez smiled. "If so, then of course! You will be fascinated by it upon your conversion. The faithful who gaze upon it are often moved to tears."

He laughed. "I'm not *that* curious. It was just an idle question. Rodriguez, I'll see you on the bridge after I wipe the blood off my face. Well," he said to Chavez, "sorry again." He dipped his head and left the room.

Outside, Karlson and a few of Mordid's guards loitered. Rodriguez's first officer Valdez and a handful of the bridge crew were waiting with them. Eryn was waiting as well. Looking very much like a cat dunked in water. The skin-tight suit was a hit, though. Clad as she was, no one seemed to notice Mordid leave their guest's quarters. Their eyes were firmly fixed on Eryn's natural assets.

She tilted her head, and her brow arched at Mordid's arrival.

Mordid gave her a toothy grin. In a sarcastic tone, he said to her, "What fun!" Then he said to his men more crisply, "Follow me."

They looked up in surprise.

Karlson swallowed. "Yes, sir!"

Mordid frowned and kept a brisk pace as he made his way toward the elevator that would take him to the bridge of the ship. He could feel his nose swelling, and his stomach was sore from the beating he'd received at Rodriguez's hands. The pain was a reminder of his failure.

"What did we learn?" Eryn whispered as she kept pace

with him.

"Nothing." He felt a bit of blood leak from his nose. "Absolutely nothing."

He wouldn't tell her about Rodriguez's choice of words, nor about one other thing mildly puzzling him. Where was Jenkins?

#

Rodriguez waited until the door was shut, then waited some more before turning to face the pope. He bowed.

"I am sorry I did not get here sooner. I had no idea he would try that!" Rodriguez straightened. "However, your Eminence, Mordid is not lying about the intruders."

The Holy Father waved a hand. "It is alright. I sympathize with Mordid. He is being paid a lot of money and knows very little about why. I would be just as curious." His lips turned into a smile. "Not quite as rash and stupid, but just as curious."

Rodriguez snorted. "Don't be fooled. He has bouts of cleverness. Such as the plan to move you and your people to another room. Before we go, though, I must tell you something."

Chavez bobbed his head. "Of course. What is it?"

"I know who has snuck aboard. The ships that attacked us were from Earth Space."

The pope paled. "Truly?"

The others in the room gasped.

Preventing panic, Rodriguez held up a hand. "It is not what you think. The ships were not modern. Err...they were by our standards, but they weren't the latest from Earth Government. They are not from Earth Force. I have a contact who believes they belonged to the false pope and that his agents mean to assassinate you. Perhaps a lie, and yet it does make sense."

"Ah," the pope said. He gestured for Rodriguez to follow and returned to the room where Mordid had nearly been beaten to death. The suitcase was on the ground. The pope knelt and picked it up. Gingerly, he secured the suitcase to his wrist.

"You expected this?" Rodriguez asked.

"Yes. The deal we have arranged with Earth Government bring ups the problem of two popes!" Chavez looked at the mess in the room and said, "I figured that any man in an exalted position would be resentful were it to be taken away." He glanced at Rodriguez. "The assassins will be fanatical. Men who falsely believe in their puppet pope. Men who think their souls are in danger should he be deposed. They are misguided." He then added, "And no doubt motivated."

"They are no more fanatical than I, your Eminence. They will not harm you!" He felt fire rush through his veins at the very thought of heretics so much as touching the Holy Father.

"Good. In the meantime, I suggest we hurry to the Khan system."

Which brought up a point he didn't think he'd be able to ask about. "Holy Father, forgive me for asking, but why the Khan system?" He lowered his gaze. "You do know it is dangerous there. More than if there were a hundred assassins aboard. It is a place cursed with war. Or blessed, I suppose, for one such as I. But for a man such as you? It is not a safe place, with respect, your Eminence."

Chavez nodded. "I know. Earth Government thinks I will be taking a direct route to Earth Space. From what I gather, they plan on hosting a parade and demonstrating their willingness to mend the fence, so to speak." He held up a hand. "Ah, but they wish to do so in such a way as to show that they are *allowing* me and the One True Faith to return. Like we are children who at long last are no longer grounded by our parents. They think I will return, and like their puppet, put on a yoke."

Rodriguez frowned. He reached up and stroked his moustache, tugging at the waxy tip. "So, you do not wish to go with your head bowed?"

The Holy Father let a laugh slip forth. "*Si.* I will not go as the vanquished exile coming home, but as the victor invited back. To do so, I must make it abundantly clear that the One True Faith is triumphant, correct, and powerful."

"May I ask how?"

"The Khan system has been the battleground for five of Corporate Space's largest companies. It has been the graveyard for countless mercenaries from the Upper Arm. It is a region that represents what Earth Government hates most about all those places not under their dominion. Yet, they have been powerless to stop it. There it lies, right next door to one of their worlds, but their bloated bureaucracy leaves them impotent. They wag their fingers, they wring their hands. Yet they can do nothing about the carnage."

Rodriguez swallowed. He had the utmost faith in, well, his faith, but he didn't like where this was going.

"Where do you fit in?"

Pope Chavez grinned. "I will end the war. When I go to Earth Space it will be as a hero. I will do, with God's direction, what Earth Government cannot. Faith will triumph over Godless ideology. Faith will bring peace to the Khan system."

He was afraid he'd say something like that. Rodriguez had faith, but the Khan system was a place that chewed up good Catholics just as fast as nonbelievers. Leading the pope to his death wasn't his idea of sound religious reasoning. "And our fleet will be involved in ending the war?" He sucked in a breath. "I am not sure if we can do that."

The pope tilted his head. "Of course you can. I can't do it without you." He held up the suitcase. "Do not worry, Admiral. The relic will let us prevail."

"Yes," Rodriguez replied and averted his gaze. Perhaps he needed to let Mordid in on the secret of who their guest really was. What would be the point in getting the pope to the Khan system if in the process the fleet were destroyed? There could be no Tyrant Rodriguez if the company was obliterated while waving about an ancient artifact.

He didn't like his religious conviction warring with his ambition. He much preferred them to be working in concert.

"Are you well, Rodriguez?" the pope asked.

"I am." He'd confess the lie later. "We just have so much to do." He bowed. "I must return to the bridge. I'll have some of my most trusted men move you to a new, and safer, location."

Rodriguez left the guest quarters. He cursed in Spanish and in English as he made his way to the bridge. He pulled out his communication device and adjusted the dials.

"Valdez. I have new orders for you. Our guests need to be quietly moved."

His first officer replied, "*Of course. Sir, I must inform you one of our men is dead. Victor Torres."*

Dead?! Rodriguez halted. "An unsanctioned boxing match, or was it the intruders?"

"No. He was killed by one of Mordid's chosen men. By a man called Jenkins."

#

A soft, soothing feminine voice woke Jenkins from his uncomfortable slumber. He opened his eyes and saw that the lights of the garbage chamber had gone from dull, cold white, to a flashing and urgent red.

The voice emanated from a speaker built into the wall. It was hard to make out without concentrating.

"Warning. Trash to be ejected in ten seconds. Space and you do not mix."

"Oh no!" Jenkins lurched to his feet and almost instantly lost his balance. He felt pain in every limb, and a quick scan of his body revealed that his clothing was ripped, torn, and blood-stained. The grenade hadn't killed him, but it had certainly wounded him.

The room rumbled. Jenkins stumbled his way to the door and yanked on the handle. It didn't move.

"Warning. Trash to be ejected in five seconds. Space and you do not mix."

"Come on!" he shouted and pulled again on the handle. Still it would not budge.

"Three, two…"

He caught sight of a dirty, mostly obscured sign on the door. It read, "turn handle and pull."

"One."

Jenkins turned the handle and pulled. The door flung open, and he grasped onto the handle with both bloody hands, expecting the floor to open up and space to suck him and all the trash out with it. He shut his eyes, bracing for the inevitable fight with the deadly vacuum of the void. He hoped that his organs didn't explode right away.

Nothing happened.

Jenkins popped one eye open.

"The door is open. Please shut it so trash may be removed."

He let out a breath and exited the room, shutting the door behind him. He rested against the cold metal and waited for his heartbeat to slow down. The door vibrated as the trash was jettisoned into space.

He was alive, but hurt. There was no telling how much shrapnel was imbedded in his body. He needed to get to an infirmary and also find Mordid. He'd failed to stop the intruders, but he could still thwart their plans. He wasn't dead as they expected.

Before him was a long hallway, similar to the many he'd trodden before within the massive ship. He walked, wearily and unevenly, and listened for sounds of life. At first, he heard nothing, but then came the distinct sound of heavy boots marching on the deck. Still, the sound was muted. He shook his head, but his hearing didn't improve. The grenade did more than just pepper him with bits of metal and fire. A high pitched whine rang in his ears and would not abate.

Moving toward the noise, Jenkins smiled as he saw down an adjoining hall a squad of black-clad, armored marines. High sloping armor hid their lower faces, and their heads were shaved. In their hands they held beamers, deadly and expensive weapons that incinerated flesh but didn't ricochet or puncture the hull of a ship, making them perfect weapons for any shipboard work, so long as the settings were kept in proper order.

"Hey!" Jenkins called out.

The squad leveled their weapons.

"It's me." Jenkins wiped his face in case it was obscured by blood, soot, or refuse. "Jenkins. I'm commander of the Tyrant's bodyguard."

The lead marine said, "I know who you are. Hands up."

"What?" Jenkins stumbled toward them, but when the marines narrowed their eyes and focused the muzzles of their weapons at his face, he halted. He raised his hands.

"Okay, I give up. Make this quick, though. I need to see the boss. We have visitors on board." Jenkins eyed the marines. "The boss will want to know—"

"Shut up," the lead marine growled. "You can talk to the Tyrant all you want. From behind bars. You're under arrest,

Commander Jenkins."

Jenkins smirked. "We have arrest?"

The man shrugged. "Yeah, sure. Just like in the real armed forces in Earth or Corporate Space. Except you don't have any rights, a lawyer, or a trial." He waved one of his men forward. "Secure him."

The chosen man tromped ahead and roughly pushed Jenkins against the cold wall. As he forced Jenkins's hands behind his back, he whispered in his ear, "Looks like the Mexican gave you one hell of a fight."

"What?" He winced as his wrists were locked in place by thin, immensely strong bands that tightened of their own accord.

The marine gripped him by the shoulder and pushed him toward the squad, who formed a ring around him. After a jarring push, the marine who had bound his wrists together said, "Don't try to deny it. You left something behind, stupid. You put your name right in the dead man's hand."

Jenkins pursed his lips. He hadn't the slightest idea what the marine was talking about. Dead man? He shuffled along and said, "Oh yeah?"

A marine next to him reached out and grasped Jenkins's collar. He tugged on it. "Didn't you notice?"

The yank tweaked his neck, but he was able to see his collar. The dark uniform looked dirty and damaged, as one might expect it to look after being within the blast radius of a grenade. He also noticed that the special rank pin he wore, denoting him as head of Mordid's bodyguard, was absent. At first, he thought that the pin had fallen off during his scuffle with the intruders, but then he thought back to something Karlson had warned him about when Jenkins first made it clear how ambitious he was.

Karlson had told him that advancing in the ranks would mean risks beyond the battlefield, that petty jealousies were just as deadly as an enemy's bullet.

His rank pin was missing, and it wasn't because of his recent fight.

"I've been set up," Jenkins muttered.

One of the marines laughed. "Uh-huh. Hell, even if you're telling the truth, it doesn't matter. I've seen more than one innocent officer kicked off the ship. I didn't shed a tear, I'll tell you that. Have fun down the tube. When your tongue turns to ice and your breath spits through your teeth along with blood."

The others began to recount tales of the various executions they'd witnessed or somehow played a direct role in.

Jenkins let out an annoyed growl. Perhaps he'd not escaped the cold grasp of space after all.

#

Thrask sat on one of the weightlifting benches in the empty gym. His battle-scarred hands were planted on his thighs and his gaze firmly fixed on the door. He ground his teeth together in anticipation.

When the door opened, he smiled. Herrin stepped in, and he had something stuffed within his tunic. He cradled it, like one would a babe.

Standing, Thrask said, "You did it. Good work."

Herrin shut the door with a jab of his elbow toward the button. His pale eyes fixed on Thrask, and he smiled in return. "I was in and out and no one saw me. I put some bits of the broken table into the suitcase. It'll buy us time unless the religious folk like to gaze at their…their thing."

"Thing?" Thrask approached. "Well, what is it?"

Herrin opened his tunic and worked out a most unusual relic. Thrask expected it to be something old, perhaps made of wood. Instead, Herrin held in his hands a metal box with a cylinder jutting up from the center. Atop the cylinder was a strange symbol that, although Thrask didn't recognize it, was clear enough in its intent. It depicted a skull.

"Huh," Thrask said.

"I know! What the heck is this thing? It doesn't weigh much, and it feels funny. I've never seen or handled anything like it. Touch it." He held the silvery box up.

Thrask hesitated a moment, but then reached a hand out and let his fingertips brush across the metal's surface. It was cold, far too cold to be any metal he had encountered before. It should have been warm due to Herrin's body heat. The metal was smooth as well, as if it had been dipped in oil. But when

Thrask rubbed his fingers together, they were dry. Whatever the thing was, it was made with state of the art technology and was certainly not a religious bauble with a storied history.

"We'll bring it to Mauss," Thrask said. "I followed my part of the bargain. He told me to bring him this thing, not to tell him what it was. He'll give me what I want." He clasped his hands together. "Maybe if I press him I can get more than that. If he knows something that can hurt Rodriguez, then maybe—"

His dreams of revenge on Mordid and Eryn were interrupted when his communication device buzzed.

Thrask pulled the item out and switched it on.

"What?"

Mordid's voice replied, "*Is that how you answer your calls? This is why no one invites you anywhere.*"

Thrask snarled, "I'm not paid to be pleasant. I'm paid to lead your armies, and as far as I can tell, this mission won't be seeing the army in action. So, unless we're invading Reconquista, I don't know why you're bothering me."

"*I wanted to thank you for your efforts in the guest's quarters. You came in at a good time. It was about to get messy.*"

Thrask grunted. "Do I get a reward?"

"*Sure! What do you want?*"

Thrask held the device close to his ear and tried to calm his voice so his rage wasn't evident. "How about you get this thing out of my heart so I don't have to worry that something stupid you do gets me killed? When I die, I'd like to know it was my fault."

"*Ha! General, even if I take the pulmonary collar out of you, there is still a high probability that you will die due to a decision of mine. I'm the Tyrant, and you're the general. It's my job to put you in harm's way. How about a pony instead?*"

"Keep your horse. Is that all, Mordid?"

"*Almost,*" Mordid said, "*Jenkins was picked up for killing one of Rodriguez's men. You don't happen to know anything about that, do you?*"

Thrask glared at Herrin, who in turn kicked the ground and pretended to whistle, while looking away in a most conspicuous manner.

"No," Thrask said. "Tell Jenkins I approve, though. I don't trust Rodriguez or his men. Neither should you. You should keep an eye on him. On everyone."

Mordid replied, "*Hmm. Pulmonary collars for everyone then? A good but impractical plan.*" The channel turned to the hiss of static.

Putting the communication device away, Thrask shook his head at Herrin. "What did you do? I don't have time to deal with your schemes. I have a hard enough time keeping track of everyone else's."

Herrin held up the "relic." "I got you your..." He frowned. "Whatever it is. You said I could have Jenkins's job, right? I'm just making it easier on all of us." He tilted his head. "Jenkins's death is inevitable, right?"

Thrask sniffed. He regarded the End Roader a long moment before nodding. "Yeah, it is. Keep me informed next time. I don't like people doing things behind my back." He narrowed his eyes. "You got it?"

Herrin offered a wide smile and nodded. "Yep. So, speaking of doing things behind people's backs. What now?"

Thrask shrugged. "We take that thing to Mauss. He tells me what I want to know, and he gets stuck with it. How does that sound, future commander?"

Laughing, Herrin said, "It sounds great, future Tyrant!"

5

THE UPPER ARM -THE MERCILESS ORBITING RECONQUISTA-

After cleaning himself up, and putting on his favorite giant military hat, Mordid strode toward the festive bridge of his flagship. Eryn had declined to accompany him. She wasn't coy about her dislike toward Rodriguez. She called him "crafty and ambitious," apparently not seeing the same in herself. A pair of his bodyguards waited outside Rodriguez's domain.

He extended his hands in the air as he emerged on the deck.

"Your admiral hit the boss, and he will live to tell the tale!" Mordid declared.

The crew cheered and greeted Mordid with whoops and various phrases in Spanish.

Rodriguez stood in the center of the command pit, and he offered a bow and devilish smile Mordid's way. He approached him and held out his hand.

"My apologies. However, sneaking about our client's rooms wasn't wise, *amigo*."

Mordid clasped his hand and gripped. Hard, but not embarrassingly so. He exchanged the customary, macho "My handshake is firm, but not overcompensating with strength" test of wills with Rodriguez.

When the admiral's hand relaxed, Mordid placed both of his behind his back. He won—as always. "No, but put yourself in my boots."

"I'd be taller. You wear lifts."

"And?"

Rodriguez laughed. "*Si, Si,* I would be curious, too. If I knew what it was, I'd tell you. I did not pry, though. Men of God should be respected."

Mordid shrugged. "I respect their money. However, what is done is done. Shall we get underway to the Khan system?"

Rodriguez's smile faded. "Yes. Mordid, when we enter the system things could get bad very quickly. I do not think any of the warring parties will like uninvited guests. We will be without friends there." He crossed his arms. "In case you aren't on the bridge when we get there, what are your orders upon arrival?"

He was right. Mordid was not contracted with any of the factions battling one another for the rights to a dead alien empire. Each company would see his arrival as reinforcements for a rival faction.

"When we arrive," Mordid said, "I want you to broadcast to the nearest company fleet that we are for hire and will work cheap. If they balk, contact the next nearest company and be bold about it, so all the rest hear. That should get a little bidding war started. Stall for time until I can get onto the bridge and work my magic."

Rodriguez laughed. "I see. And what particular trick do you have in mind?"

"I'll propose outrageous and confusing contracts to the companies until we find out what Pedro wants." Mordid shrugged. "Our contract says we need to get him to the Khan system, and it's a little vague after that."

"A decent enough plan," Rodriguez said. He reached up and grasped Mordid's shoulder. "Oh, before we go. One of your men knifed one of mine."

Mordid grasped his hand and removed it. He arched a brow. "All of the men are mine."

"Of course!" Rodriguez stepped back. "I mean, one of

your devoted followers, Victor Torres, was killed by one of *your* bodyguards. It happened in a bathroom. Very nasty. The men are beside themselves. We are already putting up a memorial." Rodriguez pointed to an empty chair by one of the many consoles on the bridge. Atop the chair were several candles, and flowers decorated the top of the darkened monitor. A tiny, white wooden cross was placed against the chair, and its base was ringed by several more glowing wax candles.

"Ah." Mordid tilted his head. "Do you know what happened?"

Rodriguez held out his empty hands. "No. The two went into the same bathroom. A knife was drawn, and poor Victor will box no more."

"Knife?" Mordid cursed. "Tolfus Herrin. He's fond of—"

"Oh no!" Rodriguez shook his head. "It was Jenkins. Commander of your guard."

Mordid blinked. "Impossible. He's not the type to do that." He pondered a moment and mused aloud, "Well, he would, but not unless it got him something. He's an ambitious sort, and not the type to knife deckhands. He's an officer now. He'd be knifing his way up the ranks, not down."

"I'm sorry, *amigo*, it's true. Jenkins's officer pin was still in Victor's hand."

Mordid opened his mouth to object.

"And Jenkins was found beaten up, as if he'd gone toe to toe with a prize fighter." Rodriguez cocked his head. "Did I also mention there are surveillance recordings?"

Damn it! Jenkins was a good man. He was young, ambitious, and more or less loyal, having opted to serve Mordid over Thrask, Eryn, and Mauss—earning their ire and his praise. Still, setting him up for murder wasn't their style. He was too beneath them for such efforts. Did his favored man slip up? If so, there was nothing Mordid could do for him. Ambitious and dangerous he could handle, recklessness was something a Tyrant could only appreciate in himself.

"It sounds rather damming." Mordid stroked his beard. "I take it the dishonor to my loyal bridge crew needs to be paid for in blood?"

Rodriguez stroked his moustache. "I think it only fair."

"I'll talk to Jenkins first." Mordid held up a hand. "And I promise you that Victor will be avenged. There is no rush, though. He's dead and Jenkins isn't going anywhere. Now then, on to the Khan system?"

Rodriguez twirled his moustache and stared at Mordid.

Mordid continued to toy with the tip of his beard.

They stared at one another long enough to make a few of the nearby crew members peek up from their stations with apprehensive glances.

"*Si.*" Rodriguez tore his gaze away and ordered his men in Spanish to get the fleet ready for transpace.

The deckhands shouted and worked furiously. The ship's lights flickered, and a deep groaning echoed throughout the ship as the Racer Rabbit transdrive warmed up.

Orders were passed to the rest of the fleet. Soon, every ship would be preparing their ancient Racer Rabbits.

Mordid watched the view port as the brown planet of Reconquista was replaced by the dizzying depths of space. The great craft was turning. He listened to Rodriguez count down and clenched his hands.

"*Tres, dos, uno!*"

It felt like being kicked in the gut as the *Merciless* was flung at impossible speeds into transpace. It was a place between places, like a separate universe of nothingness where ships could move and appear back in their own time and space, crossing vast distances in a relatively short amount of time. The technology was refined, but the Racer Rabbit in the engine room of the ship was getting old. Side effects, such as nausea and fatigue, increased with every crossing they made. He'd have to get the thing replaced one of these days. There was also the effect it had on the men. Well, most men.

Mordid looked at the view port. It was black, as if they were hurtling through a lightless cave.

Rodriguez looked over at his first officer.

"*Tiempo?*"

Valdez looked intently at a monitor before saying, "Nine weeks or so. We have eight stops to make along the way."

Mordid smiled at the news. Not bad for leapfrogging from the Upper Arm across nearly all of Corporate Space. Mordid turned and left the bridge behind him.

"We pray for justice," Rodriguez said.

Mordid glanced over his shoulder and replied, "You just need to ask, Admiral. There is no need to pray to me."

He stepped into a large corridor where a pair of his men waited. Karlson and an End Roader by the name of Bulks. Mordid looked at each in turn.

Karlson swallowed and stood up straighter.

Bulks stared back with his oversized eyes. He then began to look himself over before touching his face and wiping off crumbs that weren't there.

Neither knew.

"Off to the brig."

"Re-really?" Karlson said. He slumped. "I'm sorry about the confusion, sir, I didn't know—"

Mordid brushed him off. "It's not about that, Karlson. Your immediate boss is there, and I need to talk to him."

"Jenkins?" Karlson shook his head. "Why? Did he do something? Sir, he had the best intentions. He just goes off without thinking sometimes. Kind of like—" Karlson swallowed again and didn't complete the comparison.

"Really?" Mordid poked the old soldier in the chest. "And what were his intentions this time?"

Karlson shook his head. "I-I don't know, sir. He wasn't making much sense. Whatever he was doing, he was doing it for you." He cleared his throat. "And himself. But you, most of all."

Mordid let out a heavy breath. "We'll see."

He marched his way to the brig, a place he rarely had to visit. Crime and punishment were common aboard a mercenary ship. Fear and false promises only worked most of the time, not all of the time. Mercenaries were the type who didn't have morals when it came to killing people for money. Thus they didn't mind killing one another over petty grudges or debts—and sometimes just out of boredom. Every week someone, somewhere in the company was bound to run afoul of the law, limited as it was.

However, Mordid didn't handle such matters. His officers

doled out punishment. As far as he knew, most troublemakers cooled off in the brig for a few days, while the serious cases were fired from the company and removed from the property. The easiest means of doing so was jettisoning them out into space. Though he heard Thrask once say he was more fond of holding a public execution by firing squad and then kicking them off the ship.

The brig was large, filled with cells on two separate levels. Catwalks ringed the room where guards could stroll and get a view of the inmates. Not that such was necessary. Only one of the cells held a prisoner. In terms of shipboard employee malfeasance, it had been a quiet day.

A pair of marines sat in chairs and talked quietly between themselves in the center of the brig. When Mordid entered, their eyes widened and they scrambled from their chairs to their feet, saluting.

"Sir! Never see you down here," one said in evident surprise.

Mordid flashed a quick smile. "I should visit more often. Though, I must say, it looks quiet."

The man gave a curt nod. "Yes, sir. We just have the one. We just installed a tube that with a press of a button will send him out into the void. It's like one of those water parks, but you land in death instead of a pool."

"Really? That is great!" Mordid moved toward them. "Tell me there is a red button!"

"Oh, yes, sir. Look here." He pointed at a console that, true to his word, had dozens of large, red buttons, each one labeled with a number.

"Totally villain," the other marine said.

"Totally," the first agreed.

"Totally," Mordid concurred.

"Sir? Please don't kill me for fun," Jenkins said from within his cramped cell.

From behind Mordid, Karlson grumbled, "I kinda like him, sir."

Mordid eyed the enticing red buttons for a moment before tearing his gaze away. He marched up to Jenkins's cell.

The man looked like he'd been more than just beaten by a

boxer. His uniform was in tatters and his face blackened with the tell-tale soot of explosives. Mordid grasped the bars and pressed himself close.

Limping, Jenkins grasped the bars and leaned heavily against them. "I'm in rough shape, sir. They didn't give me much medical treatment before tossing me in here." He winced. "We entered transpace, didn't we? Damn, I can feel the years shed off of me!" He jerked back and looked Mordid up and down. "Oh no. Are you alright, sir?"

Mordid nodded and touched his sore nose. It still hurt, and he felt the sting tug a few tears from his eyes. "I'm fine. Well, better off than you, that's for sure."

Jenkins licked his lips and muttered, "I didn't do it, sir."

"So, can you explain," Mordid asked, "your officer's pin in Victor Torres's hand? How about your wounds, which more or less match up to what a boxer might do when fighting for his life?"

Jenkins took a breath, but Mordid bowled over him.

"Or how about the surveillance recordings of you?"

"Seriously?" Jenkins pushed himself away from the bars and paced back and forth—which didn't take long given how tiny his cell was.

"You can't explain any of that?" Mordid prompted.

Jenkins returned to the bars and grasped them until his knuckles turned white. "Sir, I was trying to find the intruders on the ship. I found them. Four of them with perfect teeth and faces and mocha skin. Earth, sir. Earth is here and on board!"

Mordid inwardly smiled. Jenkins would go far if he didn't get tossed off the ship in the next couple of weeks. "And all the rest?"

"Well, they attacked me and I had to—"

"The pin? The recordings?"

Jenkins drew in a long breath. He averted his gaze. "I-I don't know, sir. I don't know about that at all." He shut his eyes, and when they opened, he fixed his stare onto Mordid. "I *didn't* do it. I was beaten by others and got peppered by a grenade!"

"Who did in the boxer then?" Mordid leaned close to the bars.

Jenkins sighed. "I don't know."

"I do." Mordid turned and crossed his arms. He knew who did it, but not how. There was only one person who could clearly improve his lot in life were Jenkins to end up a frigid corpse-icle. Planting evidence would be easy, but changing security recordings was the kind of work that only Mauss or Eryn could perform, and there was no way the company's chief diplomat or PR head would lift a finger to assist the likes of Herrin, even if it meant getting back at Jenkins for his refusal to go along with their schemes back on Pristine.

"You do?" Jenkins said, "Well who? I'll put a bullet in their brain for this! I'll—"

Mordid faced him and let out a sigh. "I know who, but I can't figure out how they got away with it. I'll leave it to you to determine who might want to *knife* their way into your position."

"Knife?!" Jenkins paled. "Tolfus? He-he wouldn't. I, we, back on Pristine—"

"What?" Mordid laughed. "You helped him out? So what? Jenkins, he's from End Road. They used to eat people on that wondrous remote world. Maybe they still do. Tolfus Herrin will do anything that helps himself. If that means working with you, fine. If that means framing you, well that's also fine." He snapped his fingers. "The only question is how he did it."

"Sir, get me out of here. I'll get that inbred mutant to talk."

"Can't," Mordid said.

"Can't? You're the Traveling Tyrant. You can order my release, we can go kill Tolfus, and then we can find those Earth agents!"

He had potential, but he was young and naive. Mordid opened his mouth to explain.

"It would cause problems later," Karlson said.

"Ah!" Mordid stepped aside. "Listen to Karlson. His years of service gives him insight." He waved his hand toward the cell. "Tell him, old-timer."

Karlson bobbed his head at Mordid and approached. "Jenkins, if the Tyrant starts picking favorites to the point he lets them get away with outright murder—"

"I didn't—"

"Perceived murder! Whatever. Listen." Karlson snapped. "If he does that, then what little discipline our outfit has will fall apart. It's what caused the fall of the last Tyrant. He let his friends act without consequences and he was damned fickle…" He looked at Mordid. "Does he need to know about Gideon?"

"No." Mordid didn't want the old days revived. In truth, he much preferred men under his command that had no dealings whatsoever with the former Traveling Tyrant. It was much easier to rule over men who knew only one master. Even the stories and legend of Gideon Mordid wanted suppressed.

"So, what do I do?" Jenkins asked.

"Wait," Karlson replied.

"That's right," Mordid echoed. "We'll have a trial for you, just as soon as I remember how to run one. We've never done it before. It will take time, and I'll convince Rodriguez that it will be a great show and give his men some time to kill while we make our way to the Khan system, with your death being a good final show before we emerge."

Jenkins rolled his eyes. "That doesn't sound like a good idea at all!"

Mordid winked. "Trust me. While you get persecuted on the stand, I'll find out how Herrin set you up. I have to hand it to him, he's worked you over good." Mordid grinned. "I'd even allow it, if it weren't for the fact that you are my guy and I'm the only one who gets to determine when and how you die."

Jenkins retreated to the far wall of the cell and leaned against it. "And what about the intruders?"

"I'll find them. For now, enjoy your off time." Mordid gave him a thumbs up and one of the winning smiles Eryn taught him. It didn't exactly have the desired effect, but for the moment there was little he could do to help Jenkins out.

"Sit tight and Mordid will see you through," Karlson said.

"See. Listen to ancient wisdom." Mordid strode out of the brig. He had much to do in the coming weeks. The ship was filled with far too many assassins, or thieves, and he wasn't done trying to pry out the secrets of Pedro Chavez either. There was his admiral to placate, and somewhere through it all he needed to prepare for the chaos that would surely ensue when they arrived in the largest warzone in the Corporate Worlds. He mentally grumbled at the growing amount of burdens, but then again, he was the Traveling Tyrant. He was more than just a pretty face for the mercenary company. He was its problem solver. The weight could pile atop his shoulders, and he would handle it.

#

THE CORPORATE WORLDS -THE MERCILESS IN THE LABOR SYSTEM-

The view port suddenly went from pitch black to a starry field. Rodriguez didn't feel the shift from transpace back into reality as intensely as others did. It was just a momentarily tickle in his gut and nothing more.

He looked at the knife-like prow of the *Merciless* and the red fist painted upon it. One day, the fist would be replaced with an eagle valiantly clutching the symbol of the hated Earth Government in its talons, or, if things worked out, maybe the golden avian would be clutching a snake like it was in the old days before the exodus.

"A private call, Admiral," Valdez warned.

But the repainting of the fleet wouldn't begin today. They were still weeks away from their destination and the fall of Mordid, and this stop was the one he knew would annoy the man from Earth. It was time to set aside dreams and deal with the present.

Rodriguez swept his hair back and said, "You have the bridge, Valdez."

After a leisurely stroll, Rodriguez seated himself in the private communications hub he used when speaking with the stealthy ship that shadowed their movements. He toyed with a few buttons and reclined back in his chair.

The placid, smiling face of the Earth captain appeared on the monitor overhead. For a man who must be furious, Rodriguez was impressed with how calm he looked.

"Admiral, you are going the wrong way."

Rodriguez chuckled. "Oh, no. I'm just taking the scenic route. Besides, I need to kill some time. We still haven't found those assassins your false pope sent. Oh, and we are hosting a trial! You know, it's actually quite fun. I was even able to yell at the *gringo* who murdered my ship's best boxer."

"Your loss is clearly devastating," the captain said.

"*Si.* But in a few weeks, the jury will scream 'guilty,' and we'll watch a man turn inside out for his crimes. If we are very lucky, he'll float past the bridge. Maybe even bounce into the window! The men would appreciate that." Rodriguez stretched in place. "So?"

"So? Earth Space can best be reached by heading for New Mecca."

Rodriguez snorted. "The Most Holy Father cannot return to Earth Space by arriving in a system dedicated to another religion. I know you tolerate all religions in the same fashion, but I don't!"

The smile remained. "Then go to the Galileo system. It's the same distance away."

"Oh, no, no!" Rodriguez shook his head. "Galileo had a nasty tangle with the church. He claimed the Earth moved! Silly. Every educated man knows that the Earth is still. *Viva* the geocentric theory!"

"Admiral, we have a deal, and if you are breaking it…" The captain trailed off, and for a moment his plastic smile faltered.

"Do not worry." Rodriguez dipped his head. "I honor agreements. We are going to the Community system."

The captain's smile fell further.

"Aww, upset, *amigo*? It is in Earth Space, and that's where you wish the Holy Father delivered and Mordid."

"That is an unwise and reckless decision." The man's voice was much colder. "The Khan system lies between you and Community. Besides, Community is about as far away from Reconquista as one can get. It is a ridiculous thing to do."

"Yet it is what will happen." Rodriguez flung his hands in the air. "I think the Holy Father doesn't want any special welcome, eh? But what do you care? Everything you want will happen." Rodriguez gave a broad smile. "You'll just have to wait." It felt good nettling the man from Earth.

The captain took a deep breath. He let it out, and his smile forced its way back onto his face. "Admiral, Earth Government has sensitive operations ongoing in that region of space. I'd advise you to avoid the Khan and Caesar systems. Entirely."

"I must pass through both to get to Earth Space. *Lo siento.*" He checked himself from stroking his moustache and revealing the sense of apprehension that was replacing his smugness. What was Earth Government doing in Corporate Space? The Caesar and Khan systems were outside their dominion.

"I won't be able to alert anyone, channels are not secure. You don't understand," the captain said. "You must—"

"I must nothing," Rodriguez snapped. "We are going to Community and you may tag along, or you may go your own way. I think the Holy Father doesn't want you, or anyone, knowing the time and place of his arrival. I think that is a smart move. Who knows what you had planned for him if we went the obvious way." He stood. "Follow or do not. I don't care."

Before the man from Earth could answer, Rodriguez cut the channel. Eventually, he'd need to work with the man to ensure the Holy Father arrived in Earth Space safely, just as soon as they did whatever the pope planned to do in the Khan system. He also needed the Earth man's assistance in ensuring Mordid, and with luck the rest of the command staff, ended up in Earth's hands- or dead. This had to happen while the company's fleet remained intact. No fleet, no Traveling Tyrant Rodriguez. For now, though, he'd let the man from Earth stew. It felt good to see the polite facade crack a bit. It was almost as much fun as watching Mordid's minion Jenkins squirm at the trial. Still, Rodriguez thought with satisfaction, it would be far more delightful to watch the murderer of Victor Torres twitch, writhe, and cough out his lungs and veins in the clutches of space.

#

"Stupid trial," Jenkins spat as the marine shoved him into his bare, empty cell. He was slammed into the far wall, and he groaned and slid to the cold floor.

"Well, don't get caught committing murder." The guard shut the cell door and wandered back to his chair. He eased into it, then, as was his custom, turned his back on Jenkins and talked in quiet tones to his partner.

Jenkins didn't bother objecting to the man's words. He'd learned quickly enough to stop objecting at his trial when his demand for an expert to look over the surveillance footage was met with a flurry of Spanish insults and several items tossed his way. In fact, since the trial had begun, it had steadily become a Spanish-only environment. His defense lawyer, the cook from one of the lower levels of the ship who recalled watching a lot of law shows, had only bothered to learn a few legal phrases, which revolved around asking about bathroom breaks and when lunch was.

He had to get out. If he stayed, he'd die—Jenkins was sure of it. Mordid had shown up to none of the trials, and the sparse visits from Karlson were less than encouraging.

Rising to his feet, Jenkins rubbed his still sore arms and looked his cell over for the thousandth time. The bars were solid and the walls metal, and there were no facilities. He had to urinate on the wall and defecate in the corner. He had no idea who cleaned up after him while he was berated at his trial. His meals consisted of a pasty, wet, soggy sandwich and a cup of water. A cup and a sandwich offered little avenue for escape, but there was one aspect to the room that held a modicum of promise.

Jenkins looked up at the lights. They were fitted behind a translucent plastic sheet and hummed continuously as their cold, overly bright rays banished shadow, and any decent sleep, from the cell. They were like nearly every other light aboard the *Merciless*. When he was a soldier-for-hire without rank, he'd had to change more than a few of them. He'd been shocked silly twice.

Jenkins peered at the guards. The two marines in their black uniforms were talking to one another, ignorant of their one and only prisoner.

Swallowing, Jenkins approached the bars and placed his feet between them. He straightened himself, gripped a cold steel rod with one hand and reached up with the other. He could just barely touch the plastic cover of the lights. Using his fingertips, he moved them aside. Like sliding the lid of a coffin, he exposed the bulbs and narrowed his eyes, trying not to blind himself. He could make out little wires fastened to the glass tubes. The little wires, if not handled with care, could be dangerous. Exactly the sort of thing Jenkins needed—something more dangerous than a cup.

He glanced at the guards. They were still paying him no mind, so he reached up higher, narrowing his eyes at the mild pain from stretching. His fingers hooked over a set of wires, and he jumped, landing in the middle of the cell. The sound of his boots striking the floor reverberated in the tiny room. The wires grew taut about his digits as he leapt, and then snapped free. One of the lights went out.

"Hey, quiet up," one of the marines barked.

"I'm hungry," Jenkins complained.

"What? Well, dinner isn't for an hour." The marine looked over his shoulder. "Keep that noise up and it won't be until tomorrow."

Jenkins pulled the wire down so that it dangled halfway to the floor. "Well, feed me and I'll be as quiet as usual. I've not disturbed you for weeks. I think I've earned an early meal. Besides, I'm going to die, aren't I?"

The marine sighed. "Probably. I don't know. Hold on and don't say I never did nothing for you when you get to Hell." He stood up and walked to a refrigerator unit fastened to the wall where Jenkins's dull meals and tin-tasting cups of water resided.

"Hurry up," the other guard complained. He stretched and placed his hand behind his back. He shut his eyes and said, "I don't have all day."

The first marine snorted and retrieved the customary sad sandwich and cup of water. He shut the refrigerator door with a kick of his leg, just like he always did.

He hummed to himself as he approached Jenkins's cell, just as he always did.

"What's with the light?" the marine halted.

Jenkins stood, blocking the view of the dangling live wire from the man's vision. "Light's out. Happens all the time. I'm surprised you don't have to change them over and over."

The marine grinned. "Someone else's job. I just keep you in your cell." He neared the bars and placed the cup on the inside, reaching between the bars, as was his custom. His now free hand grasped one of the bars, and he slid the plate beneath the horizontal bar that framed the door—as usual.

Jenkins smiled as the man's hand grasped the metal. He gripped the wire by the safe rubberized coating and rammed the coppery live end onto the metal bars.

The marine sucked in a breath. His eyes widened, his sparse hair stood up on end. The jolt was not nearly enough to kill him, but more than enough to lock him in place.

Moving fast, Jenkins released the wire. The man was on his knees. Jenkins stooped so that he was face to face with the guard, who still grasped the cell bar in a deathly vice. Jenkins reached through, grasped the man by his collar and drew him close. His other hand leapt for the marine's sidearm.

With a pull, the gun was free, and he placed the muzzle squarely against the man's forehead.

"Open the door."

"Illinz?" the other asked. He stood up and reached for his pistol.

"Open it," Jenkins warned, while twisting Illinz's collar, "or I'll just negotiate with him instead. I like both of our odds if we make a deal just between us."

Illinz stood, and his trembling hand reached out to press the button that opened the door. A buzz sounded, and the metal bars slid aside with a rattle.

Jenkins released Illinz and darted into the guard's room. He pointed the pistol at Illinz's compatriot. "Don't. You're not paid enough to die."

The guard frowned, glanced at his sidearm, then sighed. He raised his hands. "True enough. What do you think you're doing?"

Illinz raised his hands as well. "Yeah, you can't escape. There's nowhere to go, Jenkins. Unless you plan on just hiding in the *Merciless* like some rat. There are beamer-armed marines all over. You'll be cut in two."

The other nodded. "You'll still get caught. How about you go back into your cell, and we'll just pretend this never happened. Besides, think about your trial."

"Oh, I am," Jenkins assured them. He kept his distance

and gestured toward his former cell. "In you two go. And toss your communication devices on the floor. And the gun too." He smiled. "You can share my sandwich and cup of water."

"Nice guy," Illinz mumbled. He and his companion did as they were told and shuffled into the cell.

Jenkins pressed the wall button and locked them in. "Next time you see me, I'll be a hero." He frowned. How exactly that would happen, he wasn't sure. He had to clear his name for sure and on top of that find the men from Earth running loose within the cavernous confines of the Tyrant's command ship. While doing so, he had to not get killed, since he had no friends. Well, almost no friends.

"Sure thing, hero," Illinz said and looked at the dangling wire. He grasped it and poked his friend.

"Ow!" the other marine rubbed his arm. "That hurt!"

"That's what he did to me. Just so you don't think I gave up for no reason!" Illinz glared at Jenkins. "And yes, it hurts."

Jenkins scooped up one of their communication devices and winked. "Sorry."

He moved for the exit and, as soon as the door opened, licked his lips. From this moment on, anyone who recognized him would likely shoot on sight. Worse, Jenkins couldn't defend himself—not even against any of Rodriguez's men, whom he'd built up a distinct personal dislike toward.

Tucking the pistol in his belt, Jenkins took a breath and made his way through the ship to try to find Karlson before the word got out that he was loose.

#

Thrask lumbered down the hall with his head bowed low and contemplated Mauss's message. He was not overly surprised when he heard Herrin's voice from behind him. Herrin was as silent as a cat when he wanted to be. His prized minion also knew when it was advantageous to be around. Or when some plotting was afoot—which usually was one and the same.

"I'm here, General. Where are we going?" Herrin asked.

Grunting, Thrask said, "Mauss says he finally knows what that thing is. He wants to tell me in person all about it." He looked over his shoulder at Herrin. "The old man sounded…" Thrask trailed off.

"Sounded what? Decrepit?" Herrin skipped to Thrask's side and looked up at him.

"Worried." Thrask cleared his throat and tried to banish negative thoughts. It was difficult. Mauss rarely showed emotion, he rarely raised his voice, and he never sounded distressed. Not ever. Until now.

"Is that bad?" Herrin asked.

"Probably."

Thrask plowed his way through the informants and minions of Mauss and approached the old man's door. The camera fixed above the doorway focused.

"Open up," Thrask growled.

The door slid open and within was Mauss's poorly lit room, a new table and atop it the relic the guest had so jealously guarded. It was only a matter of time before the fellow checked up on the briefcase and found it lacking. But lacking what? Mauss was by the table, his thin fingers were resting atop the wooden surface, and his gaze was set intently on the silvery object.

Entering the room, with Herrin at his side, Thrask crossed his arms. "Well?"

The door slid shut.

"Come closer and look at this," Mauss said. He did not tear his eyes off the thing.

Shrugging, Thrask strode to the table and peered at the item. One of the lights in the ceiling focused on it, bringing out the device's sleek contours. It looked the same as when Herrin delivered it to him. It was mechanical and rather fancy-looking for being a relic, and its purpose was unknown. The skull on the cylinder portion of the relic was the only familiar sight, and it wasn't one that Thrask particularly liked.

"It took me a while to figure out what this was. I didn't want to tamper with it and a good thing too." Mauss let out a breath. "General, you are looking at a bomb."

Thrask blinked. "Bomb?" He backed up. "Is it active? Is it on a timer? It doesn't look like any bomb I've ever seen." He pondered a moment. What would a religious sort like Cardinal

Chavez want with a bomb?

Herrin laughed. "Great. And I take it that it's not the usual kind of bomb?"

"Correct. It is not your typical explosive device. I had a trusted agent from engineering look it over. He's the type that loves conspiracy theories, no matter how outrageous." Mauss pursed his lips. "He's the type that is always afraid of *them*."

"Aren't you *them*?" Thrask muttered.

"True enough, but he's delighted to be of service so long as I entertain his most wild theories and give him a few knowing nods." Mauss reached his hand out and stroked the sides of the device. "According to the engineer, this is a bomb built by the finest of technicians. He's certain only the most adept, and well-funded, minds from Earth Space or one of the most powerful corporations could produce it."

"Okay, so it's a bomb. Listen, Mauss, you said you could help me get an angle on Rodriguez if I got you this thing. You've had it for weeks." He glared at the device. "Let's toss it out into space, and you can then meet your end of the bargain."

"Sounds reasonable," Herrin said.

Mauss arched a brow. "Tell your End Roader to get his hand off that knife or I'll shoot him someplace unpleasant. Or worse, I'll let Mordid and Rodriguez see what really happened in the bathroom. I don't know much about Mexicans, but I do know they take their boxing seriously. Given how much fun they are having torturing Jenkins in that sham of a trial, I can only imagine what they would do if they found out...."

Herrin backed away and waved his empty hands in the air. "All right, all right." He rolled his eyes. "You're right, boss, this guy is creepy."

Mauss sneered. "Creepy, mmm?"

Thrask shrugged. "Ignore him. Back to me. Tell me what I want to know. We had a deal." He clenched his fists and glared at Mauss. Herrin might be scared away, but he'd snap the old man in two if he didn't fulfill his end of the bargain.

"Summon Rodriguez," Mauss said.

"What? Why?" Thrask opened his mouth to say more, a lot more.

"Because," Mauss interjected, "I will get him to tell you what he's been up to. You'll have a confession of his poor behavior in front of witnesses. It should make for a fine piece of blackmail. For all of us." Mauss glanced at Herrin. "By us, I mean your boss and me. Not you."

"Sure," Herrin replied and stepped back another foot.

He didn't like this. Thrask much preferred something straight forward, as opposed to whatever theatrics Mauss was planning. However, if Rodriguez would reveal something useful, and Thrask could use that information, it would be well worth indulging the old man.

"Fine." Thrask rammed his hand into his pocket and produced his communication device. He adjusted a few dials and waited for the static to clear up. The *Merciless* was a powerful craft, perhaps the strongest ship in the Upper Arm, but she sometimes played havoc on communications. Sometimes her lights went dim. One time her gravitationals nearly crushed them all to death. Strong as she was, she was getting old.

"Admiral," Thrask said.

"*Si? What do you want, ground-pounder? I am very busy making sure your ride is smooth and worry free.*"

Thrask shared a look with Mauss, who nodded.

"I need you to come down to Mauss's room. Alone."

"*Oh really? And why should I do that? I have things to do, and not to be rude, General, but if you ask me to go somewhere alone, I get a bit suspicious.*"

Thrask snorted. "I'm sure. Still, you're going to do it. I have the relic, and I think you should see it. Before it blows up."

Mauss rolled his eyes. "You are a master of subtlety, General."

There was a pause from Rodriguez and Thrask grinned. He imagined the admiral furiously stroking his moustache. If life were poker, the admiral's moustache was his tell.

"Well?" Thrask prompted.

"*I'm on my way.*"

Nodding, Thrask returned the device to his pocket. He glared at Mauss. The old man always thought of himself as better, as if somehow being sly, in of itself, was the best course of action.

"Being straightforward gets things done. Imagine if I fought the Tyrant's wars with all that subtlety and deception you favor? What then?"

Mauss pursed his lips and was silent for a moment. He said, in somber tones, "I suppose we'd win with fewer casualties, but with far less stunning images for Eyrn to film." He turned his eyes to the relic. "However, General, your sledgehammer personality may come in handy when Rodriguez arrives."

"It better, or Herrin's knife-wit sure will."

"That's for certain sure," Herrin said, and his hand drifted to his side, stroking the hilt of his prized blade.

6

THE CORPORATE WORLDS -THE MERCILESS IN THE LABOR SYSTEM-

Mordid sat in bed, his back to a wall and his eyes fixed on a large monitor on the far wall. He used a remote to try out different channels. Being deep in Corporate Space meant there were thousands upon thousands of channels to choose from. Unfortunately, being deep in Corporate Space meant that nearly all of them were fixated on selling a product. There was precious real news for him to ponder. For all the wildness, dangers, and treachery in the Upper Arm, that region of space at least had truthful information to ponder. He missed Bucky Owls ranting about Earth Government's plot to rule the galaxy or Zaltrek's lengthy speeches about why he had to put a hundred people to death. Instead, he had to watch a bunch of blonde women giggle about the length of the latest sniper rifle, as if assassins needed harlots endorsing their tools!

"Are you paying attention to this?" Eryn said from beside him.

She was clad in a night gown, which contrasted sharply with Mordid's full military attire, complete with coat, hidden knife, and pistol. Even nearly naked, Eryn was dangerous, so it was only fair he was armed.

She held a pad filled with moving images and angled it toward Mordid. "Look."

Mordid watched one of the blonde women hug the silvery rifle on the big screen. "I am."

Eryn scowled. "No, look at this. I've been working all night on making the latest corporate intro, and you need to pick the best." She nudged him. "Between those girls and yourself, who do you really want to gaze at?"

He grinned. "Me!" Sighing, he took the pad from her hand and regarded the four moving images. They all were flashy, they all had him in it, but only one had that Tyrant style.

The door thundered.

Mordid tossed the pad onto Eryn's lap and reached for his pistol. "Who the hell is it?"

"Open up you tiny, insignificant, man!" bellowed Pedro Chavez.

"What did you do?" Eryn asked as she focused her dark gaze onto the door.

"Nothing!" Mordid pursed his lips and tried to think of something that might have annoyed the cardinal. While desperate to get a hold of the relic, he'd been too busy keeping the fleet operational, keeping Jenkins alive by encouraging Rodriguez to draw out the trial, going over reports from his spies, and making PR decisions with Eryn. He hadn't the time to try another peek at the relic in at least a week.

Slipping off the bed, Mordid made his way to the door and pressed the button to open it.

Red-faced, with wide eyes, Pedro Chavez pushed past Mordid into the room and slapped his hand on the button to shut the door.

Mordid barely caught a glimpse of the man's entourage outside, looking equally furious, judging by their grimaces, wild hair, and clenched fists. Two of Mordid's guards tried in vain to keep them back.

"What?" Mordid managed as he backed away from the man.

Pedro waved his hand. "Put that away!"

Blinking, Mordid put his gun away. He hadn't realize he'd

drawn it. "Sorry. Anyways, what?"

Eryn giggled. "He's mad because we're not married."

He shot her a look. "Pedro, despite what it looks like, I do not sleep with her. Or around her. Or even near her. I don't close my eyes around her. It's a bad idea."

"I'm wounded, Mordid." Eryn looked back at her pad. "Well, I have work to do, so just ignore me." She toyed with the surface of the pad with her dexterous, long fingers.

Shaking his head, Pedro tapped Mordid on the chest. "Our deal is over. Done. Drop me and my people off at the nearest inhabitable world."

Mordid cleared his throat. "Over? Pedro, I thought we came to an understanding?"

"We did!" He sucked in a breath, and the veins on his balding forehead bulged. "But you couldn't resist temptation, could you? Like Adam, you just had to have the forbidden fruit." He looked at Eryn. "Did she put you up to it?"

Without looking up from her work, Eryn said, "That would be biblical. Alas, we don't have any idea what you're talking about."

"She's telling the truth." Mordid crossed his arms. "Let's start over. What did I do?"

"The relic, *idiota*." Pedro flung his hands in the air. "It is gone!"

Not good. Mordid rubbed his face and shut his eyes tight. "Damn it all. I told you I wanted it separated from you for safe keeping. Gone? How? When?"

"You deny taking it?"

Mordid popped his eyes open. "I swear—"

"All the time. Curses like a sailor," Eryn mused.

"Not helping, woman." Mordid arched a brow and continued, "I swear I did not take it. Tell me everything. I'll get it back for you, and I'll drop you off at the nearest Corporate World." While the first part was true, the second wasn't. With so much money on the line—and the pope's contract was an outrageous sum—he'd do anything to woo Chavez back. If that meant locking him up for a while, then he'd do it.

The veins in the priest's head stopped throbbing. He

swallowed and said, "I do not check on the relic often. It is sensitive, as such things are. However, on a whim, perhaps divinely inspired, I opened up the case not a few minutes ago and," he visibly shook and the veins in his head returned, "it was filled with broken pieces of furniture."

Mordid smiled. "Really?"

"You're smiling?" Pedro huffed. "I am a patient man. A forgiving man. A gentle man. But this is the one matter, the only matter, that gets my blood on fire! It is not a topic to smile about!"

Mordid walked to the bed and sat down. "Pedro, I know you are angry and that the relic is dear to your heart. However, I think I know who has it. Or at least, the suspects are in a very narrow field. You said the case was filled with debris?"

"The very same from the day you *first* tried to steal it and—" Pedro's eyes lit up, "And therefore…"

Mordid said, "Whoever has stolen it was in the room that day. And when was the item out of your sight?"

"Only during your scuffle with Rodriguez."

Mordid thought back to those who were in the room. Other than Pedro's men, there were only a few others who could have possibly made the swap. Only one of them was stealthy and sneaky and, being an End Roader, treacherous by his very nature. The news was marvelous. It was also just the kind of dirt Jenkins could use to perhaps turn the tables on Herrin.

Mordid laughed. "Excellent. Pedro, you and your men can stay here. The quarters are cramped for such a crew, but I insist. At least for now. I'll be getting the relic back for you." He leapt from the bed and looked at Eryn. "Keep him entertained."

She paled. Impressive given how milky her skin was. "Really?"

He nodded. "I'll be summoning you shortly, but while I'm off, I want to make sure nothing happens to our guests. If, for any reason, the intruders find out he's here, you'll deal with them?"

She let out a breath. "Yes, yes. I'll kill them all for you."

"Good." Mordid winked at Pedro. "I'll be back soon."

"Wait!" Pedro reached a wrinkled hand out. His anger fled and he tensed up.

Mordid could feel the worry radiate from him. He frowned and shrugged. "What? I'll get your holy bauble back. All is well. Wait, is there something about your relic I should know? It's not alive is it? Or, something alien. I hope not. I hate alien technology. It never works right. It always has side effects."

Pedro's hand dropped. "No, nothing like that. It is an antidote to greed, nothing more." He nodded. "Just get it back. I'll reconsider ending our contract if you do this."

"Done!" Mordid sped for the door, opened it, and burst through the expectant crowd of robed figures. They shouted at him, but Mordid smiled as he passed through the throng.

"Shut it. Your boss is going to love me again!"

It was time to round up the suspects and play a bit of high theater. He looked over his shoulder at the two men guarding his door. Bulks and Rendstrot. Both were End Roaders, both were Herrin's men. While Mordid had no reason to think Herrin and his kin would be dumb enough to make a move on him, he didn't want the pair tipping the fellow off. End Roaders were loyal to one another above all else. Jenkins needed a break, and Mordid wanted the relic back with as little fuss as possible.

His communication device buzzed. Walking with a swift gait, he pulled it from his pocket. "What?"

"*Sir,*" a gruff voice said. "*This is Illinz from security. Umm, our prisoner escaped.*"

Wincing, Mordid slid to a halt. There went any plans to get Jenkins out of trouble the easy way. "Really? Come on, Illinz! Your one and only prisoner? How did that happen?"

"*He electrocuted me. It hurt, sir. I almost cried.*"

"You will cry when I get done with you," Mordid muttered. "Okay, alert the ship. I want him alive. Anyone who harms Jenkins will have me to answer to. Got it?"

"*Can we hurt him?*"

Mordid smirked. "I highly encourage it. It'll teach him a lesson not to escape unless I tell him to." Mordid cut the channel. He fiddled with a few of the dials and opened up a connection to the three men he needed to see.

"Mauss, General, Admiral. Big Room. Now."

#

Rodriguez peered over the shoulder of one his bridge crew. He watched in satisfaction as the man's fingers flew over the console and entered the coordinates to the next system. As soon as the Racer Rabbit transdrive was powered up, they'd be on their way to the next Corporate World. Each leap from system to system had been thankfully quiet, and none of the mega-corporations had even bothered to challenge them. Then again, it was unwise to challenge a mercenary horde of substantial size that was just passing through.

"Sir," Valdez said and jogged over. He grinned. "I have good news!"

Blinking, Rodriguez stood tall and placed his hands on his hips. "Oh? I would be delighted to hear it, Valdez. Lately, the only news we get is that the Earth man is mad or that assassins are on board."

"Jenkins escaped. Mordid wants him alive but..." Valdez trailed off, and he flashed an ever widening and toothy smile.

Excellent news! Rodriguez clapped his hands together. "Wonderful! The trial has been fun, and I think poor Victor Torres has looked down from heaven with joy. But to be honest, Mordid keeps delaying the truly exciting part. Justice." He flicked his moustache. "Valdez, I have a job for you."

"Do you need your socks cleaned?" Valdez ventured with a grin.

"No," Rodriguez said with a smile.

"Do you want me to get you some new moustache wax?"

Rodriguez reached his hands up and with the tips of his fingers toyed with the ends of his wide moustache. "No," he said.

"Do you want me to hunt down Jenkins and shoot out his kneecaps, then drag him to an airlock and take pictures as we decompress him and jettison him through a door that's only open," he squeezed two of his fingers together, "this much?"

"Si!"

The crew, aptly listening, cheered.

Valdez winked. "Okay, Admiral." He pointed at a few of the men. "Come with me. We will get vengeance for our lost brother!"

Those chosen leapt from their seats. Those who weren't chosen frowned, but they did not object.

The helmsman nearest Rodriguez said, "Ready for transpace, Admiral. Every ship in the fleet is a go."

"*Uno, dos, tres, vamanos!*" Rodriguez ordered.

The lights flickered, the sounds of struggling machinery echoed and an instant later the view port changed from star-laden space to depthless, eternal black.

A few of the crew members grumbled from the effects of entering transpace, and Rodriguez felt a bit of indigestion put a flame in his belly, but with a pat to his wide stomach, it went away.

Valdez and his chosen men marched off the bridge, their eyes gleaming and their smiles wide. The discomfort of transpace was clearly not on their minds.

He envied them. However, Rodriguez hoped that the group collected plenty of pictures of Jenkins suffering and dying. They could place the images around Victor Torres's shrine of crosses and flowers as a reminder to what happened to anyone who harmed one of Rodriguez's kin. He was master of the ship, and his men died on his command, and his alone. Well, his and Mordid's, but not for long.

In his pocket his communication device hummed. Stepping away from the crew for privacy, Rodriguez pulled the item out.

"*Admiral,*" Thrask said through a hiss of static.

The general then made a convincing case for Rodriguez to visit.

He returned the communication device to his pocket and addressed the crew. "Hector!"

"*Si?*" The navigational officer looked up from his console. His black brows kitted so close together they became one.

"You are in charge. I am going alone to visit with General Thrask." Rodriguez puffed his chest up, to look and sound more authoritative. "If Valdez returns with images of Jenkins's death, do not let anyone see them. Not until I do! I want us to look at them on a big entertainment screen together."

Hector smiled and let out a whoop, which meant "yes."

Satisfied, Rodriguez strode off the bridge to make his way to Mauss's den of rats to see what the general of Mordid's army was doing with the Holy Father's prized possession.

#

The marines thundered past in full armor, clutching beamers or assault rifles at the ready. Deckhands scurried for cover as the black-clad enforcers of the *Merciless* barreled down the hall in search of their prey.

From the shadows of a side passage whose lights were failing, Jenkins watched them pass by. Biting his lower lip, he mentally cursed. It was the fourth squad he'd encountered thus far. It was only a matter of time before someone recognized him or before one of the ever-growing patrols of marines discovered him. If all he had to do was hide, it would be easy. The ship was enormous enough to do just that, but he had to be somewhere. Worse, that somewhere was in the middle of the ship, which was more populated—and apparently filled with squads of marines who took great joy in marching around over and over in search of him.

When he was certain the marines were gone, Jenkins emerged from the shadows. He kept his head low and walked briskly. He ignored the men traversing the hallway. Everyone had somewhere to be, and he made no effort to derail anyone from their destination.

Someone banged into his shoulder.

"Watch it!" a soldier growled.

"Sorry," Jenkins replied and held his hand up in an apologetic wave. He passed the man by and hurried his steps.

He didn't look over his shoulder, but Jenkins could sense the soldier staring at him. At any moment he'd call him out! At any moment he'd draw his sidearm, and that would be that.

"Hey!" the man yelled.

Jenkins halted. He took a deep breath and risked the barest glance over his shoulder. Swallowing, he croaked, "What?"

The soldier, a pale-skinned, scowling sort, as was common in the Tyrant's employ, made a rude gesture. "Don't I know—" the man winced.

The lights of the ship flickered, and Jenkins felt his head spin. He tottered to the side and grasped the nearest bulkhead. The cold metal jarred him, and he let out a small gasp as his fingers fumbled against the wall.

The soldier addressing him put a hand to his head and sat down.

Other people sat down as well, one man vomited, and a few laughed, apparently unaffected.

"You'd think the admiral could at least warn us!" the soldier growled.

"Yeah!" Jenkins echoed, partially to keep him distracted and partially in total agreement. The tendency to suddenly leap into transpace was one of his least favorite parts of his job—aside from the plots against his life. For a moment, he sympathized with Mordid who apparently dealt with such plots on a near continual basis.

"See you around," Jenkins said and hurried on his way.

"Yeah, see you," the soldier said from behind him, the suspicion gone from his voice.

Jenkins stumbled a few times as he navigated a variety of passages, but thankfully the effects of entering transpace didn't linger. Well, if one didn't count the life-draining aspect of it. He imagined a few of his hairs had turned gray and that with every leap into the void he was looking more and more like Karlson. That's what was said anyways. Every leap into transpace sucked the very life out of you. Unless you were high enough up in the ranks. They didn't age so fast. They knew a secret. A secret Jenkins wanted to know as well.

Jenkins reached the door he was seeking, and he glanced either way to ensure the hallway was clear. He rapped his fist against the iron-gray metal surface.

"What?" Karlson called out.

"Open up."

The door slid open and Karlson, looking ill and pale, grasped him by his collar. "What are you doing?"

"I—"

Karlson yanked him inside and shut the door. Their joint office was cluttered with papers, data disks, and other bookkeeping implements scattered on the floor. Every locker and drawer was open.

Jenkins frowned. "What happened here?"

"You!" Karlson groaned and sat down on the nearest chair. He swept his hands through his graying hair. "They've come looking for you and tore this place apart, as if making a mess would somehow make you magically appear."

"Well, it did!" Jenkins smiled. "Good thing they've passed on by. They won't check here again."

"Oh yes, they will." Karlson stared at him. "They've been here twice already. You've pissed off the whole ship, Jenkins."

"Commander," Jenkins corrected. He held his hands up. "I have a way to get out of this. Besides, your plan was for me to wait for Mordid to save me. Guess what? It wasn't working. The big guy apparently has more important people to worry about than me, a body guard." Jenkins pointed at himself with his thumb. "Well, as I was lingering in my cell, or getting pelted with fruit at my *trial*, I realized the only person I could count on to save my skin was me."

"So, goodbye." Karlson pointed at the door. "I hope you save you. I'm glad you don't need me."

Jenkins cleared his throat. "Okay. I mean, the only person who can save me is me, and you. I need you, Karlson." He stepped over a pile of informational sticks and navigated his way to a toppled chair. He righted it and sat down.

Jenkins said, "My plan is brilliant. If it succeeds, I'm back in Mordid's graces, the Mexicans no longer hate me, and I save the contract, making me a hero everyone has to adore and reward."

"And I get?" Karlson arched a brow.

"The same fame and fortune. Before you met me, you were a soldier serving under the illustriously drab command of Plinth, right? How many years did you march about with nothing to look forward to besides retirement?"

"Decades," Karlson mumbled. "Still, don't flatter yourself, Jenkins. Ever since I threw my lot in with you I've been nearly eaten by a giant bug, I've been chased by mobs, both religiously and civilly motivated, I've nearly been executed by Mordid, and all I really have to show for it is the 'honor' of protecting him." He crossed his arms. "What's in it for me?"

Jenkins wasn't counting on the man being so stubborn. "Karlson, I thought we were friends?"

"What's my first name?"

"What?" Jenkins straightened.

"What's my first name? You've seen it on files. I've maybe even mentioned it. If we're such good friends, clearly you know my first name." He regarded Jenkins with a level stare.

This wasn't working. He wracked his brain, but he couldn't think of any other name to call Karlson other than Karlson. He needed a different tact.

"I'll pay you."

"Oh really?" Karlson rolled his eyes. "I'm not retiring, I'll probably die in the service of Mordid with a lot of unspent cash that he'll surely find a use for. Money isn't enough." Karlson huffed. "I'll help, but you need to do something for me."

"Anything!" Jenkins smiled. "Whatever you want, I'll do it."

"I want you to arrange a date for me with Eryn." Karlson smiled, and his grin made a dozen more wrinkles appear on his face.

"Are you crazy?" Jenkins leapt from his seat. "That's Mordid's girlfriend or would-be killer. I don't know yet, given the way those two act. And she's not normal, I'll tell you that. There is something seriously, seriously wrong with her."

"Okay, well, line up a date with some other attractive woman on this ship." Karlson crossed his arms.

"Well…" Jenkins trailed off. The *Merciless* was crewed almost entirely by men. There were a few members of the opposite sex, but they were hideous creatures. Only Eryn was one worth looking at.

"What about a different woman on a different ship? The *Star Wench* has plenty of girls aboard."

"It's called the *Star Wench*." Karlson shook his head. "I want a date with Eryn Sanovich. Before I die, and knowing my luck, that'll be soon, I want to be able to say I went on a date with the pretty granddaughter of a genocidal maniac." Karlson sighed. "Hey, if I drank heavily, I'd ask for booze. If I did drugs, I'd ask for that. I live dangerously. Like it or not, what's more dangerous than a date with Eryn?"

The man was insane. But he needed him. "Fine. I have no idea how, but I will get you that date." He loathed to think what he'd have to bargain away to get Eyrn to consider spending even five minutes alone with worn-out Karlson. That was a matter for another day, though.

Jenkins fixed his gaze upon Karlson. "I take it the men from Earth haven't been found?"

"No." Karlson frowned. "They could be anywhere. It's a big ship, and they probably have some pretty fancy tech."

"I bet," Jenkins said and continued, "And what about the relic they want? Where is that?"

Karlson stood and sighed. "I don't like where this is going."

"Says the man who wants to spend time alone with Mistress Crazy."

"Fine." Karlson said, "It's a secret. Only a few of us know. The relic and all the religious sorts were moved to another room, in secret. Their original quarters are being used as bait to try to lure the intruders."

Jenkins laughed. "It's been weeks and they've not come?"

"Well, no," Karlson admitted.

"Then they aren't coming. They know it's a trap. However, if they find out where the relic is, then they'll make a move on it. Perfect!" Jenkins grinned. Provided they didn't get killed along the way, caught by the Tyrant's forces, or in some other way derailed, the plan he had in mind was perfect. "I'm glad I came to you! Karlson, you've made my plan come together."

He groaned. "Great. So, what is it?"

"We hide in an empty room, and we tip off the men from Earth that the relic and the guests are there. They come to kill everyone, but we kill them first." He clapped his hands. "Easy!"

"How many invaders are there?"

"Four."

"Four highly, trained assassins from Earth." Karlson scratched at his jaw and regarded Jenkins. "I should get that date first."

106

"No way. Until I'm redeemed, that's not happening. We'll have the drop on them, and it will go by smoothly. Bang, bang, bang, bang—they're all dead." Jenkins frowned.

"What?" Karlson glowered.

"Do you have a spare gun?"

Karlson pointed to the corner of the room. Inside a discarded drawer, a sleek black muzzle jutted out from under the metal frame. "Right there. The marines who want to crack your skull open tossed it aside." He opened the door to the room and glanced out of it.

Popping his head back in, Karlson said, "You know on level eight where all the lights go off randomly? Strobe level. We can pick a room there. No guards, no people, and we'll get the element of darkness."

"Good thinking, Karlson." Jenkins picked up the discarded pistol, checked to ensure it was loaded, and slid the weapon into his belt.

"How do we get the men from Earth to go there?" Karlson asked.

Jenkins had pondered that on his way to meet with Karlson, and only one way seemed plausible. "We use your communication device. On an open channel, we make the mistake of mentioning where the relic is. If the men from Earth are lying in wait, then that's the sort of thing that should lure them out."

"It might just lure everyone else as well," Karlson warned.

Jenkins flashed a smile. "Let's just hope the assassins get there first."

The older soldier grumbled and stepped out of the office. As he led the way down the gray halls of the ship, he said, "I can't believe we're going somewhere *hoping* elite, Earth-sent assassins find us."

Jenkins nodded. "I can't wait."

#

Thrask leaned against the far wall of Mauss's shrouded chambers. Herrin lingered nearby, like a faithful dog. As for Mauss, choosing not to waste time, the balding man sat at his desk and looked over archaic paper files.

Mauss glanced at the door. "He's here." He pressed a button under the desk and the door silently slid open.

Rodriguez didn't so much walk in as waltz. His shirt was partially open, revealing gold jewelry, and he held his head back so that he stared at the room's occupants down his nose. Brown eyes stormed with evident fury.

"Here I am," he announced. "I am busy doing my job, unlike you, so make this quick."

Mauss grinned and turned his eyes onto Thrask. "General, I shall let you take the lead in this conversation. I believe you'll get from it everything you want."

Thrask grunted. He'd better, or Herrin's knife would. "So, Admiral, what do you think about that thing on the table, eh?" He pushed himself off the wall and strolled toward the desk. He reached out and tapped the table top.

Rodriguez looked at the silvery device. He stared, then stared at Thrask. "Very lovely? This is what you came to show me?"

Mauss shared a look with Thrask.

Sniffing, Thrask gestured to the item again. "Yes. Now explain."

Rodriguez threw his hands in the air. "It's a box and has silvery parts." He moved toward it and narrowed his eyes. "That looks to be a skull. I'd leave it alone. Now, if you don't have the relic, then you've wasted my time, and I will not forget the insult."

Mauss licked his thin lips and said, "Admiral, that *is* the relic."

"No, it is not." Rodriguez clamped his mouth shut and crossed his arms. "Keep your silvery toy. I do not care what it is."

Thrask snarled, "You fool, that is the relic. Herrin stole it from the priest, Chavez. Mauss researched it, and it's a bomb."

"Really?" Rodriguez shuffled closer to the table and bent over, staring intently at the item. "He brought aboard a bomb?"

Mauss nodded. "Yes." He looked at Thrask. "I will admit I was expecting a different reaction. General, I thought you were going to get something exciting out of Rodriguez. I may have been," his face twisted as if he had tasted something sour, "mistaken."

Thrask felt anger bubble up inside him. He'd wasted time and a life on getting the relic, and the only reason for it was to put Rodriguez in his place, to have leverage over him. That, so far, seemed unlikely. "Well, great," Thrask grunted. "Throw it out of an air lock."

Rodriguez stiffened. "We can't do that."

Ah, perhaps there was something, Thrask thought.

Mauss smiled. He brought his fingers together and sighed. "Never mind, General. I am right. I do love it when my instincts are correct."

Thrask laughed and his mood lightened. "Good." He pointed a finger at Rodriguez. "Start talking, Mexican, or I'll toss the bomb out of the air lock and let Mordid know his guest's idea of a religious relic is something that could have incinerated the ship."

Rodriguez's face turned red, and his moustache wiggled. He planted his hands on his hips and tapped his foot. "Bah! I have nothing to say."

"Oh, but you do," Mauss said, "and we're listening, Admiral. Thrask and I are a part of Mordid's command staff. Whatever secret you have is a risk to the company, and I for one do not tolerate risks to the company. I'm the type who likes to talk things out."

"I like to bash things apart," Thrask growled. "Explain."

"Fine." Rodriguez paced back and forth. "It was I who arranged for the contract."

Mauss clapped his hands together once. "I knew it!"

Rodriguez smirked. "Oh no, you did not! I went to great lengths to hide my involvement. You simply knew I was up to something."

"Close enough," Mauss said.

Thrask waved his hand and glared at the pair. "Enough. I want answers. You two can taunt one another on your own time about how smart you both are."

"True," Rodriguez said. His face lost some of its crimson glow. "Anyway, I arranged a contract with the Holy Father. We worked together to establish a means to get him to the Khan System."

Mauss stood up. "The pope is on board?"

Herrin whistled.

Thrask shrugged. Religious matters were of no concern to him. Regardless of how thrilled Mauss was by the prospect of an important guest, as far as Thrask was concerned, it was unimportant—except for one aspect. "Who cares? Why does he have a bomb?"

Rodriguez offered a bow. "General, I say this with the utmost sincerity." He grinned. "I have no idea. The Holy Father is the relic. The suitcase was, uh, well..." he trailed off.

"A bomb?" Herrin provided.

"Who is that?" Rodriguez asked, and he waved his bejeweled finger the End Roader's way. He glared at Herrin. "The men are talking. Shh."

Herrin reached for his side, no doubt seeking out his trusty knife.

"No," Thrask ordered. He ignored the ruffled End Roader and focused his attention on Rodriguez. So far, he didn't have much to leverage against him. The fact that the guest was the pope didn't seem all that important, and while the matter of the bomb would be embarrassing, it wouldn't quite be damning. Nothing so far was of great use. There had to be more.

Sweat danced on Rodriguez's brow. He maintained an arrogant expression, but Thrask could see his fingers twitching. It was all the man could do not to stroke his moustache. His eyes darted from Mauss to him. There was more, and Thrask knew it!

Thrask looked at Mauss. "Mauss, this isn't enough. No more games. Just get to the point so I don't feel you've played me for a fool to get what you want. I'd like to remain," he smiled and clenched his fists until they cracked, "friends."

"Point?" Rodriguez asked.

Mauss returned to his seat and tilted his head. "Once again, the general's blunt nature reveals itself. Very well, he and I had a deal of sorts. I was hoping you'd hang yourself, Admiral, but I suppose I shall provide more than just rope."

"Wh-what are you talking about?" Rodriguez backed up.

"I know you have been communicating with someone. Someone not on this ship, and someone not aboard one of our other ships." Mauss stared and his expression grew taut. "You best explain."

That was something, Thrask thought. Was it with a rival? Mordid had hundreds of them. Perhaps it was with a corporation that wanted the pope? No, no, Rodriguez was a believer. He'd not hand the head of his religion over to anybody. Thrask tried to keep his smile in check.

"I—" Admiral Rodriguez shook his head. "I have nothing to tell you, Mauss."

Thrask felt his communication device buzz. Growling, he pulled it from his pocket and was surprised to see Mauss and Rodriguez doing the same. They shared glances.

"*Mauss, General, Admiral. Big Room. Now.*" Mordid's voice echoed in the chamber. The channel cut no sooner had the order been given.

"Gentlemen," Rodriguez said, "let us take this bomb to Mordid. He should decide what to do. I would also like to break the news to him about his special guest." Rodriguez stepped toward the box.

Mauss's hand skittered over it like a spider heading for a fly stuck in its web. "I'll take it." He rose and with ginger motions picked it up. "The matter of who you are contacting, without Mordid's permission, is not over, Admiral."

Thrask nodded. "Damn right it isn't. I have half a mind to just let Mordid figure it out. He's crafty and I bet—"

"No, no," Mauss said. He stared at Thrask. "I'm sure, General, you and the admiral can work that matter out between yourselves. In private. No need to bother Mordid."

"But—" Thrask shut his mouth as he realized Mauss was throwing him a bone. He had his reward! He had rope. He grunted in agreement. "To the Big Room then."

No one moved first.

"Cowards." Thrask opened the door with a press of a button and walked out. No one shot him in the back. Herrin ghosted to his side.

"Did that go well, boss?"

Thrask grinned. "I think so. I have no idea what Rodriguez is up to, but it doesn't matter. He thinks I know something, and

Mauss has put the fear right into him! That's enough. I'll use it."

Herrin nodded. "Good. So, what will you do now? You have something over the guy, but now what?"

"Now? Nothing." He glanced down at Herrin. "Think of it as your knife. I'll use it when it benefits me the most." He muttered some of his options aloud. "Maybe if Rodriguez is clever enough to sneak the pope on board undetected, he could get me a doctor. One that you could watch over to secretly get rid of that damned thing ticking in my chest. Then Eryn! Yes, I could snap Eryn's neck and off Mordid on the same day."

Herrin nodded. "Sounds good. Do you want Rodriguez gone?"

Thrask shook his head. "Not yet. When I'm the Tyrant I'll need someone to command my ships. I don't know much about the navy. I'll let the Mexican do that until I find someone else. Know any admirals?"

Herrin sniffed. "Funny you mention that, one of my kinfolk just happens to have experience commanding fleets. Nothing as large as this, of course! Just a little pirate outfit." A smile spread across his features.

"Good! Hah. By the time I'm done here, End Roaders will be all over the company! From high command all the way down to screwing in light bulbs. Herrin, you picked the right guy to follow." Thrask looked at him. "Have any sisters?"

Herrin's smile faltered. "Wh-what?"

"Just thinking. See, if I married one of your sisters, one from the direct Herrin line, we'd be family. I'm noticing you End Roaders take that seriously." Thrask inwardly beamed. Mauss would be proud of him. Too often people assumed that because he was large and menacing he was also stupid. Stupid men did not become generals in a ruthless mercenary fleet. "As loyal as you are now, I bet if we were related, it would really seal that bond. The Thrask line! All the End Roaders would have to respect it." He tilted his head. "So get to picking me a bride."

Herrin slowed his pace. His expression turned ashy, which was impressive given his Upper Arm complexion that was akin to a dead fish.

"We… uh. It's so serious to be kin. I don'—t"

Thrask belted out a laugh. "Come now, Herrin. I'm not the sharpest, but I know strategy. I've been listening to you, my boy. I know you want more. More for yourself, but even more so for your family. You're offing Jenkins for the sake of advancement, putting End Roaders in with the Tyrant's body guard. I sense a pattern. Herrins are getting very close to the top. A knife wound away, I'd say."

Herrin shrugged. "I didn't think you'd notice with all of your plotting and problems."

"Oh, I noticed. When this is all over, I'd hate to find myself surrounded by strangers. Imagine if I were instead surrounded by blood-tied family!" Thrask marched ahead. "Your sisters, none of them are fishy, are they?"

"No," Herrin mumbled. "No, they're fine."

"I think I'll be very popular on End Road." Pleased with himself, Thrask strutted his way to the conference room to meet with Mordid.

Herrin gave a small smile. "Maybe you would at that."

7
-TRANSPACE-

Mordid sat in a chair at the head of the table and practiced rotating in it. Eryn said it was best to turn slowly and smoothly to capture the essence of villainous power. Any stutter in the turn would throw off the imagery. On the other hand, it was rather strange to be staring at a blank wall waiting for them to arrive. The broad window ran along the side of the chamber, revealing the depthless ink of transpace. A window just for him as a backdrop was needed. No one stared at a blank wall, but staring out into space, or depthless, black nothing, spoke volumes. It was very Tyrant-like. Maybe he could have a painting bolted to the wall. Something like a volcano going off with the phrase "rage of an angry God" beneath it.

He heard the door open.

With a deft movement of his foot, Mordid spun the chair. He clasped his hands together and put forth his most deadly of scowls. He frowned as he saw only Thrask and Herrin in the room. A larger audience would have been more awed by the rotation of the chair. He very well couldn't do it again and again for each person. He'd have to talk to Eryn about that.

"Where are the others?" Mordid asked.

Thrask shrugged. "Slow." He sauntered to a chair, eased

his bulk into it, and propped his booted feet atop the table. Placing his hands behind his head, Thrask threw a grin Mordid's way. "You have news?"

"Feeling impudent, today?" Mordid glared at Thrask for a moment and then fixed his stare upon Herrin. Too bad the man was siding with Thrask. Too bad he was angling to get rid of his man Jenkins. "Out you get."

"Oh, sorry." Herrin saluted and exited the room without further complaint.

Thrask watched him go and turned his attention back to Mordid. "Oh yes, I'm feeling on top of the world. I've been pursuing your interests, Mordid. And I think you'll like what I found out."

Mordid didn't like the sound of that. He countered with, "Where is the relic? I know you have it." Not true, but since he was alone with Thrask, he could try the ruse.

"On its way. You'll be thrilled," Thrask said. "And yes, I stole it, so don't even ask. And you should thank me for it."

"Cardinal Chavez may not agree," Mordid said.

Thrask smiled even wider. Mordid was surprised he didn't start giggling.

"What?"

"You'll see," Thrask said.

The door opened, and Rodriguez and Mauss entered. In his chief diplomat's hands was something roughly suitcase-sized and silvery. Neither man wanted to go into the room first, so they settled with a duo entry, squeezing past one another to fit through the doorway. Upon entering, the pair separated, choosing chairs on opposite sides of the table.

Mauss set the item, with pointed care, atop the table and brushed his skeletal fingers over its surface. "The relic."

"It's a bomb!" Thrask said. His words burst forth as if they were an explosion.

Mauss groaned and he shook his head. "Yes. It's a bomb."

Mordid fixed his gaze upon the item. He'd been chasing a bomb? Pedro had chained to his wrist an explosive device? It made no sense. He also didn't like it being in the room.

"If that thing goes off, it will make Eryn's day. Perhaps

we—"

"Pedro Chavez is the pope!" Thrask said, and he laughed so loud he nearly fell out of his chair.

"Wh-what?" Pope? Mordid shook his head. "No, no. He's a cardinal."

Mauss brought his fingers to his temples and stared intently at Thrask. "No, Thrask is right. Why not tell him Santa Claus isn't real, General?"

"Hey," Thrask replied, "I don't see a reason to dance around the subject. Mordid needs to know these things, right? The relic is a bomb, the pope himself is on board posing as a cardinal, and Rodriguez," Thrask grinned at the admiral, "well, he knew about it. Tell him."

Mordid looked at the bejeweled admiral. Mordid leaned back in his seat and tilted his head. "You better explain and fast, or else Thrask will, and I have a feeling you won't like the way he tells the tale."

Rodriguez, normally proud, blustery, and gregarious, hung his head. "It was I who arranged to take the pope to the Khan system. I used my contacts in the fleet and on Reconquista to ensure you, and even Mauss, were unaware of how it came to be. I did Mauss's job for him. But the money is real, the contract is real—I just made it so. You will never be offered such a vast sum again. We are beyond rich- if we succeed."

"I don't need help doing my job," the thin man snapped.

Mordid waved Mauss off.

Continuing, Rodriguez said, "The pope has been allowed to return to Earth Space. Free to return and reestablish the Church in Rome. It could be an end to the exile. We all could go back to our true home. As a Catholic, it is my duty to get him there. It is my duty to make it possible for Mexico to resettle the land of our fathers. Making you, well us, money was just a perk of the job." He looked up at Mordid. "Pedro Chavez is the relic. The suitcase is, well, uh—" he looked at the item and his brown eyes narrowed.

"A bomb," Thrask reminded them. He swung his feet off the table and grinned at Mordid. "Maybe the pope wants to blow us up after we drop him off?"

116

"No!" Rodriguez said. Some of the customary fire returned to his voice. "He would not do such a thing."

Mordid growled, "But that *is* a bomb, *amigo*?"

"*Si, mi hermano*," Rodriguez conceded and he hung his head, refusing to meet Mordid's gaze. "I do not understand."

Mauss said, "It's more than a bomb, Mordid. It is a very expensive, highly technical, advanced explosive device. It's not something one would carry around just to blow up a ship or kill a few people. It's specialized, but I don't know for what. It may even have some alien aspects to it."

Mordid smacked the table. "My instinct was to refuse this contract! Religion only leads to trouble. Belief in imaginary people leads to real-life killing."

Rodriguez opened his mouth to object, but a stare from Mordid had him hanging his head once again.

"So?" Thrask ventured, "Let's jettison the bomb, and—"

"Not yet." Mordid reached into his pocket and pulled forth his communication device. "I signed the contract, and the Traveling Tyrant doesn't break contracts. However, my contract is specific—to get a relic to the Khan system. If the pope himself is that relic, so be it." He adjusted a few dials on the item.

"*Yes*?" Eryn's voice purred on the other end.

"Bring Pedro Chavez to the conference room. He has some explosive matters to explain."

Static greeted him for a moment. "*He heard you, Mordid. He looks a bit piqued.*"

"I bet," Mordid replied. "Get him down here before I blow my top. Tell him I plan to be bombastic. You know what, make explosion noises with your mouth. That's an order." He stuffed the device into his pocket and crossed his arms. It took effort not to harrumph.

Mordid did not speak while they waited for Pedro and Eryn. Thrask grinned in open, unabashed self-congratulation. There was no point calling out the fact he stole the relic. He was proud that he did it, and as treacherous as Thrask could be, Mordid was glad that the general had helped sate his curiosity about the mystery item in the suitcase. The matter of getting Jenkins framed along the way so that one of Thrask's "chosen" men could replace him was a matter to be dealt with at another time. Men like he and Thrask, like Olympian gods, could nudge things, but not get too involved in the plots of their minions. Mordid wondered if Thrask was being too forward and if he should match it as their chosen champions battled it out. A matter for later. So many matters were for later.

Rodriguez stared at the table and kept glancing at Thrask. Here and there he toyed with his luxurious moustache. He should have been glowering at the general. Instead, Rodriguez had nothing but worry in his eyes.

Mordid stroked the tip of his beard. What else did Thrask know and yet have the wherewithal not to blurt out?

Mauss was Mauss. He was skeletal, quiet, and utterly sinister, and thus unrevealing, in his expression and mannerisms.

When the door opened, Eryn, clad in throat-to-toe black and gray attire, and the robed Pedro Chavez entered.

Rodriguez stood and bowed his head. "Your Eminence."

"Pope Pedro," Mordid said. "That rolls off the tongue. Kind of like Traveling Tyrant." He indicated a seat. "Please sit and let's chat about the bomb on the table."

"That's a bomb?" Eryn asked. She pursed her lips. "Can we all chat elsewhere?"

"It's not that kind of bomb," Pedro said. He sat heavily in the offered chair and waved a hand at Rodriguez, who took a seat in response. Pedro looked at Mordid. "It was not my desire to lie to you any more than was necessary."

"Thanks?" Mordid shrugged. "From what I gather, I'm involved with religion, Earth Government, and who knows who or what else! I'm a mercenary, Pedro. I try to pick fights I can win." He continued to stroke his beard. "But, since we are being truthful, how about you tell me what that is?"

Pedro nodded. "I will tell you everything." He reached out and grasped the item. While Mauss glared, he didn't interfere, and Pedro was able to pull it close. His fingers danced over the silvery surface with care.

"This was made at a great expense to the Church. Just as you were hired at great expense. It is a bomb that can only be activated in the core of a sun. Once it detonates over a period of months, the sun will turn into a red giant and then either become a black hole or collapse into a white dwarf. Either way, whatever system this takes place in will be decimated."

Mordid felt the blood drain from his face.

Mauss coughed. "That-that is impossible. A system-killing weapon?"

Even Thrask lost some of his composure, and his smile turned into a tight-lipped frown.

"Yes," Pedro said. "It is the only one of its kind, and the research behind it has been destroyed. Decades of work, of money, of spying, and of things not of human desing- all the research is gone. This was made for one purpose only. Once it is used, it cannot be made again. At least, such a thing won't be made with ease again, nor be funded by the Church. I can't speak for the evils of other men in the future."

"We could do wonders with that thing, Mordid," Eryn said. Her eyes glittered. "No system would be—"

"Or women," Pedro whispered.

Mordid shook his head and brought a finger to his lips. Such an item could get him killed. Ransom was the work of pirates, and the sort of venture that paid off once, then tended to make lifelong, dedicated enemies. Besides, what if the threatened party simply told him no? If Mordid used such a bomb to threaten a system and they refused to pay him, what good would it do to destroy their sun beyond petty spite? Incinerating Paradisa, a lonely world filled with plants, animals, and no people of note had cost him plenty in the end. What would system-wide genocide get him?

"What is it for, Pedro?" Mordid asked.

"To end the war in the Khan system. When you deliver me there, we shall launch the device into the system's sun. I will make public what I have done and everyone will have a few months to evacuate the area. Access to the system once the sun collapses will be impossible. There will be no Khan system. All the better, it has no life-giving worlds. No resources. It has nothing of true value. It only has greed and the death of men."

"If he does that, it means," Mauss said while gazing at the device, "the only route to the dead alien empire will be closed."

"The war between the corporations over the spoils of that extinct species will be over," Mordid mused. He tilted his head. "It really is an antidote for greed!"

"Exactly." Pedro said. He looked at each member sitting at the table. "I will bring peace. Then, when I go to Earth Space, they will see me and the faith for what it is. It is not powerless as Earth Government portrays. Faith is not something akin to what a person likes to watch, or wear, drink, or eat. Faith isn't a passing fashion statement. It is real, and it can bring the greediest of corporations to a halt and awe the most arrogant of governments. God's voice can be very loud."

Rodriguez whispered a prayer in Spanish and crossed himself.

"Very high ideals, Pedro." Mordid stood and stalked around the table, placing his hands behind his back and grasping his own fingers in a vice grip. "But it's foolish. Winning a game is something everyone can stomach. Ending the game before it is won?" He completed his circuit of the table and focused on the pope. "If you bring the war to an end in the Khan system and then come rolling into Earth Space calling yourself the voice of God, where does that leave me? You'll be safe. No one is going to kill the pope!"

Except the assassins on board. That is what Rodriguez meant when he used the word. They were here for Pedro. He knew it, and they all knew that too.

Everyone opened their mouths.

"Shut up. Besides the assassins on this ship." Mordid grinned. "Which we'll eventually find, Pedro, so don't worry. But back to me." He patted his chest. "If I let you get away with this, every major corporation fighting over the Khan system will come looking for me. Every mercenary outfit trying to make a profit there will make me their sworn enemy. And Earth Government? They already think I'm a criminal. They say the most outrageous and diabolical things about me, and though they wouldn't openly decry that I delivered the pope, deep down they'll be mad about it if you don't play along with them. Pedro, if you're welcome in Earth Space, then I know they'd want to be behind the transportation. Earth Government likes to control everything.

My escort is clearly a spectacle and you want an arrival that is out of their hands. They don't like things out of their hands."

Mordid frowned. "Is that why they slipped assassins aboard?"

Rodriguez cleared his throat. "No. The assassins are from Earth, but not Earth Government. They are minions of the false pope."

"The Earth-appointed man I am told I'll be replacing upon my arrival," Pedro said. "Apparently he wants to hold onto his job. Though, he need not worry. I simply do not recognize him, nor does any true Catholic."

"The fake ones will kill you just as well," Eryn offered.

Mordid shook his head. "Great. I'll also have religious fanatics enraged that I put one man in charge of Mr. Make-believe over another." Mordid looked at Mauss. "In your opinion, how is this contract sounding? Can we consider it broken due to their withholding of information?"

"Mordid!" Rodriguez said and lurched to his feet.

Pedro waved a hand. "Sit, my son."

Mauss stared ahead at nothing. His lips twitched and his fingers drummed atop the table. After a moment of silent, mental computations, he returned Mordid's look. "The Catholic Church did not provide full details in their contract. The pay they offer does not come close to the risk the company would incur." He snorted, "Not to mention the risk you, Mordid, would personally incur. Your list of foes is long, but manageable. Do this and you will have some exceedingly powerful people and institutions seeking you out. You'd be better off descending into piracy with the bomb. Extort a system or two—then hide for the rest of your life."

Mordid gave a curt nod. "Thank you, Mauss. The thought had occurred to me." He looked at Pedro. "I'm not in this for faith. I'm in it for profit and fun in the name of me." He jerked his thumb toward himself. "I see no reason to continue this affair. We'll stop at the nearest corporate world and—"

"I'll double what the contract stipulates," Pedro said.

Mordid coughed. The original amount was astronomical. Doubling it would be akin to selling off an entire planetary system, all of its people, resources, and the accompanying trade routes. It was the stuff the largest of corporations and Earth Government haggled over—not mercenaries.

"Bull sh—"

Pedro quirked a brow and gave a smile. "I'm the pope."

"You lied before," Mordid retorted. "You'd do it again to carry out your crazy crusade." Mordid shook his head. "No way. You do not have that sort of capital."

Pedro looked at Mauss. "You seem the type of man who knows his numbers and the way of the galaxy. How many systems does Reconquista hold sway over?"

Mauss pursed his lips.

Before he could answer, Pedro said, "How many members in the galaxy pay their tithe to the Catholic Church? Combine all that together. This doesn't even cover the healthy donations we get from the Upper Arm despots and from Upper Arm freemen for protection and for our refusal to accept Earth Government. We are very popular. We also control, or have influence over, a dozen of the major corporations. A spy network you would weep over and with it all comes capital."

Mauss let out a long breath. "Mordid, theoretically he has the money."

Pedro nodded. "This is the most important task of a generation, Mordid. If money is all you care about—"

"It is."

Pedro's eyes narrowed. "Then that is what you will get. Whatever enemies you make will have to contend with the fact that you are the wealthiest, most powerful mercenary the Upper Arm has ever, or will ever, see." Pedro stood and shuffled over to Mordid. He leaned in close. His brown eyes bored into Mordid's. "I see in your eyes a great and horrible sin. The same sin I'm going to end in the Khan system. Avarice. That sin has corrupted you so deeply that it goes against your very rotten nature to refuse me. You can't say no. What has poisoned the men in the Khan system has long ago poisoned you." He sniffed. "Say no. I dare you."

"I-I could," Mordid said, stuttering as he did. That was a lie. His heart was racing with excitement, his head was already full of the things he could do with such vast and absurd resources at his disposal, and for all the enemies brought upon him, there would be fame as well as money to counterbalance their hate. Money. Money could solve every problem if there was enough of it.

Mauss looked stunned. The old man never looked stunned. This was it then. The contract of a lifetime. The contract of all contracts.

"I could say no," Mordid said again, "but I won't."

Pedro nodded. "To be honest, I am disappointed. You have failed a test. But good will come of it." He smiled once. "Perhaps more than you all know."

"I am as constant as the Northern Star," Mordid replied.

Rodriguez let out a long-held breath.

"Risky, but sound," Mauss said.

"Stupid," Thrask grumbled.

"We're still going to blow up a sun, right?" Eryn chimed in last.

"Yes," Mordid said to all of their comments.

#

With the decision made and nearly everything out in the open, Mordid dismissed them. Mauss, Mordid, and the pope remained in the conference room to work out details of the altered contract. Rodriguez merely nodded to the trio before exiting.

No sooner was he a few feet outside the room than he felt a towering presence behind him. He turned and squared off against the much larger Thrask.

Thrask loomed over him and brought his face close to Rodriguez's. He smelled of stagnant sweat and gun oil. "I kept your little illicit communications a secret."

Rodriguez did not answer. He crossed his arms and met the man's hard stare head on. If Mordid were to find out who he was dealing with, all his plans were ruined, not to mention his life. However, if Thrask hadn't exposed him already, then he wouldn't. Not without cause.

"Going to thank me?" Thrask asked.

"No. But I imagine when you want something you'll be reminding me how grateful I should be?"

The battle-scarred man nodded. "Yeah. Something like that. I'll be asking for you soon enough. Herrin!"

The End Roader was lingering against the wall. He detached himself from it and stood at Thrask's side. The pair walked off, each looking disgustingly smug.

Thrask's presence was gone, but a sweet scent filled his nostrils a moment later. He faced Eryn. "Yes?"

Her painted lips formed a seductive smile. She sauntered close, and her eyes flit toward Thrask's retreating form. "I couldn't quite hear what he said, but I imagine whatever it was, it makes you dislike him?"

"Does anyone like him?" Rodriguez asked.

"Mordid. In a strange, self-destructive way. I, however think he's dead weight. I can think of someone who could do a far better job winning the Tyrant's wars." She sighed, "But my dreams will have to wait. Anyway, I wanted to speak with you."

He pushed past her. "I'm busy. If I desire to have my moustache stroked or have some need to wear makeup, I'll let you know."

She leapt ahead of him nimble as a cat, barring his path. "Not so fast, Rodriguez. I'm getting the sense you don't like me." She tilted her head and her expression fell. "Why ever not?"

He laughed. It felt good to find something funny lately. "You're a woman. I have the utmost respect for you as a woman. However, when you act like a man, it just makes me think you are *loco*."

It was her turn to laugh. "You think I should be cooking meals, mending clothes and—"

"And raising children, yes," he said, cutting her off. "Now, unless you wish to cook me some burritos and tacos, I need to get back to the bridge. I need to do a man's job. A woman's job is important. I deeply value it. You do not understand, though."

Her hand snapped out and planted upon his bare chest. Her nails dug in hard enough to nearly draw blood. He smirked and ignored the pain. He'd never back down from a woman! Not even one related to a genocidal maniac.

124

"What you need is a friend. Thrask and Mauss clearly hemmed you into a corner. I've never seen Thrask so deliriously happy, and every time Mauss wasn't staring daggers at that bomb he was staring daggers at you." She lowered her pale hand. "And most importantly, Mordid is miffed. Admiral, you are about to find yourself replaced."

If only she knew he had the same plans for her. "Really?"

She bobbed her head. "Really. If you don't ally yourself to someone in Mordid's command staff, then you'll find a majority baying for your removal. One way or another it will happen. Mordid doesn't mind when accidents occur to unpopular sorts. There are four. You can afford to anger one, even two. Not three. Anger all three, and the man at the top will let nature take its course."

He snorted. "And you suggest that I work with you? Why?"

She struck a pose. "Fame!" Relaxing her stance, she continued. "We are about to engage in a mission like no other. We are going to tweak the nose of several major corporations, piss off Earth Government, and destroy a sun!" She slid her body close to his. "Most of this will be occurring in space. The best vantage point will be right alongside you on the bridge."

He pushed her back and wrinkled his nose at her scent. It was pleasant, but far too feminine for the likes of a military ship. Like so much about Eryn—it was wrong. "So, I let you on the bridge and give you freedom to do your PR work, and in return you become my friend? I do not think you offer me much."

"If I like you, Mordid likes you." She shrugged. "Think of me as Lady Macbeth."

She was educated. She recognized Mordid's Shakespeare quote as had he.

"I can do that." He thought for a moment. An alliance with her could keep Thrask and Mauss distracted. It would definitely keep her distracted! That would be suitable. If she were busy, then she'd not see her impending downfall and that of Mordid and all the rest.

"Fine," Rodriguez said, in slow and measured tones. "I'll let you film. The bridge crew prefer Spanish. Do you have a translator?"

"No," she admitted.

Good! He waved his hands and masked his pleasure at her lingual ignorance. "Do not worry. Nothing will be said that you can't figure out, and, more importantly, you'll see what's going on."

She giggled. "Excellent! I'll have a few teams visit shortly. I'll also have a few follow around the pope. If he wants his message to be heard, then it has to be recorded."

Rodriguez placed a hand over his heart and bowed to her in a very traditional style. "We have an agreement. I will look forward to seeing you on the bridge, and I trust that when my enemies whine about how I need to go, you will triumphantly, and with feminine charm, demand that I stay."

"Agreed," she said. With a skipping gait, Eryn departed, humming as she went.

"Woman," he muttered and watched her go. Any alliance with Eryn would be incredibly temporary. Weeks at best. Soon as they arrived in the Khan system, she and all the rest of the command team had to go—and soon. He took a deep breath and grasped the end of his moustache. Just as the pope was going to try to make momentous changes, Rodriguez had to as well—for his sake, as well as for the success of the Holy Father's vision. He took a little solace in the fact that his ambition for mastery over the company fit in nicely with the Holy Father's dreams and a sum of money that would make him the richest man the galaxy had ever seen.

#

They had set up a proper ambush—or at least as proper as a pair of men with pistols, limited ammo, and time could. The room Karlson had chosen was large. The enemy would have room to maneuver, but a lot of distance to cover. Jenkins and Karlson had cobbled together a barricade of shelving units and a broken refrigerator to hide behind near the far wall, leaving absolutely nothing for those entering the room to use as cover.

True to strobe level's namesake, the lights overhead occasionally flickered as the wiring failed to provide the proper power.

All they needed was to set the trap.

"Ready?" Jenkins asked.

Karlson hefted a pistol in one hand and a communication device in the other. He thumbed a button and said, "I have the guests' dinner. I'm on level eight, but the room is empty. Where the heck am I going again?" He waved the communicator in front of Jenkins.

"Room seven-seven, you idiot. And you're not on a secure channel." Jenkins snarled, summoning up as much contempt in his voice as he could. "Thanks to you, we'll need to move the guests—again! Get their meal down here, and I'll tell them it's time to pack up. Wait. You know what? You get to tell them they're moving again. They'll be thrilled to hear it."

Jenkins nodded.

Karlson released the button and dropped the item. He wrapped his hands about his pistol and braced it against their makeshift barricade. "You sure they're listening?"

They better be! Jenkins nodded, exuding confidence. "Any minute they'll come blazing through that door and make quick work of us." He winked. "Well, they'll try to. I figure one of them might even get a round or two off before we drop them."

The communication device hissed, and a rough voice broke through the static. "*This is marine patrol zeta-nine. No one is supposed to be on strobe level. It's off limits.*"

"Damn it!" Karlson stared at the dropped device. He swallowed and looked at Jenkins.

"Don't answer!" Jenkins said, "Keep your eyes on that door. Whoever comes through it needs to die."

"Not if it's our own men!" He reached a hand out and shook Jenkins by the shoulder. "I said I'd help you out, but like hell will I fight our own men. I'll end up being pushed out an airlock with you."

Jenkins shrugged him off and kept his eyes set upon the door. The lights dimmed and flashed. "Karlson," he soothed, "if you don't answer, they'll get bored and go away."

"*We're coming down there. Do not move.*"

Karlson groaned. "Forget it!" He stood up. "Let's go. We

can be gone before they get here. I'll hide you, and when we get to a habitable planet, I'll get you off the ship."

"No. This has to work! There are Earth-sent assassins on their way here. If those marines kill them, I'm doomed." Jenkins looked at Karlson. "Trust me."

"Ah! If we don't get killed in the next couple of minutes, I might wring your neck out of principle." Karlson hunkered down behind cover.

The door opened.

Jenkins held his breath.

"It will be easy. Drop them as they run through the door."

Two metal cylinders bounced into the room.

"Are you *ever* right?" Karlson spat.

The first cylinder exploded thunderously, flashing with as much intensity as the lights above, which promptly shattered. The other cylinder let forth a red, blinding smoke.

Through the growing crimson haze, Jenkins saw figures emerge. Bastards! He aimed at the first and squeezed the trigger of his pistol.

The shadowy figure collapsed, and to Jenkins's relief the three others emerging from the smoke, with short, compact, assault weapons in hand, were not Tyrant employees.

Karlson fired off a few rounds, baring his teeth.

Another assassin collapsed.

The remaining lights above flickered randomly, causing the red smoke to glimmer as if it were a nebula.

The remaining pair of assassins slid to a halt, crouching. Jenkins could see the confusion on their faces, and the two exchanged glances.

"That's right! Surprise!" Jenkins fired again. But the surprise was on him.

One assassin darted left, the other right, and sparks bounced where they had been, as Jenkins's round missed. As the two moved, they laid down fire of their own. Their guns whined, and the rattling sound they emitted was soft and barely audible.

The sounds of the bullets smacking into the refrigerator were not.

"Ah!" Karlson cursed and threw himself flat. "I'm hit!"

"Bad?" Jenkins fired off two quick rounds toward the running killers and ducked behind the barricade fully. Bullets passed over his head and smacked into the wall. A shelving unit exploded as a series of rounds sent it spiraling from the barricade. Some rounds passed through their barricade, unperturbed by the metal in their trajectory.

Karlson rolled onto his back and moved his pistol from his right hand to his left. "Shoulder. Burns." He focused his muzzle, with a shaky grip, toward one side of the barricade.

Looking the other way, Jenkins leveled his pistol. The soft rattling ceased.

He saw a dark shape poke up from the other side of the barricade. Pointing his pistol, Jenkins fired. The shape vanished.

Over the top of the barricade, the final assassin leapt. He held in one hand his gun, and in the other a knife. His perfect features were contorted in rage, and his eyes blazed as he sailed through the air, intent on killing them both.

Jenkins sucked in a breath and flung himself backwards. He landed hard on his spine and brought his pistol to bear, firing the entire time. The gun clicked empty just as the smoking barrel fixed on the descending assassin.

He landed atop Jenkins, and the knife drove down.

Bang!

In an instant, the top of the assassin's head ripped open. Blood poured down his ruined face, and he collapsed atop Jenkins, spasms causing the corpse to wriggle. More blood flowed—and bone fragments as well. All spilled forth, covering Jenkins' face, chest, and shoulders in ample hot ichor.

"Gah!" The blood was thick and the smell coppery. Jenkins was not shocked by the gore of combat, but it was a bit different when a dead man bled all over one's face. His stomach twisted, and he kicked the corpse off of him.

"Welcome," Karlson said. He managed to get to his feet, and he looked over the barricade. "Ah! That one is still moving." He fired. "Missed." He fired again. "Got him." Looking back at Jenkins, he said, "I'm not a great shot with my left hand. You're lucky I didn't shoot you by mistake."

Wiping the blood from his eyes, Jenkins replied. "I

don't feel lucky." He set his pistol aside and stood, wringing his crimson-soaked hands as he surveyed the room.

To his satisfaction, the men from Earth were dead. One was sprawled by the doorway, mostly obscured by the hissing canister of smoke. Another had managed to crawl halfway to the barricade, leaving behind a slick red trail before Karlson had finished him off. The third was slumped on the other side of the barricade, while the last was managing to attack Jenkins's eyes, nose, and mouth from beyond the grave with his blood.

"Stings," he complained, wiping his eyes.

"Stings? I've been shot! You need a shower, I need a doctor." Karlson frowned. "Jenkins?"

He blinked, trying to clear his eyes. "What?"

"These guys are dead. Now what?"

"Easy, we show the marines what we did, and everyone forgives me. How can Mordid not intervene on my behalf?"

The door opened again. Men in black armor stormed through, and, with heavy steps, over a dozen formed a battle line. Most of them had fully enclosed helms. Others had high armored bevors that looked like black collars reaching just past the mouth. One wore no helm at all. He was bald, scowling, and pointing an oversized pistol at the pair of them. Red smoke from the assassins' canister wrapped around the marine commander like a shroud.

Jenkins raised his hands. "Don't shoot. It's me, Jenkins. These are assassins sent from Earth to kill our guests. I stopped them. Let Mordid know."

The marine's scowl didn't alter, nor did the manner in which he held his weapon. He glanced at the bodies and then back at Jenkins. "Is that so?"

"It is. Contact Mordid and he'll confirm it." Jenkins raised his hands. "I'm not lying."

Karlson, with great caution, set his pistol down and raised one hand, while the other hung limp at his side. He grimaced and said, "It's true. I'm also shot. My arm is bleeding and numb. I need a medic."

The marine commander pulled out his communication device and with a few deft movements opened a channel.

"Boss, this is Maxter. I have," he eyed the bodies. "Four dead intruders on strobe level. Is that a good thing?"

Mordid's voice responded, *"Great work, Max! I can call you Max? Max is easier. I'll hug you myself in a moment. You did great!"*

Maxter's lips turned into a smile, and his eyes twinkled. "I'm afraid Jenkins is here as well. He didn't make it. Sorry." He tucked the device into his belt. He looked at Jenkins with cold eyes.

"Valdez says there's a hefty bonus if we don't take you in alive. I think I just found a way to get two pats on the back."

Jenkins felt his heart skip a beat. He ducked behind the barricade and yanked Karlson with him.

"Great plan," Karlson whined.

From the other end of the room, Maxter said, "Make it easy on yourself. I can make it painless."

Jenkins looked at his pistol. Empty. He looked over at Karlson's weapon. "How many rounds do you have left?"

"Three, two?" Karlson shook his head. "Not enough to kill all of them!"

"Come out, come out," Maxter crooned. His voice was closer.

Jenkins heard the man's armored boots echoing on the floor. He looked at the dead assassin. Swallowing, he flung himself atop the corpse and pulled from his hand the silenced assault gun. That would have enough rounds to send the marines scurrying. Clutching the weapon, Jenkins popped up from behind cover and squeezed.

"Hello! I hope you are having a nice day. However, You are not authorized to use this weapon," came a gentle feminine voice from the gun.

Screeching, he ducked, just as the top of the barricade exploded under the concussive force of Maxtor's enormous pistol.

Tossing the weapon aside, Jenkins looked at the assassin. The knife was no good. He spied two grenades on his belt.

"Jenkins, we're going to die! Hurry!" Karlson curled up against the barricade and turned his gaze up, as if waiting for the sky to fall.

Jenkins pulled a grenade loose. He grasped the pin and prayed that the thing wouldn't say he was "unauthorized."

"Come out!" Maxtor shouted. He was close.

"Fine!" Jenkins jumped to his feet. Maxtor was right there!

The marine rammed the muzzle of his gun into Jenkins's face. He grinned. His finger flexed on the trigger of his ridiculously sized weapon.

Feebly, Jenkins held out his hands and pulled the pin of the grenade. "Go ahead. Blast me and I blast you. I'll drop it."

Maxtor's eyes focused on the grenade. He reached his spare hand up, thought better of it, and jabbed the muzzle of his gun against Jenkins's head.

"Orinzon, come put the pin of this grenade back in," Maxtor ordered.

Jenkins glanced at the line of marines by the doorway and the smoking canister that sputtered once more leaving the entire chamber obscured in red dust. He then turned his gaze onto Maxtor. "If anyone gets close to me, I'm dropping this. Sure, I'll die, but I do have the satisfaction of taking one more person with me."

"Two more," Karlson sighed.

"Right. Two." Jenkins had one more ploy to try. He licked his lips. "However, Max. Can I call you Max, too?"

The marine snarled.

"There is a way we can all win." Jenkins forced a smile. "Mordid is coming. When he walks in, you explain that what you meant by me not making it is that I have this grenade in my hand. One I bravely caught in midair as the assassins were lured into my trap."

The marine's eyes narrowed.

"I know you wanted two pats on the back. You'll get it. One from Mordid, and one from me. I'm far more valuable as a friend than Valdez. Besides, once the Mexicans find out I didn't kill their boxer, Valdez and the admiral won't care about me." Jenkins shrugged. "But, if you really want, I'll go ahead and blow you, me, and Karlson up."

"You owe me," Maxtor grunted. He withdrew his weapon and looked over his armored shoulder at his men. "Stand down.

This man here is a hero. He caught this grenade in midair. His buddy here and we, mostly we, killed the intruders." Maxtor spat and looked at Jenkins. "Deal?"

"Fair enough." Jenkins held his hands up. "However, until Mordid gets here, just stay where you are, Max. We'll sort out the matter of putting the pin back in when he arrives."

The marine snorted.

It didn't take the boss long. He strolled into the room, beaming a smile, up until he saw Jenkins. "I thought you were dead."

"Not quite, sir." Jenkins nudged Maxtor. "Max here thought I was dead. You see I—"

"Caught a grenade in midair, sir." Maxtor put an arm around Jenkins. He proceeded to tell a tale far more colorful than Jenkins could have ever managed.

Occasionally, some of the other soldiers added embellishments, Karlson continually reminded them all he was shot, and after twenty minutes, every man had somehow taken part in the killing of the assassins. Heroes one and all.

"Uh huh." Mordid eyed the bodies. "Which one did you get with a beamer?" He waved his hands. "Never mind, it doesn't matter." He pointed at Maxtor. "Get a pin back in that grenade." He pointed at two other men. "You and you. Get Karlson down to an infirmary."

Maxtor nodded and bent down. He picked up the small shining pin and handed it to Jenkins. "There you go, hero." He backed away and rejoined his men.

Nodding his thanks, Jenkins held the pin and tried to work it back into the grenade. Try as he might, it wouldn't fit. Swallowing, he shot a nervous glance at Mordid.

"See you," Karlson muttered as two of the marines escorted him away.

"Problem?" Mordid asked.

"Can't get it to fit back in," Jenkins said. He sucked in a breath. "Do you have somewhere I might throw this thing?"

"Nonsense!" Mordid walked up to Maxtor. "Tape?"

The marine reached into a belt pouch and produced a thick, black roll. "Never leave my bunk without it."

"And here's yet another reason why." Mordid approached Jenkins and grasped his wrist. He used his teeth to free up an edge of the roll of tape. Then Mordid proceeded to wrap up Jenkins's hand like a mummy. By the time he was done, the grenade could not be seen, nor any of Jenkins's hand.

"Sir?" Jenkins frowned. "Excessive?"

Mordid released the roll, and it dangled from Jenkins's hand. He scanned the ground and stepped toward the assassin with the knife in his hand. Pulling it from the dead man's grip, Mordid used the serrated edge to cut the tape. The roll fell and Mordid caught it with his left hand. Nimbly, he tossed it across the room back to Maxtor. The marines backed out of the room, leaving the pair alone.

"Excessive is breaking out of the brig when I made it quite clear I would handle the issue," Mordid whispered. "I think a little discomfort will do you some good. I hope it doesn't hurt too much when they peel the tape off, and I really hope that the grenade doesn't go off either." He whispered in Jenkins's ear, "I have a lot on my mind, and your antics aren't helping."

Licking his lips, Jenkins nodded. "Sorry, sir. But I got the assassins! The guest is safe."

Mordid flashed a smile. "In that, you did good. Which is why I'm going to help you out. Victor Torres was clearly stabbed with a knife. Just like this. In fact, I bet it was *this* knife." He held up the blade he had taken from the assassin.

Jenkins looked at the weapon and then nodded his head vigorously. "That works for me."

"When Rodriguez finds out, he'll go from hating to loving you. You remember Pedro?"

"Our guest?"

"He's the pope. The actual pope." Mordid pointed the blade at Jenkins's chest. He pushed, just a little. "And you saved him from certain death at the hands of Earth agents. Our resident Catholics will rejoice, and everything will *almost* be back to normal."

He stepped away from Mordid and rubbed his chest where Mordid's pilfered knife had prodded. Waving his tape-ensconced hand, Jenkins said, "Almost?"

"Herrin set you up, and try as I might, I can't figure out how he arranged it. He's working with Thrask and Mauss, but why those two would assist him is beyond me. Thrask maybe wants a new lapdog. But Mauss? You and Herrin are but insects to him." Mordid dropped the blade. "And I don't care in the end. I need you to get rid of Herrin, and I don't want to be involved in it. Pawns and kings shouldn't mingle on the chess board."

"Soon as this thing is off, I'll do just that." Jenkins clenched his other hand. "I'll kill every End Roader in the fleet!"

"You may have to," Mordid said. "But you need to do it the right way. If you march up to Herrin and put a round through his skull, you'll be back in the brig, and I'll be the one to press the big red button. You need to do it right." Mordid patted him on the shoulder. "And that means Herrin needs to die. He needs to die in such a way that no one will question how it happened. The chaos of battle and all that. Got it?"

It was advice Karlson had given him about the other End Roaders.

Jenkins saluted with his taped-up hand. "Yes, sir!"

The whole rotten lot had to die in combat.

Mordid sighed. "Good. Now, be careful. Soon as Herrin finds out you're clear of any wrongdoing, he'll have the same plan for you. Don't be anywhere alone with him, and soon as we enter into action, don't let him out of your sight." Mordid tapped the side of his own head. "You're in a war the likes of which you've not engaged in before. Only one of you wins in the end."

"Thank you, sir," Jenkins said. He bowed his head. "I know you didn't need to help me. I'm grateful."

"Think nothing of it! You did good work on Paradisa. Back on Pristine, you sided with me rather than Eryn, Mauss, or Thrask. That matters." Mordid walked toward the door. He said as he departed, "And to be honest, I was getting accustomed to a body guard that wasn't secretly out to get me! Loyalty has its rewards, Jenkins. So long as you are loyal to me and only me, I'll make sure you are rewarded and protected. As much as I can."

"You're the boss!" Jenkins said.

"Hellz-ya I am."

#

Thrask sat in a chair shrouded in a room of darkness. A room of secrets, papers, contracts, and other items of interest to the fleet's chief diplomat. Mauss sat across the highly polished table and moved aside a few stacks of neatly organized paper. His ancient computer cast a blue glow and brought out the skeletal lines of the Tyrant's chief diplomat and spy.

"So, you don't know who he's talking to?" Mauss asked and wrinkled his nose.

"Nope," Thrask replied. "Right now, who cares? I have him where I want him, and he'll be helping me." Thrask shrugged. "If that's all you wanted to know, then I'll be on my way. The big show is about to begin, and on the off chance the army gets to do something, I best be set."

Mauss held up his hand. "Before you go, let's talk about your heart condition."

Thrask sat heavily. "What about it?"

"You want it off."

Thrask rolled his eyes. "Of course I do. Would you want to be leashed to Eryn? She taunts me with every breath she takes. But, I can't tell Mordid she's switched it to fit to her. He'll just hook me back up to him!" Thrask narrowed his eyes. "Why are you asking?"

"I might be able to help," Mauss mused.

"But not for free."

Mauss grinned. "No. Not for free. I was hoping Rodriguez would break down and reveal to you whom he's been communicating with. Despite my best efforts, I can't break through the encoding he's using. I want to know without getting Mordid involved."

"Fair enough." Thrask scratched his lantern jaw. "Why the secrecy?"

Mauss answered quick enough. "Ah! Because I need to know the context of Rodriguez's illicit conversations. My primary task is to see to the safety of the company and to ensure its profits. Mordid doesn't always make this an easy task. Tyrants come and go for a reason."

Vulture. Thrask sneered. "Yeah, but you stick around,

don't you?"

"I do." The thin man tilted his head, and his finger tapped upon the desk. "Now then, my motives aside, let's make a deal. You find out who Rodriguez is talking to and tell no one but me. In return, I'll make sure you are no longer hooked up to Eryn's wicked little beating heart. With but a word from me, you'll be free of her and Mordid will not know."

"I'll break her pretty neck then!" He could imagine what it would feel like. He imagined the mad woman might giggle before her throat collapsed and her bones splintered in his hands. He'd get the last laugh!

"If you think you can—by all means." Mauss sighed. "Lately, she's been a bit of a liability. I believe her loyalties are conflicted." He sniffed. "We have a deal?"

"Sure," Thrask thrust his hand forth. "You get dirt on Rodriguez, I get free of Eryn." Eryn was conflicted? Thrask inwardly snorted. Was Eryn dealing with someone else as well? High Command plots could be ever so tangled.

Mauss gently shook his hand, and when he retracted it, he glanced at his fingers as if they might be somehow dirty and tainted. He arched a brow. "By any chance, do you have a plan?"

He did! "Yep. I heard Eyrn will be loitering about the bridge playing with her cameras."

"I heard the same."

"I'm going to get her to do the dirty work." Thrask flashed a grin. "Irony."

"Yes, General," Mauss nodded, "that would be irony."

8
-TRANSPACE-

With the assassins dead, the bomb safely under lock and key under his bed, the pope revealed, and a new contract brokered, Mordid felt that all was well. The last few weeks of the journey had gone by smoothly. Sure, Jenkins and Herrin were plotting one another's death, Thrask knew something dreadful about Rodriguez, and Eryn had kept nudging him to spend time with her, but such things were standard behavior in the company. Mordid had little to complain about, which was a rarity.

He had chosen a dining room of immense size—normally reserved for the officers of the ship—to share a meal with the pope. It wasn't every day that galactic scum such as himself had the chance to chat up a pontiff. They sat across from one another at a long and empty table decorated with a blood-red cover. An honor guard from the bridge mingled with two of Mordid's personal bodyguard near the doorway. Their armor clinked and clattered as they spoke in hushed tones. A massive window stretched across the whole length of the chamber, framing them. The window had nothing to reveal but a depthless, eternal black. They were still in transpace, but not for much longer.

Pedro sipped at his soup and drank sparingly of his wine. Mordid feasted on a combination of seasoned pastas and several wines, and eyed a bit of cake with heavy layers of frosting and the words "You're the Tyra" on it. Not quite right, but the chef meant well, and what did two letters really matter anyway?

"How's the soup?" Mordid asked.

"Bland. How's your impressive armada of food and drink?"

Mordid smirked. "I'm not that gluttonous. Stick with making me feel guilty for the great sin of avarice. There are days that go by where I hardly eat a thing. But this is a celebration! You are about to reach the Khan system. Which," Mordid grasped his glass and held it up, "I shall promptly blow up."

Pedro picked up his own wine glass and toasted the air. He took a sip and set it down. "I don't think there is anything I could say or do that would make you feel guilty."

"Don't get too self-righteous. You could have had someone else transport you." Mordid set his glass down and wagged a finger at Pedro. "You chose me. There must have been a reason you selected such an arch-sinner as myself."

"You came highly recommended. Your admiral is also a man I can trust, and to some extent so are you. I've watched you closely, Mordid." He smiled a moment and then shrugged. "And I think there is more to you than just greed."

"You're blind, then." Mordid took up his glass again. "I'm in it for the money. That's how I afford fancy uniforms, big hats, and wine." He peered across the table. "And money is the only deity that people worship. They spend every day doing something to appease the great money-god. Of all the souls in the galaxy, how many do you think are praying right now?" Mordid arched a brow. "And how many are chasing credits, land deals, contracts, resources, gold, and other valuables? Money is God. A God I get and understand. Money grants wishes. Money listens to all petitioners. Money rewards those who seek to earn its favor. Money will descend upon the noble scientist who discovers a cure, and the filthy criminal who finally gets that big score."

"It's not quantity, Mordid. Faith moves mountains." Pedro smiled. "And destroys suns."

"No, no, your Eminence," Mordid chided, "money did that. You won't get me to believe that the men who built your sun-buster were paid with a forgiveness of sins. The days of indulgences have long passed. And you yourself pointed out how deliriously wealthy your church is. How can you look at me with a straight face and say that you don't give as much credence to the money-god as you do to the imaginary one?"

Pedro let out a small laugh. "Your insolence is shocking, but hardly surprising."

"My audacity is what is getting you to the Khan system."

"You are *my* audacity, Mordid. I will give you that. You will assist *me* in bringing back the faith to Earth Government—the right way. My way. It will be faith that does it in the end, Mordid. It will be faith that moves us. Even you. I have proof." Pedro toyed with the spoon in the soup and took another small sip.

Mordid took in a mouthful of pasta, and once he'd swallowed it, he dabbed his beard and moustache with a napkin. "Proof? Go on, I'm listening."

"If you were really all about the money, and nothing but, then you would have turned me over to Earth Government. Perhaps you'd have ransomed me to them. Or taken the weapon and used it for ill." He waved a hand. "I'm sure you have all manner of rationalizations as to why you aren't doing these things. But you're lying to yourself. Those other paths would be easier. I know the one you are choosing will be hard. You are saying no to easy, quick, and safe money, to a lot of money you very well may never get to spend." Pedro sighed. "Earth Government will be your foe, several powerful corporations will want your head and jealous mercenaries will dream of your death. When you and I part ways, you may very well regret ever meeting me. Yet I sense you will not veer from your course. You and I are linked."

Mordid glared at the small man across from him, took up a fork, and stabbed at his cake. "Are you trying to convince me to break our contract? You're providing me with some compelling reasons to."

"Exactly!" Pedro's eyes lit up. "Reason. Reason says you should do the morally wrong thing. Your reason dictates that you should sell me or use the weapon for yourself—maybe even both! Instead, you are helping me."

"For money," Mordid added. He smiled. "For so much money, I'm curious if you'll actually pay up."

"Oh, I will. God works in mysterious and sometimes financially rewarding ways." Pedro's voice dropped. "You are a bad man, Mordid. The gates of heaven will surely not open wide for you when you die. But just maybe, if you do this, they'll open a crack. I know something about you. Something no one else does."

"Truly? I'm a man who kills for money, I've ended all life on a planet, I'm a thief and a bully, and my idols include Genghis Khan, Richard III, and Mussolini. I loved his uniforms!" He crossed his arms. "What do you really know that no one else does?"

"That you'll see this through to the end. It is in God's plan. To the ignorant masses in the dark you will bring the light of religion once more. The *real* Reconquista is not a dusty planet in the Upper Arm. It is reclamation of Earth itself. Not with ships, guns, or soldiers—but faith. You're a part of that, Mordid. Even though you have had every chance not to be. Money aside, you're doing the right thing."

Mordid ate his cake and tried not to roll his eyes. He pointed his fork at Pedro. "If you really want to see how deep my faith goes—don't pay me and see what happens."

"Oh, do not worry. Money you will have, nor am I blind to your many faults. And they are many. But I know beneath them all is good. It can be found in all men, Mordid. Sometimes it's just harder to find in some than in others." He leveled a stare. "Do you understand what I am saying?"

"Of course," Mordid replied.

"So you perhaps see that there is something more to the galaxy than money?"

"Nope. I said I understand. I do. I just don't believe. Do you understand when I tell you everything I do is for my own personal gain?" Mordid smiled wide and then finished off another bite of cake.

"Of course," Pedro replied, "I just don't believe it to be true. I hope it is not. I have faith it is not."

"Excellent! We've made unbelievers out of one another."

Mordid set his fork down and pushed his plate aside. "A mentally stimulating conversation, your Eminence."

"Likewise, Tyrant."

Mordid finished the rest of his meal in silence, as did the pope.

That is, until Mordid sniffed. "Protestants."

The pope arched a brow. "Pardon?"

"Could I turn you over to the Protestants?"

The pontiff smiled and sipped his soup.

#

The woman was insufferable! Rodriguez had tried narrowing his eyes at her, he had scowled, he had stroked his moustache, but none of it had worked. Eryn and her minions made nuisances of themselves, regardless of his displeasure. They filmed, asked questions, shone bright lights in the faces of his bridge crew and repeatedly ended up underfoot.

He stood upon the bridge, surrounded by companions, and in a place he normally felt at ease in. This time, however, he had to share his sanctum with someone who should have been in a kitchen. Or prison. He wasn't sure when it came to Eryn. He was having regrets.

Rodriguez would have had her and her ugly media-cohorts tossed off the bridge if not for their deal. He needed a friend; she needed to be able to take pictures of something more exciting than empty mess halls and corridors when they arrived in the Khan system. For now, he'd suffer her antics, but the moment he could be rid of her was a moment he'd celebrate.

She drew close to him with a camera held in one hand and a shriveled old scribe in tow who jotted down notes and did a good job of disguising its gender in rumpled attire and wrinkly flesh.

"Is it always so busy up here?" Eryn asked.

"Yes," he lied. There was no reason to tell her that the vast majority of the time they were in transpace he and his men could ease back in their seats, prop their feet up, and keep half an eye on the ship's monitors. Nothing happened while in transpace, and if it did they'd be dead too fast to do anything about it.

"Huh." She pointed at the massive flag of old Mexico hanging from the ceiling. "Now, is that flag original?"

Finally she was talking about something worth his time. He puffed his chest out and smiled. "Yes. It is from the glory days, when Earth Government struggled to force my ancestors to bow down to their will—and failed." He slapped his chest. "But today that injustice will be avenged. His Eminence will bring Mexico roaring back, along with the one true faith!"

His men dutifully cheered and whistled in approval.

Eryn filmed it all, holding her camera up and licking her lips. She winked at him.

What would a little press hurt? When the command staff were all dead, there was no reason he couldn't use Eryn's footage. A new Tyrant needed new propaganda! "Shall I tell you the story of how it all happened?"

She shrugged. "Well, I suppose, but it's common knowledge. Earth's governments united, Mexico refused, they fought a hopeless war, and as soon as space travel was possible, they left. En masse."

He snorted. "Hah! You tell the story with as much passion as a plank of wood. For a woman who loves spinning tales, surely you could do better than that!"

Eryn's lips curled into a sly and small smile. She held up her durable little camera. "I don't have to. Go ahead."

He cleared his throat, and the general chatter of the bridge died down as he prepared to tell a tale as sacred as any psalm and as dear to his heart.

"We were poor," Rodriguez whispered.

"But free!" his men echoed the proper refrain back at him.

Eryn jumped a bit.

Laughing, Rodriguez continued. "There was progress in the old days. Man had touched the stars, expansion beyond the solar system was opening up. Poor and rich alike could master the heavens. But rather than let men be free, the rich of the Earth decided to use their new technology and gifts to enslave." He paced across the deck, envisioning what it must have been like for his great-great-great-great grandfather to dwell in such dark days. "One by one the mighty nations of Earth sacrificed themselves in the name of unity, prosperity, and equality. But it was a Godless peace. What is prosperity if it is without salvation? The new government lied and said all faiths would be welcome, but we saw the truth. There would be no faith, no light, only an eternal darkness and falsehood. The Holy Father, Pope Urban IX, called for resistance. All good Catholics would stand against the unification! He saw the truth of the one government"

His men cheered, as was appropriate for this point in the well-told tale.

"Most did not answer the call. They were afraid and isolated—but not old Mexico! Where rich nations shied back. We. And only we. Fought back. Our ancestors!"

More appropriate cheers echoed throughout the bustling bridge.

Rodriguez stormed toward his captain's chair and slapped the back of it audibly. "We fought like lions!" he said, as if he were personally present. "The war was hopeless, and still we fought. When every city lie crushed, every village occupied, every worthy man dead or wounded—only then did we lay down our arms. The pope was dead. The cause was not."

He pointed at the dark view port dominating the center of the bridge, revealing the void of transpace. "But no sooner was the war over that Mexico had its revenge. We left. Bit by bit, one by one, family by family. They tried to keep us in Earth Space, but we have a long and noble history of defeating walls and borders. To the Upper Arm we went, and upon Reconquista's dusty soil a new, true, and Mexican pope was proclaimed! That flag," he pointed at it, "was taken from Old Mexico itself by the hands of my family! One day it will fly over Old Mexico again."

His men whistled and hollered. They were on their feet, and Rodriguez could not help but smile as pride and energy swept through him like a torrent of tequila down his throat.

The main doors opened behind him, and he quickly offered a deep bow to the figures that entered. Actually, he was only bowing for the sake of one of them.

The bridge crew was still and silent as the pope, Mordid, Thrask, and Mauss entered along with a pair of bodyguards who seemed more intent on eyeing one another than guarding their charges. One he knew to be the man he'd spent weeks lambasting for crimes that in fact were caused by heretical Earth-sent assassins. Jenkins was innocent, but it still would have been a highlight to the trial to see him hurtled into space. The other was Thrask's knife-wielding pet.

"Admiral," the pope said and extended his hand.

Gratefully, Rodriguez approached, fell to one knee, and kissed a ring on the pope's finger. "Your Eminence."

Mordid thrust his naked hand out toward him. "Admiral."

"Hmmph!" Rodriguez stood and planted his hands upon his hips. "*Hola, mi amigo.* I was just telling Eryn the tale of Old Mexico and that flag."

"Instead of talking about history, let's make it!" Mordid slapped him on the shoulder and slid into the captain's chair.

It was his right to do such, but Rodriguez still had to suppress a frown. "Of course. Valdez, how long?"

His First Officer looked over a computer console and smiled. "Twenty seconds."

"Good timing. I'm eager to see this," the pope said. He looked at Mordid. "Once we arrive we'll need to get close to the sun."

The Tyrant didn't respond. His eyes were fixed upon the empty view port.

The *Merciless* shuddered, and the empty void was replaced by stars and something burning and spiraling right toward them.

Rodriguez snarled. "Port! Port! Hard to port!"

Mordid leapt from the chair and took a few staggering steps toward the view port. He glanced at Rodriguez with a raised brow.

Rodriguez gave only a light shrug in reply and watched as the wreckage of some ship, or half a ship, rather, tumbled and rolled past them. What was once a craft was now a twisted bit of steel lit up by oxygen fires and trailing embers of orange-red light. It reminded him of a spent log in the fireplace collapsing into red and gold cinders.

There was no true sense of movement. The ship's gravitationals kept them steady, and space had no G-forces to contend with, yet in his bones Rodriguez could *feel* the mighty craft turning. He imagined all of the thrusters blazing as the knife-like prow of the *Merciless* narrowly missed a collision.

With the wreckage cleared, Rodriguez was dismayed to see flashing, burning light, shadowed hulks illuminated by a distant sun and the twinkling of smaller chunks of metal scattered in a broad pattern before him.

"How many?" Mordid mused, speaking in low tones, perhaps to himself.

Rodriguez knew space. He had a gift for it, and with a quick glance he had a rough estimate. "Twenty capital ships, maybe double that in smaller class vessels. Most of the oxygen fires are out." He frowned as his eyes focused on a twisted hulk, whose broken frame was silhouetted against the Khan system's sun.

"When's the last time a large scale battle like this has taken place?" Mauss said from behind the assembled notables. "Years?"

"Actually, a week ago, I'd venture," Mordid said.

Valdez swept a hand across his head, slicking back his hair. He looked away from the console and said, "Admiral, there are hundreds of distress calls in the debris field."

"We must save them!" the pope said. He locked his gaze with Rodriguez's.

"No!" Mordid barked. He shook his head. "Absolutely not. If we go on a mercy mission, I don't get paid." Mordid stared at the pope. "And what you want won't happen either. Consider them martyrs."

A sigh left the pope's lips, and his shoulders slumped. "It is a terrible price. There is nothing we can do for them? You have many ships, Mordid. Not just this one. Spare a ship. One."

"No. Not till you and I both get what we want. Then we can go about fishing people out of the deep." Mordid stroked his beard as his eyes fixated on the view port. "And whatever did this is still out there. Whoever won here is out there, and we're no good to anyone dead."

Rodriguez kept his mouth shut and turned his eyes onto the wreckage. He walked toward one of the many stations scattered about the bridge. He peered over the shoulder of the dutiful deckhand and ran an expert eye over the data.

"The whole system is a mess. I count four other debris fields and…" He couldn't believe it.

"What?" Mordid asked, raising a thin black brow.

Rodriguez looked up from the monitor and felt a chill dance down his spine. "And I detect only three operational fleets. We're larger than all of them. Mordid. We're larger than all of them combined."

"Is the war over?" Eryn ventured. "Did we actually miss it?" She sounded displeased, like a little girl being told she wasn't going to have a *quinceañera*.

"Sir!" said the deckhand at the communications center. He pulled off a pair of bulky headphones. "We have a message coming in from one of the planets."

Mordid rubbed his nose, and creases formed upon his pale brow. "Let's hear it."

Rodriguez gave a tiny nod, and the deckhand complied. A crackle of static echoed from the bridge's speakers embedded into the gray walls.

"*Welcome to the Khan system, Tyrant. Which side do you work for?*"

The voice was accented. Slavic of some sort, Rodriguez guessed.

Mordid answered without hesitation, "Whichever side pays. And looking at what's left in this system, you better hope it's yours."

"*Ha! You're funny. You have a reputation, Mordid, that precedes you. I am Company Executive Officer Sasha of Khan Operations for the Vladstock Corporation. You may approach Khan 7. I would meet with you. There is trouble here.*"

"Yeah, before I orbit your planet and land, tell me the nature of the trouble." Mordid crossed his arms and peered at the speaker as if it were Sasha himself.

"*Earth.*"

Mordid's eyes widened. He spun on a heel. "I'll be right there. Cut the channel."

The speaker hissed with static and was silent.

"Admiral, take us to Khan 7." Mordid said as he strode toward the massive reinforced doors exiting the bridge. "Eryn, you'll be with me and you too, Pedro."

Pedro?! He called the pope Pedro?! Insolent man! Still, Rodriguez said nothing and only gave a nod. He needed Mordid off the bridge, and as soon as possible. The captain from Earth shadowing them had questions to answer. Casually, Rodriguez moved toward a console and looked at the disposition of the Tyrant's fleet. Sure enough, there was a faint signal from the stealthy Earth ship. It was hardly noticeable at all, and had he not known what to look for, he might have ignored or missed it.

By the time Rodriguez looked up, the bridge was his again. Eryn's minions remained, but the rest of the command staff and the Holy Father were gone.

Valdez stepped up next to Rodriguez and whispered in his ear, "Now what?"

"Watch the bridge. I need to make a call." Rodriguez gave a long look to Valdez and then whispered, "Be ready for anything. Our time to act is approaching."

"*Si!*"

Rodriguez stomped off the bridge and marched directly to the quiet communications center he was free to use. He ensured the door was shut and locked and slipped into a comfortable seat. He typed a few commands into a keypad and waited, staring at his own reflection in the monitor that was suspended by cables from the ceiling.

The smooth, smiling features of the Earth captain appeared. He had a disgustingly smug expression—more so than usual.

"What is going on?" Rodriguez snarled.

"I told you," the Captain replied, "that going to the Khan system was a bad idea. You should have delivered the pope and Mordid as we had planned. It would have fit into our plans much better."

"Too late now. Mordid will be on the surface of Khan 7 in under an hour—with the pope." He reached a hand up and ran his fingers along the tip of his moustache. "You can have Mordid, but the Holy Father must not be harmed. Nor the fleet. It's mine!

148

The pope must come with me. I shall see him taken to Earth Space."

The Captain smiled wider. "Agreed. An easy task, too. There is a sizeable Earth Force fleet operating here in the Khan system. I shall instruct them to reveal themselves and apprehend the criminal."

Reemphasizing his point, Rodriguez said, with as much menace as he could muster, which was considerable, "The pope is not to be harmed, nor my fleet. You get Mordid." And if he had his way, the whole rotten command staff as well!

"That is the agreement. Earth honors its agreements, Admiral. We get Mordid, and with him comes a pleasant trial, and the galaxy sees what happens to unsanctioned madmen with fleets. You get to give us the pope, and with him will come unity. Earth Space isn't really whole until all faiths fully participate in the democratic process."

"Whatever," Rodriguez mumbled. He had more than a slight suspicion that once Earth Government made an example of Mordid, they'd just as merrily string up *any* mercenary they got their bureaucratic claws on. That, however, was another battle for another day. "Just keep your end of the bargain." He pressed a button to end the transmission and took a deep breath. "Now is my time," Rodriguez said to himself. He hauled himself out of the chair and walked out of the communications chamber— ready to be a Tyrant.

#

The landing craft was delightful and comfortable. Jenkins was used to having to strap himself to a bench and watch with nervous, unwanted anticipation as bolts popped free from the ship's hull as the pressures of entering the atmosphere took its toll. Not anymore! There were perks for being the bodyguard of the Tyrant.

The ship they were on was Mordid's newest, picked up during a brief layover in one of the Corporate Worlds on their way to the Khan system. The exterior was silver, the interior was gray, as was standard with all things Tyrant, but it had good lightning and its own powerful gravitational system that made even the roughest planetary descent fairly smooth for the occupants. Being a craft of luxury rather than utility, it sported a central room that had dark wood tables, leather-backed seats, and a bookshelf. It looked like a sitting room, not the interior of a ship. Nothing was bolted down, and soft, pleasant music piped in through hidden speakers. Mordid's customary landing craft was a beauty—and no doubt it was expensive. The boss must have been spending the pope's pay in advance.

Mordid sat, legs crossed, with a pad in his hand. He ran his fingers over it, while Eryn stood behind him as a pretty, if dangerous, shadow. She whispered in his ear, and occasionally Jenkins could hear her say some mildly intriguing fact about the Vladstock company.

The pope and two members of his entourage sat across from Mordid. They were dressed in plain off-white robes. Their brown skin and dark hair marked them clearly as hailing from Reconquista, but to say the little man Pedro Chavez was the pope was unbelievable! The secret was out, though, and by now Jenkins's was sure that even the most lowly deckhands on one of the smallest cruisers in the fleet knew about it. The Traveling Tyrant had in his company a most illustrious guest. Which also meant rich. For the head of an exiled faith, Pedro Chavez looked small. The briefcase cuffed to his wrist made him look even smaller. Jenkins imagined a pope should have a large hat and golden rings and should be portly. Portliness was a sign God enjoyed feeding you.

Karlson nudged him. "Stay alert."

"Hmm?" Jenkins blinked.

The older solider pointed at Herrin.

Herrin sat with two of his kinsmen, Bulks, and Rendstrot. The rats. Jenkins had brought Herrin into the elite unit that was given the lucrative task of guarding the Traveling Tyrant. He'd even let him bring his family members along. Now, the inbred End Roaders stared at him, smiling in an eerie way that only the inbred and violently depraved could truly master. Clearly, Herrin had to die! But now wasn't the time or the place. Though Jenkins didn't see himself as religious, it still was in poor taste to murder a man in the presence of priests. Besides, the last thing he needed to do was upset the pope, because if he was mad, then Rodriguez and his fanatics would be mad. Despite Mordid proclaiming his innocence, Jenkins couldn't shake the feeling that the Mexicans in the company were a little put out at not getting to see him ejected into space, innocent or not.

Herrin sharpened his knife and winked, which duly refocused Jenkins's thoughts.

Sighing, Jenkins tore his gaze away from the three smiling figures and regarded Karlson.

The man ran a hand through his salt-and-pepper hair and whispered, "Three of them, two of us."

"We have Mordid, and that means we have Eryn too. Remember what a terror she was back on Paradisa. I'm not afraid," Jenkins said.

"Hmm. I wouldn't count on either of them. Mordid pays us. He doesn't care, though, if we live or die. I should know. He's been trying to get me killed for years."

"I try to get you killed all the time, and I like you just fine!" Jenkins said and flashed a quick grin.

Groaning, Karlson said, "Don't remind me. I could have retired. I could be drunk in some Upper Arm bar talking about my mercenary days. Instead, I'm mingling with the upper echelon of the company and facing down Earth-born assassins, End Road mutants, a pontiff incognito, and your incessant boot-licking."

"At least I lick the right boots. Now cheer up. Look at all the good things we have." He gestured to the room. "A nice environment."

"Hmm," Karlson replied.

"A pretty woman to look at." Jenkins pointed at Eryn. Like a cat sensing it was being watched, Eryn glared at the pair and seemed about to hiss as well, until Mordid, without looking up from the slate in his hand, reached a finger up and poked her, recapturing her attention.

"Yeah," Karlson said without much enthusiasm. "Still owe me that date."

Jenkins ignored him. "And great people to work with, like me. Shortly, however, I think we'll be attending funerals. Three of them if I have my way."

"Your own, if this doesn't go right," Karlson warned.

"Ha! Well, say nice things about me if they do me in." Jenkins smirked. "Or not. You'll probably be lying dead alongside me if things don't go right. But don't worry. If Herrin wants to bring a knife to a gunfight, let him try."

Muttering, Karlson said under his breath, "A knife and two other men with guns."

Nums, Mordid's personal pilot, said over the hidden intercom, "*Sir, first I'd like to thank you for this toy. I hardly need to fly her. Enjoying the ride?*"

Mordid handed the slate over to Eryn and called out, "Yes! I can hardly tell we're in a ship! How close are we to landing?"

"*Already have, sir.*"

"Wow! That was money well spent." Mordid stretched and adjusted his overly-large peaked cap. He brushed his hip up against Eryn's black-clad and sinuous form. "And Mauss said it was a decadent waste."

She gave a little laugh. "Well, he's right on the decadent part. So, what's the plan? Going to share it with me yet?"

"Certainly," Mordid said. "We meet with whoever is in charge, Executive Officer Sasha, or whatever his name is, and we find out what's going on. Earth shouldn't be mucking about this deep inside Corporate space and certainly not in the Khan system," Mordid said.

"My guess," Eryn mused, "is they want access to the dead alien civilization for themselves. I'm impressed they were able to organize the effort, though. For all their technological wonders, there is a reason they had to outsource galactic colonization." She shook her head. "When my grandfather was accused by them for 'unspeakable acts,' did you know that it took the Earth Government so long to properly word the charges against him that by the time they informed the uninterested public, he'd been dead for years?"

Pedro Chavez rose from his seat. "Who was your grandfather?"

"Sanovich!" Eryn proudly declared.

The pontif wavered, and his two assistants leapt to his aid. "M-Mordid, I knew you were a faulted man, but you work with—"

"Eryn Sanovich," Mordid said. He planted his hands on his hips. "She is not her grandfather. She has not committed planetary-wide destruction."

"Unlike—" she began.

"Other people," Mordid finished.

Jenkins licked his lips and kept quiet during the exchange. It was, however, exciting to watch how business was really conducted.

"Yes." Chavez nodded. "Forgive me, the name alone does carry a certain dread with it. I pray the apple does in this case fall far, far from the tree." He held up his arm, and the suitcase dangled from the chain and cuff. "On to our task, though. Be it greedy corporations or a jealous Earth, the war and strife in the Khan system must end. So long as there is access to a system filled with vile, corrupt, inhuman, and thus ungodly technology, there will be strife."

Mordid nodded. "Agreed. And as promised, I will ensure you'll be the one to end it. But before we destroy a sun and call ourselves saints, I need something from you."

A smile danced across Chavez's features. "I had a sense you did not bring me here solely for company."

"Correct." Mordid approached him, and being both short, they were eye to eye. "I need the money up front."

"No."

Jenkins pursed his lips. Not good.

"It's the only way. If Earth is responsible for the destruction we've seen so far, that means I'll be taking an even greater risk."

The pope shook his head. "Payment is to be upon delivery. I'm good for it. I'm the pope! You, by your own admission, are a severely twisted figure."

Eryn slunk toward the pair. "It's the only way this will happen. You've made big promises, but you could be lying. You're the pope, but you've lied before and until we have the money, you're just a shady, shifty, slimy client to us. We've transported you this far, and we'll see your mission carried out, but—"

"What's the mission?" Jenkins asked. He was too curious not to ask. Besides, he didn't like how the pair of them were cornering the old man. He wasn't a suit-wearing slave-driving Corpy! He was the pope! He deserved a sliver of respect. Or did he? Jenkins frowned.

The dark-haired woman winced and shot Jenkins a deadly stare.

Mordid yawned. "Oh, nothing much. The pope here wants to kill the Khan system's sun so that the whole place becomes unstable and impossible to navigate. That way, no one can use the transpace route from the Khan system to the neighboring alien worlds and scavenge their long-dead empire for prizes and goodies. He plans to end a war that's been going on here for quite some time between five major corporations, before his triumphant return to Earth Space. Although Earth may have beat him to the punch."

"But that isn't our problem," Eryn added.

"Very true," Mordid said.

Chavez frowned and looked at Jenkins. "Happy? All caught up?"

"I-I think?" Jenkins wasn't sure. On the one hand, it was nice knowing what they were all up to. On the other hand, the mission sounded not only intrinsically dangerous, but also like the kind of mission that made powerful, lifelong enemies. And since when did popes blow up suns? He imagined they blessed babies and said prayers for the dying—on a grand scale.

"Up front," Jenkins muttered, changing his mind.

"Where was I?" Eryn mused.

"Trying to convince me to pay a profit-driven mercenary up front and trust him not to leave me here," Chavez replied.

"Right!" She straightened her shoulders and cocked her head to the side as she regarded the pope. "The company is run by very scary, shadowy investors. They are like all the bad parts of the Bible woven into one corporate board of directors. If Mordid doesn't have payment, now, and this thing doesn't go right, then he, and probably all of us, are doomed."

"They're the kind of fellows to kill your neighbor's best friend as well as everyone else in your life if you fail them. Very thorough when they are displeased," Mordid said.

The client crossed his arms, and the suitcase swayed by

his waist like a pendulum of an old-fashioned clock. "That is your problem."

"I let you have your bomb back? I kinda liked it under my bed," Mordid said and batted his eyes and put forth a pouty expression.

"It's *my* bomb! Er, device," Chavez said, throwing his hands in the air, causing said bomb to sway erratically. "Besides, you have a rather vital piece of it."

Mordid patted his coat. "Just a little insurance. I'll give it back, I promise. I have to make sure *you* don't decide to solo this."

"We tried the nice way," Eryn said.

Mordid sighed. "We did."

The Tyrant looked at Jenkins. "Right! When we get off the ship, Eryn and I will talk to whoever is in charge. You and your team will escort the pope to the nearest inter-galactic bank and get payment. In full. Guard the pope, that suitcase, and most of all, the money with your life." His eyes flit to Herrin and then back to Jenkins. "Try not to get killed. It's a dangerous place." He cleared his throat. "So I'm told."

"I will not comply!" Chavez said. "This is robbery."

"No," Mordid corrected, "It's extortion. A robbery is theft. I am not a thief. I have every intention of completing our deal, but not for free. You remember when we had dinner together and you hinted that I might just possibly have some redeeming qualities?"

"Yes," the man said in glum tones.

"You were wrong. I'm a mercenary." Mordid snapped his fingers. "You understand your mission, Jenkins?"

Holding the pope hostage wasn't Jenkins's idea of a good time. It definitely wouldn't make the Mexicans like him, or any Catholic for that matter. "Uhhh," he mumbled. His mind raced to find some way out of the task.

"Sir!" Karlson said.

Ah! Good old Karlson. His years of experience in weaseling out of things was sure to save them from the odious task ahead.

"What if," Karlson said, "the pope refuses to comply?

What if he won't pay up?"

"No problem!" Mordid grinned, and he pointed at one of the pope's assistants. "Shoot that one." He pointed at the other. "Then that one. If that doesn't convince Pedro, get creative."

"Er," Karlson said.

"Uhh," Jenkins said, still struggling to find the appropriate way to say "no."

Chavez frowned.

"Yes, sir," Herrin said smoothly. "You can count on me. I mean us." He looked at Jenkins as he slid his knife into its sheath.

"Perfect!" Mordid clapped his hands and strutted to the doors of the ship. He pressed a button and they opened. Recycled air *wooshed* out of the ship and was replaced by the scent of heavy population. Smog, fuel and heated air from machinery tainted the room.

"Mordid," Pedro said, while his eyes narrowed into tiny, black slits.

The Tyrant looked over his shoulder. "Yes?"

"There is a special place in hell for you, Mordid."

"At least it's special. I'd hate to find myself in ordinary hell. Get my money, and I'll get you your sun-bomb put back together. I get rich, a star dies, we all win." Mordid descended the ramp, followed by Eyrn. He said as he departed, "Jenkins! Get that money and get back to this ship. I'll meet you here." He paused and looked at Jenkins. "Oh, and don't get any funny ideas while you're holding so much cash in your hands that you could buy several worlds. The idea will pop in your head, but don't act on it. If you slip up on that account, you're dead." He stared hard.

Blinking, Jenkins dumbly made his way over to Chavez. He looked at the man and shrugged. "Sorry, Pope. Er, your Popeness."

"Hmmph!" Pedro Chavez whispered in Spanish to his two men, and they fell in behind him as he made his way to the ramp.

Jenkins looked over at Herrin. The End Roader and his two goons, Bulks and Rendstrot, were making their way down the ramp ahead of them, but all three spared the time to give Jenkins sinister and murderous looks. It was a nice reminder for

156

Jenkins that not only would he be responsible for shaking the pope down for money, he'd also have to watch his back or he'd find Herrin's knife in it.

Karlson let out a low whistle, and he stood alongside Jenkins as the crew disembarked the landing craft. "Pleasant environment. Nice company. We get to meet interesting people. Yeah, this is great, Jenkins."

"Shut it." Jenkins rubbed the bridge of his nose and tried to think of a way to turn the whole rotten affair to his advantage. He wasn't having much luck at it.

#

The skeletal diplomat sat in his seat, his hands clasped together and his eyes fixed on the object in Thrask's hand. The glow of the ancient computer cast the man, as well as the room, in stark shadows.

"A present?" Mauss asked.

Thrask threw a portable camera on the polished desk. A few of the papers Mauss had stacked toppled. Baring his teeth, Thrask tapped the recording device. "I think you'll like this."

Mauss arched a brow, and he reached out to rearrange the papers. He muttered, "I better." Once the stack was orderly, he peered at Thrask. "That looks like a camera."

"Smart guy. And I thought Mordid kept you around for your charm." Thrask crossed his bulky arms and regarded the diplomat. "I offered some perks to one of Eryn's lackeys. A rather wrinkly old woman who seems a bit miffed that Eryn insists on being fairest of them all." He laughed. "A few flirty words and she handed it right over."

"You're as bad as Mordid," Mauss said. He picked up the camera and swiveled in his seat toward his computer. With quick motions, his hands moved and a cord was strung from one device to the other. To the keyboard his hands next flew, and despite his age, his digits moved with the greatest of ease. The tapping of each key blended into a blur. His head bobbed as he looked up at the screen, and upon it images appeared.

"Ah, so you have footage of the bridge."

Thrask nodded and placed his hands upon the desk.

Leaning forward, he looked over the hunched shoulders of Mauss at the monitor. So many images appeared and vanished that he couldn't keep up, let alone make any sense of it. That wasn't his problem, though.

"Boring, boring, useless," Mauss said. His hands continued to move, tapping and typing away relentlessly. "Boring, more pointless footage and—" His hands froze.

"And what?" Thrask arched a brow. All he could see was one image frozen on the computer's screen. It looked like one of the consoles on the bridge.

"Your spy was able to film the disposition of the fleet. Each ship is labeled and signified by a green dot. See?" He moved his chair aside and pointed with a crooked finger.

A bunch of green dots was not exciting. There was, however, something not right. Leaning farther forward, Thrask narrowed his eyes and noted that within the sea of green labeled dots was a pale, white dot. It was hardly visible, and not labeled. He pointed at the object. "What is that?"

"Good eye." Mauss tapped the screen, right beneath the white, blurry dot. "That, my dear General, is a ship."

"One of the wrecks?" Thrask ventured. He hadn't been on the bridge when the *Merciless* exited transpace, but he'd heard the tales quickly enough. The whole system was littered with recent hulks from a titanic battle they had the fortune to miss out on. Battles in space were entirely unfair and outside his element. Shooting at an opponent from essentially a million miles away was not nearly as satisfying, or as honest, as shooting a man in the face.

"No. It's alone and hovering at the edge of our fleet. It's an active ship, but stealthy. We're lucky we even saw it. I imagine it comes and goes." Mauss linked his fingers together and reclined in his seat. "I believe that is who Rodriguez is communicating with."

"A ship?" Thrask frowned. "So what? What does it mean?"

"It could mean anything, General." Mauss stood and unplugged the camera from the computer. He handed it back to Thrask and pursed his thin lips.

"Well," Thrask said as he took the camera, "let's go find

out. We can commandeer a shuttle and—"

"Take pictures," Mauss said. A sly smile slid across his face. "We'll then have something solid to hold over Rodriguez. Excellent! And now that you've done me a favor, it's time I repay you. I told you that with a word I could free you from your slavery to Eryn."

Anger boiled up inside Thrask. It would be good to get the pulmonary collar off. "You did."

"Poof, you're free." Mauss slipped around the desk and fetched his long, gray, and battered coat from a nearby wrack. His uniform was, like so much about the man, old. It was a design from a former Tyrant, perhaps even from the days of the first.

"What do you mean?" Thrask stomped toward him. "We had a deal."

"And I'm honoring it," Mauss shot back. "Eryn lied to you. The collar is still tied to Mordid's vital signs. If he dies, you die." Mauss spread his hands out wide. "I'm sorry she deceived you. She bid me to keep my silence and I did. Until now. You have earned the truth."

He nearly reached out and throttled the man, but instead gripped the camera tighter. Fortunately, the thing was bulky and durable. It was perfect for combat duty or as a stress reliever in Thrask's paw-like hand. "How long have you known?"

"Since Pristine. I had no reason to tell you and every reason not to anger her when she said, 'shhh.'" He shrugged. "Do not be cross, General. Believing you are beholden to Eryn is the same thing as actually being beholden to her. Now that you know she has no hold upon you, you are free to snap her neck. Isn't that what you wanted?"

"I feel a fool for working hard for you, just so you could reveal a lie!"

Mauss snorted. "My dear General, all I do is deal in lies. But hold on to your hate. I think I have some plans for you. You know that were Rodriguez to be placed fully under our thumb, and Eryn removed, that would make Mordid incredibly isolated. You could be the Tyrant in all but name."

"Ha!" Thrask snarled. "What good is that?"

Mauss said, "It's about the best you can expect. If

Mordid pulls off this contract, it will be big. Huge. It will be the most financially rewarding mission this company, or probably any mercenary company, has ever accomplished. My job is to ensure the success of the company. Lately, Mordid has been only moderately useful. Paradisa was a wash. Pristine was successful in the end but needlessly complex, and the pay was not very exciting. All good reasons to perhaps swap Tyrants." He smiled. "But if Mordid wins this one," he spread his hands out wide, "Then I will do everything in my power to protect him."

The old bat was hard to understand. Thrask shook his head. "So, if I understand you, you wanted him dead not that long ago?"

"Perhaps. I was looking into it."

"And now you don't?"

Mauss shook his head. "Of course not. He's about to make the company a lot of money."

"But you still want to force Rodriguez to bend a knee, kill Eryn and isolate the man you now want to protect?" Thrask scratched his jaw. "I don't get it."

"Mordid, I think, will work best if he's limited in his ability to inflict harm upon himself. I like him, I really do, but how many contracts has he accepted that, regardless if they were successful or not, have led to unexpected and needlessly risky situations?" Mauss arched a brow. "Name just a few."

That was easy enough. "Well, there was that time we invaded the wrong planet and killed off those pale little dancing aliens. Um," Thrask glanced at the ceiling. "Paradisa, of course. Dead client and a dead world. Yep, that was bad. On Pristine, he got mixed up with a bad woman and got shot." He thought back to the early days and laughed. "Oh yeah, and there was that time we were supposed to chase off the what's-it-called company."

"The Hakama company, yes." Mauss sighed. "And he did, but not before jilting our employer, which nearly resulted in her not paying us." Mauss cleared his throat. "If Mordid had been a bit better managed, all of those would have gone smoothly and quietly."

"So, you have the company's best interests in mind, eh?" Thrask shrugged. "Fine. I'll toss Eryn out an air lock or have

Herrin stab her in the back and call it a suicide. We'll find out who Rodriguez is chatting with and blackmail him, and I'll gladly help keep Mordid in line."

Mauss shuffled toward the door. "Good. Let's go get that shuttle. Where is your knife-wielder?"

Thrask followed him out and said, "Mordid specifically wanted Herrin with him, along with Jenkins."

Mauss smirked. "You might lose your man."

"Might, but men are cheap. And if things go my way, well, then Mordid will be all the more under my power." He reached out and with his free hand grasped Mauss by the shoulder. With a twist of his wrist, he spun the man about.

The diplomat's eyes flashed.

Before he could say a word, Thrask loomed over the smaller, much thinner man and poked him. Hard. "I want this thing out of my chest."

"I'm sure you do," Mauss muttered.

"You're going to make it happen. I think I'm on to you." Thrask smiled and bared his teeth. He straightened his stance and said, "You like to control people. You want this thing in my chest so it keeps me in line. Well, it's not happening. I'll help you remove Eryn, lock down Rodriguez and muzzle Mordid, but you'll do your part. I'm not your dog. We're partners. The pulmonary collar goes." Thrask grasped Mauss's hand and slammed it against the hunk of metal hidden under his shirt.

Mauss slithered his hand free and wiped his fingers along his coat as if trying to clean them off. "I see. Fine. Soon as this operation is over, you'll get your operation. In secret, of course. Mordid is taking pains to prevent you from doing this. I am not a genie, but I can try."

Thrask nodded and gave a grunt in the affirmative. "Naturally."

"To the shuttle then?" Mauss didn't wait for an answer and turned on a heel and walked away.

"One more thing."

"Yes?"

"The payout on this one is insane. Enough for all of us: you, me, Mordid, Eryn, Rodriguez and, hell, every crewman and grunt out there. Enough to call it quits." Thrask sniffed. "You ever thought about that?"

The skull-like face split, revealing yellowed teeth in what was supposed to be a smile. "And do what? Sit on a porch and watch the grass grow? All of us are meant to live and die in this company, my dear General. It is our purpose. Mordid was a nobody, and yet he was born to be somebody. Born to topple Gideon. Eryn? She comes from the loins of a genocidal maniac. She was destined to bring terror to the galaxy. Rodriguez would never sit in a rocking chair unless it was at the helm of a ship. And you? You will never know peace. You are meant for war. Rich, poor, it does not matter. You will fight. Even with that leash wrapped about your heart, you will fight." Mauss strode away.

Smiling, Thrask followed behind the wretched buzzard. The idiot thought he had all the angles covered. He was too clever for his own good, though. As soon as Thrask was free of the collar, only Mauss would stand in his way on the path to take on the title of Traveling Tyrant. Clearly, Mauss had no intention of seeing him promoted to the top. And that meant, in the end, Mauss would have to be removed. Mauss was right about something, Thrask thought; they were all bound to the company until the end of their lives.

9
KHAN SYSTEM –KHAN 7–

Mordid watched as the pope, the sun-killing bomb in a briefcase, his boy Jenkins, the should-have-retired Karlson and Herrin and his inbred cousins departed to go fetch an absurd amount of money. He wished he could come along with them, just to see who killed who and when.

Eryn stepped alongside him and crossed her arms. "Think they'll be ok?"

He smirked. "No. But everything will work out, one way or another." Mordid paused to take stock of their surroundings.

His luxury landing craft had touched down upon an elevated pad ringed by flashing lights. Above, he could barely see the blue sky and white clouds, thanks to the towering structures of steel and glass that dominated the area. It was like being an ant in an enormous forest of man-made reeds. Above him, smaller aerial transports zoomed past, and occasionally the face of one of the buildings would ripple and the windows would swivel and make up a mosaic depicting some advertisement or another.

The air smelled of rank pollution that the city's filters couldn't handle. And the city exuded an aura of slimy, unethically, and yet hard-won, wealth.

The people he saw, including the corporate security

officers heading his way, had plastic smiles and flinty stares.

All in all, it was a typical Corporate World. This was the part of man's domain in which all that mattered was getting a fair deal, and to Mordid, the standard Corpy's idea of a fair deal was one in which he won and everyone else lost- but didn't know it.

The first officer to approach him was clad in green and white attire. A pistol rested snugly in a holster at his side, and while he waved with one hand, the other rested on the butt of his gun.

"Welcome to Khan 7," the officer said, "Our Executive of Operations is eager to meet you, Tyrant." His eyes darted after the retreating forms of Jenkins and all the rest. "Are they—"

Mordid interrupted him. "They are going to carry out some business for me. This is a Corporate World, so I have things to do and people to see. Since when has anyone tried to stop the flow of business in Corporate Space? Now then, stop eyeballing my men, and look at me." Mordid held a finger up to his own blue eye. "And take your hand off your sidearm. If I so much as sneeze, nuclear warheads, beamers, fighter craft, and frightening individuals will come descending from the heavens above to rain down hell."

The man's hand on the gun went limp. "Of course, it's a habit. Sorry, Tyrant. Please, follow me." He looked at Eryn and then nodded. "Are you his bodyguard?"

"No, I work for the PR department." She struck a pose and adjusted her cap while letting her inky hair fall loose upon her shoulders.

"Uh-huh," the officer said, clearly not impressed. He led the way toward the twisting walkways that sprung from the landing pad like the strands of a spider web. These strands ran into the depths of the towering city. The Corpy's armed companions waited for Mordid and Eryn to walk past before they fell in behind them. Their fake smiles never faltered.

Mordid kept his thoughts to himself as he walked. He was sure Eryn had the same sense he did. There was most assuredly something rotten going on. From what he could make of the situation, the Vladstock Corporation should have been throwing themselves at his knee-high boots begging for his favor. He had enough firepower in orbit to challenge every fleet left in the system. With a single stroke, he could win the war for Vladstock, or one of the other competing companies. Not that he would do it! But they didn't know that.

They walked in silence, and he paid his surroundings little mind until Eryn cleared her throat. He caught her eye, and she glanced up.

Casually looking in the indicated direction, Mordid saw one of the tall silvery buildings that loomed over the winding, bridge-like path they were on. It was currently in advertisement mode with its windows making up the parts of a corporate visual. Nothing unusual about that. He looked closer.

The ad! It wasn't an advertisement for a new gun or a flying transport or a pill to make hair grow atop the pates of balding, insecure men. It was an ad that depicted a man with dark, flawless skin, a smile with the utmost perfect teeth, and the words "Remember to Share" floating above his visage. If there was one thing Mordid never expected to see on a Corporate World, it was a public service announcement about sharing. It was like telling a nest of deadly snakes not to be poisonous and to be kind to mice.

A quick scan of the other structures revealed that mixed in among the more traditional advertisements were the typical messages from Earth about unity, prosperity, and equality. The very antithesis of what the Corporate Worlds were about. They should all be saying things like, "I Got Mine" and "Sucks to Suck."

Frowning, he followed the corporate officer toward a shining silver structure that was taller than all of its by no means small neighbors. A green and white banner with a logo of a white bear hung limply from a pole by the door. Opposite it was an empty pole. It should have had the flag of the Corporate Worlds, a black banner with the letter C, and the Hindi and Chinese symbols for "Corporation" proudly blazed upon it in gold. Gold: the symbol of money. While the corporations hated one another with an entrepreneurial passion, they proudly clung to their original charter giving them the right to settle worlds and turn a profit. Their shared flag was what separated them from being a mismanaged—or rather, over-managed—colony of Earth.

The clues were painfully obvious.

Eryn sighed as they entered the lobby of the building. "This place is being held hostage," she murmured.

"Pardon?" their lead escort said.

Mordid gave Eryn a little kick with his boot. They could state the obvious facts later.

The lobby was immaculate and richly decorated with imported wood, marble, and gold inlay and littered with corporate advertisements that were worked into every chair, fountain, statue, and floor tile.

A few Corpys in their finely pressed suits eyed Mordid, but none greeted him. The officer walked toward an elevator and gestured for Mordid to follow.

They all piled in and listened to mind-numbing music. Be it on the *Merciless* or on a Corporate World, at least elevator music was the same. Whoever came up with the forgetful tunes must have made a fortune.

The elevator rapidly shot them up to one of the upper floors, and the doors opened to reveal a long hallway. The floors were tiled and white; above was a curved, glass ceiling, held in place by iron supports. The sun shone brightly, and the sounds of birds and other wildlife echoed. Of course, there were no animals beyond the human variety, but clearly the Vladstock company wanted its more lofty employees, on the equally lofty floors, to work in a pleasant atmosphere.

Mordid found it too bright, and he winced.

Down the hall they walked, their heels clicking. Mordid noticed two guards in the same green and white as his escort stationed by a set of wooden double doors.

Their handler halted at the doors and faced Mordid. "I shall come collect you when it's time for you to return to your fleet, Tyrant." He bobbed his head once, and he and his men walked back toward the elevator.

The two men by the door had particularly blank expressions on their faces, shaved heads, and what looked like antennae sticking up from their skulls.

Eryn smiled. "By the pope's blessed toe clippings. Are those? Are those drones?"

166

"I need to get men like this!" Mordid said, and he reached out to touch one of the man-made attachments rising out of the guard's skull.

Before he could touch it, the guard's mouth dropped open and his thick throat flexed. Through the guard's open jaws, Mordid just barely noticed a small speaker lodged in his mouth.

"Please," came Sasha's accented voice from the expressionless man. "Enter. And don't touch that. Bad reception means a bad drone."

Withdrawing his hand, Mordid shrugged and opened the doors. He strode in, brandishing a smile like one would a weapon. He heard Eryn's heels click on the floor as she followed behind him. The doors banged shut.

The room was bright and, like the long hallway, sported a glass ceiling high overhead and white, gleaming floor tiles. The walls were clean, white, and unadorned. At an enormous wooden desk sat a man in a gray and finely tailored suit, with a green and white button holding the jacket closed just above his sternum. His face bore the signs of surgery to remain youthful in appearance. Such medical work was a bad decision in Mordid's opinion. People who opted on too much age-related surgery traded wrinkles for a perpetual look of surprise. Eryn's makeup was far more subtle about beating back the years. And drugs. High-grade life-enhancing drugs.

The man's hair was black and piled up high in what looked like a wave of gleaming tar, and his sideburns were long, though the rest of his face was clean-shaven. His smile was the fake and overly-earnest grin Mordid had come to expect from the Corporate Worlds. Their host woodenly gestured at a pair of chairs across from his desk.

"Please, do sit."

Eryn said, "You're Executive Officer Sasha?"

"Yes! I am Sasha Toylatev, but please, call me Sasha. Toylatev too often gets shortened to just Toilet. So, I much prefer Sasha." He leaned back in his seat and looked Eryn over. "You have your grandfather's eyes."

Eryn swept past Mordid and giggled. "So I've been told. I hope you don't hold anything he did against me?"

Mordid cleared his throat. "Let's talk about me. I'm a jealous Tyrant and demand attention." He took the seat next to Eryn and removed his hat, setting it upon Sasha's desk.

The arch-Corpy laughed, though his eyes narrowed slightly as he glanced at Mordid's absurdly-sized hat. "Of course, Mordid, forgive me. Your reputation precedes you, though I am surprised you are here. The war for the Khan System is an old one, and your mercenary company never seemed all too interested in it."

"I am now," Mordid said. "It seems Earth has run rampant here, and now I count only a handful of operational fleets. Who's on your side?"

Sasha let a laugh leave his lips again, but it lacked mirth. "Well—"

Eryn added, "And where are the corporate fleets? The three left are all mercenary outfits. There should be five of you claiming various regions of the system."

Mordid nodded. Rodriguez had identified the fleets as major, or formerly major, players in the Upper Arm mercenary circuit.

"You saw the wrecks?" Sasha asked, and his brow rose.

"Earth did that?" Mordid pursed his lips. "Interesting. Well, before I make my outrageous demands, tell me what has happened here."

"Demands?" Sasha blinked.

"Storytime first!" Eryn prompted him as she crossed her arms.

"I see." Sasha said and his smile faded into a worry-filled frown. "Things were going slowly, but well. Vladstock was making major gains in the Khan system, and in a few years I am certain we would have prevailed." He sighed. "Then Earth came along and ruined the game. Their fleet was very advanced and descended upon the system with a skill I thought not possible of them. They spend decades debating laws on how to best dispose of dog poop. I never thought they had this in them."

Licking her lips, Eryn said, "What happened?"

"They came in shooting!" Sasha swept his hand across the desk and knocked Mordid's hat onto the Tyrant's lap. "And they swept the system. None of us realized what they were doing or else we may have unified to fight a common foe. All you see left are cowards."

Mordid laughed. "You mean those smart enough to run away. Well, the Upper Arm breeds scum, but not stupid scum. They were smart to withdraw while they could. Who do they work for?"

Sasha threw his hands in the air, almost wildly. "I do not know. They have made no hostile moves, but they haven't answered my communications either."

"Licking their wounds," Eryn said. She grinned. "And like bad gamblers, with so much money invested, they're afraid to just pack up and go home."

"Mmm," Mordid agreed. He picked his hat up, propped it atop his head, and gave a winning smile, one of the ones Eryn liked best for her promotional pieces. "So, I must be very important to you." He held up a hand to forestall Sasha. "Well, don't even try to court me. I'm just stopping by to pick up some money and then I'll be off. I still have no interest in your war here. Rest assured, I am entirely neutral, and if your competitors on the other planets pester me, I'll tell them the same as you. Not interested."

Sasha tilted his head. "Indeed. And your demands?"

"Well, as master of the most powerful fleet in the system, I demand you tell me a bit more about Earth. I want to know what Earth Government is doing this deep in Corporate Space. What happened to the charter? This is *your* territory."

"Where are they now?" Eryn asked.

"Why are you hosting their charming public service announcements?" Mordid asked.

"I noticed your flag is missing," Eryn quickly added.

"I did too!" Mordid clapped his hands. "Sasha, you haven't made a terrible mistake, have you?"

The corporate man's head tilted. He slammed his fist upon his desk. "No!"

"So," Eryn said, using soothing tones, "tell us what we want to know."

"Bah!" Sasha said, and his form jerked. "After Earth Force destroyed or crippled every fleet in the system, they paid each of Khan's worlds a visit. I assume they told my competitors the same thing as me. We could continue doing business but without violence. They said we were now citizens of Earth Government. They said law and order had arrived, and it was our own fault."

That wasn't good! Mordid cleared his throat. "Did you mention the Corporate Charter?" While those who settled the Upper Arm were a collection of individuals striking it out on their own, without Earth's permission, the Corporate Worlds were nominally legal. After grinding to a halt in an attempt to colonize, burdened by its own legal framework, Earth had given companies permission to settle the stars. Thus, the Corporate Worlds were born. Semi-autonomous, legal companies who had Earth's blessing when it came to colonization. So long as the goods flowed from the Corporate Worlds into Earth Space, all was well. Earth even turned a blind eye to how the various corporations interpreted the word "hostile" in hostile takeover. The "deal" was centuries old. Everyone got what they wanted, and the law bent and twisted to accommodate that fact.

"Revoked," Sasha said and hung his head.

"Oh my," Eryn breathed. She looked at Mordid and leaned across the desk. "Revoked where? Just here?"

He shook his head and glanced at her and then at Mordid. "I don't know. I think everywhere. This planet is now under Earth's jurisdiction. If I play by their rules, I think the company will be left alone. Maybe."

Eryn groaned. "Mordid, we need to get out of here."

Mordid's heart dropped. The whole of mankind had just been upended, and it wasn't even his fault! Earth was making a power play. Something on a galactic scale. He made a motion to leave.

Sasha's tracked them. "Do not be so hasty."

"Hah! Why not?" Mordid said, "I have no interest in solving your war. I have absolutely no interest in tangling with a fleet from Earth. Especially a fleet that decimated not one, but at least five corporate fleets." Mordid rose from his seat. "I demand you let me fulfill my business needs here, and I'd very much like it if you could personally wave goodbye to me when I depart. It would greatly stroke my ego."

170

Sasha said, "If you want your ego stroked, listen to this. When the representatives from Earth met with me, they mentioned you."

"Me?" Mordid asked.

"You?" Eryn said as she stood next.

"Yes, you!" Sasha pointed at him. "They gave me a warrant for your arrest. They say you are accused of crimes against an entire planet. They say you are to be an example. They called you 'arch-criminal.'"

Eryn let a laugh slip forth. "Mordid, you're to be Earth's poster child for villainy!"

"Huh," Mordid said. Fame was wonderful! It led to lucrative business proposals, and infamy was just as good as fame. However, technically all mercenaries were nothing but pirates in the eyes of Earth. But no Upper Arm outfit ever ventured near enough to Earth Space to ever let the bureaucrats make good on threats about law and order. Sure, Gideon was in their hands, but that was Mordid's doing. For Earth to single him out was unsettling. War with a government was bad for business.

"Something big is happening," Sasha said, "And so now, I have demands of my own."

"Oh really?" Mordid placed his hands on his hips. He looked down upon the Corpy, or former Corpy, or whatever he was. "I have a rather large and menacing fleet in orbit. If you think to hold me hostage, believe me, my admiral will vaporize your planet and *weep* for me after the fact. My general will invade, heedless if I live or die, and he'll consider it a chance at promotion. Piss me off, and your life becomes something rather thermo-nuclear."

Sasha stared up at him, and his false smile slid into place. "Earth is looking for you. Leave here, and I tip them off. Harm me, and believe me, my men will blindly avenge my demise, and it doesn't much matter what your minions do then. Dead men don't care!" Sasha stood up and smiled wider. "And so I have a deal. One you can't refuse."

"Uh-huh." Mordid cocked his head to the side and clenched his right hand.

"The other mercenaries cannot oppose you; my

competitors are weak. It would be a simple task for you to visit each of their worlds and lay waste to it. You can win the war for a grateful Vladstock Corporation, and I shall simply tell Earth, if they even ask about what happened, that you intimidated us, while our competition foolishly tried to resist."

Eryn said, "Sorry, we don't have the time."

Sasha shook his head. "You will make time. I insist. Leave here, and I guarantee Earth will know about it. Their fleet is still in the system."

Mordid felt his heart skip a beat. "Wh-what?"

"Impossible. Still here? They're hiding by the damned sun, or close to a world!" Eryn said. She rushed to Mordid's side and gripped his arm. "We need to warn Rodriguez."

Sasha laughed. "Like I said, something big is happening. But do as I ask, and I can stall Earth. I can mislead them. I can ensure you can carry out my task easily! And you will be paid. I know how your kind work." He tilted his head, and his brow rose in a high arch. "Refuse me, and you'll regret it."

For a man without a fleet, a sizeable army, or mercenaries at his beck and call, and with Earth breathing down his neck, Sasha had played his hand well. Too bad the whole sun was going to go out and make his final power play a moot point.

"Fine," Mordid said. He'd just lie. "I'll do it."

"Excellent." Sasha placed his hands upon the desk and leaned forward. "Pay will be arranged after the fact. And she," he looked at Eryn, "stays behind. As collateral. I shall keep her safe and when the deed is done, I shall ensure she ends up back in your hands. I absolutely will not budge on this. I want a hostage, and she will do nicely. No negotiation."

Before he thought much of it, Mordid pulled his pistol out and fired.

Sasha's didn't even flinch. He fell back into his chair. His mouth gaped like a fish's, and then his maw opened impossibly wide. Within, Mordid saw a tiny, black speaker.

"A foolish mistake," Sasha's drone said, "No matter. I shall be a good citizen and hand you over to the proper authorities." The body went still, and a bit of smoke rose from the dead drone's agape mouth.

"Damnit!" Mordid glared at the body. "Did you know it was a drone? That was a very nice model. Expressions, hand gestures! And—"

"Mordid," Eryn grabbed him and pulled him close. Her eyes sparkled.

The door burst open, and the two guards with antennae jutting from their heads entered with weapons in hand. Their expressions were as blank as those of space zombies.

Without breaking eye contact, Eryn's hand rose. She had a gun, too. She braced her wrist on Mordid's shoulder and fired twice. The gun's sound was silenced. The two guards slumped, with holes in their foreheads.

"Uhh," Mordid said.

"You love me!" She pulled him tight to her chest. "When he said I had to stay behind as collateral, you shot him! You love me!"

Mordid slipped his hand between them and pushed her away. He rushed toward the door, tucked his pistol back into its holster, and dragged the two bodies inside the room. With a swift kick, he shut the doors. Looking over his shoulder he said, "No, Eryn. I shot him when he said I'd do the work for free."

Her brows knit, and she pointed the pistol at him. "He didn't say that. He said he'd pay you." She pointed. "Do not lie. You shot him dead as dead can be when he threatened me. You. Love. Me."

He had no time for this! It was confusing as well. Why did he shoot so fast? It didn't matter. She needed to be mollified.

"Fine, fine, I love you." It sounded strange coming out of his mouth. It needed more to let her know just what kind of love it was. "But like a little male spider loves a giant black widow." He waved his hands at her. "Now get a rescue organized. The real Sasha is already calling Earth's fleet by now."

Seemingly satisfied, and glowing with a bit of blush in her cheeks, Eryn pulled forth her communication device and set her still smoking pistol on Sasha's desk. She fiddled with the dials and held the item close to her ear.

Wasting no time, Mordid pulled his own device from his long gray coat and twisted the dials to get a hold of Jenkins.

"*Sir?*" came his bodyguard's voice. The static was heavy. Earth, or the Vladstock Company, was already trying to jam communications. However, the connection was still strong enough. The *Mercliess,* whose communication hubs routinely failed, was on her game today and when at full capacity, she could jam whole worlds.

"Do you have the money?" Mordid asked.

"*Yes. I think it's funny that a galactic fortune is the same size as gambling dice.*"

"Good," Mordid licked his lips at the thought of how much wealth would shortly be in his hands. "We'll talk about the oddities of high finance later. Get to the landing craft. Consider this planet hostile. Kill anyone in your path. Above all else, get Pedro safely to that ship!" He cleared his throat. "Well, that and make sure the money gets safely to the ship, then Pedro. He's like a close second. Money. Pope. Got it?"

Mordid cut the channel without waiting for a reply and looked at Eryn. "How's Rodriguez doing? Am I going to have a horde of iron-gray ships spilling out of the sky to aid in my escape?"

She smiled and nearly giggled, having to stifle it with a hand over her mouth. "Nope. Earth's fleet emerged. I was right, they were hiding by the sun! We're in reeeaallll trouble."

He blinked. "Oh good," he said dryly. Mordid tilted his head and regarded Eryn. Her eyes twinkled, her smile was radiant, and for a woman trapped in a hostile high-rise with an entire fleet bearing down upon her, she seemed far too happy. "So why are you so giddy?"

"You love me! You love me!" she sang.

#

Rodriguez glared at the view port. He could see the blue-green curve of Khan 7 and, beyond it in the depths of space, twinkling lights that were not stars or planets. His eyes were well-trained in spotting things that didn't belong.

His crew worked swiftly and spoke only in Spanish. Eryn's minions filmed from the corners of the bridge, unaware of the conversations around them.

"How much time do we have, Valdez?" Rodriguez asked.

His First Officer hovered by a consol and patted the crewman manning it on the back. Looking at Rodriguez he said, "They'll be on us in a few minutes, Admiral. They have as many ships as we do, and I'm having problems identifying some of them on the sensors. Some have stealth." His eyes focused with great intensity, and he then looked over at the admiral. "They have landing craft heading for Mordid's position."

Before Rodriguez could utter a command, his communications man perked up. "Message from the planet, sir. It's Eryn."

Rodriguez nodded and reached up to stroke his moustache.

"*Hello!*" came the woman's voice over the speakers. She sounded entirely too pleased.

Rodriguez said, "Hello. Tell Mordid a fleet from Earth Force is here, they were hiding by the system's star. The pope will need to be evacuated instantly." There was no need to inform her that the landing craft from Earth were coming.

The channel faded to static.

Though he didn't much like hearing her voice, he needed her now. Glaring at his communications man, Lupe, he said in Spanish, "The Holy Father's life is on the line! Do not let them jam us! I don't care if you need to cut life-support to make that happen!"

The man licked his lips. "Yes, Admiral! The planet is trying to interrupt us and the enemy fleet. But I'll-I'll keep the channels clear."

The lights dimmed, and the entire ship shuddered as Lupe engaged in a battle of epic, and entirely technological, proportions. Eryn's voice returned. "*-loves me! Isn't that great?*"

"Where is the pope?"

"*Huh? Oh, with Jenkins getting the cash. Mordid and—*" static blared.

"Wh-what?" Rodriguez pulled at the tip of his moustache till it hurt. "I'm sending down some marines. Get back to the landing craft." He waved his hand, and the channel went dead.

"Valdez!"

"Sir?"

Rodriguez approached him and placed his hands on his shoulders, drawing the First Officer in close. While everyone on the bridge knew they were supporting the pope and faith had sealed their lips about it until Mordid knew the truth, only Valdez knew of Rodriguez's plan to take the company for himself. If he had told the bridge crew, Rodriguez wasn't entirely sure it could stay a secret for long. No doubt, he thought, when he was Tyrant they would rejoice and forget all about Mordid. Had he been good to them? Yes. But, really, how good, Rodriguez thought with self-serving satisfaction.

"Go down with the marines," Rodriguez said, staring intently at Valdez. "Kill Jenkins, kill the man with the knife that Thrask keeps around, Herrin, and anyone else who might be a witness. Get the Holy Father back here." He brought him closer and whispered in his ear. "Mordid must not leave the planet. We are leaving him for Earth."

Valdez's brown eyes locked with his. "Eryn?"

"Kill her."

Valdez frowned. "She's a woman."

"True," Rodriguez said, "I sometimes forget. Forgive me. Leave her. She can't come back here. Soon as you have the Holy Father secured, come back. We'll leave Mordid and his madwoman to their fate." Rodriguez smiled. "We'll deal with Thrask and Mauss when you get back."

Valdez smiled and gave a curt nod.

Rodriguez released him and pushed him away. "Go! Go! Save the Holy Father!" He whooped and the bridge crew joined in the calls and whistles, unaware of Valdez's ulterior motives.

Valdez darted off the bridge, cheered on by the men.

One of Eryn's cameramen stepped closer from the edges of the festive bridge and waved a hand. "Uh, Admiral? What's going on?"

Rodriguez felt nerves warring with elation. His moment was at hand! He looked at the cameraman and forced a broad smile to form.

"You are witnessing glory!"

176

#

The city was impressive, Jenkins had to admit. The skyscrapers kissed the very heavens and, as far as he could tell, went on forever. It was as if the whole planet was one, giant, rich urban center. Upon the silvery surfaces of the buildings, advertisements appeared. More than a few depicted men that looked suspiciously similar to the assassins from Earth, along with quaint phrases such as, "Harmony is Best!"

For as many structures as there were crowding the skyline, there were relatively few people walking about, and most moved as if in a hurry. Above, transports flew this way and that, but their numbers were not what Jenkins would expect. Shouldn't there be a swarm of them, like the bees of some great hive?

Karlson pointed toward one of the many walkways that stretched from the landing pad and wound its way into the city. "There's a bank down that road."

Jenkins smirked. "How can you tell?"

The pope answered, "Outside the door is a Foo-Dog. Can you see it?"

Peering, Jenkins could. The building was not too far away, and outside its doors was a small, perhaps knee-high, green dog-lion-thing, molded in an oriental form.

Jenkins had been to banks before but only in the Upper Arm where they were decent enough to post clear signs and endless armed guards. An Upper Arm bank was where electronic money was kept, but also strongboxes. On Freebird, he had several valuables stored away in vault for his retirement, such as a jewel that he stole from the palace of Zaltrek on Pristine and a few other quasi-valuables he'd looted during his career from a variety of hapless worlds. Some goodies he sent to his parents so they knew he was alive and were happy about the fact.

The pope stood next to Jenkins as the group walked toward the bank. Herrin and his lot took the lead, whispering among themselves and pausing to give Jenkins sinister glances.

The pope smiled and looked up at Jenkins, distracting him from the threat of Herrin and the End Roaders. "The statue," the old man said, "is supposed to bring luck and ward off bad spirits. A little on the demonic side for my tastes. But banking is not something the Church condones, so it's perhaps a fitting guardian."

"Huh, you don't bank?" Jenkins cleared his throat, "Your Popi-ness."

"Your Eminence will do, but since we are incognito, Father will work just as well." The pope reached out his dark and wrinkled hand to pat Jenkins on the arm. "And yes, I bank. It is a necessary evil and one I pray about nightly. However, the material universe runs on money, and like it or not, the Church has to adapt. It is not easy. We must bend but not break, or we'll become no better than the false Catholicism Earth Government has feebly propped up." He rolled his eyes. "And a religion with no standings at all might as well not be a religion."

Karlson sniffed. "I think that was Earth's intent."

Chavez nodded. "I wholeheartedly agree. It is why I must return *my* way and we must see Earth for what it is."

One of his assistants muttered, "We shall see."

"Have faith," Chavez reminded him.

"So," Jenkins said, not wanting to linger on the topic of religion. "The Tyrant is going to get a large sum of money from you, correct?"

"Correct," Karlson said and cleared his throat. "That's our orders."

The pope's lips tightened, and he inhaled a sharp breath.

"Well," Jenkins said, "what does that look like, exactly? Are we going to have to have another one of those?" He gestured toward the suitcase.

"No, no." Chavez held up his free hand and brought his thumb and forefinger close to one another. "Your Tyrant's money will be stored in an electronic cube that is not large." He then said, "At this level, money isn't raw electronic cash. It's that and more. The cube will contain land deeds, corporate contracts, trade agreements, and so on. It's a large package of deals, resources, and other legal contracts that make up the fortune your avarice commander demands." He lowered his hand. "And all of it will be in Mordid's name."

"Ah, so I can't steal it for myself," Jenkins said with a laugh.

Chavez chuckled, but his eyes took on a hard gleam. "No, my son, you cannot. You could try, but his warning to you was one of wisdom."

When they reached the bank, Herrin was already inside. The lobby was richly decorated, sporting banners, comfortable furniture, and a long counter, behind which stood pretty women in green and white form-fitting attire. A single guard—with a shaved head, blank stare, and metal rod sticking out of his head—stood by a door to one side of the room. He cradled a shotgun in his hands.

"Drone," Karlson mumbled.

Jenkins stepped closer to him. "Eh?" Karlson was a fount of knowledge.

The old soldier nodded at the guard. "A drone. I've only seen them once before. That fellow might as well be a space zombie, except his actions are controlled by someone else, not by a desire to eat his fellow man."

The thought sent a chill through Jenkins. "Is he alive?"

"Yeah, yeah. They eat, poop, and pee and all that, but no one is really home upstairs anymore. I was younger than you when I had to fight a whole damned army of them. Nowadays, their electronics can be jammed, they can be tampered with, so you don't see them too often." He shrugged. "They're cheap, though. They never complain, are happy with no pay, and will merrily march into gunfire."

The pope and his assistants drifted toward the counter. Chavez spoke to one of the women, but his words were so soft Jenkins couldn't pick them up. The pontiff smiled and waited patiently as the woman reached under the counter and produced a hand-held "gun." Before Jenkins could react, she swept it across Chavez's face and it went *beep*.

Herrin must have never been in a proper Corporate Worlds bank, either. As soon as the woman produced her "gun," his knife slid halfway out of its sheath, and his two kinsmen tensed up, reaching for their compact sidearms. Seeing no harm, however, Herrin, Rendstrot, and Bulks relaxed.

Herrin crossed his arms. His eyes met Jenkins's. "Soon," he mouthed.

Jenkins mouthed something more crude back at him and raised his hand to make the matter more clear with a gesture. Karlson battered his arm down.

"Not now," Karlson muttered under his breath.

Jenkins crossed his arms in the same manner as Herrin. "Well, we can't just make eyes at each other all day. Remind me never to trust anyone again. I can't believe I let him bring his mutants into our outfit. He's an ungrateful pig."

"I'll be sure to remind you," Karlson said. He glanced left, then right. "When the pope has Mordid's blood money, we can make a move. Remember how we planned to let the End Roaders lead the charge and get killed in action?"

"Yeah?" Jenkins said. "What of it?"

Karlson glanced at the drone and then back at Jenkins. "Those things are like robots. When Herrin reached for his knife, it leveled its shotgun."

"Ahhh," Jenkins said. He hid a smile and whispered. "So, if I get Herrin to draw first, you think that drone will blast him?"

Karlson gave a curt nod.

"Good work." He frowned. He needed this to happen a bit more privately, though.

"Thank you, sir."

Jenkins frowned. "But I don't want to kill him with the damned pope in the same room. It-it-it's not right." He wasn't sure why it felt perfectly fine to shoot Herrin in an alley, but not in the presence of someone like the leader of the Catholic faith. He blamed it on the slight chance that God existed. He'd mumbled a prayer here and there, and in dangerous situations he had hoped, even prayed, for a miracle. It would be a shame to ruin any favor he had with the big guy in the sky by getting his top man spattered in Herrin's blood.

Karlson stared at him as if he'd grown a third eye and sprouted horns. He whispered, "Who the hell cares? Remember, get him to draw first."

The pope lingered by the counter, and eventually the pretty woman he was talking to placed a tiny cube in his hand. It quickly vanished into his pocket. Jenkins found it hard to believe that a galactic sum of wealth was tiny enough to become lost among the lint of a man's pocket.

His communication device buzzed. The sensation startled Jenkins, making his heart jump. He crouched, staring at the trio of End Roaders.

His swift actions caused them to do the same.

"Is there a problem?" Chavez asked. His two assistants shuffled closer to the pope and looked around. Their eyes were wide and nervous as their necks craned this way and that for a threat that wasn't there.

"No," Jenkins said. He pulled the device out and held it to his ear. It was the boss.

Mordid asked him how things were going, and Jenkins replied that he found it odd that one could put an insane amount of wealth into such a tiny package. Couldn't one lose galactic wealth as easily as they did spare change?

Then Mordid told him the bad news.

Jenkins lowered the device and placed it in his pocket. Clearing his throat, he said, loud enough for everyone to hear.

"We need to go. This place is—"

The drone opened fire.

#

Thrask sat at the controls of the small shuttle, while Mauss was slumped in the seat beside him, wrapped up in his gray coat. The diplomat peered at the instruments on the panel of the ship as they coasted through space.

Thrask kept his eyes focused on a point of light that not only didn't blend with the rest of the field of stars, but was also on the same course as the mystery ship, according to the film he'd smuggled off the *Merciless's* bridge.

"It's a ship, all right" Thrask said.

"Maybe you should have been an admiral instead of a general," Mauss replied. He reached his bony hands out and grasped the consol to act as a brace. Leaning forward, as if reading an eye exam, Mauss stared through the shuttle's window at the same point of light as Thrask.

Silence filled the cockpit once more as the glittering anomaly revealed more of a shape. The form was pale, the angles modern and new. The craft wasn't the cheap, efficient design of the Corporate Worlds, nor did it have the bulk and hardiness found in the products of the Upper Arm's shipyards.

"Earth," Thrask spat. "Do you think it's left over from the attack back at Reconquista?"

Mauss slid back into his seat and crossed his arms. His beady eyes narrowed. "No. Rodriguez wouldn't allow that. Traitorous as I think him to be—"

"And we're not?" Thrask said with a grin.

Mauss cleared his throat. "Rodriguez wouldn't let the pope come to any harm. According to Pedro Chavez, the first attack was launched by the soon-to-be ex-pope on Earth with subpar ships. Well, subpar by Earth standards. This is something different." He pointed at the craft as more of its white hull became evident. "I've never seen that design. The stealth abilities are impressive. Our sensors barely see it, and were I not looking right at it, I might think they were in error."

"Could Rodriguez have missed it?" Thrask hated to think that was the case. He much preferred his rival to be engaged in damning activity rather than just ignorant—though that too could be used to Thrask's advantage.

"No. Stealthy is not invisible. He knows it's here, and the captain of that ship knows that as well. They have an arrangement of some sort." Mauss frowned. "My instinct is that it's an Earth liaison to ensure the pope's return to Earth Space goes smoothly. If I were in their shoes, it's what I would do." A small smile appeared on Mauss's face for a brief moment. His teeth were yellowed, like dry bones. "Earth will be miffed, I think, when Khan's sun goes out like a light and the pope returns to them with an interesting bit of propaganda."

Who cares, Thrask thought. Religion and Earth politics mattered very little to him. The pope was a passenger going from point A to B. He was a passenger with a powerful bomb, but a passenger still.

Thrask veered the shuttle to one side and looked at the vessel in more detail. It was long, slender in places, and bulbous in others, and the white paint looked very much like star light. Thrask saw no markings upon it. Every ship in the Tyrant's fleet bore paint. Most were emblazoned with the red star and fist that Mordid chose as the company's symbol. Some chose to go with the white backdrop and rearing black snake in honor of the independence of the Upper Arm. Still others bore faded markings from past employers and companies that had yet to be removed and replaced with the reds, grays, and blacks Mordid fancied. This ship was indeed different. It was almost a bit lifeless in his opinion, with its lack of insignia and its almost ghostly hue. It looked…alien.

"So, we know Rodriguez's secret. What do we do?" Thrask peered at Mauss.

"A good question." Mauss looked back at Thrask. "We can hold this over Rodriguez, but not for long. Soon as this operation is over, the Earth ship will leave, and Mordid won't care about it."

"Fine, let's tell the boss." Thrask shrugged. Getting points with the Tyrant was not entirely what he wanted, but whatever made Rodriguez look bad was good in the end. If Thrask couldn't blackmail Rodriguez into obedience, then he'd just throw him to the sharks—or rather, into the jaws of Mordid.

The ship's console went wild. Hostile dots appeared across one of the monitors, and moments later, a swarm of smaller icons were picked up by the shuttle's sweeping sensors.

"What?" Thrask yanked the shuttle's stick to veer the craft toward the *Merciless* and away from the newly arrived fleet. "Who are they?"

Mauss brought his face nose to nose with the monitor, and its red glow cast his wrinkled, clean-shaven face in a fiery hue.

"It's the Earth fleet that already wrecked this system," Mauss said, and his lips twisted into a frown. "They're heading for the planet. They were hiding! Bah, I'm fixated on a lone stealth vessel and didn't think about the rest of their fleet using the oldest of tricks. Hiding close to the star! Damn, damn!" Mauss's hands flew over the console, and the ship's communications array clicked on with a buzz of static.

"Mordid, this is Mauss, you need—" Static hissed.

"Mordid," Mauss said again.

Thrask banged his fist on the console, and the static cleared up. "There, see? Need to be rough sometimes."

"*Hola.*"

Damn it! That was not Mordid. Thrask narrowed his eyes. "Rodriguez, this is Thrask. We were inspecting something, and now look! Earth Force is here. Tell the boss, and get ready to earn your pay."

"*Is Mauss with you?*"

"Yeah, so what?" Thrask sneered.

Mauss winced and rubbed his brow. His eyes fixed on Thrask. "Yes, I'm here," he said and then added a resigned sigh.

"*Excellent and adios.*"

Thrask perked up. "What?" He reached over and grabbed Mauss by the arm. "What does he mean? What does ady-oss mean?"

The diplomat inhaled a sharp breath and let it out. "It means Rodriguez is planning to kill two birds with one stone. And if I'm correct, he'll get two more in a moment." Mauss smirked. "The man, I believe, is far more ambitious than I thought."

The ship's warning lights flashed. Missiles were inbound.

Thrask released Mauss and looked at the monitor. "The *Merciless* is firing on us! That dirty, untrustworthy—" He let out a rage-fueled cry. He felt a little better afterward, but that didn't stop the fact that missiles were streaking toward them. "He's trying to take the company over before I can!"

"Ponder your career later." Mauss tapped the console. "We need to get to the planet. If Mordid dies, you die."

"If we get hit by a missile, you and I both die." Thrask directed the ship toward the planet and fixed their course to match the location of Mordid's personal shuttle. His fingers moved over the controls in an effort to guide them.

With little emotion in his voice, Mauss said, "Those missiles will hit us before we reach the planet. Do you have a plan?"

"Hah! Do you have a plan for how to stop Rodriguez from taking the company over?" Thrask punched a few buttons and worked the control stick to try to make their shuttle as elusive as possible. He saw on one of the monitors the signal of a pair of missiles getting closer and closer.

"If I was aboard the *Merciless* or able to communicate

with the rest of the fleet, yes. However, I'm stuck here with you."
Mauss gave another annoyed sigh. "Twenty seconds before we're
dead."

"Yeah, yeah, I see that." Thrask tried spiraling the ship
and moving it in wild directions to throw off the "scent" that the
inbound ordinance was tracking. The view of the planet before
them spun accordingly. "And if I was back on the *Merciless,* I'd be
strangling the Mexican myself."

"I should have known better." Mauss shook his head.
"Soon as I knew Rodriguez was up to something, I should not
have allowed the entire command staff to leave the admiral
entirely unattended. Well, no use complaining about the past."
He pursed his lips momentarily. "Ten seconds and I won't be
complaining at all."

"I KNOW! I have a trick I learned chatting with Mordid's
pilot. Maybe it'll work. Cut engines close to the planet and the
missiles might get confused." Thrask tried to cut the engines and
let the pull of the planet draw them in. He bit his lower lip and
sucked in a breath.

"Two-one." Mauss shut his eyes.

Nothing happened.

The old man's eyes popped back open. "Did it work?"

The signal of the missiles was still there, but the missiles
were moving away, seeking out new targets. Thrask grinned.
There were also other images all over the monitor. Earth ships,
Tyrant ships, and plenty of ordinance sailing this way and that.
His eyes couldn't keep track of what was what, but one thing was
certain. They had not exploded.

"Yeah, it worked." Thrask reached for a button to restart
the engines. As he did, the ship rocked violently, and warning
lights and sirens screamed. Smoke spilled from behind them to
cloud the cockpit in a noxious haze.

As the choking pall increased in volume, Mauss coughed.
"It worked? What was that then?"

Thrask banged at the controls and tried, with little luck,
to get the ship to respond. He narrowed his eyes as a fighter craft
zipped ahead of them. It was a fighter craft painted white with
a roughly tear-drop shape. Unlike the larger ship hiding among

the fleet, this one had a symbol upon it. On the bottom of the fighter's hull was the image of Earth, with a collection of golden stars haloing the mother-planet. Thrask raised his hand and shot a rude gesture toward the passing craft that had strafed them.

"Although I share your sentiments, I don't think that will work," Mauss said in droll tones as they headed, out of control, into the atmosphere.

10
KHAN SYSTEM -KHAN 7-

Mordid stared at the dead corpse of Sasha, or rather, the Sasha drone. Just barely, he could see a glimmer of silver in the piled up hair. Somewhere on the planet, maybe even in the same building, the real Corpy was getting his security forces ready to avenge his non-death. It was a stupid act to shoot him! Why had he done it?

Cursing, Mordid moved to the desk and started to push it toward the doorway. It was a heavy thing. "Come on, help me." He looked at Eryn, but she was busy combing out her long, inky hair and adjusting her hat.

"Eryn!"

"Hmm?" She spun on a heel and skipped toward him. "What are we doing?" She pushed on the desk and helped guide it toward the doorway.

"Making a barricade. We are several stories up, and I imagine the place is filled with blindly loyal automatons who are going to march up here and try to kill us." He glanced at the walls. They were bare and unexciting. He looked up. The roof was made of iron arches with glass between them. It was quite a way up, though. There was no easy way to get there.

"I think—"

Eryn cut him off. "We're trapped."

"Yeah." He reached into his pocket and pulled out his communication device. He toyed with a few dials. "Jenkins."

No response.

"Jenkins!"

Eryn's head tilted. "Are we being jammed?"

Jamming led to a hiss of obscuring static. There was some low level noise, but not the squealing that he associated with interference. He shook his head. "No, we're still clear."

He adjusted the dial again. "Rodriguez. *Hermano*?"

Nothing.

"Are you doing it right?" Eryn asked and crossed her arms as she rested her flanks atop the dead man's desk.

"Yes, I'm doing it right!" Mordid slammed the device into his pocket and stroked the point of his beard. He sat on the desk beside Eryn. Sucking in a breath and feeling his pride wilt, Mordid said, or rather mumbled, "You try."

"Hmm?"

He shot her a narrowed, steely glare.

Laughing, she pulled out her own device and tried to contact Jenkins, then Rodriguez. No one answered her. She switched a few more dials and cleared her throat.

"Mauss?"

Silence.

"Hmm." She tried another channel. "Thrask!"

Nothing.

Eryn bit her lower lip and cast a long look at Mordid. "No one in the command staff is answering. Neither is your bodyguard."

"Who I purposefully teamed up with a man who tried to frame him for murder." Mordid took off his hat, wiped his brow, and replaced the large cap. "I may have shot myself in the foot, or stabbed, rather. We may be alone."

She stood up. "You think everyone has betrayed you?" She looked up to the impossible-to-reach ceiling. "I can't believe it. They'd never *all* work together."

"Not at the same time, maybe not all. But I have a sense enough have betrayed me to make it count. Even if it isn't all."

Mordid sighed. The treachery of his command staff, Eryn's included, generally meant their machinations were spent on one another. The incident on Pristine was a fluke. Time and again the command staff sparred, while Mordid enjoyed life as the Traveling Tyrant. Today, however, he had a sinking sensation something had gone wrong. This was likely it; he was to meet the fate of all Tyrants.

"No one is coming to get us," Mordid said with a touch of finality.

"Well, besides an army of mindless corporate drones," Eryn nudged him. "See, someone still loves you!" She flashed a smile. "And guess who loves me?"

He ignored her. They needed to escape. Perhaps Nums could guide the shuttle to the ceiling of the building. But then what? The ceiling was too high to reach, and Nums would need to man the craft and wouldn't be able to provide assistance.

"Guess who?" She poked him in the side.

"Quiet, I'm scheming," he scolded.

The glass panes in the ceiling rattled in their fittings. Mordid turned his eyes up and saw a pale ship pass overhead and heard the groan of its engine.

From outside, on more than one speaker, Mordid heard a broadcast.

"*Citizens of Earth Space, remain in your homes. Mordid, also known as the Traveling Tyrant, also known as the Scourge of Interpretive Dance and Arch-mercenary—you are hereby under arrest for crimes including, but not limited to, planetary destruction, illegal warfare, cruelty to animals, false imprisonment...*" the list was long.

Earth. They had discovered the fact that he had incinerated Paradisa in a childish—but cathartic—fit; they had also apparently bothered to research his past crimes. Mordid rolled his eyes. "Well, it seems Earth loves me!" He leapt from the desk and paced across the room and back again.

The sound of boots marching echoed from outside, while the message proclaiming Mordid a criminal echoed over and over.

Eryn sucked in a breath and drew her pistol. "Someone's coming."

Judging by the sound of the boots, lots of someones. Mordid strode toward Eryn and pulled his pistol out. "We're stuck in a boring room with one desk, a body, and a glass ceiling too high to reach." He stared into her dark eyes. "The only door leads out to a hallway filled either with mindless Corpy cyborgs or self-righteous soldiers from Earth. Maybe both."

"So, we're screwed, right?" Eryn's nose wrinkled. "No way out. Doomed. Can't win?"

Help was not coming. There was no way out. She had the right of it. No winning.

"Right." Mordid sucked in a breath. "I'll pull the desk aside. You go out with your hands up. Say I held you prisoner." He swallowed. "I'll stay here."

She giggled. "Oh really? And then what?"

"I'm not sure." He brought his pistol to his temple. "I mean, this would be the historically correct thing to do, right? A quick shot and avoid the trial they'll have set for me. Bang. Done."

She frowned. "Well, yes. How about a blaze of glory, though, a last-stand action?"

"Oohhh, I don't know." He used the cold muzzle of the weapon to scratch his head as he considered her option. "I might get really hurt and not die. And you know what? I'm not that keen about being taken alive. Could you imagine it? On Earth they'd parade me around, and not in a good way. I'd be made a fool of. I'd be there in a cell for a century talking to my lawyers about all the rights I was blessed to have before ever seeing a judge and jury. I'd die, quietly, likely in bed. A boring, boring bed." He shook his head. "That sounds terrible. I hate cells. Suicide for me. You can escape."

She put her pistol to her head. "Well, if you die, I die."

Mordid frowned. Insane devotion was touching in a morbid way. But there were other issues as well. "And Thrask dies too. He's linked to my heart."

She grinned.

He glared at her and tilted his head. "He *is* still linked, right? You don't know something I don't?"

She batted her eyes. "I promise, as far as I know, his heart still beats in time to yours, and he hates you for it. So, this will be a three-way suicide of a sorts."

"Well, two suicides and one murder." Mordid shrugged. "It's a shame he has to die for no reason. But I'm sure he had something nasty planned for me. In fact, I bet he's up to something right now."

"Entirely justified," she concurred. "Well, should we wait till they burst in or count to three? I've never done this sort of thing before."

Mordid hadn't ever considered suicide either. It seemed a reasonable option at the moment, and he wasn't afraid. Pain scared him, alien monsters scared him, the investors he served put a chill through his bones, but a shot to the head would be quick and far less agonizing than having to fill out endless forms while in Earth custody.

"Let's wait till they burst in, and I'll say something Tyrant-y. Then we'll do it."

She grinned. "Sounds good. Well, let's stand in the middle of the room side by side. By the time they break the door down and get the desk out of the way, we should have plenty of time." She guided him with her free hand to the center of the chamber and faced the doorway. Eryn struck a pose. Her eyes found his and her lips curled into a smile.

"You can get out of this, Eryn." Mordid sniffed. "This doesn't—"

She cut him off. "You die. I die. If you try to talk me out of it, I'll shoot you now. Then myself after. You're ruining this." She stared. "Don't."

"You know," Mordid mused, "I think I have something to tell you." Mimicking her dramatic posture, Mordid placed the pistol firmly against his own skull and gently rested his finger upon the trigger.

"Yes?" she cocked her head to the side. Her eyes glittered.

"Hold on." He forced a smile. "I'd like it to be the last thing I ever say."

#

The Earth fleet had moved on Rodriguez with efficient speed, appearing out of the star's cover and likely aided by stealthy ships. It was not a small fleet and it was advanced, hosting technologies he was not fully aware of.

In Spanish, he said, "Hold position, tell the entire fleet no one is to open fire. Our mission is to save the Holy Father above all else." He reached up and gripped the end of his moustache.

"Sir!" Lupe said, "Message coming in from one of our shuttles. They are trying to contact Mordid directly."

Rodriguez tilted his head and gave a gesture with his hand.

He heard Mauss's voice.

What luck!

It took considerable effort not to fall to his knees and thank God for the fortune dropped into his lap. In Spanish he said, "Hello."

Thrask's voice answered next. Even more impossibly good luck! "*Rodriguez, this is Thrask, we were inspecting something and now look. Earth is here. Tell the boss and get ready to earn your pay.*"

"Is Mauss with you?" Rodriguez asked in the common language.

"*Yeah, so what?*" came Thrask's terse reply.

"Excellent and," switching back to Spanish, Rodriguez said, "goodbye." He waved his hand, and the channel was cut. The men of his bridge turned in their seats to regard him.

"Brothers! An opportunity the likes of which we shall never have again has presented itself. Mauss and Thrask are on a little ship, all alone. Eryn and Mordid are on the planet below, without soldiers or an easy way back to the fleet. The pope is moments away from being returned to us." He crossed his arms. "We could let this moment of God-given chance pass us by or we can seize it. The fleet, the company, the wealth, everything!" He felt his own heart stirring. "Can be ours."

One of the men stood up. "But sir, Mordid has been kind. If it were not for him—"

Rodriguez raised a hand and barked, "Twenty percent raises to everyone on the bridge and new uniforms with lots of gold braid and some proper glittering buttons!" Rodriguez glared at the men seeking out other challengers. A chance like this would not come by again. This was his moment now and all secrecy had to be flung aside.

The objecting crewmen sat down, and his hands worked over the controls of his station. "Firing on the shuttle now, sir!"

"Good man!" Rodriguez pointed to the man in charge of communications. "Keep that shuttle quiet and open a channel with that little ship nestled in our fleet. The one we all agreed not to talk about." They would have to deal with that as well. But now that the men were agreeable to betraying Mordid, what was the harm in revealing that he had dealings with Earth?

Lupe worked fast. "Open."

"Captain," Rodriguez said to his Earthly counterpart. "We shall stay on our side of the fence, you on yours. Agreed?"

"Not entirely," replied the voice of the captain whose name he never bothered, or wanted, to know. "Something of a show is needed. You'll weather it fine, I'm sure." The channel went dead.

The crew murmured to one another.

There was no time for Rodriguez to explain all of the machinations he had been involved in. Now was the time for action and boldness.

Licking his lips, he said, "Fine. They wish to fight? Order the fleet into battle formation. I want fighters out there, quickly!" He stormed across the deck and planted his hands upon his wide hips. He sneered at the distant white shapes of the Earth fleet as they barreled toward him, set against the backdrop of Khan 7. Their fleet's size roughly matched his, and given the wreckage they'd seen strewn all over the system, their ships were superior. Thus, the odds needed to be evened out.

"Lupe!" Rodriguez reached up to tug at his moustache. "Contact the other three mercenary fleets. Put me through to all of their ships."

The man nodded, and his fingers flew feverishly over his station's controls. With a final swipe of his hand, he pressed a button and looked up expectantly.

Static popped and hissed, but not enough to drown out a broadcast. Lupe was going to get his raise before anyone else!

"This is the Traveling Tyrant, Gustavo Esteban-Carillo Rudolfo Rodriguez. Earth has shattered your forces and put you all to shame. Now is your chance for revenge. Join with me, and we will put these dogs to flight. Flee and you might live, but believe me, if I fail here today, then Earth will come after you. Maybe not here, but in the next system, or the one after that." He trembled as he spoke. Not out of nerves, but out of anger. Giving a speech could always be troublesome, but when it was truthful, it was easy. And he was being truthful, well, mostly truthful.

"They have already sought to teach us Upper Arm folk a lesson. They are bringing a future we want no part of. We have never wanted a part of it! If you will not side with me, then run like cowards, sell your ships, and prepare yourselves for long lines, smiling faces, and electronic forms. If you wish to fight again, and fight for pay and want to ravage the galaxy in the name of profit!" He laughed. "Well then, fall into formation and witness the destruction the Traveling Tyrant can wreak, even on 'mighty' Earth! The *Merciless* has no equal and she comes with a hundred maidens! This is a fight for the right to be free, to be mercenaries and peddle our deadly wares. Now, fight for your livelihoods or change your careers! And I need not say all of you will be well, well, well paid."

His crew exploded into applause, shouts, and yells. Their whistles and cries filled Rodriguez's heart with supreme joy. A pity, though, that it was all for show. He waved his hands to quiet them down. Of course, they, the patriots of Old Mexico, loved him. But would the others listen, or would they guess at his true intent?

Static popped and crackled.

The ship went silent. Men halted their work, and Rodriguez felt a trickle of sweat dance across his cheek. "Answer," he whispered.

"Answer!" Rodriguez roared. "I have a battle to win."

"This is Captain Xothres. We're in. You damn well will pay, though."

"This is Captain Geventis. Is Mordid dead? Good. Hated the guy. I'm in. I expect proper compensation."

Rodriguez let out a breath and smiled.

"This is what's left of the Red Company. We're in. Let's kick these guys back to Earth. And maybe you have room for us in your

outfit after."

Rodriguez stomped his foot upon the deck. "Yes! Now, fall into our formation; we're going to get in close, and victory shall be ours." He pointed at the view port. "Helm! Find the biggest enemy ship and head that way. Fire. Fire. FIRE!"

He signaled Lupe to cut the channel with a slicing motion of his hand. When they had privacy once more, Rodriguez lowered his voice. "Cancel that order. Move slowly. As soon as the pope is on board, we are disengaging. Those fools will cover our retreat."

The crew moaned.

"Now, now," he chided them as if they were children, "Faith comes before money and glory. Cross yourselves. Pray."

And so they did.

#

The drone's shotgun blast threw Bulks against the far wall. Well, most of him. Large hunks of Bulks remained on the floor in a growing pool of red.

Jenkins drew his pistol and crouched, popping off two rounds into the drone.

Karlson and Rendstrot joined in, and the drone jerked and wheeled as puffs of smoke and blood blossomed on his chest. Stumbling, the drone collapsed to the ground.

"Get the pope—" Before Jenkins could say another word, Herrin was on him.

While Jenkins had focused on the drone, the End Roader apparently had no such instincts and used Bulks's death to close the distance. His knife was in hand, and he delivered a low thrust.

Cursing, Jenkins backpedaled and used the butt of his pistol to batter the oncoming blade aside. Herrin responded just as quickly and reached out with his free hand, gripping Jenkins's wrist in a cruel, nail-digging vice.

Jenkins tried to free his hand and ended up firing a shot into the floor. The round sent spider-web cracks through the tile. Pain then burned across his cheek as Herrin's knife snapped up.

"Stop!" Chavez cried. The pope's assistants flung their arms in the air and spoke in Spanish with an equal amount of excitement.

Karlson fired at Rendstrot, who in turn returned the favor at the same time.

BAM! BAM!

Just as their shots were simultaneous, so were their cries. "Gah!"

Both men staggered.

"I keep getting shot," Karlson howled.

Jenkins saw the knife, red with his blood, arcing back toward his face. With a desperate growl, Jenkins surged forward and brought his forehead into Herrin's face.

The bone and cartilage of Herrin's nose collapsed, and he lost his grip on Jenkins and flew backward. Blood streamed from his face, and his eyes narrowed.

"I said stop!" Chavez racked a shotgun. The suitcase, still cuffed to his wrist, swayed.

Jenkins momentarily took his eyes off of Herrin. "Where did he get that?"

"From the dead guard, you idiot," Herrin said. His voice sounded exceedingly nasal.

Karlson and Rendstrot clutched at their wounds and lowered their pistols as they eyed the armed pontiff.

"Why are you shooting one another? Have you gone mad?" Chavez handed the shotgun over to one of his minions. He pointed. "Keep an eye on them. Shoot whoever seeks to harm his fellow. I'll personally forgive you for the sin, if it comes to that."

Jenkins pointed at Herrin. "That traitorous mutant has been trying to kill me for weeks! He framed me for a murder I didn't commit, and now this."

Herrin brushed his hand across his busted nose, and his face twisted up as he saw how bloody his palm and fingers were when they came away. He looked at Jenkins and said to the pope, "It's pure business, Chavez. Jenkins, and his old beaten dog, need to go so that me and my family can rise. Blood is thick. You'd do anything for your faith; I'll do anything for my family."

"I promoted you and your family! I'm the only reason you're not locked up in the brig." Jenkins jerked his head in Herrin's direction. "Shoot him."

"No, we are not shooting one another." Chavez pointed at the door. "What is going to happen is this. You are all going to lead the way back to the shuttle. If any of you turns upon the other, then father Rojas will send your wicked soul to a place of gnashing teeth, darkness, and destruction." He shook his head. "The sanctity of the one true faith is at risk. Does that mean nothing to you?"

"Not really," Herrin said.

Karlson muttered, "More of a Protestant man myself, with respect, your holiness."

Jenkins shrugged. "I like to think there is a God. I pray in foxholes."

Rendstrot groaned and clutched his side.

"Fine!" Chavez inhaled a deep breath and pointed at the door. "You lost heathens and apostates may not believe in God, but you do believe in shotguns. Move, or taste the fury of father Rojas."

Emphasizing the point, Rojas swept the barrel of the gun across the room and back again, making it clear he'd shoot anyone.

"This isn't over," Jenkins said to Herrin. He walked for the door, wincing as he felt the burn on his cheek intensifying. He could feel blood running and imagined the scar would be impressive.

"You're right," Herrin replied and followed, a few feet behind.

Jenkins looked over his shoulder and nodded in appreciation at Karlson, who, with one hand pressed upon his wounded leg, limped behind Herrin, and after him Rendstrot fell into line with a limp of his own. The papal group was last. If anyone started shooting or knifing, it would be an amusing conga line of bullets in the back.

Outside the bank, the buildings of the corporate city all displayed the same advertisement. Jenkins tilted his head and blinked.

"Huh," Herrin said. "That's no good."

Though he hated the man and hoped Herrin would never leave Khan 7, he had to agree. Upon all of the buildings' shining surfaces, which numbered in the hundreds, were giant images of Mordid, and written above him in bold, impossible-to-miss letters, "WANTED BY EARTH GOVERNMENT."

The streets were clear, but from above, Jenkins heard a low groan. He scanned the sky, but much was blotted out by the immense skyscrapers. He glimpsed something, something white.

"Earth," Herrin said.

"Great." Jenkins jogged along the walkway back to their landing pad. The groans from above grew louder and more numerous. Every time he glanced up, he saw more white ships with the blue markings of Earth on their frames.

He looked over his shoulder to make sure the rest were following. Herrin flashed him a deadly smile, Karlson looked pale, Rendstrot was trailing blood and limping heavily, and the pope and his minions followed along. Rojas's shotgun remained at the ready.

From some of the passing ships above, and out of hidden speakers dotted about the city, calls for Mordid's arrest rang out.

By the time they reached the landing pad, the sounds of Earth's ships were continuous as the repeated audio messages calling for the apprehension of the Traveling Tyrant.

As Jenkins strode toward Mordid's personal ship, he heard a scuffle behind him. Whirling, he leveled his pistol and saw Karlson grappling with Rendstrot.

"Stop!" Chavez commanded, but neither listened.

Herrin glanced at the fight, before launching himself at Jenkins, knife in hand.

The man was fast, but Jenkins was ready and delivered a low kick toward Herrin's shin. His boot landed squarely on target, and the End Roader's charge stuttered to an ungainly halt.

Jenkins smiled and stepped back while leveling his pistol at Herrin. "That's what you get for bringing a knife to a gun fight."

"Stop!" Chavez cried again.

"He started it," Karlson grumbled as he rolled to the ground with Rendstrot. The larger End Roader wrapped his fingers around Karlson's neck. Karlson banged his fist into Rendstrot's wounded leg, eliciting a cry. Karlson's assailant released his hold on the older man's throat.

Both of their pistols were on the pad, just out of reach. Rojas loomed over the pair, shotgun leveled and eyes wide. He glanced at Chavez and then back at the squabbling soldiers.

Herrin crouched, and his eyes glittered.

Jenkins arched a brow. "Don't even, or I'll shoot you in the face. More than once." Looking over Herrin's shoulder, Jenkins said to Karlson, "Stop playing around. That's an order."

"Really, sir?" Karlson said through gritted teeth while wrestling with Rendstrot.

Chavez entered the fray, despite the excited verbal protests of his two men. The small man reached down, grasped the two by their collars and yanked.

Karlson rose to his feet, and Rendstrot snarled and did the same. The End Roader pushed himself free of the pair and limped toward the discarded pistols.

"Don't!" Chavez said.

"Shut up." Rendstrot bent over and grasped the pistol.

Jenkins shifted his aim toward Rendstrot, but no sooner had he done this than Herrin took a step closer and swirled his knife in a lazy pattern with a twist of his wrist. Jenkins jerked the muzzle of the weapon back at the knife-wielder.

"Drop the knife," Jenkins ordered.

"Drop the gun!" Chavez said to Rendstrot.

Neither End Roader listened.

Cursing, Rendstrot took aim at Karlson.

BOOM!

Rendstrot toppled to the ground, though there was little left of him above the waist to identify him *as* Rendstrot. Blood flowed in thick rivers.

Rojas lowered his smoking shotgun and then threw it to the ground and flung himself to his knees. He bowed his head and crossed himself over and over.

Chavez shook his head, a look of disappointment heavy on his face, and he stepped past Rendstrot's gruesome corpse and laid a hand upon Rojas's head.

Karlson dusted himself off and pointed at Herrin. "Shoot him now, sir, and be done with it."

"No!" Chavez shot Jenkins an intense stare. "No more

199

killing. You are acting like dogs. If you have the least bit of a soul, you'll not risk it in murder. You have that man at your mercy."

Herrin kept his eyes on Jenkins and slid his trusty knife into its sheath. He raised his hands. "You got me." He winked and smiled.

"Shoot him, sir," Karlson said again, his tone firm.

Chavez pointed at Jenkins, shook his head, and went back to administering to the weeping Rojas. "I tell you now, if you shoot that man, your soul, believe in it or not, is irrevocably damned to hell."

Jenkins stared at his rival. His finger twitched. "You murdered one of Rodriguez's men. You repaid my favor with treachery!" Every word caused his face to flare up in agony. He had to spit the words, not say them.

Herrin shrugged. "Then shoot me. You killed my kin. Kill me, or am I going to the brig again, sir?"

"Yes," Jenkins said.

"Bad idea, sir," Karlson warned.

"Noted, Karlson." Jenkins gestured with his pistol for Herrin to back away. "You tried to set me up, and you know what? You'll pay for it. When I go back to the *Merciless* I'm not going to worry about one of the bridge crew throwing a grenade under my bed. They'll know I was an innocent man. You'll tell them what you did. You."

"Will I?"

"I'll ensure it."

Karlson approached and tilted his head. "Hmm, not a bad plan. They'll deal with him, and you don't need to worry about any bad blood with the Mexicans." Karlson smirked. "And I thought you'd got religious on me."

"Nope." Jenkins glanced at the pope.

Chavez offered a fleeting smile and a nod.

So, only one man knew the truth of it. It wasn't as if Jenkins planned on going to church or following the rules of the Good Book. A mercenary on the rise couldn't afford such moral luxuries. But it didn't hurt to win a few points with the Almighty. Besides, it rubbed him the wrong way to murder people, even deserving ones, in front of Chavez. Did the old man have some aura about him? It felt like it.

A shuttle descended, passing between the towering structures. It was gray and bore the red star and fist of the Traveling Tyrant.

"Reinforcements?" Karlson asked.

Jenkins shrugged. He hadn't had time to check in with the boss to find out what to do once the pope was brought to the landing pad.

The bulky, battle-scarred ship touched down next to Mordid's more elaborate and clean shuttle. Jenkins had to turn his face away as the ship blasted the air aside.

The ramp of the gray ship lowered, and naval marines in black armor stormed out, with high protective collars hiding half their heads. They clutched, in their gauntleted fists, beamers and other high-powered compact weapons. Among them was a man in a black naval officer's uniform. His skin was darker, and his eyes were bright with intelligence.

Dimly, Jenkins recognized him as Rodriguez's right-hand man, Valdez.

"What are you doing here?" Jenkins asked.

The marines formed a protective ring around them, and a group of the soldiers ushered Chavez and his men into the shuttle.

Valdez waited until the pope had boarded and then barked, "Back on board! Go!"

The remaining marines obeyed, rushing back into the shuttle just as quickly as they'd exited.

"I have a prisoner here. He tried to mutiny," Jenkins said, pointing at Herrin with his pistol. "I'll need him secured. What's Mordid's plan? I've been out of the loop for a bit."

Valdez sneered. "You will be out of it much longer."

"What?"

He didn't hear the shot so much as feel it punch into his side. Jenkins fell to the ground, and his pistol spiraled out of his trembling hands. His head banged against the landing pad and further jarred his senses.

Dimly, he made out the mutilated corpse of Rendstrot.

He saw movement but couldn't tell who was moving where. Sound didn't register in his ears, either.

Planting his hands on the pad, Jenkins tried to rise. His side burned, and worse, he felt increasingly dizzy. A boot kicked him in the stomach.

Pain flooded him, and Jenkins rolled onto his back. Herrin was on him. He heard the sound of the shuttle's engines roaring.

Jenkins saw the gray shuttle carrying the pope rise into the air, and he felt the heat from its exhaust. Herrin's knife was held high in his hand, and the End Roader was straddling him. A broad smile formed across his lips.

"Thanks to you, two of my kin are dead. I'm going to enjoy slicing you up." Herrin's knuckles turned white around the handle of his weapon.

"I wouldn't do that," Karlson said.

Jenkins groaned and saw the older soldier, unarmed and grasping a freshly wounded arm to go along with his bleeding leg. He'd not made a move to get any of the numerous pistols on the ground. Some help he was!

"Oh yeah?" Herrin spat. "Soon as I'm done with Jenkins, you're next, you wrinkled old bag. I'll have your guts on the ground before you get to a gun."

"Then what?" Karlson asked. He looked at Mordid's shuttle. "Think Nums in there is going to fly you back to the *Merciless*? Even if you force him to, do you think Rodriguez won't shoot you down?"

"What are you blathering on about?" Herrin said. His knife remained poised.

Jenkins coughed and felt tired. He groaned and fought off the black wave of unconsciousness that wanted to sweep over him.

"That was Rodriguez's first officer that just shot poor Jenkins. He bundled the pope up and flew him back home. Without Mordid. I know our boss. Do you think he'd summon a team of heavily armed soldiers to rescue just the client and not himself? He's been betrayed."

Herrin lowered his blade a fraction. "So what? Give me a

reason not to kill you both."

Karlson smirked. "Son, you're not getting off this planet alone. You can kill Jenkins, and you can hope to get to me before I pick up that shotgun and splatter you all over the pad, or," he winced while tending to his own bullet wound, "you can patch up Jenkins and come with us to find Mordid. He'll know what to do. He's not the Tyrant for nothing. And he likes us a hell of a lot more than you."

Jenkins shut his eyes. It was simply too hard to keep them open. He mumbled, "He's right. Save me now, and we'll kill each other later."

The darkness was becoming more than just a visual experience. Jenkins felt the entire world going numb.

The last thing he heard before sliding into unconsciousness was Herrin.

"Fine, we'll all murder one another later. I need bandages. Karlson, use whatever Rendstrot has left on him that isn't blood-soaked. Jenkins, don't bleed out on me. Not today at least. Not on a bullet. If you die, it's on my knife."

#

The ship's gravitationals were shot, and Thrask felt his stomach flipping about as they spun out of control through the atmosphere.

"Get this thing working," Mauss said as he coughed and waved his hand in a futile gesture to clear away the smoke in the cabin.

"Let me try this." Thrask clenched his fist and slammed it onto the control panel. Lights flickered off, then back on.

"Don't tell me that worked," Mauss said.

"HA!" Thrask clutched the control stick with one hand and pounded his broad fingers into a variety of buttons to try to regain more stability. He glanced up, and through the cockpit's reinforced window Thrask saw clouds of feathery white giving way to a near-barren world. The ground was almost a uniform rust color. He could see no water or distinct land formations of any sort. The only feature of note on the ruddy landscape was an island of gleaming, enormous towers.

Thrask directed the trembling shuttle toward the man-made structures. They were on course for Mordid's shuttle, as far as he could tell. As the ship drew closer to the ground he spotted rusty and decayed buildings hidden among the red terrain. He imagined they were mines, water-collection plants, and the usual world-raping devices the Corporate Worlds were so fond of. They were idle ruins now. And if the shuttle didn't hold together, it would be just one more rusted hunk of steel dotting the landscape.

A few Earth fighters streaked past them, but fortunately none of the enemy opened fire on their stricken vessel as it closed in on the city at a quick rate.

"If you don't get a better handle on this thing, we'll end up colliding with a building." Mauss pointed at the nearing structures.

"Shut up and do something other than make obvious comments." Thrask felt the stick in his large hands jerk, and he growled, grasping it in an ever-tightening clench. The buildings all displayed some sort of advertisement in a simultaneous broadcast, but he couldn't make much sense of it. Within moments they were in the forest of steel and glass. One wrong move and they'd veer into a skyscraper.

"There!" Mauss coughed once more and pointed. "Can you see the pad?"

"Yes!" Thrask focused his vision, and he could also see movement. One of their ships was taking off! At first, he thought it was Mordid, but no, the Tyrant's personal "yacht" was still on the landing pad and stationary.

There was no time to ponder. Thrask guided the ship between the buildings and pulled back on the handle to try to slow the descent. The stick fought, and so Thrask fought harder and put his back into it.

"Land, you subpar piece of junk." He yanked on the stick.

Pop!

"Now what?" Mauss said.

Thrask stared at the control stick in his hand and eyed the wires dangling out of it with dismay. The control panel where it was once seated sparked in defiance. Grumbling, he pressed the broken stick into Mauss's frail hands.

"Here."

"Wonderful."

The ship collided with the pad, rather than landing upon it. Thrask heard the screech of metal, more smoke spiraled into the cockpit, and the smell of fuel stung his nose and caused his eyes to water. The impact was enough to toss him this way and that, but the restraints of his chair thankfully held.

When the rocking sensation stopped, Thrask unclipped his harness and stood. It was nearly impossible to see, and he reached out to grasp Mauss. He then paused his act of charity. Why bother?

Grinning, Thrask stumbled and fumbled his way out of the cockpit. The door leading to the shuttle's interior was jammed, so he kicked it. Once. Twice. With a third brutal kick, the door collapsed and more smoke blinded him.

He coughed and wretched and fought his way forward. He could see light and crawled over twisted metal to reach it. It was a breach in the hull! Snarling, he pulled himself through the hole, wincing as a sharp piece of jutting metal snagged his pants and gashed his leg.

He tumbled out of the craft and landed on the pad, coughing violently. Thrask struggled to his feet and jogged away from the stricken ship. Glancing over his shoulder, he saw that there was little left of the vehicle, save the cockpit. Thick black smoke billowed from the wreckage into the air, blotting out what little sky would have been visible between the towers.

Throughout the city, automated calls for Mordid's arrest repeated themselves, as well as warnings to stay inside. The boss was no longer popular on the planet.

"What is that saying about a landing you can walk away from?" Mauss said from behind him.

Turning to the source of the voice, Thrask frowned at the sight of Mauss standing on the pad, coated in soot, but otherwise unhurt.

"It's a good one." Thrask gestured to their ship. "Well, it's done for. We'll need Mordid's ship for sure now."

"Sir?" a voice came from within a passing swirl of acrid smoke.

Through the haze, Karlson emerged, and his wrinkled brow grew yet more wrinkles. He had a shotgun in one hand. "What are you doing here?"

"Shut up," Thrask said to the old soldier, "Mordid is in danger, and so are we." He growled, "Rodriguez is making his move, and he's jammed our signals. See if you can get through to our employer."

Karlson snapped a salute and said, "We tried a moment ago and got nothing. Then you came out of the sky." Karlson frowned. "Worse news, sir."

"Eh? Now what?" Thrask punched his hand into his palm, making a sound similar to a gunshot. "I'm wanting some good news right about now."

"Well, er," Karlson licked his lips. "Rodriguez sent down a team of marines led by his First Officer. He shot Jenkins, grabbed the pope, and took off." He pointed up. "Oh, and Herrin is patching Jenkins up now."

"He is?" Thrask and Mauss said in unison.

The old soldier nodded. "Yes sir, er, sirs. I told him he needed to think of pleasing Mordid more than you, General. Begging your pardon. Mordid is how we get off this planet, and a dead Jenkins is an unhappy boss. He kinda likes him. I do, too."

"Well, desperate times makes for interesting bedfellows," Mauss said. "Where is Mordid now?"

Karlson pointed. "He went that way. But with so many buildings, he could be in any of them. This was supposed to be a quick bank run."

A landing shuttle, painted a glorious white, dipped through the smoke and hummed as its streamlined shape traveled between the gleaming buildings.

Karlson frowned and tracked the passing craft. "So, is there something else going on, sirs?"

"Yes," the diplomat said. "Earth has taken this place over. It's a trap, I think. I haven't quite figured it out," Mauss said with a shrug. "It doesn't matter. We need to get Mordid, then fly out of here. Rodriguez might have control of the *Merciless*, but Mordid has the loyalty of several other ships. I'm certain of it. And not everyone on Rodriguez's bridge is entirely loyal to him.

206

I'm certain of that as well. So long as Mordid lives, we may have allies up there."

Thrask nodded in agreement. "And if I can get aboard the *Merciless*, then every soldier will rise up in the name of me."

"Mordid," Mauss corrected.

"Yeah, him." Thrask looked at their surroundings and noted a dead body and Herrin crouching by a living one. He strode toward his minion. "Will he live?"

Herrin sighed. "Probably. If you want, I can finish him off. The bastard has led to the death of two of my men. My kin." He spit on Jenkins's bandaged face. The wounded man didn't stir.

"He deserves to die." Herrin frowned till the creases in his face seemed like canyons.

"No, no," Thrask flashed a smile. "We need to stay on Mordid's good side. Kill him later, when it is convenient. For now, we're going to hold up here."

Karlson said from behind him, "Yes, sir. What about Mordid?"

Thrask faced the old soldier. Was Karlson pointing that shotgun at him?! Surely not; his expression was blank. It was poor discipline. Thrask swept his hand around. "This city is massive, and there's no telling where Mordid is. Can you call him?"

Karlson fetched his communication device out. He turned a dial, pressed a few buttons, and sighed. "No."

"Then we wait for a sign. He knows where his shuttle is." Thrask pulled his pistol out from its holster and cocked the weapon. "And until the boss shows up, we hold."

Mauss drifted toward him. He regarded Thrask and mused, "There will be lots of them."

"Them?" Karlson asked.

Before Thrask could answer, the first squad of Earth Force's soldiers arrived. They were there to secure the pad and the arch-criminal Mordid's ship.

11

KHAN SYSTEM -KHAN 7-

Waiting to die was exciting at first, then nerve-wracking, but finally it was boring.

"Now?" Eryn asked.

"Does it look like they're trying to get through?" He watched the door for some sign of the men from Earth. He imagined they—or legions of Sasha's drones—would be kicking their way in at any moment.

A moment passed.

Then another.

Mordid lowered his pistol and cursed. He looked at Eryn. "Call Nums. If they won't oblige me with an appropriate death scene, then I'm going to try to escape." He approached the barricade and clambered atop the table. With caution, he placed his ear against the door. He heard nothing on the other side.

Eryn fiddled with her communication device and let out an annoyed hiss. "Guess what?"

"Jammed?" Mordid crawled off the table. "Fine, we'll do this on our own. Back to the other plan you had. We'll fight our way out. We have enough ammunition between the two of us to be a mild nuisance before they gun us down." He braced his shoulder against the desk and moved it aside, panting with the effort.

She laughed. "I don't need a gun. I'll poke their eyes out. I'll kiss them and then rip out their tongues. I'll die choking on their blood." She flushed suddenly, and her pale, almost corpse-like skin blossomed with life. "Wait!"

"Eh?" Mordid was trying to not envision Eryn gagging on hunks of flesh she'd bitten out of people. He gave the desk one more push and then turned to face his head of PR.

Eryn flung herself at him. Her arms wrapped tight, and she looked down into his eyes. Her own eyes were wide and black and sparkled with the gleam of madness. "I want to know what your last words were going to be." She smiled, baring teeth as she did so. "Tell me."

He tried to push her off. "Well, not now! It's not right to say my final words in advance."

Her arms tightened their hold. She was surprisingly insistent and powerful, given how supple her frame was. "Uh-uh. Soon as we walk out of that door, a bullet will probably find a home in your skull. Then, I'll never know! Tell me!"

He squirmed. "It's embarrassing, no." She'd hold it over him forever if he admitted a thing.

"I'm strong enough to pick you up," Eryn warned him. "Do you really want me to kick open that door while cradling you?"

The thought was as disgusting as it was terrifying. He was Mordid! Wanted by Earth, feared by billions, well, at least millions. He placed his hand and the muzzle of his pistol against her hips and pushed with all of his might. She was as sticky as a web, but did break free, staggering back a step.

She laughed and spread her arms out wide to try again.

Mordid leveled his gun at her head. "I *will* shoot you."

"Tell me!" She bent forward and rested her forehead against the muzzle. "Or shoot me."

He rolled his eyes as she called his bluff. Fine! The truth was better than her trying to cart him around. Such an unseemly sight would ruin any Tyrant's career. Being saved by Eryn, more than once, he could and had handled before. Scooped up by her? Never! How unmanly.

"Well?" she goaded.

"I was going to say," Mordid licked his lips, "That if I ever retired I'd probably marry you."

"Really?" She batted her eyes and took a step back. "You would?"

"Well, if I didn't have to kill you before such a time, sure." He looked away from her. "But Eryn, as the head of the company, I can't do a thing like get married. You understand?" He met her dark eyes.

She nodded and giggled. "I do. I hope I don't have to try to kill you. I. Love. You. I know it. I feel it! It's like torture!"

He frowned. "Right. Well. I…" He coughed. "Love you, too. It is like drinking an entire bottle of alcohol not being sure if it is poison." He sighed. "I hope I don't have to murder you." He strode up to her and wrapped his arms around her and picked her up, cradling her as she so threatened to do to him. With his pistol still in hand, he glared at the door. His back hurt from the effort. As the Tyrant, he usually had someone pick up things larger than his coat for him. Still, this was a matter of pride, of which he had a small sliver left.

"Let's do this right." He marched to the door. He tried to grasp the knob while still holding Eryn and his pistol. It was a cumbersome affair.

"I got it," she reached out and pulled the handle.

It would be a sight! He charged into the hallway, ready to watch the stunned expression of his foe's faces, or if they were drones, the lack thereof.

Instead, he saw an empty hall.

"All of our dramatic moments are getting ruined," Eryn said. She looked at him and shook her head. "Where is our audience?"

He dropped her. She landed on her feet, like a cat would.

"I have no idea." Mordid scratched his jaw with the cold metal of his pistol. "Come on, we'll go down to the lobby and try this again."

"You won't carry me?"

"No." He stormed past her and marched down the gleaming white hall toward the elevator. He stabbed his finger into the button and waited. He shook his head. "I don't have the energy to do it like that again." Before she could offer up an alternative he snapped, "You are not carrying me. Don't even."

She grinned.

The doors opened to reveal two dead men. One was dressed in the colors of the Vladstock company. Additionally, the fellow was bald and bore the lackluster expression of a drone. The other was a man with mocha skin who wore gray combat fatigues and sported a blue helmet that was entirely out of place compared to the rest of his uniform. The pair were a mass of blood, and each held a weapon in hand.

Eryn scooped up an assault rifle.

Mordid took the Vladstock drone's shotgun. He entered the elevator and used his pistol, still firmly in his other hand, to press a button to get them to the ground floor.

"Do you want to carry me still?" Eryn asked as the light, airy music common to all elevators played.

Mordid shook his head. He could only manage such a physical task here and there. "No. We'll go out, guns blazing. Two-fisted style. We're done for this time. Two people in an elevator in a combat zone? So, let's make it good." He hefted the shotgun in one hand and waved his pistol about with the other.

"I wish I'd brought a camera! Imagine the footage." She sighed and mirrored him, ready to blaze away with pistol and assault rifle.

The elevator slowed to a halt.

"I still love you," she chimed.

"I love you. There. Let's die."

"Ahhhh!" Mordid charged forward as the doors opened, firing as he ran. The shotgun bucked in his hand, the pistol twitched with every pull of the trigger. The roar of gunfire gloriously echoed.

His bullets smacked into a reinforced window that was already riddled with cracks and pockmarks, and the mighty blast of his pilfered shotgun sent pellets across an empty lobby.

"Seriously?" he spat.

The lobby wasn't empty as much as it was lifeless. Drones and gray-clad, blue-helmeted soldiers were strewn about in a grotesque and tangled mess. Blood stained the floor in great pools, and no one so much as twitched.

Eryn was smiling and she danced through the war-torn room, skipping as she made her way through the maze of corpses and hopping over a pile of what looked like entrails. "They murdered each other trying to get to us! This is irony, right?" She spun and faced him.

He nodded. "I suppose. I'm just really not happy, though." He tucked his pistol in its holster and clutched the shotgun with both hands. "That's three times my last moments have been foiled."

"Well, they weren't your last moments, so cheer up," she reminded him.

"Yes, yes," he agreed. He was by no means suicidal by choice, but having prepared for death, it wasn't so much a relief as disappointment having not found it. Then again, living was awesome. "And that is what's important. Me." He let out a heavy breath. "Come on, the shuttle isn't far. Let's take our money and run. We have a star to kill."

"Eryn," he murmured.

"Mmm?"

"Why are they killing each other?"

She shrugged. "I don't know. Us?"

He smirked. "I sure hope so."

#

The admiral laughed to himself as the coaxed mercenaries barreled headlong into the clutches of the Earth Force fleet. By the time they had realized the entire fleet of the newly-raised Traveling Tyrant Rodriguez was reversing course, it was too late. They were like ancient wooden ships that had come too close to a whirlpool. One by one, they were being sucked into the deadly, and hopeless, maw of Earth Force.

Rodriguez could see a flash of light as one of the duped mercenary ships met its end in a short-lived blossom of fire. He had told Lupe to try to jam them to make their fate all the more certain. They would die, and in their death throes provide cover for his escape. As a side benefit, every mercenary who met his end meant less competition for Rodriguez in the future. It was shaping up to be a wonderful day.

The doors to the bridge opened, and Rodriguez turned to see Valdez and the pope. The infamous suitcase dangled safely from the pontiff's thin wrist.

"His Eminence!" Valdez said by way of introductions and bowed low in the old-fashioned and courtly manner.

The crew crossed themselves, and a hundred prayers were murmured.

Rodriguez smiled and strutted toward the Holy Father. He knelt and took the man's small hand, kissing his golden ring. Just then, he saw out of the corner of his eye, another flash in the view port. Yet another potential rival was no more!

"Wh-what is happening?" The Holy Father retracted his hand, and his brows knit together. "Where is Mordid? What is going on?" He stared at the view port. "A battle?"

Rodriguez lurched to his feet and belted out a deep laugh. "Everything is going well! The entire command staff is stuck on Khan 7. Earth is distracted, fighting hapless mercenaries, and the entire company is mine! I am the Tyrant now!" He pounded his hand to his chest, thumping it in delight. "And, thus, it is all yours, your Eminence. We can demolish this system's sun, and you need not pay a thing for it. My gift to you." He could feel himself flushing with pride. "We have won, your Holiness. We have utterly, entirely, won."

The slap across his face struck him as entirely inappropriate for the occasion. He blinked and staggered back while the crew gasped.

"Your Eminence?" Rodriguez said, raising a hand to his still stinging cheek. He looked around, confused, and then stared at the Holy Father. "What have I done?"

"Done?!" Chavez's dark skin turned purple, and he trembled in visible rage. "Done?!" He shook his head and flung his hand in the air. "You have nearly cost the Church everything! I had a deal with Mordid and you, without my permission, decide to not only break it, but bring about wanton murder in the process? I shall put this in plain terms, my son. We are the good guys." He craned his neck, meeting the gaze of the bridge crew, who promptly lowered their eyes.

"So we must act the part. God will not tolerate the

wicked," the pope said. The room went silent, save for the beeping of machines and the static-laden transmissions flowing in from other ships.

Rodriguez pursed his lips and took a moment to soak in the righteous indignation leveled upon him and the crew. He decided to counter it with the truth, but he felt small, as if the tiny bent man before him was towering over him.

"Forgive me, your Eminence," Rodriguez said, "We are the good guys? Then let us rejoice! Mordid is a nonbeliever; the men dying out there are either Earth-born and godless or mercenary-scum who have committed countless atrocities for pay. Villains of the worst sort are now at one another's throat, while we, the pure and holy, are clear to carry out your great task!" He spread his hands out wide. "Is it our fault that this happens to cost the church nothing? Is this not God's reward manifesting itself?"

"Don't try to interpret His ways," the pope snapped. He held up his arm, the one from which the suitcase dangled. "You see this?"

"Yes. It is the bomb that will destroy this system's sun. It is why we are here." Rodriguez planted his hands upon his hips. "Shall we go deliver it?"

"It is missing a part." A tight, mirthless smile, formed upon the pope's face. He stared long and hard at Rodriguez.

The elation that once filled Rodriguez was gone. The confusion as to why his most beloved Holy Father struck him was also gone. There was only one sensation left. Shock.

"No," he whispered.

The pope nodded his head. "Oh yes. Guess who has it?"

Rodriguez stormed toward the view port and pointed a bejeweled finger at it. "Get this fleet turned around! We're going back into action! Line ahead! We do this the old way. Broadsides and point-blank range. Fancy Earth toys be damned! The *Merciless* will take the lead!" He cursed and clenched his fists. Everything had slipped from his grasp! All thanks to a blasted widget. No! Not a widget. "Damn you, Mordid!"

"Damn all of your ambition and greed," the pope said from behind him.

#

The sound of gunfire ended Jenkins's slumber, and the smell of something wonderful baking mingled with it. He blinked his eyes and stared up at a pale light. He hurt all over, but not quite as bad as he thought he should. There was an overarching numbness dulling everything. Jenkins looked around to get an idea of where exactly he was.

He was sitting in a nice leather chair. The place had a roomy interior and gray walls. He was in Mordid's personal ship. He looked down at his chest to see his tunic open. Wrapped around his pale form were white, but blood-stained, bandages, and beneath them a lump. It smelled odd. Like food. The ship appeared to be empty, but it was not quiet. He could hear the sound of gunfire beyond its thick walls. A great volume of it.

"Nums!"

Jenkins winced. His cheek hurt, but that too was bandaged.

The pilot's voice filtered through the speakers, "*Glad you're not dead, Jenkins. They slapped a Gut-Shot on you, so you should pull through or be filled with bread. Weird, huh! The boss is on his way, and we'll be leaving soon. Maybe.*"

He tried to stand, but found his legs entirely useless, as if each limb was filled with water and not flesh, muscle, and bone.

"What-what's happening out there?"

"*I'm not entirely sure myself. I just fly the armored space-limo. From what I can tell, Earth Force is here and going to kill us all. Uh, and Rodriguez may have gone rogue. The chatter on the coms is pretty bad. I sure wish the pope was on board. Now he's a lucky charm!*"

"Lower the ramp; I'm going out there." He tried to stand, but his legs were still being uncooperative. Jenkins looked around for a weapon but found none. Still, he had to get out there. Herrin was there, and the last thing he needed was for that traitor to get any amount of glory in front of Mordid.

"*Negative. That ramp lowers when the boss is ready to come on board. For now, Jenkins, you're out of this fight. Besides, I think we're about to get overrun. Safer in here.*"

"Damn it!" Jenkins slapped the edge of the chair he was

lying in. "Nums!"

"*Yes?*"

"Mordid is a rewarding kind of guy. Neither of us are earning any points with the big man by sitting here." Jenkins grasped the arm rests of his chair and hauled himself as straight as he could. He looked around, finding it awkward to talk to the air. He needed something to look at! He fixed his gaze upon the blank reinforced door to the cockpit.

"*And?*"

"And we don't get rewarded by just sitting here. Do something. This thing have guns?"

"*What? Of course it does, but it's meant to take out other ships. We have missiles, beamers, the whole lot, but that kind of destruction isn't precise. I might vaporize the boss by accident.*"

Cursing, Jenkins glared at the door. "If the boss can't get here, what's it matter? Nums, do something and we'll both make out as heroes."

"*Really now? I'm the one who would be doing all the shooting. I think all the credit or blame would be on me. No, Jenkins, you sit tight.*" He coughed. "*We'll sit tight.*"

"Nums!"

Nothing.

"Nums!"

Nothing.

"If it goes well, we share the credit, if it goes bad, say I put a gun to your head. Win win, Nums. But doing nothing is a loser's proposition. Losing is all on you."

A long silence persisted, broken only by the gunfire outside the ship.

"Nums! Give me an answer."

"*Fine. But if I turn the boss to a pile of ash, I might put a gun to your head before I concoct a story. Or fly you out into space and open the doors.*"

Jenkins let out a long sigh of victory. That did hurt, even with all the drugs they must have pumped into his system.

#

"Almost out of ammo!" Thrask barked. He remained

crouched behind a piece of the crashed shuttle while rounds skipped around him, sparking across the pad's surface. He peered around the jagged edge of steel and saw men in gray uniforms with stupidly painted blue helmets advancing on their position from one of the streets. Overhead, an Earth Government shuttle swept by. It sported a chin-mounted gun belching forth a flurry of rounds that blasted apart rock, steel, and glass in a deadly line.

"A few left," Karlson said. Like Thrask, he was using a bit of the downed craft for cover. He thundered off a shotgun blast and sent the men from Earth scurrying out of sight.

"Boss, I'm down to a knife." Herrin had his favored blade in his hand and was pressed against the hull of Mordid's yacht, whose immaculate paint job was marred with countless black streaks from gunfire.

His hands were stained with Jenkins's blood. It was a pity it was from efforts to save him.

"Mauss, ammo?" Thrask glanced at the old man, who was lying prone behind a smoking piece of machinery that had once powered their ship.

"Saving one round for myself. Imagine the indignity of being captured by Earth Government." He looked over at the Tyrant's craft. "We'll need to go find Mordid at this rate."

"If he's not already dead!" The thought churned within him. In an instant, he realized that if Mordid was dead, he'd know it. Or rather, his heart would explode and he wouldn't.

A silver cylinder landed next to him. It took a moment for Thrask to realize it was a grenade. It wasn't at all like the clunky, fragmented hunks of iron he was used to.

"Ah!" Thrask grabbed the explosive, hurled it back, and threw himself flat against the pad. The explosion came a moment later and deafened him. A pall of smoke descended in its wake.

"They're closing in on us!" Karlson said over the staccato of gunfire. He fired off his remaining rounds at the Earth Force soldiers as they went from cover to cover, closer and closed in on the pad.

"What is the plan now, General?" Mauss asked. "Out of ammunition, outnumbered, and waiting on Mordid. I don't like it."

It was a good question, and one Thrask didn't have an answer to. If Mordid wanted off the planet, he should have been there by now. He wasn't. Perhaps he was wounded and Thrask's heart would erupt later? Maybe he was captured? Maybe he just needed a little more time? That was the best scenario, so he clung to it like a man lost at sea would to a piece of driftwood.

"We need to give him more time!" Thrask bellowed.

Mauss laughed dryly. "Indeed, you are quite loyal, General."

Thrask took a breath and stood up, with his hands in the air. "Don't shoot! Don't shoot! We surrender!" He closed his eyes. If he'd been fighting anyone else in the damned galaxy, he'd be hit by every single gun that could draw a bead on him.

From the adjacent street, a smooth voice called out. "Everyone raise your hands. You are all under arrest in accordance with Earth Government laws. Please slowly and calmly approach us."

Thrask smiled. He opened his eyes to see the enemy all over the city and dozens of them moving toward him with their weapons raised.

With looks of confusion on their faces, Mauss, Herrin, and Karlson set aside their weapons and stood, raising their hands high in the air.

Gunfire echoed through the city and Thrask saw black smoke rising from a distant building. Someone was fighting Earth, but he wasn't sure who, or even why. One thing at a time, he thought to himself. He had Earth to stall.

"Do we come over to you? Or over there?" Thrask jerked his head in a random direction.

A dark-skinned man with perfect features and a winning smile peeked his head up from a bullet-ridden power-box. "Over here. You will not be mistreated. Walk slowly this way."

"We have wounded!" Thrask nodded in the direction of what was left of one of Herrin's kin.

The Earth Force officer frowned and tilted his head in obvious confusion as to how half a man could be considered wounded.

Karlson dropped to a knee. "I'm shot."

218

Mauss shrugged. "I'm old." He sat down.

Thrask shook his head, and he tried to sound as stupid as possible. "They're hurt. Should I drag them to you or you come to us? I don't want to die. Please, tell me what to do! I give up!"

The officer emerged from cover. "Please be calm. You will not be harmed. Lie face down, and we will come to you. Make no sudden moves or I cannot guarantee your safety."

Thrask nodded. "Ok! I am lying down. Everyone is lying down."

He went to his belly.

Nearby, Mauss glared at him. "What is your plan, General? If you do not have one, I'm shooting myself now." The man's eyes turned to slits. "And don't say you have no plan just to see me off myself. Now is not the time."

Thrask snorted. "I'm stalling. I'm improvising. Maybe… maybe…" Mordid was better at this. Damn him! He *was* better at this.

Thrask blinked. "I'm not meant to *be* a Tyrant." The thought stung, stung worse than any wound he had received. He chased it away.

"What?!" Mauss hissed.

The Earth soldiers were creeping forward, while others stayed safely tucked behind cover. Calls for calm were repeated.

The guns of Mordid's private craft opened up on them. On all of them.

12
KHAN SYSTEM -KHAN 7-

Mordid strode through the demolished room looking for threats. There were none.

Eryn picked her way through the ruin, stepping over bodies and nudging a few with her foot. She looked toward a set of doors.

"That's the way we came," she said with a gesture.

"Right. Back to the ship we go then." He led the way and reached the doors. To his surprise they opened. More to his surprise were the pair of drones pointing shotguns in his face. Even more to his surprise was the bearded bear of a man in green and white standing behind the drones and sporting a massive furry hat.

"Mordid!" The man's voice had a thick Slavic accent.

"Sasha," Mordid said cautiously and backed away.

Eryn was at his side, and her weapon pointed at the Corpy. "I'm faster than your drones. Don't even think about making a move."

He waved a hand. "You misunderstand me. I am your escort back to your ship."

Mordid snorted. "Are you? Do you remember our last conversation?"

"That was a long time ago, and besides, it never happened." Sasha cleared his throat. "Lower your weapons, my drones."

The blank-faced men lowered the muzzles of their shotguns in eerie unison.

Sasha squeezed between them and he held a hand out to Mordid. "Let us work out a new deal. As friends."

Mordid's hands were full, so he placed the barrel of the assault rifle in Sasha's hand so he could shake it as if it were quite natural to do so. Mordid's mind slowly, but eventually, caught up.

"They're screwing you," he said.

"Yes. Total occupation. The company is having its well-earned, hard-fought-for territory taken from it. Stolen, you might say. The men from Earth truly want you in their grasp, but they are taking Vladstock's planet as well. For good measure, I suppose." He stretched. "When they told me to have all my drones stand down, I agreed. Who was I to interfere in your capture? When they then demanded I hand myself over to them, well, I did not like their tone. As if I had done something wrong! Me?! When I made excuses they said I was under arrest…" He shrugged.

Mordid understood perfectly. At least, he was starting to. "They're up to something very big, Sasha. Something bigger than you, than the Khan system, and even me. Me!" He tossed him the assault rifle and waved his pistol about. "They're taking over."

Catching the weapon, Sasha nodded. "Yes. Fools. Had they been more polite, you would be my prisoner, or dead. But they are fools and I am not stupid." He bowed low. "I humbly ask for employment. My current contract has been, I believe, rescinded."

Eryn shrugged. "Alright. We don't have time for double dealing, though. If I have the teeniest, slightest inclination you're going to hand us over to Earth, I'm shooting you. Groin shots only, mind you."

Mordid nudged Eryn. He could handle his own affairs and that of the company, and he chose who was hired and who was not. It didn't matter if he agreed with her. One marriage promise and she thought they were partners!

He cleared his throat. "You need to earn your keep then.

Your drones. I want as many as you can get to descend on the platform. I want my shuttle secured. Then, all of us will escape."

Sasha straightened, and his eyes were wide. He smiled. Then wider. Then too wide.

"What?" Mordid snapped.

"I have two drones under my command. The rest I sent on a final command to attack anyone armed and not wearing our colors of green and white." Sashsa waved a hand. "I had no choice. Earth's technology is superior to what we have here, and they're jamming everything. The drones included. They'll perform their last command, though. These two," he pointed at each, "are commanded by my voice. You can't jam that, oh no!"

"A challenge," Eryn cooed. "I think I could jam your voice quite well."

Mordid ignored her. "Two it is then. Lead the way. We need to get back to my shuttle, and we need to find out what's going on."

Sasha nodded. "Indeed." He looked at the drones. "Escort us to the shuttle pad. Shoot anyone not wearing our, er, rather, shoot anyone in gray and blue."

The drones blankly stared, then turned and walked back the way Sasha had come from. The burly man stroked his beard and followed after.

"Mordid, you do not know how angry I am." He smiled. "I worked hard for all this and to have Earth take it. The system, the planet, my job, my drones! I was like a king here." He sighed and gave a shrug. "Today has been a terrible day." He sighed then laughed. "Ah, well."

"You're taking it awfully well, Sasha," Eryn quipped.

"There is a saying where my family is from. They say, on the worst day of your life, do not worry." Sasha picked up his pace as they left the ruined building and headed toward the distant pad, which was covered in smoke. "Because there will be a day worse than that. That, and it is the Vladstock way! Laugh in the face of adversity!"

"A solid bit of advice," Mordid said. He gazed at the pathway leading to the landing pad. The black smoke that billowed up from it parted at times, revealing his personal landing craft.

That was good. There was something burning on the pad, but it wasn't his ride.

Red beamers tore through the city, gleaming tracer rounds smashed into buildings, missiles whose trajectory was marked by white streaks of smoke fired forth – all from his landing craft. A second later, buildings exploded, glass panels shattered, and massive blossoms of flame erupted. The pad blazed, the buildings blazed, and the pathway blazed, which was very much like a bridge. It cracked and sparked where cables had been exposed. Were it to fall…

"Run! Run! Sasha, get these drones running!" He dropped his pistol and reached out for Eryn's hand. She dropper hers and grasped his hand. They shared a look.

"Drones, run! Run!" Sasha prodded at their backs. Run they did, but nothing like people. They took long strides and tottered. They looked like puppets being pulled along by strings. Every movement was stiff, but it sufficed.

As they charged forward, the gleaming pathway was marred by pockmarks, chunks of sparking light from internal wires set free, and fire, lots of fire. Parts of the path shattered and fell far below in a crumbling mess. Smoke stained the sky black, and as they ran, the world shook beneath their feet. Below was more paths, and somewhere so far down he couldn't see, the ground.

"This thing will fall out from under us!" Eryn leapt like a gazelle and pulled at Mordid's hand with angry tugs. Above, an Earth ship sailed past. Its engines droned, and there were things crawling on it. Not things!

A drone fell from the ship and smacked atop the pathway, shattering like a doll a few paces in front of Mordid.

Another fell, nearly landing atop him.

Morid cursed and turned his eyes to the sooty skies above.

The white tear-drop shaped craft above him had drones crawling all over it. They must have leapt upon the thing from one of the high-rises, Mordid thought. As the Earth ship continued on its way, mindless men fell from it like rain, while others pounded at the ship's impervious hull.

The world wobbled again.

"Go, go! Be sure to laugh at death!" Sasha darted across a crumbling section of the pathway.

Mordid and Eryn followed. Mordid glanced back and gasped as a huge section of the path broke and fell to one side, smashing into buildings and further breaking apart into a cloud of debris.

When his foot landed on the metal of the pad, Mordid let out a sigh of relief. The pad, thankfully, was still firmly rooted in place. He gazed at the utter destruction his ship had caused.

Men in Earth's uniform lay strewn about. Fires burned. He could see what looked like one of his men. Or at least, half of one of his men.

Not everyone was dead. Some of the gray-clad men of Earth were moving, moaning, and trying to crawl.

Eryn was on them in an instant. She shot one with her assault rifle. She leapt upon another and snapped his neck. Yet another she strangled with a screaming hiss.

Let her have her fun.

Sasha's pair of drones tottered along until one of their heads suddenly exploded.

The other drone turned, just as a huge man crashed into it. Man and machine-man tumbled to the metal ground.

"Thrask?" Mordid tilted his head.

The bloodied general looked up as the drone, who was not fighting back, lay beneath him. It blinked and looked nonplussed by the whole affair.

"Mordid? Mordid! I'm…" He snorted. "I'm actually glad to see you."

#

The Earth ship was white, gleaming, and beautiful to behold. It had better weapons, sensors, and engines than any ship in Rodriguez's fleet.

But it was smaller and already covered in long, black, scoring marks from the touch of his ship's deadly beamers.

The admiral watched through the view port as the giant knife-like prow of the *Merciless* crashed into the Earth ship.

White metal rippled and buckled. Explosions briefly flared in the void of space, and the elegant craft was bisected.

Golden-hued tracer rounds sped toward each half, beamers of angry red flashed against the broken hull, and missiles glowed bright and hateful before exploding against its hull.

The two pieces of the ship glowed brighter and brighter as they were consumed from within by flames. Then they were out of sight, each section sent spiraling into space or into the atmosphere of the planet.

His crew did not cheer. There was too much work to do.

"Sir, the *Star Wench* reports that—" the crewman looked at the view port.

A distant ship exploded. Rings of fire blazed from the core of the vessel before fading into darkness.

The crewman lowered his head. "The *Star Wench* reports that they will not be captured. Captain Silla gives her regards."

Rodriguez ground his teeth and crossed himself. The men did the same, and the Holy Father, standing at his side, whispered a prayer.

In his view, war was no place for women. But, if Captain Silla had wanted to play the role of a man, she had done so. Spectacularly.

There was to be no retreat. Rodriguez had driven his fleet into point-blank range with the ships of Earth. He had done so partially to mitigate their superior technology and partially to prevent his mercenary fleet from making a run for it. The ships under his command would have to fight, die, or give up.

A deep clunking sound echoed on the bridge, and the lights flickered. Something else had struck the *Merciless*. Somewhere along the massive ship's hull, a hole had been punched, and men were likely being sucked out into space. None of the crewmen spoke up. Whatever it was, the damage was not enough to prevent the ancient ship from doing its job.

The view port was filled with the colors of battle. Beamers sparkled, red opposed to blue, and gleaming tracer rounds filled the dark heavens. The white hulls of Earth ships mingled with the iron-gray of the Tyrant's fleet and with the other colorful vessels of the mercenaries now fighting side by side for their lives and freedom.

Normally, a battle in space was conducted at great ranges. Rodriguez had been in battles in which he couldn't even make out his foes with the naked eye. Not this time.

He gave the middle finger to a long white craft, imagining that the captain of said vessel could see him. They were close enough that he could even make out individual view ports. The enemy blazed away, and glowing rounds peppered the *Merciless*, which returned the favor. Anti-fighter weapons were being used against capital ships. Damn they were in the mix!

"*Bastardos!*"

"Ehem," the Holy Father said.

Rodriguez turned and bowed to the pontiff. "My apologies, your Eminence."

He strode toward Valdez. "How close are we?"

His First Officer loomed over a console and patted the crewman's shoulder who manned it. "Close." He glanced over at Rodriguez. "How close shall we make it, Admiral?"

He stroked his moustache and turned his gaze back to the view port. "Closer. I want to feel it."

Valdez licked his lips and whispered in the crewman's ear. The man thrust his jaw out, and his hands played over keys and dials.

The lights flickered once more. The view port's starboard side filled with the curvature of Khan 7.

The *Merciless* shook heavily. This subsided into a low and steady vibration.

"Now!" Rodriguez shot a glance Lupe's way. "Are we clear on the planet?"

Lupe nodded and said in Spanish, "Yes! We're close enough that we are free and clear and everything else is jammed."

Rodriguez pulled out his command communication device. He cleared his throat and fiddled with the dials.

"Mordid?"

A pop and crackle echoed back.

"Mordid, can you hear me?"

The Tyrant's voice answered back and was crisp and clear. "*Yes. I do hope you plan to rescue me. I am in need of it.*"

226

Rodriguez replied, "*Si, Hermano.*"

"*Excellent! Who…woah. I see you. You don't need to land the Merciless. It doesn't land. It's a space ship. SPACE!*"

"*Si,* I am coming with everyone and everything." Rodriguez looked over at the Holy Father who gave a stern nod in return.

#

Thrask stayed prone behind a hunk of twisted metal from the shuttle he crash landed. He raised his arms high and pulled the trigger of the Earth gun. The pilfered weapon had at first refused to fire, but after Herrin cut the trigger finger off the former owner and bandaged it to the trigger, all was well. The gun rattled, showering Thrask in hot shells. He ignored the pain and let the rounds fly. Quickly, he jerked his arms back.

Bullets sparked and banged against his choice of cover. Many more bullets were shot at him than he was able to fire back, but that didn't matter. Every barrage of theirs had to be answered or they'd get closer. As it was, they were buying time.

A cannon from Mordid's personal craft thundered, and another building was struck. Black smoke puffed out in a concentric ring, while shards of glass, metal, and what appeared to be people fell far below. Other structures nearby were dotted with gaping and smoking holes.

A rocket from the roof of a building hissed through the air, but before it struck Mordid's ship, it arched suddenly and vanished among a row of buildings. The ship was impressive with its defenses!

They were holding out on the elevated pad. However, Thrask knew they could not do so forever. A stray shot would find its mark. The Earth soldiers would get close enough to throw grenades or accurately strike with some other explosive ordinance. It was only a matter of time before the electronic defenses of Mordid's craft failed and a missile exploded above them. All of it was a matter of time. Mordid and Jenkins were aboard the ship, leaving precious few to hold the pad.

"We surrender!" Eryn cried out as she crawled on her belly toward Thrask.

Bullets answered her and roaring gunfire from multiple directions.

She smiled at him as she rolled close. "I don't think they'll fall for it a third time."

Thrask smirked. He had been surprised they got it to work a second. "Doubt it. If we are to get out of this, we need…" Thrask's eyes turned skyward. His eyes widened, and he could not suppress a toothy grin. He pointed.

Eryn glanced up. Sighing, she rolled onto her back like a cat and stared up at the sky. "We need that."

It was the *Merciless*. The giant triangular vessel was entering low, low orbit. Red light gleamed off its hull as it surfed the waves of the atmosphere. From its aft, a trail of pale smoke extended and…something else. Dozens upon dozens of gray dots. Then hundreds. Then what looked like thousands.

Thrask pulled forth his communication device. He turned it to the channel that was linked to every colonel, captain, and commander in the company.

The channel hissed. It sounded clear. Crystal clear.

"This is General Thrask. Sound off!"

The various colonels barked their names, one by one.

He sighed with relief. "I see you all. There's a landing pad in the city center. I want that secured and every high rise around it. Anyone with a gun who is not us, shoot. This place is crawling with mindless drones, Earth government soldiers, and civilians."

Colonel Samson's voice replied, "We'll be with you shortly, sir. The Navy is clearing the skies, and a squad of marines is being dispatched to your location."

Thrask snarled. "Marines? No. Rodriguez is a traitor. He's mak—"

Eryn tugged his sleeve and shook her head no.

Thrask jerked his arm away, but she continued to stare. A bullet snapped overhead and he cursed, huddling closer to the bit of metal cover he and the PR woman shared.

"Fine. Hurry. Thrask out." He switched the device off and looked at her. "I told you what happened."

Eryn nodded. "And clearly things have changed. Either he's dead and someone else is guiding the *Merciless* to our rescue, or Rodriguez has had a change of heart." She stressed the word heart and smiled at him.

Anger bubbled up within him. He could break her neck. Then and there and she could not stop him.

Another staccato of nearby gunfire and the sound of rounds striking the metal wreck banished the thought. Roaring, Thrask raised his arms and let fly with a flurry of bullets. The weapon soon clicked empty, and he tossed it over the barricade in defiance. Rolling to one side, he grabbed another gun, which also had someone's finger strapped to the trigger with tape. "Eryn. I have an army to lead. You need to do your job. Meaningless as it is."

She licked her lips. "You're right on the first part." She shimmied to one side and reached toward her waist. A small camera was produced. "Look suitably commanding. Your men are going to want to see this, and so will our clients."

"You want commanding?" He spit and risked rising to his knees. He opened his mouth and thrust the pilfered weapon out as if it were a spear. His bellow was almost as loud as the gunshots. Bullets whistled past him. One nearly hit him in the head, and he could feel flame against his temple. Sparks bounced as rounds smacked into his cover. He roared all the same and fired back.

Only when his weapon was empty and hurtled at the enemy did Thrask take cover again. He felt blood flowing down the side of his face, but he didn't care. "How was that?" he snarled.

Eryn's eyes were wide and dark. "Beautiful," she said with a flick of her tongue, like some snake.

She continued. "If they get close, very close, do you think you could kill some with your bare hands?"

"Count on it."

#

Jenkins remained lying in the rather comfortable chair, unable to be useful. Praise that he should have earned for ordering Nums to let loose with a barrage on every living foe the craft could reach was instead stolen by Nums.

Mordid had thanked Nums for it before Jenkins could explain that it was his idea. Mordid had then excitedly told them that the *Merciless* was cutting through the skies above and the sight was magnificent. Not that Jenkins could go outside to see it. He was too hurt to walk, and a battle was raging.

He shifted, and this caused pain throughout his torso. "Sir, I can help." He wasn't sure how, though.

Mordid was seated at a table with some bearded man wearing green and white. The newcomer was tapping at a holographic display and occasionally huffed. Mordid had his communication device close to his ear.

The Tyrant shot Jenkins a warning look, then continued speaking. "Take the whole planet. How many cities does it have?" He smirked. "Just this one? Easy then! We're taking it. Which means, *mi amigo*, we need to win up there. I will be along shortly, but for now, my orders are for you to smash the hell out of them. Tell Pedro he'll get his grand statement all right, and tell him I'll keep the relic safe. With my very life."

"What's going on?" Jenkins risked asking.

Mordid held up a hand. He listened intently before setting the device down. "To catch you up, Earth Government has sent some super-fleet here and cleaned house. When we popped in, they thought to capture me because I'm suddenly the bad guy. Very unfair if you ask me." He shrugged. "Sasha here worked for the Vladstock Corporation and planned to turn me over, but in turn he was betrayed by Earth, which plans on taking this whole system for itself and me along with it. They'll also nab the pope while they're at it."

The man called Sasha perked his head up. "The pope?"

The boss flashed a devilish smile. "I keep illustrious company, Sasha. You're lucky you're signing up with me. How are those drones looking?"

The bearded man with the Slavic accent nodded. "I have them converging on every Earth Government outpost and set them to ignore your men. They are going to be wiped out eventually."

"If that's the case," Mordid said, "See if you can get them to carry live grenades and totter toward the enemy at full speed. It will be like those children carting bombs on Paradisa, eh, Jenkins!"

Pastor Kestor's fanatics were the last thing he wanted to think about. Jenkins answered with a small nod and changed the subject.

"Sir, what now?"

Mordid grinned. "Now? We make sure the skies are clear, and then I'm going back to the *Merciless* to take command of the fleet."

"What about the admiral? He betrayed you! He planned to-" Jenkins bared his teeth and tried to swings his legs to the side. They barely moved. His hands moved to brace against the armrests.

Mordid seemed not to notice his pain and eagerly explained. "He slipped up. He can't kill me because I have a piece of the bomb that the pope needs. I underestimated him, but it's still me we're talking about here. Me. Mordid. Tyrant!"

"Bomb?" Sasha asked.

"We're going to blow up your sun," Mordid replied in an offhanded manner.

"Oh. Ah, well. It wasn't like I was overly attached to it." Sasha went back to trying to direct his army of corporate drones.

"Won't he kill you the second you set foot on the *Merciless*?" Jenkins tried once again to rise. "Sir, if you're going back there, I have to be with you. To guard you."

"You might be able to crawl very slowly, Jenkins. If I had more time I would let you slowly, slowly crawl ahead of me on my way to the bridge." Mordid spread his hands out wide. "I don't have the time though. Nor am I powerless, so don't you worry. Pedro and I have a deal worked out. Now, he's willing to deeply bend the rules, but I know he won't betray me. I have the utmost faith in it. In fact, I'm entirely counting on faith from this point on."

Jenkins paled. "Sir?"

Mordid winked. "God is with me. This time. This one and only time."

13

KHAN SYSTEM -THE MERCILESS-

A pair of armored marines followed Mordid as he marched his way to the bridge. He had made sure his beard was in perfect shape, that his coat flourished with every step, and that his boots shined.

The ship shuddered and the lights dimmed, but Mordid did not hurry his pace. He needed to exude calm, total control. Soldiers who darted by were favored with a smile, busy technicians were given thumbs up, and when one of Eryn's hags put a camera in his face, he gave a quick speech. It didn't matter that it was one of his usual speeches that just swapped out a few names to be relevant. It worked. Focus groups had said so.

He entered the elevator, and when his marines piled in, he pressed a button.

When the doors opened, Mordid strode into the chaotic but manageable mess that was Rodriguez's bridge. Crewmen chattered. Officers peered into monitors. Dials were repeatedly turned and levers flipped, while many a button was pushed.

The view port revealed a space battle of suitably epic proportions. White Earth Government ships were dueling with both his ships and those of several other mercenary companies lured into the fray by Rodriguez.

The duplicitous admiral stood by Pedro Chavez. Both were too busy to notice his entrance. He had not announced his arrival to Rodriguez, and he had ordered everyone on the *Merciless* to keep quiet about it. One thing Mordid had that Rodriguez didn't was intimate communications with all manner of people aboard the *Merciless*. He had in his personal graces lowly deckhands, stalwart marines, soldiers, officers, and even bridge-crew members. Most were bought, though some he had personally assisted in the past and had more than just their monetary loyalty.

"*Amigo!*" Mordid flourished his coat by sweeping back its tails. "Are we winning?"

Rodriguez spun on a heel. His face turned scarlet for a moment, and then he strode towards Mordid, extending a bejeweled hand. "Fierce fighting, *hermano*."

The pope approached and dipped his head in a form of greeting. "God will not let us falter."

"I agree," Mordid said. "Ah!" He licked his lips and stuck his hand in his coat. He drew forth a silver cylinder and pressed it into the pope's hands. "For you. I told you I would bring it, and you met your end of the bargain. You were true to your word. You kept it, and I deeply, deeply appreciate that."

Mordid looked past them at the view port. "Rodriguez, we're fighting awfully close. The *Merciless* can punish at a range, you know."

"*Si*. They need to have the guns of our ships rammed down their throats. Sometimes they need to be just rammed!" Rodriguez's hand lowered to his side, drifting close to the butt of his pistol. "Where are Eryn, Mauss, and Thrask?"

Mordid paid the subtle hint of violence no mind. "Them? Oh, surviving. Have you identified a command ship? Who is our counterpart?"

Distracted, the admiral pointed. "You can see here. That long white ship with towers jutting from it. They swarm about her like bees and sting any who draw too near."

"Ram her. I want her boarded."

Rodriguez paled. "Wh-what? I do not think you understand how this all works. When I say we need to ram ships,

I am selective. That is a big girl you're wanting to hit. Are you sure?"

"Oh, yes." His eyes found Pedro's. "God is with us this time, right?"

The pope scowled, but he nodded his assent.

"Rodriguez, I'm feeling the divine spirit take and fill me. Ram them. Order every ship in the fleet to converge on her. Order every assault craft to board and take her. That ship is mine, and I'm going to do something very holy with it." Mordid swept past them and planted his hands on his hips.

"Mordid, you are talking crazy." Rodriguez followed after him. "As your admiral, I must insist that you reconsider."

"Are you my admiral? I don't think my admiral would try to murder my chief diplomat and my general. I don't think my admiral would order my favorite bodyguard shot. I don't think my admiral would try to leave me for dead." Mordid looked over his shoulder at the man. He could see him flushing and his hand resting firmly on the pistol tucked in a belt holster.

"My admiral," Mordid continued, "would not do such things. He'd at least be very, very apologetic about it. He would also go about making amends by following the orders of his employer. Of the Traveling Tyrant. The one and only." Mordid looked at the view port and smiled.

He was not worried. He had faith. God, this one and only time, would deliver. Not that Mordid prayed for it. God was a mercenary, in his opinion. One who backed the winning horse. Once you were picked, you won the race, and that was that.

Pedro Chavez cleared his throat. "I think you should listen to him. In fact, I insist that you do."

What did it matter that God probably was picking Pedro that day? Mordid smiled as he merrily hitched his wagon to the pope. He smiled wider when he heard Rodriguez huff and carry out his orders.

#

He had one more shot at being the Tyrant. Literally. Just draw the gun and shoot him, Rodriguez thought.

But the Holy Father himself was glaring. He had spoken.

God himself might as well have come down and commanded Rodriguez. He nodded at Lupe, and the communications man set to work relaying the fleet's orders.

"Full power to the engines. Most of the army is on Khan 7, but we have plenty of marines. Valdez!" Rodriguez barked.

"Sir!" His first officer straightened.

"I want you personally leading the assault. The Tyrant wants that ship. So he gets that ship." He pointed at the craft that was rapidly increasing in size. Lights danced about its white hull as thousands of fighters challenged thousands of others.

Valdez saluted and exited the bridge, jogging as he entered the elevator.

Ahead, moments later, Rodriguez saw gray capital ships converging on the Earth command vessel. A bulky ship painted in the red color schemes of another mercenary outfit moved ahead. Its frontal guns were blazing away continuously as blue enemy beamers sliced across its hull. The red ship exploded, yet even as it died, even as it was immersed in flames, it kept firing. The dead vessel was replaced by another capital ship and then another, and then a dozen more iron gray vessels crept into view. All of them were heading for one target.

The *Merciless* shook hard.

"We're breaching their escorts. We're taking a lot of fire, Admiral!" an officer shouted from his console.

Mordid placed his hands behind his back and stood rigid. He gazed silently at the view port.

Monitors lit up with damage reports. The bridge crew was speaking into communication devices, pounding at keyboards, and working the controls, levers, and buttons that directed the massive vessel onwards.

Minutes passed, and with each one the *Merciless* rocked. A bank of lights dimmed and switched off. The already dimly lit ship was cast into further darkness, illuminated only by emergency lights, monitors, and a few devotional candles, like those piled about the shrine for the murdered boxing champion.

When another tremor rumbled through the ship, the giant, wooden crucifix nearly tumbled from its wall mount. The cross cocked to one side.

Before Rodriguez could say a word, Mordid sprang into action. He leapt toward it, and his hands braced against the crucifix's wooden base. With a grunt, he shoved it back into place.

He gave a glance over his shoulder as he braced himself, looking not at Rodriguez, but at the Holy Father.

The two men nodded.

Bastard! You ruthless, lying bastard, Rodriguez thought. Mordid was putting on a show. A show for the pope and a show for his men, and worst of all, it was working.

Some of the men cheered. A few clapped. The Holy Father even let a smile slip.

Of course they were all falling for it. Mordid was back. He was not dead, and therefore all of Rodriguez's promises were empty.

Mordid lived, and so long as he did, they loved him. Were he to die, though? Why had the Holy Father forbidden it?!

Inwardly snarling, Rodriguez came to Mordid's aid. He leaned against the cross and assisted his employer in making sure the wooden symbol was firmly in place.

He whispered, "What are you doing?"

Mordid whispered back, "I'm being a Tyrant. I'm being the leader these men need. I'm being loyal to our client. Besides, there's absolutely no way you could replace me. I know something you do not."

With a grunt, they secured the cross and stood back. As battle was waged in space, they each turned their eyes to the symbol of faith.

"Oh?" Rodriguez drawled.

"Remember how you became my admiral in the first place? You came to my aid when Hurth had to go. I have dozens of captains waiting to turn on you. I have marines who are prepared to shoot you. I have crewmen who will rig your toilet to suck your ass out into space. And here on this bridge?" Mordid flashed a wide smile. "I have men who will clap and hug you the day you call yourself Tyrant. And later, maybe that very same day, maybe months later when one of them shoots you in the back, you'll be absolutely surprised who it was that did it."

"You're lying," Rodriguez snapped, though he could not help but turn his gaze upon his crew. They had to be loyal. All of them believed in a cause, all of them were of the same blood and heritage. Who would dare turn against that?

"I saved one man's mother from poverty," Mordid said, as if reading his thoughts. "Another, I paid for his little brother's surgery that he couldn't afford. Another, I gave him a little bonus in honor of the birth of his baby daughter back on Reconquista, with a rider attached that every year I live, she gets a nice birthday present." Mordid smiled. "I bought their families. The day you became admiral, I bought them. I know where their loyalty truly lies. You never will."

"You monster," Rodriguez said.

Mordid ignored him. "Never plot against me again. Or Eryn. Well, unless she tries to kill you. But not before."

Rodriguez took a few paces back. He wiped a cold sweat that had unexpectedly formed on his brow.

The two stared at one another.

"Oh dear," the Holy Father said.

Rodriguez looked away from his employer at the view port. The Earth ship was a magnificent vessel—long, white, and narrow, with gleaming white control towers jutting up from its surface. It was akin to the seaborne aircraft carriers of old. It had a gray ship of the mercenary fleet skating dangerously close to its hull. Fighters swarmed about it, and assault craft were attaching to the white ship like black ticks.

Mordid raised a hand. "Lupe, I want to be on every channel. Make it happen."

He knew his name?! Rodriguez glared at the communications officer. Was he one of the men in Mordid's pocket?

The lights went out. Gravity wobbled, and Rodriguez reached out, grasping the crucifix for support.

Mordid floated up, slowly. His coat billowed, and he waved his hands to quiet the men. He looked like some conjurer performing a levitating trick.

Lupe nodded and whispered, "You are on, boss."

Boss?! Rodriguez gripped the cross so tightly he felt his

nails dig into the venerable wood.

"Earth Government ships. I am Mordid, the Traveling Tyrant. You have violated the Corporate Charter and attacked my person, property, and most of all, my beloved men and women. I have every right to defend myself, and in doing so I have every right to kill you to the last man. Khan 7 is mine. The Khan system is mine. The pope is my honored guest. Your fleet burns, and your army is shattered. I have your command craft. I am not bloodthirsty, I am not a murderer, I am not a killer. Unless you want me to be. I am a mercenary. This is not personal. Not yet. You have this one and only minute to surrender. Every ship is to power down. Every fighter to return to their bays and every soldier to lay down his arms and put up his hands." He lowered his arms. "Agree, and you will all be returned to Earth Space in comfort and safety. Defy me, and there will be no respite. You have this one chance. All of you surrender, or all of you perish. To my legions, to my vast fleets, to the endless reinforcements who will enter this system, for one minute cease fire. After that? The *Merciless* will crash into the Earth flagship. I am Mordid the Traveling Tyrant, I have already won."

Mordid pointed at Lupe and whispered, "Cut it."

The man nodded. The lights partially returned and gravity as well.

Rodriguez shook his head. "Will it work?" He looked up at the view port. The gleaming beams, the shining tracer rounds, the glowing ember of missile exhaust was nowhere to be seen.

"Order everyone to stop jamming. Give them this one minute to make up their minds. Keep on course for a collision."

The crew obeyed, and Rodriguez watched. His plans were foiled, and the Tyrant was rubbing it in by stealing his glory. He glared at him, but Mordid's eyes were fixed on the Earth command vessel. It grew larger and larger in the view port.

"*Tyrant*," a woman's stern voice came from the speakers above. "*I formally surrender my person and my ship. Allow the rest of my fleet and men to depart in peace.*"

A woman! They had been fighting one of the most epic battles in recent history with a woman? Rodriguez muttered and cursed. "The world is turning upside down."

Nodding to Lupe, Mordid cleared his throat. "They are to power down. I will let them leave later. All in all, I accept. Prepare to be boarded. I expect your sword delivered to my admiral with all due proper ceremony in the presence of the Holy Father."

"*I do not have a swo—*"

Mordid made a slicing gesture across his own neck and the hiss of static ended. The communications were cut.

"We won?" Rodriguez frowned. He couldn't believe it. Mordid had *talked* his way to victory.

"That we did, *mi amigo.*" He pointed at him, and his smile was wide. "I know how these people work. They aren't mercenaries who are fighting for pay, and they aren't corporations who are weighing risk and reward. Earth Government is guided by its idealism. Deep down they think we think like them. They truly believe our rotten nature is just a matter of ignorance and a lack of understanding. They think that when we are presented with a crisis that we will act as they would act. I gave them the exact same offer they would have given us, had they taken us by the throat. A chance at mercy and they took it. Were they mercenaries I would have offered pay, were they a company, I would mention their bottom line. With these people it's all about feelings."

Rodriguez blinked, astonished.

"Well," the Tyrant confessed. "I may have been a bit draconian with giving them just a minute before annihilation, but I'm an ignorant barbarian from the Upper Arm. They have to cut me some slack." He raised a finger. "Ah, let's not ram them. Full stop."

The Earth vessel we quite close, enough to make out individual panels, damage, and blue insignia on its white hull.

The man was, on occasions, amazing. "I see." Rodriguez nodded. "I see." He felt some of his anger cool. "Now what?"

"Now?" Mordid pointed at the ship. "I want you to put on a show. Full dress uniform, mariachis, crosses, candles, and the Holy Father! I'm going to have a painting of that woman kneeling and offering you her sword."

"She doesn't have one." Rodriguez shrugged. "We'll bring her one to give to me. You are allowing me to accept this? You are allowing me to be master of this ceremony? Does not my gracious Tyrant want to be the centerpiece of the drama?"

Mordid stepped close. "I forgive you for your naughty actions. I'm offering you this token of my esteem to win back your loyalty. I threatened you, now I reward you. Will you take it?"

"You're playing me." Rodriguez crossed his arms. "You're playing me like you did that woman. You're playing me like you—"

Mordid cut him off. "Like I play everyone. Yes. I'm the Traveling Tyrant. That's why this all works. All of you need to be motivated. I can do that in many ways. Now do you wish to be guided by fear or by my false promises and winning smile?" Mordid extended his hand.

Rodriguez looked at the proffered hand. He was beaten. Beaten just as much as the Earth fleet was. However, in defeat he would taste glory. He grasped Mordid's hand. They both squeezed, and as was fitting, Rodriguez relented first.

#

The infirmary was filled with moans and groans, but Jenkins was thankful that at least he was given his own bay with a privacy curtain.

The doctors had come to see him, declared him wounded but not likely to die, and that was that. The Gut Shot would remain latched to him, smelling like baked bread, until such a time they could remove it. There were far worse cases than him. The battle for the Khan system had been brutal if brief.

The curtain parted, and Karlson stepped in. He had a black brace around one leg, and he was stripped to the waist with a primitive bandage wrapped around his shoulder.

"Nothing but the best care for you, eh?" Jenkins leaned up from his cot, then winced.

"You should see the other guys. We're stretched thin on medical supplies." He grabbed a nearby stool and dragged it close to Jenkins's cot. He sat heavily in it.

"So?" Jenkins asked.

Karlson's wrinkled face tightened up. "I don't know

240

everything. You want the basics or everything, including rumors."

"Everything," Jenkins said at once. "I'll sort out truth from lie later."

"Well," Karlson sighed. "We won. Clearly. That's why you're there and I'm here. We took it hard, though. Several capital ships are just…gone."

"Damn," Jenkins whispered.

"*Star Wench* was about to be boarded, and they chose to detonate their Racer Rabbit. *Impending* fell to pieces, and parts of her are still raining down on Khan 7. *Ruthless* rammed an Earth ship, and both of them were locked together. Neither side heard the call to surrender, and they damned near wiped one another out. In hand to hand."

Jenkins rubbed his face. "Morale?"

"Confused," Karlson said with a shrug. "The boss says we're going to get serious bonuses for this, but that we might be in for a fight that we can't sit out. Rumor is Earth Government has invaded Corporate Space. I'm not sure how true that is, but we just tangled with them far from their border. I've heard all sorts of crazy things like the Charter is revoked and that the Upper Arm is to be conquered. Some are saying the war is upon us. The. Like, the big one."

"Like hell!"

"You asked for it all."

Jenkins nodded. "I did." He let out a breath. "Please tell me Herrin bought it on Khan 7. That he died fighting, bravely, with a knife in hand."

"Herrin died on Khan 7, sir." Karlson blinked slowly, like some placid turtle.

"So," Jenkins let out another sigh. "Where is he really?"

"Alive and well. He fought like the devil himself to keep that landing pad clear. It got messy. I saw him use that knife on a dozen Earth soldiers. I saw Thrask break a man's back on his knee. I saw Eryn as she pulled out someone's eyes. You know you can do that? Pull a man's eyes out?" He tried to gesture what the motion looked like.

"Herrin," Jenkins prodded.

"General Thrask asked that he be moved to a special

squad. A bodyguard squad. One that will stick close to him and keep him safe. The boss seemed fine with the idea." Karlson looked pointedly at Jenkins. "He's Commander Herrin now. The last I saw him he said that he would kill you. He wasn't subtle in the least. You know how some men are? They say something with two meanings and—"

"Yes, yes. I get it, Karlson. So, while I lay comatose, he gets the hero treatment. What about that bastard who shot me?"

Karlson shrugged. "He visited you while you were asleep."

"What?!"

"Calm down, I was there the whole time cleaning my shotgun. He apologized to you and said something about lighting candles. Then he left." Karlson cleared his throat. "Leave him be."

Jenkins coughed. "Leave him be? He shot me!"

"Yeah, but I don't think it was anything personal. Also, son, if you get into a squabble with him, then that means you're in a squabble with the admiral. You want Thrask and Rodriguez pondering how best to be rid of you? Herrin you're going to have to deal with, but the other guy? Valdez? Leave him be."

"You're a forgiving sort, Karlson." Jenkins forestalled him with a wave of a hand. "I'll focus on Herrin. Fine. So, we won, Herrin got promoted, my would-be assassin is going to light a candle for me, and Earth Government is possibly conquering every colony it can get its hands on."

"About sums it up."

"So, what now?"

Karlson scratched his jaw, where graying stubble was growing in unsightly patches. "Not sure. We're delivering the pope to Earth Space, but I don't know the details."

Jenkins scooted up higher in his cot. He bit his lower lip and looked at the floor. "Well, we need to find out. We need to be by Mordid's side."

"We need rest."

Jenkins snorted. "Karlson, we're wasting opportunity here. I'm no good to anyone lying in bed."

"Well, you're going to stay in bed until you can properly do your job." Karlson stood up. "I paid some guys to keep an eye on you when I can't be around. But as for any schemes, forget it.

We're done for now, sir. You need to rest up. So do I. Remember, you need to get me that date."

The old soldier gave a half-hearted salute and left without another word.

Jenkins watched the privacy sheet sway in his wake, and he slapped the surface of the cot. There was nothing to do, though. No way to act. No way to improve his lot in life.

Well, perhaps one way. He could think. He had nothing better to do. With an audible sigh, Jenkins put his hands behind his head and took in the scent of warm bread. He thought about the past few weeks and thought about the weeks to come. The future was never all that clear to him. He went by the adage that opportunity would present itself. It always had in the past. This time, he had earned shrapnel, bullet, and knife wounds in the search for opportunity.

"Risk," he mused aloud. "And reward."

#

Thrask sat comfortably in his seat in the Big Room. The command staff and their honored guest were gathered around the table, along with some bearded newcomer from the planet. Mordid sipped on a glass of wine that he not so discreetly checked and re-checked for poison.

Things were confusing. It was easy when his only goal was to kill Mordid and take his place. Now that he found out his heart was still linked to that of the Tyrant and not Eryn, it meant things had changed. Mordid had to live and she, at some point, had to die.

There was more, though. When the short man had come striding out of the smoke and ruin of the city, Thrask had been genuinely overjoyed to see him. Things were getting desperate and out of hand, and Mordid did what he did best.

He could take complete chaos, something that was spiraling out of control, and somehow steer it. Mordid would smile, threaten, lie, and bribe, and in so doing he could lasso the comet of fate and make it twist and turn.

He hated him.

He envied him.

He respected him.

He missed just hating him. The conflicting thoughts had to be put away, though. War was at hand, and while he might not fully understand politics, or how battles in space worked, he understood war as a whole. Something big was happening in the galaxy.

Mordid looked at the bomb displayed on the table. "Well, we'll jettison this into the sun after we enjoy our wine. Cigarettes?" Mordid reached into his pocket and produced a pack marked with the Vladstock company seal.

Mordid gave a polite nod of thanks to the former Corpy, who in turn nodded back.

Thrask reached out and grabbed one. He pulled the stick free and jumped when Mauss's hand was suddenly by his face. A lighter flickered and an orange flame grew.

He puffed, drawing in the nicotine, and gave a nod to the skeletal man. The tobacco was of a fine quality, meaning it came from Earth originally. The damn planet outlawed such products in Earth Space but even Earth had its black markets. The whole fleet had been lacking the good stuff for quite some time, resorting to low-grade, material. Thrask in truth did not smoke all that often, but he encouraged his men to. It relived stress. It raised morale. He even purchased vast quantities for his soldiers when able. It cost less in the end to have his older gun-bunnies hack out their lungs and die of cancer than it did to keep them around for too long. If bullets didn't end one's pension plan, the cancerous sticks did the trick.

Mauss drifted around the table and lit Mordid's cigarette and then Rodriguez's as he took one for himself. Eryn and the pope waved aside the offer, while Sasha was content to not partake of his own gift.

Pale clouds of smoke hovered in the air. Wine was sipped, and a quiet reigned.

"Let's get to it. What next?" Thrask said and tapped the cigarette so ash fell to the floor. Someone else would clean it up.

Mordid waved his hand around, and pale smoke followed in lazy lines. "A fine question. I plan to take the pope to Earth."

"Earth Space, you mean," Mauss said with an arch of his

thin brow.

"Nope. Earth. We can make it." Mordid sipped his wine with one hand and puffed on his cigarette with the other. "We've shattered their operations here, and so we'll blaze a path to Earth itself. If they really are reaching out their overly-clean and washed hands, I bet the door to Earth is open. They won't expect it."

Rodriguez drew on his cigarette and exhaled a great cloud of white. "That is very daring. Earth will have defenses. The enemy has wrecked us. We are in no condition for a fight and wont be until we have time to refit. We are in absolutely no condition to threaten the mother planet."

"They don't know that," Mordid replied. "We are going to Earth. Well, close to Earth. We'll be placing our great guest aboard their captured command ship and return it and him to the mother planet from a suitably safe distance. It will be a demonstration and nothing more."

The pope nodded. "I take it I will be the one to escort the prisoners home, then?"

"You wanted to arrive on Earth not as a puppet, but as a force to be reckoned with and to make a statement. Well, you will be able to." Mordid licked his lips. "Now, I'm going to be a bit uncharacteristic here. Yet, I'm feeling swayed by a bout of conscience."

Thrask laughed. Actually, everyone but the pope laughed.

Mordid ignored them. "I don't think it will be safe for you at this point. Consider this. One, you're going to essentially wipe out the Khan system. That means there is no southern approach from Earth Space into Corporate Space. That alone will make enemies. And, if you know your celestial maps, you do know you'll be cutting off the King system. You'll be dismantling every Corporate World operation there. In essence, you're getting rid of two systems. It will be decades, if not half a century, before safe routes to King can be plotted."

"Everyone will have months to evacuate," the pope said. "The Khan and King systems' inhabitants will be spared, so long as they leave. If I know my maps," the pope said, "the Khan system was dedicated to raiding a dead alien empire. It was a place of carnage. A place of sin. And the King system was but an armed outpost where corporations and mercenaries rearmed before going back into the pointless fight. Sodom and Gomorra."

Mordid tapped his cigarette. "So, you don't care if you make the mega-rich and mega-powerful angry. Fine. Let's talk about Earth Government. I can bring you to Earth, but they're going to arrest you. They'll say you're some sort of criminal. They'll make an example out of you. Their offer was never serious to begin with. At best? You'll be a kept "guest" for all time. I should know, I sent my mentor to Earth and as far as I know, he's in total comfort and captivity."

"True. I will be in their hands. The whole of mankind will know it. They will imprison me, kill me, or honor their agreement and allow me to rebuild an independent Catholic Church in the Eternal City." The old man raised a finger. "If they do the first," he raised another finger, "or second, I become a martyr. I will suffer or die for a cause I believe in and that suffering or death will have an impact. History is full of those who suffered and died for a reason. Good ones at that." He raised a third finger. "If the third occurs, then the blind people of Earth and its wayward citizens will once again be given a taste of faith. Not the government filtered variety, but true faith. I will cry out against Earth's many sins. Something I have done quite freely everywhere else. The flock there has, for too long, not heard condemnation."

Chavez then added, "And I sense war. Earth's influence is about to spread unless..." he shrugged.

Thrask snorted. It was to be expected that a man of the cloth would throw his fortune and life away for some foolhardy belief. He shook his head. "It's your life. Mordid, if he wants to pay us a ridiculous sum of money and then to go and die, that's his choice. Let him." The old man was a fool, but a fool with money, so he would be entertained.

"He's right," Mordid chided the holy man. "You're heading into danger."

"My choice remains the same."

"All right," Mordid said, "don't say I didn't warn you." He drew on the cigarette and blew a few rings of smoke. "Now then, back to the more important matter. Me."

"I know what you are going to do," the pope said.

Thrask crossed his arms and flicked another shower of ash onto the floor. "Oh yeah? What's he going to do?"

"Yes, now that you're committed to dying for a cause, I'm sure the big guy has blessed you with foresight and vision. What are my plans?" Mordid set his wine glass down. "Steal my thunder, I dare you."

"You," the pope began, "will make your grand entry into the Solar system and make a declaration. It will have to be brief. Your fleet is in no condition to fight, yet in your pocket you have every means to fight another day."

Mordid touched his coat. No doubt he was feeling for the cube that held untold sums of money.

"You will return to the Upper Arm," the pope said, "and you will assemble everyone and anyone who will listen. You will tell them of a great threat from a corrupt government. You will tell them—"

Mordid coughed. "Enough! I will reveal my plans later."

Thrask blanched. "What? You have to be kidding. Tell me he's crazy. Tell me this old man is just posturing and you're posturing back. Tell me, Mordid, that nothing he said is true."

"We have to fight," Mauss said. He settled deeply into his chair. "We have no choice. The fight is coming to us and soon. What we saw in the Khan system is not an isolated incident. I don't know how far Earth will reach, but I have a sense. I'm worried."

Mauss was always worried, but the way he said it made Thrask shift in his chair.

"All this talk of faith has made you people stupid!" Thrask flung the half-smoked cigarette into the air. It landed on the table near the bomb they had all grown accustomed to.

"Think it through, silly," Eryn said while smiling.

Thrask glared at her, then at the pontiff. "You're not thinking like mercenaries. We promised to deliver him to Earth Space. So, we do that. The moment we enter one of their systems, off he goes. Then we head back to the Upper Arm to recruit and repair. Then, as always, we look for a new contract. This isn't hard."

Mordid had a glum expression on his face.

"What?" Thrask snarled. "You all look like corpses."

"If Earth is moving in," Mauss began.

"If Earth is coming for the Corporate Worlds," Rodriguez added.

"Then what will happen to the Upper Arm?" Mordid asked.

Thrask blinked. Impossible. The Upper Arm was far, far, far from Earth, and it was free. It was a place of no law, not even pretend law. It was the "eat or be eaten" part of the galaxy. It was home.

"Earth is coming," the old man in the robes said slowly while meeting everyone's gaze one by one. "I have ears everywhere. I have eyes everywhere. Earth has become far stronger than you remember her, and she will sweep everyone into her unifying embrace. And those who squirm she will crush, but she will be very apologetic as she does so. There will be one government, one religion, one people, and one way of doing things. Left alone, like an octopus, she will slither in and strangle every system that she touches. She will weep for every death she causes, and yet she will kill you all. You do not fit in her vision of what is right. All of you and your way of life and my faith do not fit with her vision." He reached for the pack of cigarettes and drew forth a white stick. He eyed it before smashing it on the table's surface. "I will go to Earth and resist her there. I will die a martyr or live and accomplish my mission. I cannot stop her alone, though."

Rodriguez crossed himself. "We are with you!"

"Like hell we are," Thrask snapped. "What does any of this have to do with us?" He didn't like where all this was going. Earth was coming? She was like an octopus?

"It has everything to do with us," Mordid said. "And Pedro here has tied us together. He's paid us great sums of money to fight a war." Mordid stared at him. "He's hired us to fight Earth. He planned it so, well in advance."

The pope nodded.

Thrask stood up. "This has been all a trick? A lie?" War he knew, but war with Earth? The friendly, waving, smiling, murderous despots that drowned everyone in laws and taxes and didn't have the decency to let people kill one another for money?

The foe that was, were it able to marshal its forces, unstoppable?

"No trick," the pope said. "I really did need you to take me to Earth in a way that would guarantee attention. I really did need you to help me end the conflict in the Khan system. It was for that you were paid. The rest?"

"The rest we are being forced into." Mordid shrugged. "Which, by the way, I was aware of. So, you all can calm down. I have plans, too." He took a deep draw on his cigarette. After he took time to puff out a few clouds of smoke to join the haze above them, he continued. "Earth is going to paint me as more of a villain than I already am. I could take my billions and billions and billions of billions and hide. Where though?"

"Where indeed," the pope murmured.

Mordid stood. "Everyone, I am going to give you riches. After we drop off Pedro here, you can stick with me, or you can leave. I'll hold no grudges. From this point on, we're going to be engaged in the mother of all contracts whose risks are so great that they exceed your employment contracts. The Upper Arm lives free or dies. If you stick with me, that's your fate, too."

Thrask narrowed his eyes at Mordid. "Well, I supposed I have to come along?" He straightened. "Unless, you plan to…" he trailed off. He felt a twinge of elation. Had Mordid lost himself to the old man's fantasy and thus faith? Was Mordid going to show kindness to them all and think they would rally around him as true brothers and sisters in arms? Would he take the pulmonary collar off?

"Not a chance!" Mordid smiled.

Bastard. He was still a rotten, sneaking bastard. If there was a God, that meant there was a hell, and Mordid would burn in it for all eternity.

"Thrask, I'm going to need a general. So, everyone is free to take their riches except you. You stay." Mordid turned his eyes to another. "And you, Rodriguez."

"Me?" The admiral put a hand to his chest and pursed his lips.

"Yes, I am very sorry," Mordid replied with a mock sigh. "Pedro is going to command you, as if he were God's elected representative on Earth to stay with me and fight the good fight."

The pope cleared his throat and then gave Rodriguez a long and apologetic look.

"I see." The admiral brought the cigarette to his lips and took a deep, deep draw.

"Eryn," Mordid began.

"Oh, I'll stay!" She gave a cat-like stretch. "I'm actually not here for the money. So, you may put aside whatever scheme you had planned to keep me here."

"Figures," Thrask muttered. He then looked at Mauss, huddled deep in his chair. "And what do you have over him, Mordid?"

"Nothing," Mauss interrupted. "However, our shadowy investors, who will be taking a piece of the aforementioned billions of billions of billions, will likely be interested in Earth's machinations being thwarted." His hands came together, and his bony fingers formed a steeple. "And I have no other home than this company. I will die doing my job. I made my peace with that when you all were children."

"You are," the pope said, "freedom fighters now. Paid ones, but freedom fighters all the same. You will defend the freedoms of a most wicked galaxy because this wicked galaxy can be saved, but not if it lies under the thrall of Earth." The man gave them all, except Rodriguez, a piercing stare. "I have watched you all closely. I hope you are successful in what you must do. But I must also say. Clearly. Loudly. Let there be no mistake! Your souls are likely damned. The good works you will do cannot make up for the vile deeds you commit daily." He smiled then. "That said, I pray you are successful in the trials to come."

The bearded Sasha, who had thus far kept quiet, laughed. "God has hired the Devil!"

14

EARTH -NEW DELHI-

The life of a bill in the bureaucratic halls of Earth Government was a treacherous and uncertain one. For a bill even to exist, it had first to be born.

To birth a bill, a percentage of the population had to petition for it, or a subcommittee of the General Council had to draft it. At its very first waking moment, the bill could be extinguished with ease. If a primary committee of duly elected officials could not agree by majority to preserve it, then it was returned whence it came, and for decades it could languish before getting another chance at life. More often than not, the bill was scrapped and remained in the realm of the dead.

However, were a bill to be born and survive its first trial at the hands of the primary committee, then it had to be passed along to the appropriate technical committee. While the primary and subcommittees were made up of elected members, the technical committees contained the brightest technocrats, chosen and appointed to serve by the lower committees. They were free from the burdens of winning an election term after term. Here, most bills were sent hurtling back, never to be seen again. The technocrats were cautious experts and not the type to allow any poorly drafted legislation to slip past their watchful gazes.

Were a bill to make it past them, then it was like a baby bird taking flight. It needed to flap its wings and succeeed or plummet to the ground. The near-top of the General Council was made up of leaders who were, like their lesser bretheren in the sub and primary committees, elected. However, unlike their lesser brethren, the leaders of the General Council had long terms of office. Yes, they needed to campaign and be voted in, but once the people had chosen them, it was best to leave these titantic personalities with the time they needed to work without the bother of campaigning. Government was about governing, after all, not being elected. Twenty-year terms sufficed. When they killed a bill, it would likely never return in their lifetimes.

If a bill still yet lived, then it was a penstroke away from becoming law.

At the top of the General Council were experts in the field of politics, society, and science appointed by majority agreement from the leadership of said council. There was no set number of such experts, though two to ten was not unusual. They served their entire lives, free from political concerns and thus free to be the wise minds behind Earth Government. Were they to approve a bill, then it would be law.

Laws had once been made in a great abundance within the gleaming white halls of New Delhi, but for many years that had not been the case. There were hundreds of other and more effective means of enacting legislation than having the General Council approve a law. The subcommittes had the ability to issue ordinances, while the primary committes could decree a much wider range of various codes of law. The technocrats could put forth restrictions in the name of safety without lengthy process, and the leadership of the General Council could adopt policy protocols. The experts who guided them had near dictatorial power should they need it. When in doubt, an emergency provision was much quicker than passing a law.

Laws were just plain old rare these days. Even if one were to pass, the Earth Government courts had plenty of means to reduce, limit or, if need be, kill a law.

"Laws are already set. What we need are codes, ordinances, and restrictions!" the saying went among the people of Earth.

Especially the bright people of Earth who knew what was best.

Thus, it was quite a bit of news when the bill passed and became law. Not only did the bill pass, it passed through the hands of every committee and every technocrat all the way to the top without hardly a pause for breath. No law had been officially created in some time. Now, not only had the bill passed, it had been passed in record time. Unity, cooperation, and agreement had been found quite easily on the matter.

Earth was facing a crisis the likes of which it had never before seen. The solar system had been breached. A terrorist of epic porportions had embarrassed the military and made bold, barbaric statements. Like Attila the Hun, he had paraded about before leaving. In the days of ancient Rome, it had been the pope who had convinced the barabrian warlord to spare the city. This time, it was the pope again who had disuaded Mordid, the Traveling Tyrant, from attacking the mother planet. So the rumors went. There were other rumors as well.

The people said that the Tyrant had burned to cinders yet another planet. Some said a whole system! Everyone knew he was behind the destruction of Paradisa, a garden world that he torched because he hated its beauty. What was one more act of galactic terrorism to the Tyrant? Most everyone agreed he was the largest threat to mankind in a long while, not since the mysterious alien from centuries ago, had Earth faced such dangers.

The people said the pope had tried to reason with the Tyrant and failed. Yet others said the two were thick as thieves. It was little wonder, so most thought, that the pope from Reconquista was being kept isolated for medical observation, while the Earth-born pope would remain in charge till such a time it was deemed safe to let Pedro Chavez free. Some believed, and it was quickly gaining favor, that perhaps the Earth-born pope and Reconquista's pope could work together. Two minds would not only be better, they would be more fair. Others believed the matter could wait. In fact, most everyone believed the matter of the two popes could wait.

The bill that had been born and taken flight so swiftly was the topic at hand, and it was discussed on every news and entertainment channel. The passing of the bill was talked about in New Delhi, New London, New Moscow, and even New Pittsburgh. That news quickly made its way to the Corporate Worlds, whose charter had recently been revoked for good reason. One day, it would even be talked about in the Upper Arm, although by then it would be old news. It would be established law and well on its way to being executed.

The bill, now law, was historic.

And for the first time in a great, great, long time, Earth had passed a law. A law that declared war and gave Earth Force every tool it needed to prosecute that war. A war, not on an alien species, not on a defiant corporation, but on a single man. Earth was at war with Mordid.

END

CPSIA information can be obtained
at www.ICGtesting.com
Printed in the USA
LVHW050126050719
623232LV00008B/229/P